THE ATLANTIAN CHRONICLES

FIGHT FOR SURVIVAL

NICK BAETA

BOOK ONE

MILTON & HUGO L.L.C.
4407 Park Ave., Suite 5
Union City, NJ 07087, USA

Website: *www. miltonandhugo.com*
Hotline: *1- 888-778-0033*
Email: *info@miltonandhugo.com*

Ordering Information:
Quantity sales. Special discounts are available on quantity purchases by corporations, associations, and others. For details, contact the publisher at the address above.

Library of Congress Control Number:	2024926937	
ISBN-13:	979-8-89285-390-3	[Paperback Edition]
	979-8-89285-391-0	[Hardback Edition]
	979-8-89285-389-7	[Digital Edition]

Rev. date: 12/26/2024

To Carson, Alex, Elizabeth, Thierry, Tyler, Matt, Matty and Alyssa,
thank you for your love and support in achieving this lifelong dream.
To those who have helped shape me along the way thank you as well.
And to all those looking for their next dream never stop chasing.

CHAPTER 1

"It's round three in this exciting middleweight MMA bout. The underdog Bryce Hillcrest has been taking a beating." The announcer's voice rang out as Bryce limped back to his corner. "He will need a knockout or submission to come away with the victory now in his professional debut."

"Bryce, deep breath in…" Rhys said as his hands motioned slowly up from his stomach to his chest and then back down mimicking the flow of breath entering and exiting the body. "I'm not going to lie, you're losing. But you can beat this guy, he's strong but he's sloppy. He drops his hand when he throws that big right hand, the one he's been hitting you with all night. When the bell rings, take the center of the ring. He's going to rush forward and throw everything he has trying to finish you. Let him back you up and when you see the right coming slip to the outside, drop to the body with a hook, pivot and then throw the cross straight to his jaw, put everything you have behind it, he'll drop, trust me." Rhys said as he slowly gave Bryce water. "You've got this." Rhys finished, as the ten second blocks clacked together. Before leaving he poured one last bit of water into Bryce's mouth and hurried out of the ring.

Center of the ring, draw him in, drop, hook, pivot, cross; Bryce repeated this in his head as the referee gestured to him. "Fighter you ready?" He called. Bryce nodded preparing himself, the smell of blood in his nose and the taste lingering in his mouth. "Fighter you ready?" The referee called as he gestured to the opponent.

"You're dead!" He snarled as he nodded.

"Fight!" The referee declared, his hands slapping together as he backed away from the center of the ring. Bryce rushed forward and took the center just as Rhys had said to. And like clockwork his opponent came out swinging.

"Ortiz has Hillcrest on the ropes!" The announcer remarked as Bryce backed up his hands, blocking the onslaught of punches.

Just as Bryce saw his opening everything went silent. It was as if the whole world went quiet. But it wasn't just that, it was as if time had slowed down. He watched in slow motion: Ortiz's crooked blood covered teeth clenched, his split lip dripping blood as he threw punch after punch. Bryce easily dipped below the punch, throwing a hook to the body and using it to pivot himself so he was perpendicular to his rushing opponent. Ortiz hadn't even finished the full range of motion when Bryce lined up his punch and threw it with all his might. The connection was clean, and Bryce felt the punch land perfectly. Then as if someone hit the play button on a slowed video, the whole world came rushing back. Ortiz tumbling unconscious from the blow as the crowd went wild.

"BRYCE! BRYCE! BRYCE!" The crowd chanted.

"Bryce, wake up, it's time for our morning run." The dream world slipped away and just like that Bryce was staring into the grizzled face of his father, Rhys; his thick gray beard and short gray hair tucked into a black hat.

"Do I have to?" Bryce questioned rolling over wanting to return to his dream.

"Yes." His father said, pulling the sheets off of Bryce. "Prepare for the worst, hope for the best. And that starts with being physically and mentally ready for anything. Now get dressed or I'll tack on another mile." Rhys commanded in his best drill sergeant voice.

"Prepare for the worst hope for the…" Bryce whispered mockingly under his breath.

"Excuse me?" Rhys questioned rhetorically over his shoulder as he left the room.

"Nothing." Bryce said back his voice soft and timid.

"That's what I thought, now hurry up." Rhys asserted as he made it to the door. "Oh, and Bryce, it's cold out, dress warm." He said slightly softer than the rest.

"We live in Texas; how cold can it actually be?" Bryce called back as he pulled on a pair of workout shorts, a thermal shirt and t-shirt.

Bryce hated morning runs with his father, at seventeen he valued sleep far more than the "endorphin rush" of running. But whenever he looked in the mirror and saw his six pack, muscular chest and broad shoulders, and toned arms, he remembered why he suffers through these morning workouts with his dad. At fifty-six Rhys was as fit as any twenty-five-year-old you see posting on Instagram. His high intensity cardio, morning runs, Jiu Jitsu, Muay Thai and Krav Maga training supplemented with a calisthenics routine had kept him fit and naturally Bryce had been forced into participation as well.

Rhys and Bryce ran five miles every other day, trained martial arts every day, and did body weight calisthenics on the days they didn't run. Rhys's work had afforded him some luxury in that he could afford a modest house, with a detached garage he easily converted into a gym. When Bryce was born Rhys left the military to start his own private security business. While he didn't like to talk much about his service or his time 'Down Range' as he put it, Bryce had been able to piece together over the years that his dad alongside his business partner Anton were part of a Special Forces group who specialized in removing high priority threats across the globe. As a civilian, he'd done well for himself and while he could afford to expand his business and take on more clients, he never did, stating it would take time away from Bryce, their training and his sanity. Though Bryce thought the last part was a bit more of a joke; it still baffled him. But Rhys always said, "Why risk further exposure, more eyes, and more issues when I make enough money for you and me to not worry about anything?" And Bryce couldn't argue with that, as much as he would have liked for his dad to be away a little more often so he could skip a few days in the gym.

"You were slow around the last half mile, are you feeling okay?" Rhys questioned Bryce as the two drank water standing around their kitchen island.

"You mean besides being sleep deprived? I feel fine, maybe a bit hungrier this morning but nothing out of the ordinary." Bryce replied in between gulps of water.

"And whose fault is that? You know what days we run and what time we wake up, but you chose to play video games with your friends until far later than you should." Rhys retorted his inner drill sergeant coming out as he opened the back door and led the way to the gym.

"I'm seventeen, I'm allowed to have friends and fun." Bryce said as he slowly made his way out of the house, closing the door behind him.

"You are but when your fun does not allow you to perform at your best, it could cost you. In the field there are no second chances or do-overs. No second lives, when it hits the fan, I need to know you're ready and that you'll remember what I have taught you." He replied as he wrapped his hands for their Muay Thai training session. "Bryce, I don't do this because I enjoy torturing you, I do it because one day I won't be here, and I want to know you can protect yourself against any threat that might arise. And with more and more of these terror attacks happening on our home soil, I would assume I raised you to know, we need to ensure we are always ready. Even if that means cutting our fun short. Just last week an arsonist set fire to a power station causing three FBI agents and two other workers to be killed in the blaze, and that was before they were stopped. It's a cold world out there and you need to be ready. That's all." Rhys said softly the concern in his voice only trumped by the fatherly tone he asserted into every lesson he tried to teach his son.

"Well, it sure doesn't feel like you don't enjoy this torture. And the terror attacks are a joke, you and I know it. It was an attack on a government building and they didn't even get past the front gate." Bryce retorted as he began to shadow box.

"There is always more to the story than what you read in the paper. If I know anything from my time down range, it's that the story they publish and what really happens are often two very different truths. Remember that. Now stop dropping your hand on your cross." Rhys said as he corrected Bryce's form with a swift slap of the pad to the side of Bryce's unblocked head.

Bryce and Rhys trained for another hour until 7 A.M. and then left the garage. "Did you close the door behind you when you left the house?" Rhys said as he exited the garage side door. His hand hitting Bryce in the chest stopping him dead in his tracks.

"Obviously, why?" Bryce questioned trying to get a glimpse of what the large man was blocking.

"Stay here, count to one hundred and if I am not back or do not call for you to come, run to the police station, don't stop, just run. Could it be them?" Rhys said as he glanced back at Bryce his brown eyes steely in their resolve.

"But... Wait, who is 'them'?" Bryce began as Rhys grabbed a pistol he kept stashed in the garage and began approaching the house.

"Bryce never mind who, just do as I say." He commanded as he pushed his son back and closed the door. Bryce worriedly began counting, his ears straining to hear anything.

"56,57,58,59,60." Bryce counted as he thought to himself. *What could it be? Terrorists? No, it couldn't be that. Robbers? Maybe? But Rhys wouldn't act this way for any old robber. Maybe some kind of gang banger? Rhys did work with a couple of lawyers who were working against gang members. And what did he mean by is it them? Was it something he did when he was in the military? No, it couldn't be, he'd been out for seventeen years now.*

"Bryce, it's fine. You can come out." Rhys called from the back door. Bryce quickly poked his head out of the door and cautiously exited. "Come on, it's just Anton." Rhys said as Bryce jogged over to the door and entered the house. Inside the house sat a man around the same age as Rhys, clean shaved with a long graying ponytail. Anton stood a little shorter than Bryce's six-foot-one stature at around five-foot-ten, he was in as good of shape as Rhys but as he put it, enjoyed beer a little too much, and it showed around his slightly pudgy stomach. "You almost got yourself killed, you know that right?" Rhys scolded Anton as Bryce entered the house.

"Rhys relax, you think I would miss Brycey's first day of school? Guy's a Junior, that's a big year for him." Anton joked. "Plus, you couldn't kill me, I'm too quick." He said as he pretended to dart back and forth around the much larger Rhys.

"Whatever, I'm going to shower. Bryce, fix yourself some breakfast and then get ready for school. I'm sure Carter will be here to pick you up soon enough." Rhys said as he walked out of the kitchen. "Anton, just don't break anything." He called over his shoulder as he climbed the stairs.

"Whatever you say big boy." Anton called back. "So Brycey, you getting any tail?" Anton said, elbowing Bryce in the side lightly. "Guy like you is probably fighting the girls off with a stick."

"No, I'm not getting any tail. What are you like a hundred?" Bryce replied sarcastically as he looked through the fridge before finding the milk, grabbing the cereal and fixing himself a bowl of honey bunches of oats.

"What about that little brunette girl you used to hang out with. What was her name... Betty... Bethany... Bertha?" Anton began.

"Bennett. Her name was Bennett. And no, we don't hangout anymore, she's kind of dating the biggest jerk in the school now." Bryce said thinking back to middle school and the beginning of high school when Bennett Douglas, Carter Pearson, Harry Wilson and him were four best friends until Ashton Danier came into the picture. He was the quarterback and most popular kid in school. Not to mention Bryce's biggest bully. He and his two goons James and Jonathan tortured Bryce, Harry and Carter. Ever since Bennett started dating Ashton, the three had drifted apart. Bryce hated it but she had made her choice and so had he, just then Anton snapped him back to reality.

"So... kick his ass... we both know you can do it." Anton said gesturing to the garage. "Kick his ass, take his girl, be happy. Didn't you kiss her like two years ago anyway?" Anton questioned as Bryce dug into his cereal.

"Who told you that?" Bryce snapped looking around as if he'd been caught. It was true, it was the first dance of freshman year and Bennett had pulled Bryce aside and drunkenly kissed him at a party afterwards before rushing off to the bathroom promising to return, and after twenty minutes of waiting Bryce realized she wasn't coming back and left. Embarrassed and assuming she regretted it, Bryce never mentioned it and two weeks later Bennett began dating Ashton.

"Your friend Carter is not to be trusted, the guy crumbles under the slightest pressure." Anton chuckled. "Well kid, I'm sure she'll come around. And if not, you can always sleep with her best friend. That was how I met my second wife." Anton chuckled as he took a long sip of his coffee.

"Remind me never to tell him anything or to come to you for dating advice." Bryce returned before finishing his cereal and rinsing the dish off in the sink. "It's good to see you Anton, thanks for not missing today." Bryce said, giving Anton a soft punch in the arm. Bryce had never known his mom, according to Anton and Rhys, she'd died in childbirth. But as long as he could remember, Anton would come see him off for his first day of school and slip him twenty bucks on his way out the door. It was a tradition; and while cheesy and lame, Bryce secretly looked forward to it.

"No problem kid." Anton said softly as Bryce darted upstairs and got ready for school.

Bryce showered and got ready quickly, his clothes laid out the night before. He had picked out a white, loose fitting, t-shirt that kept his athletic build under wraps *so you don't draw undo attention to yourself or give bullies another reason to try and test you* Bryce heard his father say in his head as he lifted up the sleeves and flexed his surprisingly toned arms. He styled his shirt with a pair of blue jeans with faux rips throughout the legs and completed the outfit with white Chuck Taylors. Throwing on his black backpack filled with school supplies over his back. Bryce gave his medium length purposefully unkempt brown hair a once over, and then winked his light brown eye at his reflection before setting off.

"Could you be any slower?" Carter called up as he saw Bryce crest the top of the stairs.

"His hair doesn't style itself." Anton replied as he came around and placed an arm across Carter's shoulders.

"I'm coming, I'm coming." Bryce said walking down the steps and waving a hand at the pair.

"Remember my advice kid." Anton said reaching a hand out and shaking Bryce's hand subtly sliding him a twenty-dollar bill in the process.

"What advice?" Rhys called out from the other room.

"Don't worry Dad, I won't follow it." Bryce called out as he nodded to Anton and headed towards the door.

"Probably the best decision he could've made." Carter said while he ducked as Anton tussled his blonde crew cut. "Watch it." He snapped back as he sped out the door behind Bryce. Carter stood about five-foot-eight on a tall day as he put it. Slender and skinny, Carter had been best friends with Bryce since the first grade when Bryce put his bully in a perfectly executed rear naked choke. Bryce had earned a best friend as well as a five-day suspension from school. And a threat from Rhys that if he used his training in any circumstance other than life and death, he would be shipped off to military school. "Dude, we have to finish that level tonight." Carter said as they began their walk to school.

"I know we're so close to finishing the game." Bryce said as they passed Bennett's house, and he looked up at it.

"Dude, let her go, she's on the dark side, now. Ashton has made sure of that." Carter scoffed as he caught Bryce looking at the once familiar house. Bryce wanted to but he couldn't. He'd always had a crush on Bennett ever since he began noticing girls, she was the neighbor from two houses down, she was cute, the girl next door combined with a cheerleader. Not to mention, as they'd grown up, she developed into a beautiful girl, five-foot-six of pure beauty, her toned legs leading to a butt Bryce would check out whenever he had the chance ever since he'd noticed it in seventh grade, a toned stomach Bryce had realized rivaled his abs far too late in life, and a chest that developed early and caught the attention of every guy in class and some from the years above. But Bennett's best physical assets were both, her blue eyes- a stunning perfect ocean blue- and her smile that her father had paid far more than necessary to ensure his little princess had the best smile around he'd even sprung for the invisible braces before they were popular. On top of all the physical attributes she had though, Bennett was smart, funny, kind, and caring; that summer she'd even spent half of it in Nicaragua building wells for the less fortunate.

"I know, I know." Bryce replied, snapping back to the matter at hand. "Once we get past the dragon we have to double up on our buffs and then grind until we can get the armor of Karak then we can beat the knight and boom, we are done."

"Finally, only took a whole summer of grinding to finally get you to a point where we can do the final raid." Carter teased as the two kept plotting their after-school plans as they walked to school.

"What class do you have first?" Bryce questioned as the two arrived at school.

"Spanish with Ms. Diaz, you?" Carter said the excitement palpable in his voice. Ms. Diaz was every teenage boy's dream Spanish teacher. Her curvy figure was always on display in class accentuated by her signature tight black skirts and low-cut tops and Bryce would bet money that Carter only took the class to stare at her.

"World History with Mr. Jones." Bryce grumbled; he'd almost forgotten he had his least favorite class with his least favorite teacher.

"That blows, Mr. Jones is such a jerk." Carter said sympathizing with Bryce. "He always helps Ashton, I'm pretty sure he worships the ground he walks on."

"Well, well, well, look who decided to show up." Bryce heard an all too familiar voice from behind him. "If only he'd done that last night, we'd be ready for the raid." Bryce turned around and was greeted by Harry, his glasses pushed firmly up his nosed. "Bryce, Carter, how's it going? Carter you ready for Ms. Diaz's Spanish class?" Harry said his pudgy round frame shifting over to the boys.

"Harry you fat bastard, I already told him how much he sucks." Carter laughed, clapping Harry on the shoulder and rubbing his belly. "As for Ms. Diaz, of course, I have my cologne in my bag, I'm going to spray it before I go in."

"Quit it." Harry said, swatting Carter's hand away. "But that is brilliant, I am so doing that tomorrow. My God she is so hot, what I wouldn't do to see her after class." Harry said, nudging Bryce.

"Yeah, yeah lucky you." Bryce said half paying attention as he watched Bennett walk in from the other end of the hallway. It was like the world slowed down when she entered Bryce even felt slightly dizzy afterwards. As noises faded and her movements were almost slowed down. She looked amazing every inch of her was perfect to him. But suddenly Bryce's fantasy came crashing down around him as he saw Ashton following her just a few steps behind with James and Jonathan making gestures and gawking at Bennett's butt. "God, I hate that guy." Bryce mumbled under his breath.

"Dude, are you okay?" Carter said as he nudged Bryce. "You look a bit pale." He continued trying to place the back of his hand on Bryce's forehead.

"Yeah, why does everyone keep asking me that?" Bryce said, thinking for a moment.

"I don't know all of a sudden you looked a bit off." Carter replied quizzically.

"I'm good. I just don't like him." Bryce nodded thinking how now that Carter mentioned it, he did feel a bit dizzy, his vision blurring slightly before snapping back.

"I think the feelings are mutual considering he has bullied you for over two years now. But stay quiet here he comes." Carter said, trying to avoid eye contact as Ashton strode up his two best friends and partners in crime following close behind.

Ashton, James and Jonathan had been torturing Bryce ever since the party in freshman year when Bennett kissed him. Friends since near birth, James and Jonathan were always close behind Ashton. Ashton was the star quarterback, dating the most popular girl in the school and was set to become Homecoming King if he played his cards right, and the court jesters James and Jonathan would follow him right to the top. Both playing football, their hopes of life being any good outside of high school relied on Ashton playing well and leading the school team the Broadway Hill Bobcats to victory. As such, they protected him, kept him happy and joined in his relentless bullying of Bryce and anyone who associated with him.

Bryce knew he could easily take each of them on, maybe even all at once, but his dad would reign a fury down on him so great he wouldn't see Broadway Hills or his friends until he was Rhys's age, that is if his father let him live. Rhys always said; "Never fight unless completely necessary. Fighting brings attention to both of us, puts you in the system, and heaven forbid it ends up on the internet." Bryce never understood his father's view and wanted more than anything to end the trio's bullying once and for all. But it wasn't worth it. Only Junior and then Senior year left, and then he was gone, off to college to be whoever he wanted to be.

"Hey boys, how was your summer?" Ashton called as he waved to Bennett and rushed over to the group. Grabbing Carter in a head lock and tussling his hair.

"Let me go." Carter called out as Ashton's cronies strode up and pushed Harry.

"Hey!" Harry yelped as he stumbled.

"Shut up Porky." Ashton retorted. "Bryce how was your summer? Hope you didn't mind me and Bennett making some noise this summer. I know your houses are close by and oh boy does she like to scream." Ashton teased making inappropriate gestures after he released Carter and shoved him into Bryce.

"I... I have to get to class." Harry said, collecting himself and scurrying off. James and Jonathon only letting him pass once Ashton gave a nod of approval.

"Not so fast." Ashton said nodding to James, who was the taller of the two goons with dark skin and even darker eyes. Quickly, he grabbed Carter as he too tried to escape. James was on him in a moment and easily guided him back in to the group giving him a slap in the back of the head for good measure. "Bryce, I asked you a question. Or are you too busy with Short Stack and Lard Ass's dicks in your mouth to answer me? Did you enjoy your summer of listening to me bang Bennett?" Ashton asked again, getting up in Bryce's face mocking him. Ashton stood about the same height as Bryce and was built like a football player, broad shoulders, big chest and arms that looked like it was all he ever worked on at the gym, and never correctly, often wearing tight shirts under his letterman jacket to accentuate them. His dirty blonde hair was cut short and styled after the quarterback Joe Burrows which someone had compared Ashton to one time, and he'd since made it his entire personality.

"I heard you; I just chose not to respond." Bryce replied through a clenched jaw. He could end Ashton's whole football career in one move. But Rhys's wrath would be ten times worse, and he knew it. Kicking himself for not just risking it to teach Ashton a lesson for all the years of bullying he'd endured for no reason; all the shoves into lockers as they passed in the hall, all the rumors spread to anyone who ever showed an interest in him, the books he'd slapped out of his hands. More importantly though, for how he treated Bryce's friends, picking on people smaller than him, like Carter or Harry; or for how he treated Bennett. There was many a time, he would hear tires screech and the sound of Bennett crying as she ran into her house, or him cursing her as he left declaring they were over only to return hours later and make up. It made Bryce sick.

"You little bi…" Ashton began before he was interrupted.

"Boys? Something going on here?" Mr. Alfonso cut in. "Ashton, I hope you got the assigned readings and are ready to contribute to the discussions this year. I can't keep letting things slide because you play football. English might be the language you speak but if you turn in more work like last year, it will be the class you fail. Now off to class." The short plump teacher motioned with his hands to dissipate.

"Of course, Mr. Alfonso, I plan on working extra hard this year to prove to you all the work I did over the summer with Bennett Douglas, my girlfriend, will have paid off. I was just talking to Bryce about it actually." Ashton said giving Bryce a shot in the arm, harder than necessary but not so hard as to draw attention to it.

"I see, well I hope you are correct sir." Mr. Alfonso said shuffling forward. "Umm… Bryce, a moment if you please."

"Uhhh, sure." Bryce said as he watched the group spread out, each going their own directions.

"Bryce, I noticed you are in my Advanced English, this year. I hope this means I can expect more of your poetry, maybe this year you will take my advice and submit it to the Charleston contest." Mr. Alfonso said quietly to Bryce his voice slightly giddy, as he leaned in his bald spot clearly showing through his combover.

"I'm not sure sir. I will think about it, but I don't really write poetry anymore." Bryce said timidly. He liked the short teacher. His large belly always jiggled when he talked and he, unlike Mr. Jones and the rest of school, he seemed to see through the facade of Ashton.

"Well, that is a shame, the poem you submitted about a love lost in the ninth grade was both moving and inspired." Mr. Alfonso said a faint touch of positivity and excitement in his voice. "I hope to get the chance to read more of it."

"Uhhh… thanks, I've got to get to class." Bryce replied as he readjusted himself, rubbed his arm where Ashton had punched it and left with a wave.

CHAPTER 2

Bryce arrived just in time to slide in the class as Mr. Jones closed the door. "Almost late Mr. Hillcrest. Don't make a habit of it. If you are on time, you are already late. Five minutes early is the latest you should get here so as not to disturb your fellow classmates." Mr. Jones lectured. "And let that be a lesson for the rest of you." The tall old man sported a military-like haircut that had gone gray, and then white, long before Bryce arrived at the school. He was skinny almost like if someone had stretched skin over the biology lab skeleton. His teeth were yellowed from years of drinking coffee and his breath reflected it.

"Sorry I was talking with Mr. Alfonso." Bryce said flatly.

"Mr. Hillcrest, regardless of whom you were speaking to, it is not an excuse for being late. Now sit." He said as he pointed to the only seat left. The front of the class. Beside... Bennett?

Bryce slid into his seat and looked over at Bennett who smiled slightly and then shot her hand up. "Mr. Jones, my announcement." She said as she waved her hand, her manicured nails matching her black and white checkered dress, that cut just above her knees. Her tanned legs showing off both how toned they were and how much sun she got during the summer. Topped off with crisp white sneakers.

"Ahhh... yes Miss Douglas, please go ahead. But for future reference, please wait to be called upon before speaking." Mr. Jones said as he waved his skeleton-like hand at Bennett.

"Sorry sir. Anyway." She cleared her throat. "Hey guys and gals, I hope you had a great summer. I just wanted to say I am raising money to help get us the best prom possible this year. We're going to have a bake sale next week and other events throughout the year but if you are feeling extra generous, or your parents…" She said with a wink. "You can donate directly to me or if you want to sign up to help feel free to ask me and I will get you involved. Thanks, I hope to see all of you shaking your tail feathers this year at our safari themed prom." Bennett said giddily as she finished her sales pitch and sat back down to murmurs throughout the classroom.

"Quiet, quiet. Please, can we begin our learning now?" Mr. Jones asked as he waved his hands like a conductor and silenced the class.

"It's nice to see you Bryce, I hope you had a good summer." Bennett whispered to Bryce.

"Thanks, you too." Bryce replied in the same whispered tone.

"Quiet please, I am going over the syllabus." Mr. Jones said, looking directly at Bryce. The next hour dragged on far longer than it should have but by the end of class Bryce was happy to be finished and ready to leave, but strangely looking forward to seeing Bennett every day without Ashton. Bryce followed Bennett out of the class and as he exited the door Ashton appeared.

"Hey, perv don't look at my girl." Ashton said storming up to Bryce who had his head down texting Carter. Not paying attention, he began to walk as Ashton slapped his phone out of his hand and pushed him, sending him sprawling to the floor. As he raised a hand for another strike.

"Ashton!" Bennett screamed as she watched Bryce fall. "What the hell are you doing?" She questioned as she placed herself between Bryce and Ashton.

"That pervert was staring at your ass as you walked out. Probably getting his phone ready to take a picture up your skirt so he can get his rocks off later." Ashton said pointing his finger at Bryce who had since picked himself up off the floor and pocketed his phone. His hands up ready to defend himself, his blood boiling as he stood there, looking around as phones came out and videos were more than likely beginning to be recorded. One wrong move and Bryce might end up as the next YouTube meme or school laughing stock.

"Is that true Bryce?" Bennett questioned.

"No, I was texting Carter. You know, your friend, well that is before you sold out for popularity?" Bryce spat back as he readied himself for a fight.

"Watch your mouth punk." Ashton said as he saw Bennett's face flash with sadness. Bryce saw it too immediately regretting his actions.

"Bennett I'm..." Bryce began before he was cut off by Mr. Jones.

"Gentlemen, I do not care, nor do I mind, if you fight but do not do it in front of my door or I will be required to get involved and I do not wish to do more paperwork than I already have to do." He said sternly.

"Of course, sir, I will use my better judgment and remove myself from this situation. Please though keep an eye on this one as Bennett should not have to dress differently or be scared to act certain ways for fear of sexual harassment." Ashton said in his most prim and proper voice.

"Mr. Danier, I will see what I can do about Mr. Hillcrest and Miss Douglas's interactions being kept to a minimum, but please do refrain from violent outbursts when in my presence as I do not wish to be the reason our star quarterback is suspended from games. Now take Miss Douglas and go that way..." He said gesturing the opposite way of Bryce. "And Mr. Hillcrest you go that way. And go to your next class." He said pointing his wrinkled finger the other way.

Bryce began to walk the other way angrily. But looked back only to catch Bennett doing the same, a clear face of pain showing. As Ashton followed her gaze, placed an arm around her, and flipped Bryce off with the same hand so only he would see.

"Dude, I heard you were taking photos up Bennett's skirt, what's that about?" Carter said at lunch through a mouthful of sandwich.

"I didn't." Bryce said for the millionth time. "Ashton attacked me for no reason and then said that after Bennett stopped him from—" Bryce began to explain.

"Beating you to a pulp?" Harry interjected. "Either way the whole school thinks you're a sex criminal now."

"Well, I'm not." Bryce said angrily, biting open his lunch.

"We know that. You just have to convince the rest of the school. Plus Harry, Bryce could totally beat the tar out of Ashton, he's like a ninth-degree black belt in ass-kicking. Him and Rhys train like every day. I don't get why you don't just end him, and his two neanderthal friends." Carter said, patting Bryce on the back softly.

"I've told you, Rhys said if I ever got in a fight that wasn't completely necessary, I would be sent to military school somewhere far away from here." Bryce explained angrily, as he agreed with Carter but didn't want to risk Rhys's wrath. He was a man of few jokes and even fewer empty threats.

If Rhys threatened Bryce with a punishment, he always followed through. One time Rhys caught Bryce sneaking in after a party he was told he couldn't go to, that had earned him a three-week grounding, extra chores that included moving a whole cord of wood from one side of the backyard by hand to the other, then when he'd finished Rhys made him put it back saying he liked it better on the other side of the yard. Some of the logs were even over sixty pounds. Bryce ached for a week after that. So, if Rhys said Bryce was going to be sent to military school he meant it. Plus, unlike his father, Bryce didn't want to pursue a career in the military. He didn't mind the idea, it did give Rhys a good life, skills to get out of almost any situation, and a level of insight and awareness that he'd attempted to pass down to Bryce, but Bryce fancied himself more of a business career, or maybe marketing, either way he knew unlike Rhys he wasn't meant to be a soldier.

"I also heard you called Bennett a whore and a fake." Harry said in between bites of food.

"I didn't. I said she sold out her friends for popularity. And I regret it." Bryce whimpered as he ate the rest of his lunch.

"Well, you have a week before Ashton's birthday party to figure it out and apologize otherwise you definitely cannot come to the party that I got us invited to." Carter said, swiping and tapping on his phone as he spoke. Bryce and Harry's phones dinged at the same time.

"No way! How did a loser like you get us invited to the party of the year?" Harry said, opening his phone and looking at the party page.

"Sarah Mulligan, her and Bennett went on her trip this summer to build wells and became close. Plus, you know she's always had a crush on me, so when I heard her talking about it, I turned on the charm and boom three invites." Carter bragged as he faked brushing dirt off his shoulder.

"Sweet, you're so going to hit that aren't you?" Harry joked as he smiled ear to ear.

"A gentleman never tells, plus she got way hotter this summer so maybe." Carter shrugged.

"Bryce you better not blow this for us." Harry threatened jokingly with a plastic knife.

"I won't. I'll talk to Bennett tomorrow in World History and figure it out." Bryce said as he ate. The rest of lunch was spent laughing, joking, teasing and planning their gaming excursion for that evening.

The rest of the day went by without much incident, outside of the occasional murmur and dirty look Bryce made it through the day without any issue. As he and Carter said goodbye to Harry and walked home, Bryce pondered how he would apologize to Bennett.

"Bro just say sorry, compliment her and tell her you'll never bother her again so her and Ashton can live happily ever after. Until they both grow older, resent each other after three kids and he cheats on her." Carter said as Bryce had thrown out the idea of flowers for her. "Whatever you do, do not get her a gift and especially don't give her flowers."

"Yeah, you're probably right, that's a bit much. It's not like I actually did anything wrong. Maybe I'll just text her." Bryce said as he pulled out his phone.

"You still have her number?! It's been two years, delete that crap and move on." Carter said, reaching out at Bryce's phone.

"No. Stop. Carter!" He cried as Carter grabbed his phone, dodged his attempts to grab it back and deleted the number.

"I'm doing this for your own good. Apologize to her tomorrow and then say you'll never bother her again. Promise me." Carter said sternly, looking Bryce in the eyes.

"Whatever, just give me back my phone." Bryce angrily replied. Passing Bennett's house as they did. The two went their separate ways with a promise to see each other online that night.

Bryce walked into his empty house and tossed his backpack into the couch angrily. *Screw that school, screw Ashton, I should've kicked his ass, I know I can. But nooooo, you can't use your training in non-life-threatening situations. Screw this place...* Bryce thought as the anger built inside him. His hearing starting to go as he worked himself into a fit of rage, punching the couch and his backpack the indent far deeper than he intended. After a few moments Bryce felt dizzy as the sounds around him returned and he laid down exhausted for some unknown reason. He felt oddly similar to how he did when he saw Bennett this morning. And within a few moments he slowly slipped into sleep, the world around him closing in as his eyes had an almost tunnel vision effect.

"Bryce, wake up." Rhys said as he shook him awake. Bryce opened his eyes unsure how long he'd slept for or why he'd been so tired all of the sudden, but felt very stiff from the unnatural position he'd fallen asleep in.

"What time is it?" Bryce asked, rubbing the sleep from his eyes. The feeling of anger long since subsided.

"6:30, I came home, and you were asleep on the couch, your backpack on the opposite end with a huge dent in it, your one binder looks broken. Is everything okay?" Rhys asked the concern in his voice, slight but noticeable.

"Yeah, I was a bit mad when I got home, then all of the sudden, I kind of just lost all my energy, got a bit dizzy and then fell asleep." Bryce explained hoping the honesty wouldn't backfire on him.

"Why were you mad? Something happen at school?" Rhys questioned as he felt Bryce's head for a fever just like Carter had. "Good you're not burning up you're probably fine. But no video games tonight, you need to rest." He commanded sternly.

"Yeah, just the typical crap. Ashton was in true form today. God, I wish I could beat the crap out of him just once. And how is that fair? You said I was fine, and the guys are counting on me." Bryce pleaded the frustration building again.

"Bryce, beating up Ashton is going to lead to you getting charged or would make me send you off to military school where I am sure there will be far worse people than Ashton Danier. Show some control and let it go. If things become life-threatening then you can strike hard and finish the fight. But until then just leave it be, bullies will follow you everywhere in life, if you go around punching every bully you come across then soon, you'll become the problem yourself, and I taught you better than that." Rhys asserted sternly. "And it is a video game, it will be there tomorrow and the next day and the day after that. Your friends will understand. Now that is the end of discussion."

"What's the point of you teaching me how to defend myself if I am never able to use it?" Bryce argued.

"To defend your life or the life of those around you who cannot. And be thankful you haven't had to use it. I have had to use what I have taught you many times, and it haunts me, so while I teach you these things, I do it in the hopes you never have to. So, count your blessings people like me sacrificed themselves to give you a life where the biggest issue you have is a bully and which skeleton, orc monster game character you have to fight." Rhys replied softly lowering his voice to calm the situation while keeping his tone stern, a warning to not question anything further.

With that, Bryce got up and stormed off to his room. Texting Carter and Harry the news which was met with more joke insults and teasing. *Show control, screw control, I'm going to snap his arm let's see Mr. Jones cheer for the star quarterback when he can't even carry a book.* Bryce thought as he stomped around his room the sound of his stomps slowly fading away again. Then after a few moments it came back, he became dizzy, and then everything went black.

"Bryce, wake up, you've had a fall." Bryce heard the soft echo of Rhys's voice.

"Anton, it happened, be ready. Yes, yes, he's fine but make sure things are ready in case they come looking. Yeah, yeah, okay bye." Bryce heard as the distant sounds of a call ended and he opened his eyes to see Rhys standing over him, a concerned and slightly panicked look on his face.

"What's wrong? Dad? Be ready for what?" Bryce questioned groggily.

"Nothing son, just making sure Anton could watch the business if I needed to take you to the hospital. You collapsed. But you seem okay now." Rhys said as he shone a light into Bryce's eyes. "Yeah, you're okay. Probably just low blood sugar. Let's get you up on your feet..." Rhys said straining as he helped Bryce to his feet. "And... careful now, slowly... slowly. Okay let's make our way downstairs, I've got dinner for us." Bryce shakily got to his feet and made his way to the dinner table. He ate dinner slowly and slowly the feeling of confusion, fatigue and stiffness faded.

"Dad, what happened?" Bryce asked in between big bites of food.

"Slow down, the food isn't going anywhere." Rhys said as he reached out and stopped Bryce's hand from shoveling more food into his mouth feeling better with each bite. "That's better... You were stomping around your room and then I heard bang and then nothing. I thought you'd knocked something over and went to see then I found you laying on the floor. Are you feeling better now?" He asked with a kind, more caring look on his face.

"And what you were saying to Anton when I was coming to, something about someone coming..." Bryce questioned.

"Bryce, it was just work stuff, if you didn't come to, I was prepared to carry you to the hospital on foot. I was just telling Anton that he may need to take the clients for the next few days. But you seem to be okay. Just take it easy tonight and I'll check on you before we train tomorrow." Rhys said to find a disappointed look on Bryce's face who clearly had hoped passing out qualified him for a day off. The two of them spent the rest of the night watching tv, Rhys occasionally checking on Bryce and making sure he drank plenty of water mixed with electrolyte powder.

CHAPTER 3

Bryce awoke feeling far better but disappointed he'd still have to train. But when he didn't wake up to Rhys getting him up him for training. Instead, he awoke to the sound of metal sliding, scraping and clanking together. Slowly he made his way out of bed and to the top of the stairs listening carefully, unsure of what time it was.

"Yeah, it happened. I'm not sure how many times it's happened now but it for sure happened. All the signs are there, the dizziness, the loss of consciousness and strong emotions bringing it on. I'm not sure which one he has yet. No, I'm not going to tell him, do you know how life changing that would be? We were brought into it as adults, we chose to be in it, he didn't get to. No listen, I'll tell him when he's ready. For now, things remain as usual, if things get worse, I will let you know, but keep an eye out, they might not have caught the first couple, but it'll have triggered something and if it happens again, they'll definitely be looking. It's only a matter of time." Bryce heard the whispered talking of Rhys as he moved closer to the stairs. Just as he did the floor creaked. "Crap, I've got to go. I'll talk to you later. Yeah, just be ready." Bryce slowly made his way back to his room as he heard his father quickly slide whatever he was working on, off of the table and the hurried footsteps make their way up the stairs. "Bryce, time to wake up." Rhys said as he poked his head into Bryce's room. "How are you feeling?"

"Dad, what's going on? What were you talking about?" Bryce asked as he moved away from Rhys at the door.

"Work Bryce, just work. We've got a big client and they're demanding a lot, that's all. Nothing you should worry about. Are you ready to train?" Rhys said in a dismissive tone. He'd had demanding clients before but never like this, it was 4 A.M. why would he need to work this early, what couldn't be handled at the start of the work day? Bryce shrugged it off thinking Rhys was just catching up on work he missed the day before dealing with his collapse.

"Yeah Dad. I'm ready." Bryce said slowly as the two made their way out to the garage. After an hour of intensive bodyweight exercises and an hour of grappling with Rhys, practicing different escapes from positions where the opponent was larger or stronger, Bryce was about two pounds lighter, and the floor needed a serious mopping. "I'll clean up." Bryce volunteered hoping to avoid getting ready and delay his apology to Bennett.

"No, no it's my turn, you go get ready and I'll clean up." Rhys said, opening the door and glancing quickly up at the house before letting Bryce pass by. Bryce made his way slowly to the house and got ready for school. When Bryce came down stairs a breakfast of bacon, eggs and toast with strawberry jam and butter was waiting for him. "Eat up, Carter will be here soon, and I want you to leave on a full stomach, so we don't have any issues like yesterday."

Bryce tucked in and ate quickly, the food hitting a spot he didn't realize he had. Bryce finished his plate as Carter arrived. He then stood up, fixed his white long-sleeved shirt, pushed the sleeves up to his elbows, fixed his black jeans, smiled at his dad and left.

"Dude, you passed out?!" Carter exclaimed as they walked down the street towards school. "Maybe you have a brain tumor, it's tough to be mad at the guy with a brain tumor. I bet Bennett would forgive you and let you come to the party if you did." Carter joked as he looked closely at Bryce. "Maybe that was why you looked pale yesterday."

"I do not have a brain tumor!" Bryce yelled as he swatted Carter's prodding hands. "I'll say sorry to Bennett but that might not fix things. You didn't see her face… she was really upset." Bryce said his head dipping slightly as he explained how he hurt her.

"Whatever man just fix stuff so we can go to the party." Carter said as the two strolled into school. Bryce made his way directly to class, trying to avoid the possibility of bumping into Ashton or someone else who believed the lies Ashton was spreading about him. Even just the thought of it made his blood boil. *What did Bryce do to Ashton to have him constantly messing with him?* Just as Bryce was scribbling in his notebook Bennett walked in.

"Oh hi." Bennett said, clutching a book to her chest.

"Hey." Bryce said softly. "I'm sorry about yesterday, I was upset and said something I shouldn't have, I didn't mean it." Bryce mumbled trying his best to get the words out quickly before others showed up.

"It wasn't nice of you. I didn't sell out my friends. I made new ones." Bennett said, setting her book down in her seat.

"I know, but why him? He's a jerk." Bryce questioned.

"You don't know him like I do. He... he... he means well. And as for an apology, calling my boyfriend a jerk doesn't really land in the book of good ones." She proclaimed.

"I know, I know. I'm sorry. Can I start over?" Bryce asked and Bennett waved a hand gesturing for him to continue. "Bennett I am really sorry, for everything. I wasn't taking photos of you or staring at your ass. I was texting Carter I swear. And as for what I said afterwards, I didn't mean to, I was mad and took it out on you. And I'm sorry we used to be friends, and I just hate we aren't anymore." Bryce said, looking at her in her blue eyes. His heart racing, wishing he could tell her how much he missed her.

"It's okay. I forgive you. But maybe keep your distance from me in the halls." She said softly, touching Bryce's hand. "Next time flowers would help you a lot more." She whispered.

"I told Carter that exact thing." Bryce chuckled, relieved she accepted his apology.

"I know silly, I heard you two as you walked by my house. Also give me your phone." She said as she extended a hand. Bryce handed her his phone, and she punched in her phone number. "I'm not saying you can text me, because I'm still not happy with you. But don't delete me." And with that she saved her name in his phone. Bennett sat down and as people rolled in, Bennett's phone began to buzz. "Yes James, I am okay you don't need to worry, he didn't do it, Ashton was mistaken. Now drop it or you can't come to the party Friday. And that goes for anyone else." She exclaimed looking over her shoulder and then winking as she caught Bryce's eyes on the way back.

"Okay, okay class calm down. Today we will be learning about secret societies, secret police and the combination of both." Mr. Jones said as he pulled down the projector screen. At the end of the class Bryce watched Bennett leave, waited a moment and then got up to leave. "Mr. Hillcrest, is there something you wish to discuss?" Mr. Jones said as he looked up from his notes his glasses magnifying the size of his eyes as he looked.

"No sir, just doing my best to avoid any issues." Bryce replied as he slung his bag over his shoulder. "Good lesson today, it was interesting."

"All history is interesting Mr. Hillcrest, but yes, the occult and secret societies that allegedly run things are quite the topic. Some even say some of the lost civilizations had technologies far superior even to what we have in modern day. Others say they were the next step in human evolution. All I know for sure is I have another class to prepare for. So, if you would be so kind Mr. Hillcrest." Mr. Jones said as he gestured for him to leave with two hands sweeping him out of the class.

Bryce went about the rest of his day without incident and made it home, ready to play some games with the guys and relax. But just as he walked in, his phone buzzed. It was Rhys.

"Hey Bryce, how are you feeling?" His voice crackled across the phone.

"Hey Dad, umm, I'm good. Is everything okay?" Bryce questioned as his dad never called him unless it was bad news.

"Yes, yes everything is fine, I'm just stuck at work and won't be home until late. Just thought I'd let you know and tell you to order a pizza. Anton says to use the twenty he gave you and I'll replace it when I get home." Rhys's voice sounded nervous, but Bryce brushed it off.

"Okay. Cool good luck. See you later." Bryce replied with the clear excitement at a night of video games and pizza in his voice. With that Bryce hung up the phone and dialed the Pasquali's Pizza. He ordered his favorite pizza, pepperoni, feta and black olives.

Within twenty minutes there was a knock at the door. Bryce opened it and there stood a stocky older boy he'd gone to school with. He paid the boy and told him to keep the change. With a nod the boy walked off, but as he did, he saw someone. Ashton. The boy waved to Ashton who waved back and then looked at Bryce who was in a pair of sweatpants and a t-shirt. Ashton looked up at the door and watched as Bennett ran out to hug him. With a smile at Bryce during the hug, Ashton broke away, spun her and kissed her, picking her up as he did. Bryce turned around and slammed the door shut. *Jerk.* He thought as he stormed upstairs, grabbed a slice of pizza and threw on his gaming headphones.

Chapter 4

———————————————

Bryce spent the better part of five hours, playing games, eating pizza and enjoying his night when his phone buzzed. Bryce glanced at it. It was Bennett. She'd sent a flower emoji. "Do you have a moment to talk?" The message lit up his screen as he looked at himself in the mirror. His mouth showed the remanence of his dinner, and his hair had an indent from his headset. Thank God it was over text he thought.

"Umm yes what's up?" He quickly replied.

"Oh, good I'm at your front door." His phone buzzed. *Oh crap*! He thought as he wiped his mouth, ripped off his shirt and threw on a fresh black one that was slightly tighter than he thought. As he raced out his bedroom door, he tussling his hair hoping to look somewhat normal.

"Hey." He said as he opened the door.

"Hi. Did I catch you at a bad time?" Bennett said softly. She looked amazing in a short white dress and jean jacket, with her hair tied back in a high ponytail, Bryce had to almost pinch himself to make sure he wasn't dreaming.

"No, you're good." Bryce replied, gesturing for her to come in. The two made their way to the living room where they sat on the larger couch across from the television. "Can I get you some water or something?" Bryce offered as Bennett sat on the opposite end of the couch from him.

"Sure, that would be nice." Bennett replied as she curled up on the couch in a ball making herself as small as she could. It was then Bryce noticed her eyes were red, and her jacket had a tear-soaked cuff.

"Bennett are you okay?" Bryce said moving closer to her and reaching a hand out.

"Yeah… I… Yes… No… ugh I don't know." She said her voice quivering as she spoke. "Ashton and I got into a fight. Over you." She said her hands covering her face as she spoke. "He was mad I forgave you. He accused me of making him look bad. And he started screaming at me. Saying I don't do enough with him, and he has needs, and maybe he should find another girl." She sniffled as she spoke. "And, I said he was more than welcome to, but I wasn't doing anything I wasn't ready for. Then I tried to leave, and he grabbed me, really hard." She said rolling up her sleeve to reveal a set of finger shaped bruises. "I broke free, and he sped off. And I don't know I just needed someone to talk to and you were right here, and my Dad is on a trip to Japan for work." She whimpered as Bryce gently took her arm.

"Bennett are you okay?" Bryce said taking a look her arm. "I'm going to kill him." He snapped through clenched teeth. *How could he do this to Bennett? For sticking up for him? Did he cause this?* But Bennett brought him back to reality.

"No, you will not. He's not a bad guy, he just got upset and overreacted. This was a mistake I should've never said anything. He's probably blowing up my phone trying to say sorry." Bennett shakily said getting off the couch and to her feet. "I should go." She said making her way towards the front door.

"No Bennett. You didn't." Bryce said as he pulled her into a hug, her face pressing into his chest and her arms wrapping around him. He squeezed slightly and she squeezed back. "Don't go." He whispered. "Why don't we go sit on the roof like we used to?" Bryce suggested without letting her go and felt the nod of Bennett. Bennett sniffled and looked up a Bryce who loosened his hug slightly.

"No talking? Just listening to music like we used to?" Bennett sniffled and looked at Bryce with tears in her big blue eyes. Bryce nodded and began to make his way to his top floor. "Umm… Bryce one more thing?" Bennett said meekly as they walked.

"Yeah?" Bryce replied softly trying his best not to scare her off.

"It's cold out, can I borrow a sweater and pants? This dress isn't really made for climbing up on roofs." Bennett chuckled softly.

"Yeah. Let me grab it." Bryce said as he made his way to his room. He quickly grabbed a sweater for himself and Bennett as well as another set of sweatpants for her. Remembering when he and Bennett were little the two found out they could sneak onto Bryce's roof through a window at the end of the long upstairs hallway. By opening the window and carefully climbing out, the two could make their way to a larger flat part of the roof where they used to lay out for hours listening to whatever new music Bennett had found. Bryce let Bennett change in the bathroom and chuckled a bit when she came out. She looked as though she was swimming in his sweater, somehow though, she still looked beautiful to him. Bryce shook the thoughts out of his head. Bennett needed a friend right now. "I got the speaker; do you want to put on your music or mine?" He asked as he slid open the window.

"My music on your phone." She replied as she took his hand and climbed out the window after him.

The two spent two hours out there listening to Nic D, Noah Kahan, Luke Combs, Dylan Gossett and Zach Bryan on shuffle. Just beside each other as the world passed them by. Bennett was the first to break the silence. "Do you think I'm stupid for forgiving him?" She asked as the songs played softly behind her. Bryce almost didn't hear her.

"Why would I think you're stupid?" Bryce said as he sat up and looked at Bennett in the dim light of the surrounding houses. "I don't like him but clearly you see something in him that I don't." Bryce said softly.

"He's a good guy Bryce, he just puts a lot of pressure on himself, and he just let it get to him today." She replied, looking at him as she lay there in the dark.

"Bennett, he hurt you today, that doesn't sit right with me. But if you say he's a good person maybe I'm not seeing something you are. But you're not stupid for forgiving someone. You forgave me. And look where that got us." Bryce chuckled as he gestured to the open air.

"Yeah, maybe I should've just stayed mad at you. Would've been a lot easier and then I wouldn't have tree sap on my back." She joked as she shifted around and reached out for Bryce's hand.

"Yeah, but then you wouldn't have gotten such a great hug from me." He joked back running his thumb across the back of her hand in his. "Bennett you are one of the strongest, kindest, and smartest people I know. I know you'll do what's best for you. But don't hurt yourself to make others feel better." Bryce pleaded as he looked at her, her blue eyes barely visible in the light.

"Bryce, I think I should go. It's late." She said, her voice suddenly cracking as she spoke. She quickly scrambled off the roof and through the window. Just as Rhys walked in the house.

"Bennett?" Rhys asked as the little figure shot down the stairs and out the door, her clothes in her hand as she quickly ran home. "Bryce?" His voice boomed through the house.

"Dad it's not what it seems." Bryce said, trying to scramble through the window and down the stairs. He made it to the front porch when he saw Bennett slip into her house. *What did I say?* He thought as he turned on his heels and re-entered his house. Rhys gave Bryce a look as he entered. "It's not like that." He scoffed, marching upstairs and pulling off his tree sap covered clothes.

Chapter 5

Bryce woke up to Rhys standing over him. "Time for a run and were adding an extra mile of sprints for your little roof top excursion."

"Dad, that's not fair, it wasn't like that." Bryce pleaded, but it fell on deaf ears as his father ripped the blankets off of him. "You suck sometimes, you know that right?" Bryce said as he was dragged out of bed.

The two ran seven miles at a much faster than normal pace, Bryce could tell his dad was not in the mood for anything but focused running and training extra hard. By the end of the training Bryce could barely feel his arms and had fought out of scenarios with someone coming at him with a gun, a knife and their bare hands. Each time he failed Rhys made him do twenty burpees. Bryce learned and learned quickly, today was not the day to slack off.

"Clean up. Then go inside and get ready for school." Rhys said coldly as he walked out of the garage and towards the house. Bryce did as instructed, cleaned up and then went inside where Rhys was at the table looking over documents while his coffee was heating up. "Go get ready, breakfast will be done in a couple of minutes." Rhys croaked without looking up.

"Did I do something? You seem extra upset today." Bryce questioned as he walked by his father. In an instant Rhys grabbed his wrist and looked up from his papers.

"No but you need to focus on being prepared for the worst. Things are getting worse out there. Just be ready." His steely glare shot through Bryce.

"Okay. I'll be ready. And I'm sorry for not letting you know Bennett was over." Bryce apologized as he walked away from him and upstairs to get ready.

Bryce emerged from his room fifteen minutes later wearing a pair of brown chinos, and a button up, short sleeved, maroon shirt with white accents, topped off with a pair of black Vans sneakers. He made his way down to the table where a similar breakfast to the previous day was sitting in front of him. "Eat up. We're increasing your caloric intake, building more muscle and increasing energy, you'll need it." Rhys said as he continued to read his documents and sip his black coffee with a spoonful of honey in it. Bryce made quick work of the food and left for school. On the way he wondered if he should tell Carter about Bennett's and his late night, but he decided against it.

"I can't believe Bennett told the whole school to forgive you or they couldn't come to the party! Did you offer to clean her entire house in a maid outfit or something?" Carter joked as Harry chimed in.

"Yeah, or did you offer to buy her lunch for the school year?"

"Harry, not everything is food related, you pudgy bastard." Carter cut in. "Plus, he definitely offered to dress up as a chicken and accompany Bennett to the mall where he would carry her bags around for her." Carter continued to joke.

"You caught me, it's actually all of those and then some." Bryce said as he pushed his two friends away and began his walk to Mr. Jones's class. When he arrived, he sat down in his usual seat and saw Bennett. She was wearing a black long-sleeved shirt, and a pair of blue jeans. As Bryce sat down, he smiled at Bennett who immediately looked away. Bryce sighed and focused on the lesson or as much of it as he could. *Why was she mad at me? Was she mad at me? What did I do? Should I ask her? Should I mention my clothes?* Bryce thought over and over his mind racing questioning every possible avenue of thought as he sat there in class.

"Mr. Hillcrest, do you care to join us?" Mr. Jones spoke, snapping Bryce back to the present. "Where is Plato talking about in this statement?" He questioned Bryce.

Bryce quickly scanned the quote and thought. "Rome?" He responded.

"Class this is a prime example of someone who while physically present is not mentally present. No Mr. Hillcrest. He's not talking about Rome."

Mr. Jones sarcastically said. "Please could someone tell me what Plato is discussing here?"

"Atlantis, he is describing Atlantis. He describes a city made by half-humans half-gods, their entire city made up of concentric ring islands that are separated by wide moats that were all fed by the ocean." Bennett interjected looking over at Bryce and then back to the quote on the board.

"Thank you, Miss Douglas, you are correct. Plato is describing the naval superpower and utopian society of Atlantis. As he saw it during his life. The lost city of Atlantis. And if you will look at this, Mr. Hillcrest, what is this?" Mr. Jones said, clicking the slide to the next photo. In the photo was a series of large rings that got smaller as they approached the center, and a large channel going throughout the circles. However, everything was covered in sand.

"That's the Eye of the Sahara." Bennett answered as Bryce looked longingly at the photo.

"Correct Miss Douglas but I will remind you that your name is not Mr. Hillcrest and when I direct a question to someone, I expect that person to answer not you. But that is correct, this is the Eye of the Sahara, a monument visible from space but while few believe it to be Atlantis it does share many similarities to it. But that brings us to our lesson today, lost cities and the myths surrounding them." Mr. Jones lectured for another thirty minutes before the class ended.

"Mr. Jones, why haven't people looked into the eye of the Sahara and Atlantis being the same place more closely?" Bryce questioned the idea calling to him for some reason.

"It's simple Mr. Hillcrest, there is simply not enough evidence to support it. One person's account of one description does not make a fact. Plato was a lot of things but an all knowing being he was not. There are no other pieces of evidence to support this claim and so therefore it is not worth looking into. Now if that is everything, good day and please pay more attention in class." Mr. Jones said, doing his typical shooing motion. Bryce did as instructed and left the idea of the lost city pushed to the back of his mind to be forgotten.

The rest of the week went by quickly and by Saturday Bryce was actually looking forward to the party. While he wasn't a fan of Ashton, Carter pointed out nearly everyone in the school was going, lots of girls would be there and it was their first party as Juniors. Bryce couldn't help but look forward to the idea. "You can go but no drinking. Bryce promise me." Rhys sternly said as he looked Bryce in the eye.

"Dad, everyone will be drinking, I'll be the only one not drinking. It's only a couple of beers." He pleaded with his father.

"Bryce, you lost consciousness four days ago, I do not want to risk you passing out at this party when we have no idea why it happened." Rhys said, trying to get his point across. "Take the car, it'll give you an excuse not to drink and that way I don't have to worry about you drinking or about how you're getting home." Rhys slid the keys across the table as he spoke.

"You're serious, I can take it?" Bryce questioned not believing his father.

"I'm trusting you, home by midnight, and no drinking." Rhys said wagging his finger.

"I promise." Bryce excitedly replied as he collected the keys and bolted to his room to text the guys he was driving them to the party. Bryce got ready and wore his best red and black flannel shirt buttoned up over a pair of black jeans with his black Vans, ready to enjoy the night. Bryce left and picked up Carter, then Harry, his Dad's SUV making the group feel far cooler than the Hawaiian shirt Harry wore made them out to be.

"Harry, what the heck are you wearing?" Carter replied as the pudgy boy climbed into the car. "You look like a divorced father on vacation."

"It's called peacocking, grabs the girls attention and then boom I have an in. Plus, it's a nice shirt." Harry replied matter of factly.

"You have to stop watching those videos on how to pick up girls. They will not work." Carter exclaimed as Bryce drove, chuckling at the argument.

"When I have girls crawling all over me, don't ask for advice. And it's not a video, it's a podcast." Harry replied ending the conversation as the group pulled up to the party. "Watch and learn boys, give me twenty minutes and I'll have the girls feeding me grapes."

"Why is it always food with this guy?" Carter said, elbowing Bryce in the side. Ashton lived in a large house with a big front yard surrounded by stone walls with black painted fences, currently filled with kids from school. Bryce, Carter and Harry strode through the party looking around at the chaos of the party. In the living room the couches had been pushed to the side and a pseudo dance floor was set up with people dancing to the DJ who was in the corner playing music. The group moved their way deeper into the house and saw in the kitchen several liquor bottles and juices were spread across the counter with cups placed in front of them. Bryce gestured and the two made a drink while he poured himself a cup of fruit punch from the bottle so as not to stand out. The group reassembled after that and pushed their way to the backyard where the rest of the party was, beer pong and other drinking games were set up as well as a keg which had people lined up around it as James and Jonathan held Ashton's legs up as he did a keg stand.

"It's my birthday baby!" He exclaimed as he finished his keg stand, wiped his mouth and kissed Bennett, who looked less than comfortable with this display of affection.

"Sarah! Girl, you look good!" Carter called out as he waved over to a much taller blonde girl who smiled back at Carter as he smirked to Harry and left.

"Just you and I, big guy." Bryce said to Harry who looked at him shrugged and walked towards the beer pong table. Bryce followed and watched a bit trying to get the gist of the game. After watching a bit Harry was up and on his set of throws sunk three out of four. He was on fire. By the end of the game, Harry was surrounded by people and when he sunk the last cup with his eyes closed the crowd went crazy. Bryce smiled and walked away deciding to see what else the party had in store.

After wandering around the party for an hour, Bryce decided to try to find his friends and check in on them. Bryce checked the dance floor, the front yard, and the kitchen but no luck. Giving up hope, Bryce made his way back to the backyard and leaned against the fence.

"Hey Stranger." Bennett said, walking up to Bryce and leaning against the fence beside him. She looked stunning. She wore a pair of tight blue jeans with rips in the knees, a pair of black shoes, and a white crop top with a black, small leather jacket over top. Her hair was straightened and fell just past her shoulders and laid softly on her chest. Bryce had to take a second before he replied.

"Wow. You look... yeah... hey." Bryce stumbled over his words as he spoke.

"You are a man of many words, Bryce Hillcrest." Bennett teased as she looked around the party. "Where are the guys?" She questioned.

"I'm not sure to be honest." Bryce replied. "Thought you weren't talking to me. You kind of left in a hurry the other day." Bryce jabbed back.

"Yeah sorry, I panicked and yeah here we are. Plus, a little liquid courage didn't hurt." She smiled as she tipped her red plastic cup up to her mouth and sipped.

"I see, glad it could help. Where's Ashton, I'm not trying to start any more drama." Bryce said as he glanced around.

"I can leave if you want." Bennett replied sharply.

"No, no stay. I just don't want to cause problems at the party I almost wasn't allowed to attend earlier this week." Bryce hurriedly reassured Bennett. "But where is the birthday boy?" He questioned.

"Passed out in his room. I'll probably go check on him shortly. But don't go far. I want to chat more. Been too long." Bennett said, taking a long sip of her drink and then turning it upside down to show Bryce it was finished. With a wink Bennett walked away putting a little more swing in her hips than her normal walk. He watched for a moment before he caught himself and went back to people watching; after a few moments he walked into the house.

"Bryce!" Harry called from the couch on the dance floor.

"Harry!" Bryce exclaimed back as the pudgy boy shot up and hugged him.

"Told ya." He hiccupped, clearly a little drunker than the last time Bryce had seen him. "I won five games before I decided to retire as a champion." He slurred as he swayed in front of Bryce.

"That's great Harry, you feeling okay?" Bryce questioned leaning close to Harry's ear as he spoke, smelling cheap beer and liquor on his breath.

"Great, I got Serena Pollard's number, we're going to go out next week, and she digs the shirt." Harry exclaimed, yelling into Bryce's ear.

Just as Bryce was about to reply a loud scream came from the upper floor. "With her?" Bennett yelled. "You're messing around with her, at the party I planned for you?" Just as Bennett screamed one of the doors on the upper level opened and slammed shut. "We are over." Bennett yelled as she stormed down the stairs and out the front door. As the whole party went silent.

"Time to leave Harry." Bryce said as he maneuvered Harry through the gathering crowd. As Bryce and a group spilled out onto the front yard, Bryce spotted Carter who seemed in far better shape than Harry and aside from being covered in lipstick, seemed no worse for wear. Bryce nodded to Harry, and Carter ran over grabbing Harry's arm as Bryce ran to catch up to Bennett. "Bennett wait." Bryce called to the small fury as she stormed off.

"Screw you." Bennett called over her shoulder, not bothering to look. Bryce took a few more strides and placed a hand on her shoulder. As she turned around Bennett cocked a fist ready to swing when she saw it was Bryce and lowered her fist. Her eyes bloodshot and her makeup running as she cried. "He was with another girl." She sobbed as Bryce looked at her.

"I'll drive you home. Just go with the guys." Bryce said, as he nodded to Harry and Carter who on cue continued their walk towards the car.

"Where do you think you're going? She's staying here." Bryce heard the words and felt the impact before he could react. A fist connected perfectly with the side of his head and sent him sprawling. Bryce heard ringing as he looked around trying to find the source of the blow. Just then he saw Ashton as a foot behind him connected with his ribs. James had kicked him. Bryce clambered to his feet just as Jonathan tackled him. "Bennett babe it isn't what it looked like. She said you were cool with it." Ashton drunkenly said as he grabbed Bennett and pulled her towards the house.

"No, I want to go home." Bennett replied, pulling her arm back, unable to free it from the grasp. At this point Bryce had scrambled to his feet once again, angry and determined.

"You're staying here!" Ashton yelled as he wrenched Bennett's arm back and pushed her towards the house. Bryce didn't think he just reacted. In one movement he bolted forward, elbowed Ashtons arm downwards breaking the grip he had on Bennett, and hip checked him onto his back.

"Bennett go." He said as he readied himself for a fight.

"No Ashton, leave him alone." Bennett said as Ashton stood up, his eyes wild with fury.

"I'm going to kill you, Bryce." Ashton screamed.

"No Ashton, go inside." Bennett said softly trying to defuse the situation. "I'll stay, it's fine." Bennett called as she stepped in between the two guys.

"Shut up. Maybe if you put out once and a while I wouldn't have to go elsewhere." Ashton bellowed as he pushed Bennett to the side causing her to fall hard on the grass. The crowd of people growing with every second.

Ashton rushed Bryce from the front as James and Jonathan rushed from Bryce's left. Bryce was tackled from the side as a fist connected with his jaw. He tumbled over as Ashton and his goons rained down kicks. Bryce covered and waited for an opening. As James stepped back for a soccer kick Bryce rolled and attacked his knee diving for it and putting all of his weight directly on the joint. With a sickening snap Bryce felt the joint snap and in one movement was back on his feet as James screamed in pain.

Jonathan rushed next. In one movement Bryce jumped in the air throwing a perfect flying knee to the jaw of the oncoming boy, the knee hit, and Bryce felt the boy's jaw dislocate as he landed, stumbling forward. Jonathan lay unmoving on the ground. Just as Bryce regained his footing a bottle hit him in the shoulder. Clearly meant for his head, Ashton stood wielding a broken bottle sharp as a knife ready to attack. Just as Bryce saw the bottle Ashton rushed. But it was like he was moving at half speed?

Quarter speed?

Slow motion?

What was happening? It was as if time had slowed, and just like in his dream it was as if the whole world went quiet. Ashton was swinging the bottle knife as Bryce gathered his sense, the blow was moving but with ease Bryce ducked under the blow, then just as in his dream, Bryce threw a hook to the body of Ashton, his body crumpling under the force of the blow, then with a pivot Bryce was perfectly in line with the now concaving body of Ashton. Bryce waited a moment and then with all his power punched Ashton in the face, feeling the flesh wrap around his fist as he struck true. Then in a snap the screams of James, roar of the crowd and the sound of the world returned. Bryce stumbled backwards into Carter.

"How did you do that?" Carter screamed. "You moved so fast." Carter said, grabbing Bryce and supporting him, as the two made their way to the car. "Bennett, come on, get in the car." Carter said, ushering the still shocked and grass-stained Bennett into the car. "Bryce, can you drive?" Carter questioned as he slammed the passenger side door closed.

"What?" Bryce questioned in a fog, as glass fell out of his collar.

"Can you drive?" Carter shouted.

"Yeah, yeah, I can. Let's go." Bryce said, throwing the car in drive and racing home.

As his adrenaline began to wear off Bryce pulled in his driveway, his vision beginning to tunnel and the voices of everyone beginning to fade.

CHAPTER 6

"Bryce, wake up. Come on, wake up." Bryce heard the faint sound of Carter's voice as he felt sharp pain shoot through his face.

"Is he going to be, okay?" Bennett cried out.

"I think he's coming to." Carter exclaimed as Bryce opened his eyes, the light blinding him as he did. "Bryce you're okay!" Carter shouted as he dabbed a cold compress on Bryce's bruised face. "I thought we were going to have to get Rhys for a second there." Carter said, breathing a sigh of relief.

"What do you mean? Where am I?" Bryce questioned as he tried to sit up.

"Stop moving. You parked the car and passed out. We didn't know what to do so we brought you to my house." Bennett said softly as she pushed lightly on Bryce's chest.

"Bryce, you beat the tar out of Ashton, James and Jonathan, and at one point moved super-fast. You were there one moment and then the next Ashton is on the ground and you're finishing a punch. IT. WAS. AWESOME." Harry called out from the couch as he drunkenly ate crackers.

"He tried to stab me." Bryce said softly. "But he was so slow." He mumbled softly.

"Slow? Bryce, Ashton was moving quickly. I don't understand what you mean by slow." Bennett questioned.

"Probably adrenaline like when a mom lifts a car off a baby or something." Harry said through a mouthful of crackers. Bryce looked around at the group and wiggled his way into an upright seated position.

"So, what happens next?" Bryce questioned. "Do I go home?" Bryce asked the group who continued to look at him.

"We'll clean you up first but it's probably a good idea. People are already saying they've uploaded the fight to YouTube. It's only a matter of time before Rhys finds it." Bennett said checking her phone and then placing it back down on the table. She then reached across and dabbed the bruise around Bryce's face with the wet cold compress. Bryce winched away. "Let me help you." Bennett blurted out as she pressed the cold towel on him once again.

"Bryce, you have no idea how awesome that was. Saves the most popular girl in school, from the abusive boyfriend, then beats him and his two cronies single handedly. That movie writes itself." Carter spoke as he looked around the room to less than happy looks. "I mean come on, it's true. Plus, I was coming in to back you up when you did the whole snap a guy's leg thing, which by the way was crazy cool." Carter continued the excitement building as he described each move with actions included.

"I'm just glad everyone's okay." Bryce said, looking around the room. "Well, everyone here." He corrected.

"Me too." Bennett nodded as she dabbed Bryce's face again. "Rhys is going to freak out if you don't clean up a little."

"I think he'll freak regardless. But thanks." Bryce said, grabbing the towel from Bennett, their hands lingering on each other for a moment longer than they should have.

Bryce cleaned up as best he could, gathered his senses and made his way home, Bennett promising that Carter and Harry would get home safely. The walk home felt a mile long. And as Bryce felt his hand turn the knob the door flung open. "You're la— what happened to you?" Rhys questioned, a glass of whiskey in his hand.

"Ashton and his goons. Attacked Bennett, then me. I defended myself." Bryce said wearily. Rubbing his hands together and preparing for the worst.

"Get inside." Rhys said, pulling Bryce in and closing the door. Then in one movement the large man pulled his son into a hug. "I'm glad you're okay. When I saw the car in the driveway, and you weren't home or answering my calls I feared the worst." Rhys mumbled as he squeezed Bryce.

"Ouch." Bryce said as his ribs contracted, suddenly he remembered being kicked there.

"Sorry. I'm just glad you're okay." Rhys released Bryce and motioned to the couch. "What exactly happened?" He questioned. Bryce quickly relayed the story leaving out the slow-motion part, chalking it up to adrenaline just as Carter had said. He didn't want to sound crazy, and it didn't seem important. Rhys had told him to defend himself whenever necessary and that's what he did.

"Well, I bet you're glad I force you to train as much as I do now, aren't you?" Rhys asked rhetorically. "I am glad you're okay and am proud of you for doing what was right. Go get some rest son." Bryce nodded in agreement and made his way to his bedroom and then to bed. Sleep didn't come easy that night. He thought about how things had slowed down for him. *Carter said he moved quickly, but he felt like he moved normally and everything around him slowed.* He shrugged it off and after some time drifted off to sleep. His last thoughts of Bennett.

"You broke three ribs and his jaw." Harry exclaimed over the gaming headset. "With two punches Bryce you are a certified badass."

"I don't know if that's true. I heard it was one rib and his eye socket. Either way, it's still pretty badass." Carter replied. "I had your back though." He added quickly.

"Thanks, Carter, you don't have to keep mentioning it. Plus, I'd prefer if we didn't, my Dad has questioned me about ten times already." Bryce said, looking at his reflection and seeing the bruises from the fight.

"So now that Bennett is single…" Harry began but was cut off.

"Bryce, come down here please." Rhys called up to Bryce from the bottom of the stairs. Bryce slipped off his headset and made his way to the top of the stairs where his dad waited with two police officers flanked either side of him. "You're not in trouble, these officers just want to hear your side of what happened." Rhys motioned for his son to come downstairs and take a seat sitting calmly beside him once he did so. The two officers followed him. One was a tall brown skinned man with a five o'clock shadow and a short buzz cut. The other was a small blonde woman with small features similar to Sarah, a quick glance at her name tag revealed it was her mother she must get her height from her dad, Bryce thought to himself.

The woman spoke first, pulling out a pen and notepad, flicking it to a page and beginning to write. "So, Bryce, what happened yesterday at Mr. Danier's party?"

"Ashton attacked me with his two friends, tried to stab me with a broken bottle, and I defended myself." Bryce replied quickly and quietly looking at Rhys and then around the room.

"And what happened leading up to him attacking you?" She replied quickly, jotting down what Bryce had said. "Because the way Mr. Danier and his friends explain it, you had issues with him earlier in the week and went to his party looking for a conflict, considering they had been drinking and you chose to remain sober." She said, reading off her notes as she did.

"That's not true. Ashton made up something as an excuse to attack me in the halls earlier this week, then I spoke with his girlfriend... I mean his ex-girlfriend and we settled it. He then attacked me at his party after she caught him with another girl and tried to leave. I offered her a ride at which point he and his friends attacked me. There's videos of it. All over YouTube." Bryce spat back angrily at the accusatory tone of the officer. "Are you going to arrest me?" Bryce asked bitterly.

"Not as of right now. We're getting conflicting stories, and these videos show you being attacked but if you went there to start a fight the blame could fall on you. We're just trying to get a report of the facts right now. But it would help you in the future if you filed this report as soon as possible because if things go to civil court, you could be liable." The officer explained as she scribbled down a few more notes. "Well, that is all the questions I have right now but if we have more I will reach out. If you can think of anything else, please feel free to reach out." She said sliding a business card across the table. "I've written the report number on the top of the card as well." She said as Bryce looked at the card and the number as Rhys showed the officers out.

Bryce returned to his room and spent his time, icing his bruises and watching the videos that had been posted to YouTube. Some had already racked up eighteen thousand views. Bryce watched the video over and over again, watching the last moments as slow as possible. It was weird. It was like he was there one moment Ashton moving towards him as he began his swing with the bottle. Then within the blink of an eye Bryce was beside Ashton, and Ashton was on the floor unconscious. Over and over, he watched it, still unable to explain it. Then his phone buzzed. Bennett had texted him.

CHAPTER 7

"The Police stopped by today but didn't stay long, just asked if I was at the party and if Ashton was my boyfriend, and then left. Bryce I'm sorry you have to go through this. It isn't fair. I should tell them that it was all Ashton's fault, just get it all to go away." Bennett said as she laid beside Bryce on the roof, the music barely audible as she spoke.

"Don't bother. It'll only lead to you getting involved. You don't need to be dragged into this any further." Bryce replied unmoving; to him getting anyone else involved would just cause more issues.

"Bryce… I'm not letting you get in trouble for something you didn't do. Ashton came after you because of me. This is my fault." Bennett pleaded as she sat more upright. "Let me help you." She took his hand as she spoke and squeezed it between hers. Bryce sat up and looked out into the small forest behind his house.

"Bennett, if you get involved, you're going to have to speak against Ashton. He'll drag your name through the mud and make up lies about you. He did it to me and within a day the whole school believed him. It's not worth it. He got what he deserved." Bryce said softly, placing his free hand on the bruise across Bennett's face. "You don't need to get hurt anymore." Bryce whispered, his voice breaking slightly.

"I'm fine. You're the one who got beat up if I recall." Bennett replied, turning over Bryce's hand to see the bruises on his forearm. The two sat in silence for a moment, holding each other. Bryce laid back down and Bennett crawled closer, cuddling up to Bryce laying her head on his chest as she did. "Your heart is racing… are you nervous?" Bennett whispered as she listened.

"No… I'm… never mind." Bryce whispered back trying his best to come up with an excuse and failing. The truth was he was nervous, nervous about school tomorrow, nervous about this whole police issue, nervous about his future, and most importantly, nervous that Bennett Douglas was cuddled up to him laying on his chest just listening.

"You can be nervous Bryce. I don't know why you're pretending to be fine after everything. It's okay to not be okay." Bennett said softly as she pressed into Bryce slightly more. "I'm here for you." She whispered as she lay just listening.

Bryce must've fallen asleep because he didn't remember hearing the music stop, the crunch of tires on the stone driveway of his house or seeing headlights brighten the driveway. But when Rhys called his name, something snapped him back to reality.

"Bryce!" Rhys called out from the base of the stairs. "Come here kiddo." *Kiddo?* Bryce thought to himself. Rhys was a serious man; kiddo was not something he would say willingly or purposely. Was it a warning? Were the Police back? Bryce questioned as he wiggled out of Bennett's embrace.

"Bryce? Who is it?" Bennett whispered. "It's like midnight, do you think it's the cops?" Bennett whispered as she followed Bryce down the roof.

"I don't know. My Dad called me kiddo." Bryce replied as he slid down to the window.

"Kiddo? What does that have to do with anything?" Bennett questioned.

"When have you ever known my Dad to be a kiddo guy? Anton, maybe, but my Dad? Something doesn't feel right." Bryce replied, the hairs on the back of his neck standing up. Could it be Bennett's Dad? He never liked Bryce, ever since he broke the photo of Bennett's late mother during a nerf gun fight in the house.

"I guess but I think you're being paranoid." Bennett whispered as she joined Bryce brushing the pine needles off her sweat pants.

"See he's not here." Bryce heard Rhys call out to the room. Bryce waved at Bennett signaling her to stop.

"Then find him." A raspy deep man's voice replied. Bryce slowly moved away from the window and placing an arm on Bennett slowly moving her backwards. "Search the house. metadata shows that he was here recently. And you. Get him outside." The voice commanded and as Bryce shifted his weight back, he heard the aggressive stomping of boots throughout the house.

"Bryce, who is it?" Bennett whimpered as Bryce shifted her further up the roof. Bryce turned and signaled once again for silence and gestured to move further back on the roof. The two made their way quietly to the top of the roof just as a head peered out of the window. Bryce couldn't make out much as their face was obscured by a balaclava, but he could tell they did not seem friendly and the P90 machine gun they pointed out the window solidified that fact. "Bryce I'm scared." Bennett whispered barely audible. Bryce wrapped an arm around her and slid back so the two were hidden even more.

"Get your hands off me." Rhys shouted as he was pushed sprawling out onto the back grass. Bryce peered over the roof's peak with Bennett as the scene played out below them.

Rhys was picking himself up as the backyard lights came on and two men armed with the same gun as the man earlier pointed them at Rhys. The two men were well trained as they maintained a distance from Rhys, close enough to easily hit their target while far enough away to ensure he could not disarm them if he made a move. *My dad taught me that same technique...* Bryce thought to himself. Just as Rhys had clambered to his knees, a man approached. He was huge. He was easily six-foot-five and maybe three hundred pounds, with a bald head and thin eyebrows. Bryce couldn't make out much besides that, but he could tell the man was very fit and had a large scar across his face going from the top of his left eye to the bottom of his right cheek. Whatever and whoever did that to a man this size must've had a death wish. "Where is the boy?" He called out as he approached Rhys. "You know we'll find him, it's only a matter of time." The man said as he squatted down beside Rhys. "You did a good job hiding him. We were looking in Georgia for you." He chuckled as he grabbed him by the cheeks pinching them together.

"You must be bad at your job then." Rhys mumbled through his pursed lips.

"House is clear, Sir. No sign of the boy." A man said as several armed men filed out of the house.

"Hmmm." The man said, scratching the back of his head thoughtfully with his pistol as he held Rhys. "Guess we do this the hard way." As he said as he struck Rhys with the gun, sending him sprawling down again. Bryce began to move anger and impulse taking over his body, but as he moved, Bennett grabbed his arm and pulled.

"Bryce, no." She whispered the fear and concern clear on her illuminated face. Bryce slowly lowered himself and continued watching. Bennett's hand found his and the two watched on in horror.

"Rhys, you know how this ends." The man negotiated. "I can make it quick, end it before you suffer much more. And I promise I'll kill the kid quickly too, just because we go way back." He said as he paced in front of Rhys.

"The way, I remember it, you screwed around and found out, or do I need to remind you what happened last time we fought, I figured that scar would be enough of a reminder." Rhys spat as blood filled his gray beard turning it red. He was met with a swift kick to the chest for his insubordination.

"Guess we're doing it the hard way then?" The man chuckled as Rhys picked himself up again. "Grab his hand." The man said as he nodded at Rhys. "Last chance Rhys, where's the boy?" The man said as two more men flattened Rhys out and two more stretched his arm out from his body.

"Go screw yourself." Rhys said through clenched teeth.

"I was hoping you'd say that." The man laughed as he grabbed onto Rhys's thumb. With a scream of agony from Rhys, the man pulled and wretched the finger breaking it painfully, as the group all cheered.

"How is no one hearing this?" Bennett said as she looked around the street. The houses were all dark, not a single light could be seen throughout the entire street, dogs weren't even barking. Bryce had wondered the same thing but was too shocked to speak.

"You've got nine more chances Rhys, now tell me… where is the boy?" The man said as he grabbed the next finger. Rhys said nothing. With another scream another finger was broken hanging there bent at a sickening angle. "Tell me!" The man shouted as he snapped another finger. Rhys screamed in agony but remained silent. "Commander, this can end whenever you want. Just tell me where he is." The man said as he paused, waiting for Rhys to weigh his options.

"I. Don't. Know." Rhys spat. His voice shaking with each word. "But I can get him here." Rhys muttered his voice hoarse from the screaming. "Just… Just bring me my phone." Rhys mumbled sadly.

"That's more like it." The man said with a smile. "Now that wasn't so hard, was it? You, get me his phone." The man said, pointing at one of the seven men not part of the group holding Rhys down.

"Bryce, your phone." Bennett whispered, pulling at his pants pocket. "The ringer." She whispered. Bryce couldn't have pulled his phone out faster, mashing the silent button until it buzzed signaling vibration mode was on. Bryce stuffed the phone back in his pocket and once again peered over the top of the flattened area of roof, Bennett beside him once again taking his hand in hers. Just as the two peered over the man emerged from the house holding a phone and jogging over to Rhys and the big man.

"Call him." The man said, stuffing the phone into Rhys's cut and bloodied face.

"He's seventeen you think he'll answer his father's phone call?" Rhys questioned only to be hit again with the pistol.

"Do I look stupid? You'll call him. You think I'm stupid enough to let you text him and send some code? Ha!" The man cackled as he forced Rhys to dial. The call went through, and Bryce felt the buzzing in his pocket. He didn't answer. As the voicemail beeped the man hung up. "Call him again. And you'd better hope this time he picks up, otherwise…" the man threatened, waving his pistol in the air as he did. Rhys redialed the phone and Bryce felt a familiar buzzing in his pants. Bryce slid back on the roof and pulled the phone out of his pocket.

"Hello?" He whispered trying to keep his voice as calm as possible.

"Bryce?" Rhys questioned. "Where are you kiddo? Are you with Ashton, watching that horror movie?"

"Ummm… yeah, I am why?" Bryce replied softly.

"Don't come home! Anton for my sins! Run! Don't let the—" Rhys shouted before an all too familiar pop cut through the air and Bennett gasped.

"What was that?" The man shouted as he turned and looked at the roof just as Bennett's head slid out of eyesight. "Clean this up." The man said his eyes still on the roofline as he spoke. "Torch the house and then get some of the locals on the payroll to pin in on the boy. Cut off his options. I want him found by sun down tomorrow."

"Yes sir." A masked soldier replied as he was handed the pistol by the large man who made his way out of the backyard and into his blacked-out GMC Yukon in the driveway. As they heard the gravel crunch under the man's boots, Bryce and Bennett slowly moved around the roof, so they were hidden from the man's view as he pulled out of the driveway. It was at this point Bryce saw Rhys's limp body being pulled into the house by two armed men.

"What are we going to do?" Bennett whimpered as the two remained hidden on the roof, as the men below began pouring gasoline around the house.

"I don't know. If we can get inside, I can grab the go bag in my Dad's room. That way we'll have some money." Bryce thought as he watched the scene below play out. His eyes burned with tears as he sat there waiting.

"They're going to set fire to the house!" Bennett reminded Bryce the fear prominent in her voice, pleading for him to think of a better option.

"I know. But I don't see another option. We get the bag and then we go out the back and into the woods." Bryce said, pointing to the trees that lined his house. "When we get outside, do not stop running, for anything." Bryce said fearing the worst.

The two waited several more minutes in silence mentally preparing for the task ahead, when the movement in the house and the sounds of doors closing echoed through the night air, the two inched towards the window, Bryce entered first and then Bennett shortly after.

As Bryce entered the house the heat was already building, they'd set the fire in the lower floors, but he could feel it building fast. Pulling his shirt up over his nose and mouth Bryce pulled Bennett into the house and silently placed her hand on his back. The two made their way as a group down the hall and into Rhys's room. The smoke began to build the room's roof invisible through the thick black smoke that plumed through the house. Bryce knelt down and began feeling his way through the room past the bed to the closet until he felt the familiar fabric of the black, tactical, twenty-four-hour pack, Rhys had so often made him practice grabbing and fleeing the house with it in case of an emergency. Once Bryce had slung the pack over his shoulders, he grabbed Bennett's hand and the two began to make their way out to the hall. The smoke was unbearable and burned Bryce's lungs as the two descended the stairs smothering their coughing as they went. Bryce's eyes, nose, and throat burned as he pushed his way though, flames billowing up the sides of the walls as they raced through the house to the back door.

As the two made it to the kitchen Bryce froze. Rhys's body was laid on the floor, flames licking at the now blackened body. "Bryce, come on, there's nothing we can do now." Bennett coughed as she pulled on Bryce who was stuck in place. It took all her might, but Bennett forced him out the door. "Bryce, come on!" She shouted, snapping Bryce out of his trance and back onto the task at hand.

The two had nearly made it to the trees when Bryce finally felt the cold night air. His eyes, nose and mouth burned from the smoke and with a glance over at Bennett he could tell she was in the same state. They had just entered the trees when he felt the pull of her on his clothes. "I… I need a moment. I can't breathe." She pleaded in between coughs. Bryce nodded and the two found a spot just inside the forest where they could catch their breath. The dim glow of the flames illuminating the trees. The sound of the fire filling the night air.

CHAPTER 8

It was nearly twenty minutes before Bryce heard the sound of sirens, and the flash of lights. By that time the two had snuck their way through the forest and into Bennett's house. "What is going on Bryce?" Bennett said as she paced her bedroom. The pink walls and soft rug, the stark opposite of Bryce's gray room with video game posters and hardwood floors. He'd been in Bennett's room before as kids, but the years had changed the look. Long gone were the boy band, teenage heart throb and newest pop star posters. Now they were minimalist art prints, dream boards, a full body mirror by the closet and a desk clearly set up to do makeup with a large ring light mirror on it. Bryce didn't mind the changes, it suited Bennett.

"I don't know. I need to think." Bryce said ruffling his hair and looking over at his phone that sat on the bed charging. "My Dad is dead Bennett, they burned down my house. And I have no idea who killed him or why." Bryce choked up as he spoke, burying his face in his hands.

"I know I'm sorry Bryce. For what it's worth, I know he died doing what he thought was right. He was protecting you until his very end. Anyone would tell you that makes him an amazing Dad." Bennett spoke softly as she placed an arm around Bryce. Bryce buried his face in her shoulder and held her close. "We need a plan." Bennett said, pushing Bryce back and looking at him.

"There's no 'we' Bennett. Being close to me is dangerous." Bryce whimpered, pulling away as he did. His soot covered face streaked with tears.

"What do you mean? I am not leaving you." Bennett said, grabbing Bryce by the arm and spinning him around to look at her. "You don't get to cut and run from me. Not after what I just saw. I am a part of this now. Whether you like it or not." Bennett forcefully spoke, puffing her chest as she did trying to command some authority to Bryce who loomed over her. "If they come looking for you, they will almost certainly come here."

"No, you're not. Bennett, they just killed my Dad. My Dad. The strongest, most well-trained man I know. And they beat and killed him in front of me." Bryce cried. "They don't know you. And I plan on keeping it that way. As soon as my phone is fully charged, I am calling Anton and leaving." Bryce asserted as he walked over and checked his phone.

"No, you are not. We don't know who we can trust. Rhys said atone for his sins. You think running is what he meant." Bennett said, pushing Bryce away from his phone and looking at him. Tears of frustration and fear staining her cheeks now too.

"He said Anton. Not atone. It's a clue. Like asking if I was with Ashton. They're going to look for him not you, I'm sure they're talking with him right now, which means he's going to deny it and they'll come looking for..." Bryce snapped back, grabbing Bennett by the shoulders and shaking her.

"They'll come after me. Because when they finally get Ashton to talk- which will be hard considering his jaw is wired shut after you broke that and his ribs with two punches- he'll point the finger at me. Or Carter or Harry. People who will then be in danger. So, you might not like it, but you are stuck with me. And Anton for his sins might be a sign that we can't trust him. Did you think of that?" Bennett pushed back, breaking Bryce's grip on her shoulders. "You don't get to make all the decisions Bryce. Not now."

"I... I never thought of that." Bryce mumbled looking at his once white shoes now stained with mud and soot. "What do we do then?" Bryce asked without breaking eye contact with the floor, digging his shoe into the floor as he did.

"Now it's we?" Bennett snapped, picking up Bryce's chin so she could look at him in his soft, light brown eyes. Her blue eyes held a steely resolve as she spoke. "We meet him somewhere he can't control. Somewhere public, busy and full of people. Somewhere with lots of exits. Somewhere like..." Bennett thought out loud as she paced.

"The mall?" Bryce questioned.

"Exactly, like some cheesy spy movie. We meet him there, and if he comes alone then we're good. If not, then we know he's in on it." Bennett nodded, stopping in her footsteps and looking at him. "What's your phone at?" She snapped, her mood changing drastically.

"Sixty-seven percent why?" Bryce asked, clicking the screen on and off.

"Turn it off and unplug it now." Bennett yelled while diving for the phone.

"Bennett what are you doing?" Bryce said dodging out of the way as he did.

"They can track phones. They have your Dad's phone. We need to leave now." She shouted. Bryce grabbed the go bag and pulled Bennett off the bed towards the door. Just as the two did, they saw the beams of flashlights scanning the entrance of the house and pounding on the door. The two stopped dead in their tracks. "Crap, crap, crap." Bennett whispered. "We're too late, they found us again." Bennett quietly cried. Bryce backed her up into the room shielding her as they did.

"Check the window." Bryce murmured nodding to the window that faced the street in her bedroom, his eyes fixed on the door ready to attack the first person who entered.

Bennett slowly made her way to her curtains and with as little movement as possible shifted them just enough to see the front yard. As she did, the lights from outside filled the room. Red and white lights flashing.

"It's firefighters, probably making their way house to house to evacuate all people inside." Bennett whispered as she returned the curtain to its original orientation and crept back to Bryce's side. "They must not think anyone is home since my Dad's car isn't in the driveway and all the lights are off." She whispered reassuringly.

"Maybe but I say we wait until they're gone and sneak out the back. You heard that man, they have locals on their payroll, could be anyone really." Bryce whispered back as his hand found Bennett's hip and directed her further behind him.

"Good idea. But we should leave soon. If they're evacuating houses, it might not be long before they break down the door to check if anyone is in here." She whispered in his ear.

"We wait until the lights leave and then we go." Bryce nodded in agreement. As Bryce waited Bennett packed a bag. Bryce directed her as to what to take and what not to. Bennett managed to pack an overnight bag, blue jeans, a sweater of hers and the one Bryce let her borrow, two t-shirts, two pairs of socks and when it came to packing her underwear Bryce told her to pack what she needed, a rush of blood making him blush as he spoke about it. It took Bennett just under three minutes to pack her bag and as she zipped it up, the flashlights seemed to trail off to the next house. "Should I bring my phone?" Bennett questioned holding her phone in her hand.

"No, leave it just to be safe. We'll keep mine off until we make the call and then dump it as well. If we need to, we have money to get new ones." Bryce whispered as Bennett turned off the phone, before returning to his side. "Time to go." He said as he made his way out of her bedroom and down the hall.

Bryce let Bennett lead the way as she knew her house better, the two creeping out of the house and quickly sprinting to the forest. Once they had made it deep enough into the forest Bryce stopped. Looking back at his house he saw the streams of water arcing through the air as plumes of smoke filled the once peaceful night sky. "I'm really sorry Bryce." Bennett said, sliding her hand into his.

"Thanks, let's get going." Bryce said, wiping his face and nodding towards a path that led through the forest.

The two walked for over an hour through the forest before they exited nearly three miles away from the house. Feeling it was now safe, the two sat on a nearby bench. "I should have changed at the house." Bennett said, slapping her hand to her forehead.

"Probably wouldn't have been a bad idea." Bryce chuckled as he rubbed his shoulder where the backpack had been. "We should try to find somewhere to clean up. A motel maybe?"

"You're not funny." Bennett said, slapping Bryce's arm. "But you're right. We look like people who escaped a fire. And you need new clothes." Bennett pinched Bryce's singed and soot covered hoodie and giggled.

"I think there's one not too far from here." Bryce nodded as he began to stand up.

"One more minute?" Bennett said, pulling him down to sit as she nuzzled herself closer to him. Bryce sighed and sat down relieved to have an extra moment, and more relieved to have Bennett cuddled up to him. He placed his arm around her and let her body warmth mix with his on the cold September morning. "Okay let's go." Bennett said, picking herself up off of Bryce and slinging her pink JanSport backpack over her shoulder. Bryce chuckled at the irony of trying to hide with a bright pink backpack and then followed Bennett's lead.

After another thirty minutes of walking the two came to the Sunshine Motel. The dual level motel boasted a sun-faded blue and yellow sign with a smiling sun pulling down a pair of black sunglasses and winking. Bryce approached the front desk. As he entered the lobby, Bennett tucked in behind him as the two were greeted by a busty black woman who was reading a romance novel by some author Bryce had never heard of. The lobby smelled like a vacuum had just been run over the multi-color and patterned floor. "Welcome to the Sunshine Motel, what can I do for you sugar?" The woman said, putting her book down and looking up at Bryce and Bennett. With a quick glance up and down the woman spoke again. "Do not touch anything I just cleaned and do not want to clean again."

"We'd like a room?" Bryce requested as he quickly removed his hands from the front desk.

"Hourly rate is five dollars, or the nightly rate is fifty." The woman said typing quickly on her computer screen. The light glowing off the lenses of her glasses.

"We'll take it for the night." Bryce said, slinging his backpack off his shoulder and rummaging through it for the Ziplock bag of cash he knew was in there.

"Make that two." Bennett called over his shoulder as Bryce stripped off a hundred-dollar bill and resealed the bag.

"Ouu… splurging I see." The woman joked as she clicked the keys on the computer. "I just need a name for the room and a form of ID." She said as she looked over at Bryce her glasses slid down the bridge of her nose.

"Umm… you see…" Bryce began.

"Can we just pretend we gave you one? My… boyfriend and I really need to get away from our parents for a few days and would rather they didn't find out where we are." Bennett interjected as she peaked around Bryce. "Dad doesn't like this one too much, but I know he's the one." She whispered as she placed a hand on Bryce.

"Oh sugar, I know all about that. Tell you what. Give me an extra twenty and I'll put you under John Smith, that guy has a lot of rooms booked here if you know what I mean." The woman winked as she nodded to Bennett. Without a second thought Bennett stuffed her hand in her pocket and pulled out a crumpled wad of money. Counting it out as she did.

"Here you go… Wanda. Oh, and I like your book choice. Can you believe how cute the first time they met was? The way James thought Sarah was his friend and confessed to wanting to talk to her… ugh… so cute." Bennett said as she placed the crumpled twenty onto the hundred-dollar bill and flattened it out.

"Girl… I know right, it's so cute. Here you go. You're in room 118, just outside and down that way." Wanda pointed as she spoke, sliding a key across the desk. "Oh, and here, take extra complimentary shampoo and soap… you two need it. Now go have fun but be safe young ins like you don't need a baby trust Mama Wanda." She finished sliding the remaining items across the desk and returning to her seat where she'd been when the pair had entered.

"Enjoy the book. The twist is so good." Bennett smiled as she helped Bryce collect their items and rushed to the room.

The pair's room was as standard a room as they come. One queen sized bed in the center of the room, pushed up against the wall across from a LG TV that hadn't been new in almost a decade, propped up on a dresser, with a small table and two chairs pressed against the large window beside the door they had just entered through. Bryce quickly drew the blinds closed and placed his bag on the opposite side of the room from the door.

"Boyfriend?" Bryce questioned as Bennett tossed her bag on the floor beside him.

"It beat the stuttering you were doing. Plus, it's kind of believable until they realize how awkward you are around girls." Bennett joked back as she kicked her muddy shoes off. "I'm showering first. Don't sit on the bed. You're still covered in ash and mud." Bennett called out as Bryce watched her enter the bathroom and was halfway through collapsing into the bed. Reluctantly Bryce listened and made his way over to the table and chairs.

While Bennett showered Bryce unpacked his bag and took an inventory. Inside the bag was: a basic first aid kit, nine thousand nine hundred dollars in cash, with varying dominations, a Leatherman multi-tool, a solar blanket, a small toiletries kit, and a flashlight with batteries. Bryce couldn't help but feel disappointed there wasn't more in the bag. For a man prepared for everything Rhys had really skimped on the basics of a go bag, where was the paracord, the change of clothes, the other basics every prepper guide available on the internet mentions? But Bryce was happy to have what he did. Clothes were easy to get, and realistically he wouldn't need a bunch of rope or survival items, he was on the run from a group of men who wanted him dead, not surviving after an earthquake or flood. Content with his inventory, Bryce packed the bag up making sure to know where everything was so he could access it quickly.

After he was all packed up Bryce turned on the in-suite TV and flipped to the local news. A woman with perfectly styled blonde hair and brown eyes, smiled her bright white teeth at the screen before beginning to speak. "Tragedy has rocked an otherwise quiet neighborhood. Rockwell Street is an otherwise quiet sleepy street, just outside of the local Broadway Hills High School, that was until last night when 84 Rockwell Street caught fire, with at least one occupant still inside. Rhys Hillcrest -no photo found-was described as a quiet, kind neighbor who kept to himself and caused no issues." The woman said as footage of Bryce's house flashed across the screen with several firefighters spraying down the now smoldering pile of ash that was once his home. "While they cannot confirm for sure it has been reported to this station that the body inside the house is suspected to have been deceased prior to the fire and police are suspecting foul play. While many believe the body to be Rhys Hillcrest, his son Bryce Hillcrest has yet to be found, and this station has been asked to post a bulletin stating if you have any knowledge of Bryce's whereabouts to please contact the local police. Any help is greatly appreciated. With that, I am Stephanie Wilkinson with BHNW." She finished with a smile and a nod to the camera. Bryce quickly shut off the TV.

"Crap." He whispered silently to himself. As Bryce glanced at the clock on the nightstand. Its red numbers illuminated the time, 5:28 A.M. Mall doesn't open until 9, *hopefully Wanda doesn't watch the news or if she does, hopefully she didn't recognize me. At least Bennett wasn't mentioned in the report.* Just as Bryce finished his thought, the shower shut off and Bennett emerged from the bathroom, a towel wrapped tightly around her, her sun-kissed skin a slight shade of red from the heat of the shower and the scrubbing needed to get the soot, dirt and grime of their travels off. Bryce watched as she finished tucking her hair into a towel.

"Take a picture, it'll last longer." Bennett called out as she walked over to the bed and sat down. "Feels so good to be clean." Bennett said, rubbing her skin and smiling. "What's wrong?" She asked, seeing the concerned look on his face. Bryce took the next few minutes and explained to Bennett what he'd seen on the News and how he worried Wanda would have seen it and that the group could be here any second. "Dang it. Well, go shower and I will make my way over to the front desk for… ice." She said gesturing to the shower and then grabbing the ice bucket. "And I'll check and see if there's anything to worry about. They're looking for you by yourself so I doubt anyone will think of a couple." Bennett reassured Bryce as she waved him towards the bathroom. Bryce hesitated not wanting to risk showering when the group could be in the parking lot as he did. But after some more persuading, Bryce reluctantly stepped into the bathroom.

The water felt amazing. The black soot began to run off into the drain staining the tub as Bryce stood there unmoving as the water hit his body, the warmth like a hug, embracing him and washing the pains of the day and night away. Bryce spent ten minutes in the shower scrubbing and washing, before he emerged. After a deep breath and a wipe of the mirror, Bryce looked at his reflection. *Who are you?* He wondered as he looked at himself. *What do these people want? Is Anton involved?* Bryce felt the water slide down his muscular back and chest. As he fixed the towel wrapped around his waist, stood up straight and exited the bathroom.

Bennett sat in the opposite chair he had as the News played again she looked far more put together than Bryce expected, her hair was in a ponytail just below the top of her head, she had a gray high school cheerleading hoodie on, over a pair of light blue jeans that cut just before the ankle to show off her now slightly less dirty white air forces. As Bryce emerged Bennett glanced over, her eyes widening when she saw Bryce's body. "Take a picture, it'll last longer." Bryce joked as he scratched his head with one hand and clutched his towel with the other.

"Those look painful." Bennett said nodding to the bruises on Bryce's ribs.

"Only when I breathe." Bryce chuckled as he sat on the bed.

"Sorry." She replied.

"It's fine, somehow these earned me a girlfriend." He joked back.

"Funny. Anyway, I spoke to Wanda, not a TV in sight in the lobby. I also managed to convince her to let me look through the lost and found, which lucky for you she washes every two weeks. So… these are fairly clean, for a motel lost and found. But we can see about getting stuff at the mall before our meeting. Since we have some cash. I also raided the snack machine, with the last of the money I brought. So, we have mini powdered donuts, KitKats, fruit snacks, and two packs of Ritz cheese crackers. Oh, and Wanda hooked me up with two cups of tea. We really bonded over that book she was reading." She said nodding to the bed and then the pile of food in front of her.

"I don't know how you do it?" Bryce laughed as he slipped his boxers on under his towel and then jumped into the pair of chinos Bennett had scrounged from the lost and found. Bryce did a quick shiver at the thought of who's pants these were but thanked the lord they were just a little too big for him. Nothing cuffing the pants and pulling them up every so often couldn't fix.

"I'm cute, charming, and smart. That's how." She replied, tilting her head to one side and smiling.

"Don't forget humble." He joked back as he walked over to her shirtless.

"Can you cover up please, you're distracting." Bennett said, blocking the view of Bryce's shirtless body with her hand as she threw him the sweater of his she'd packed. Bryce slipped it on and nodded, before grabbing the mini donuts and opening the package. After offering Bennett one, Bryce devoured the pack not realizing how hungry he actually was. "Slow down there, don't need you choking on one and dying before we figure out what is going on." Bennett said as she watched Bryce barely chewing.

"Sorry." Bryce replied, his mouth half full of donut. Bryce proceeded to eat the rest of the donuts, the KitKat, and a pack of Ritz crackers as Bennett ate the rest and sipped her tea. "The mall doesn't open until 9. When should we call Anton? And where?" Bryce said once he'd finished his food and tea.

"I don't know. We have no car which means we're walking to the mall, which is dangerous considering you're a wanted man. So, I guess keep your hoodie up, and we need to get you clothes, at least something that fits, in case we need to run or fight or something." Bennett said, gesturing to Bryce's current outfit. "This is not it. As for Anton, why not call him at the mall, we call, ditch the phone and we're already there so less hassle?"

"Maybe…" He replied thinking hard. "Only thing is how do we know when he gets there?"

"We'll tell him to meet us in a certain spot. On the main floor so we can be above him watching and see if he is actually alone." She strategized as she moved the wrappers of their food around almost as if she was using them as game pieces. Bryce nodded and the plan was set. The two glanced at the clock which now read 6:47 A.M. The two agreed it was best if they set an alarm, blocked the door and got an hour's sleep. Bryce was the first to wake up, Bennett had cuddled up next to him as the two had fallen asleep, trying his best not to wake her Bryce slipped from the bed and made his way to the window, glancing out of it as he did. The coast seemed clear.

"Leaving without me?" Bennett yawned as she stretched and sat up looking at Bryce.

"No, just checking to see if any masked killers were waiting outside for us." He joked back as he returned to the bed, sitting at the edge. With a deep breath he looked at her. "You don't have to do this. You can stay here, and if it's safe, I'll come back and get you." He looked at her hard for a moment, trying to convey that this was her out and he wouldn't fault her if she took it.

"Shut up. If I don't come, who's going to make sure you look stylish while kicking butt?" She said pushing him and springing out of the bed. "Plus, I know a thing or two about fighting." She said putting her fists up in front of her face bouncing around like a boxer.

"Bennett, I'm serious, you do not have to do this, these guys are not playing around, and I don't know if I can keep you safe." He said looking at her as he pushed her hands down.

"You make me feel safe. If it wasn't for you, I'd be dead, those guys probably already raided my house, and I'd be dead for sure. You might not think it, but I am safer with you than without. And I'm not going anywhere. No matter how much you try to get rid of me." She softly said looking at him before giving him a big hug and holding him tight.

"Okay then let's do this. I don't get how you're so calm through all of this." He said pulling her in close and hugging her tight.

CHAPTER 9

It was nearly 10 A.M. by the time Bennett and Bryce arrived at the mall. "The American Eagle is this way." Bennett said quickly, leading Bryce through the now crowded mall. Bryce kept his hood up as the two moved through the crowds of people clustered throughout the mall.

"Hi, welcome to American Eagle can I help you with anything?" A small redheaded girl wearing a baggy beige sweater, and black jeans asked as the pair entered the store.

"No thanks we're good." Bennett replied with a smile as she ushered Bryce into the store. "Here take these, and these." Bennett said pulling a pair of blue and black jeans out of the stacks that filled the wall. "Oh, and this." She called out as another pair of black jeans flew through the air. "Now we need… a sweater, a shirt and what else?" She asked as she moved through the store with an efficiency Bryce only saw in movies as Navy SEALs cleared buildings. "Go change." She said as she piled two more shirts onto his growing pile of clothes and ushered him into the change room.

Bryce tried on the jeans, and they fit surprisingly well, he did a few squats and moved around testing the fabric to ensure he could move if needed. They passed the test with flying colors. "Bryce?" Bennett called as he unbuttoned the last pair of jeans.

"Uhhh…. Yeah?" He replied, trying to quickly pull on a pair of pants.

"Oh perfect, here." She said throwing a long-sleeved shirt, a flannel, and a hoodie over the door. "And I think you'll want this." She said waving a belt over the door as she did. "Everything fit well?"

"Yeah… thanks." Bryce replied, pulling up the blue jeans. And ripping off the tags. Bryce tried on the rest of the clothing, opting for the blue jeans, a white t-shirt, and a red and black flannel. Bryce exited the room carrying the pile of clothes and the tags for everything he was currently wearing. Walking to the cash register, he placed down everything and handed the tags to the red-haired girl. "I'm going to wear these out if that's okay?" Bryce said as the girl scanned his items making small talk as she did.

"I'd ask if you had any trouble finding things but clearly someone knew what they were doing." She joked as she scanned another item.

"Yeah, it's a lot easier when people pick out the stuff for you." Bryce replied, rubbing the back of his neck.

"Oh, you left some clothes in the change room too." She replied as a tall black boy walked out waving the chinos and hoodie at the girl.

"You can throw those out." Bryce said shyly as he glanced over at the boy.

"Oh yes and these too." Bennett said, setting down two black baseball hats and a pack of boxer briefs.

"Are you currently a rewards member?" The girl asked as she scanned the remaining items and looked at Bennett.

"No and I don't want to sign up right now." She replied as the girl folded the remaining clothes and stuffed them into a bag.

"Okay your total is 289.20 how would you like to pay?" The girl looked at Bennett and then over to Bryce who had slung his bag off his shoulder and quickly rummaged through it peeling three hundred-dollar bills off the wad of cash.

"Cash please." Bryce said, sliding the three bills over to the girl. The girl quickly returned the change and handed two large bags over to Bryce.

"Have a great day." She called out as the two left.

Bryce and Bennett found a bench just outside of the store and neatly transferred the newly purchased clothes into his bag. Before pulling the black hats down low enough to block their faces. "Good call on the hats." Bryce said, adjusting his to fit snuggly.

"Thanks, I saw it in a movie once and figured it wouldn't hurt. Plus, I think I look cute." She replied, adjusting hers and pulling her ponytail through the hole at the back. "We should call Anton now." She said, elbowing Bryce who was looking all around.

"Right. Good idea." He answered, pulling out his phone and powering it up. The apple logo greeted him before his phone erupted with notifications. Harry, Carter and Anton had all called him at least ten times, texted him nearly one hundred times and several other numbers had reached out to him as well. Asking where he was, what was going on, if he was okay and telling him to turn himself in. Bryce quickly texted Harry and Carter saying he was fine and to not say anything to anyone. He then pulled up Anton's contact information, took a deep breath and pressed call.

The phone rang four times before the sound of a click was heard and Anton's voice came through. "Bryce? Are you okay? Where are you?" Anton asked his words barely coherent with how fast he was speaking.

"Yeah, I'm fine." Bryce replied holding the phone in a way so Bennett could listen too.

"Where are you? I'll come get you." Anton asked as quickly as before.

"They killed him, Anton." Bryce said softly his voice twinging with pain as he spoke those words.

"I know Bryce. There's a lot I have to tell you. But first I have to get you to safety." He replied slower this time. "Now, where are you Bryce?"

"How do I know you're not with them?" Bryce asked sternly.

"You don't, simple as that. But I'm not, you have my word." He said softly. "You're in danger. Now tell me where you are, and I'll come get you." Anton pleaded as Bryce sat there Bennett's hand on his knee as he spoke.

"Give me one good reason why I should trust you." Bryce replied coldly.

"Because if I worked for them, I would have killed you the first time your father told me you passed out unexpectedly." Anton said the sound of keys jingling on his side of the phone. "Now tell me Bryce, where are you? I can get you to safety but only if we act fast. You're already all over the News, it's only a matter of time before they find you."

"Fine. I'm at the mall. First floor by the food court. Come alone or I run." Bryce said sternly before hanging up the phone and throwing it in the garbage can beside the bench. "Let's go." He said standing up and grabbing Bennett's arm.

Bryce and Bennett found a good position just above the food court, that could see the only three entry points. "Okay so we wait until Anton arrives and then when he does, IF he's alone you go down to meet him. And I'll stay here keeping an eye out for anyone who looks weird." Bennett restated the plan for the third time as Bryce waited in silence, occasionally looking back and forth between the entrances.

"Yes, but if you see anything just shout and then run." Bryce said as he watched carefully. Just as he finished speaking, he watched Anton enter the food court. He was wearing a pair of dark blue jeans covering a pair of what looked like black combat boots, a baggy white shirt with the left sleeve pushed up, and a faded, black baseball hat his long gray hair was pushed into. "There he is." Bryce nodded as he watched Anton scan the area before pulling out his phone and making a call.

"You think he's calling you?" Bennett asked as she watched the man listen to the call before pulling it away from his ear and pressing buttons on the screen, then jamming it back into his pocket and looking around more.

"One way to find out." Bryce said standing up and slinging the backpack over his shoulder. "Remember, we meet at the back entrance if anything happens." With that, Bryce looked at Bennett who nodded, grabbing his hand for a moment before he pulled away and made his way to a staircase across from the bench she'd been seated at.

Bryce made his way through the crowds and was about thirty feet from Anton when he noticed him. He rushed over and wrapped Bryce up in a big hug. "Thank God you're okay." He said as he squeezed Bryce tightly. "I called you all night, what happened?" He questioned looking at Bryce, his arms still placed on the boys shoulders.

"They killed him. A group of men, led by some big bald guy with a scar across his face. They kept asking him 'where I was' and then they shot him and burned the house down." Bryce explained, leaving out as much detail as he could without the story sounding too farfetched.

"Dang... I'm so sorry Bryce." Anton said, placing a hand on Bryce's cheek before pulling him into a hug once again. "There's a lot I need to tell you."

"Then tell me." He replied, pushing out of Anton's hug.

"Not here, we need to get you somewhere safe before I explain anything." He said as he pulled at Bryce's arm trying to lead him out of the mall.

"Get off of me." Bryce called as he shook out of Anton's grip and pushed away from him. "I'm not going anywhere until you explain what is going on?"

"Bryce now is not the time. They could be here any moment." Anton said, looking at Bryce, his eyes shooting a calm but forceful look at Bryce. "We need to leave... now!" He shouted back.

"Bryce! Look out!" Bennett shouted as two men wearing all black outfits flung their jackets open revealing machine guns, raising them up as Bryce saw where Bennett was pointing.

"Move!" Anton shouted as he pushed Bryce away and drew a pistol from his waistband, raising it and finding the first man's torso as he squeezed two rounds off into the man's chest. He crumpled as the bullets struck him. As he did the second man fired, his first burst landing just beside Bryce as he stumbled away from Anton. "Run!" Anton shouted again as the mall erupted into chaos, people running every direction as the two men exchanged gunfire. Anton running for cover, firing his gun under his arm as he dashed to the nearest food cart for some semblance of cover from the oncoming gunfire.

Bryce sprinted away, trying his best to make his way to the first exit he could. As he burst through a crowd, he saw two more men before they saw him. The men blocked the exit fighting through the crowd, their hands in their jackets as they scanned the rush of people. Bryce turned around and fought his way through the wave of running teens and adults, dodging and weaving through the gaps as quickly as he could, the screams and gunfire nearly deafening him as he ran. "There he is!" One of the men screamed as he drew a pistol from beneath his jacket and sighted it in on Bryce. He ducked as the first round was squeezed off by one of the shooters, the bullet hitting the wall just beside his head, inches from him. Bryce scrambled back to his feet and began running in a zig zag, trying his best to put as many obstacles as possible between him and the shooters. Two more shots popped off, but Bryce didn't see where they hit.

He made his way to the next exit as another man emerged from the crowd this time far closer to Bryce, without thinking he dove at the man, grabbing the barrel of his pistol and controlling it as the two fell to the ground, people stepping on the two as they rolled around fighting for control of the gun. Bryce realized he was wasting too much time and soon the other men would be on him. In a moment of pure panic, he released the barrel with one hand and began raining down elbows on the face of the man he fought. The Middle Eastern man gritted his teeth as the blows landed to the side of his head, eyes, and mouth. The two rolled around more until Bryce was able to pop up, the man grabbing his backpack and pulling him back as Bryce kicked the man once more in the side causing him to release the bag. Bryce looked back to see the two men from the last exit were now only fifteen feet away. Bryce cursed as he scrambled through the crowd as more shouting, and gunshots rang out. Bryce fought his way to the side of the crowd, dipping and ducking as much as possible in the hope the men would not fire. He was wrong, as he rounded a corner, he saw a woman collapse as the sound of a gun rang out again, a loud exhale releasing from her throat as she fell. Bryce sprinted as hard as he could towards a door marked exit.

Bursting through the door Bryce found himself in a back hallway. *Think! Think! Think! Where do I go?* He thought as he looked around at the long gray hallway. *Anywhere but here.* He thought as he sprinted down the hallway. "He went in here." Bryce heard as the sound of the door flung open and the once quiet hallway filled with the sound of boots running as screams slowly died away. Bryce was at a full sprint when he hit the door and burst into a parking lot full of people, the sound of police sirens and ambulances filling the air. Bryce looked around in panic, before he saw her. Bennett was being dragged away by one of the men in all black. Without thinking he ran towards the two, the sounds of the world fading away as his adrenaline and fear took over. Then everything went silent, and Bryce felt the familiar feeling of the world slowing down, he watched as the man and Bennett began to move slower and slower until they were almost completely still. Bryce pushed harder and within moments he was upon the two. Bryce lowered his shoulder as his momentum carried him forwards and he collided with the man sending him flying into the front quarter panel of a nearby car. As if hit by a truck the man's body wrapped around the car and he laid there unmoving. Just then, the world snapped back, and the sounds of sirens, screams and shouting filled Bryce's ears.

"Where did you come from?" Bennett asked as Bryce grabbed her arm and pulled her.

"Just run." Bryce shouted as he pulled at her arm once again, the two taking off at a full sprint as Bryce looked back at the three men emerging from the exit he'd just seconds earlier come from. As Bryce looked back, he almost ran into Anton's truck.

The brakes squealed as the large red and black Ford Raptor pulled up. "Get in." He shouted as the two skidded to a stop in front of his truck. Bryce and Bennett shared a look before deciding to jump in. The engine revved and Anton took off, blowing stop signs and zig zagging through cars, before popping a curb and driving over the median and onto the road. "Are you two, okay?" Anton asked as he breathed heavily zooming through the streets, making wild turns and running red lights just trying to put distance between him and the people with guns.

Bryce looked at Bennett who had tears running down her face. "Yeah." She sniffled, wiping her tears on her sleeve as she did.

"What the heck is going on Anton, those men, they opened fired in a crowded mall?" Bryce asked, trying to catch his breath as he felt his pulse in his head.

"There's so much you need to know Bryce. But for now, all I can say is that you and now Bennett are in grave danger." He replied looking in his rearview mirror and then back to the road in front of him which seemed to blur as Bryce watched it pass him by, his vision beginning to tunnel. "Here, drink this." Anton said, stuffing a warm bottle of coca cola into Bryce's hand. "You need the sugar."

"What?" Bryce questioned his vision becoming blurry as he spoke.

"Drink, we can't have you passing out." Anton said, tipping the bottle up to Bryce's mouth. Silently Bryce gulped down the drink, his vision slowly becoming clearer and the darkness around his field of view beginning to fade.

"How did you..." Bryce began before Anton cut him off.

"Know? Because Rhys and I aren't just security consultants. Hell, we aren't even that. Bryce, what do you know about your father? Like what do you really know?" Anton questioned slowing his truck down as he pulled down a dirt road.

"I know he was in the military." Bryce replied as he finished the last of the coca cola.

"That's correct. What else?" Anton asked gesturing with his hand for Bryce to continue that train of thought.

"And he left it because they asked him to do something he couldn't." Bryce half asked, half said, straining to remember more about Rhys's military service.

"Exactly." Anton said as Bryce sat there thinking. "Bryce, your father and I were part of an elite group of operatives. Picked from other units for various reasons and given a new task. In our eyes we were preventing the next 9/11 before it could take place. We didn't always agree with the jobs, but we followed orders. Bryce you're one of the people we would have hunted down. The things you can do... well they're not normal. Haven't you noticed?" Anton asked rhetorically before continuing. "It took four years before we realized we were killing innocent people and before we realized we weren't helping save people we were helping with a genocide. Our unit wasn't killing terrorists, we were killing the next step in human evolution. We were killing people who possessed abilities we normal humans could only dream of. I'm not proud of it but you have to understand, when we worked for Unity, we thought we were saving people. Instead, we were carrying out a task the elite of the world set out to do over two thousand years ago." Anton said as he pulled down a path barely big enough for his truck. The sound of branches scraping the sides and roof filled the silence as he took a deep breath. "Bryce, I'm sorry I wish

I could've told you earlier, but Rhys made me swear not to. He wanted you to grow up normal, without the fear of this looming over your head."

"Anton, tell me what?" He asked the shock setting in as he felt his whole world, the one he once knew crumbling around him.

"Bryce, Rhys isn't your father, we were on a mission with Tyson -the giant prick you have already had the pleasure of meeting- when we found you and your mother. She died protecting you. Tyson shot her as she shielded your cradle, in an abandoned factory just outside of Detroit. She was kind of like you. But she was called a Nar-Asam meaning she was able to create and control fire with her mind. Rhys fought with Tyson who wanted to kill you. They call your kind a 'cancer', saying you only want to enslave normal humans. I grabbed you as the two fought and fled out the back. Rhys and I had already planned to escape Tyson and leave Unity on that mission. We had stashed a car not too far from the factory. I just didn't expect to end up with a child. Rhys was barely alive when he made it to the car, four broken ribs, a fractured jaw and dislocated shoulder were his victory prize. We thought about giving you up, it was safer for us that way. But we knew Unity would find you sooner or later, and foolishly we thought we could protect you." Anton explained as the truck pulled up to an old cabin, the wooden exterior had seen better days, weathered and dirty, the cabin looked more like a run-down structural nightmare than a safe house from a death squad of well-armed, well trained, and overzealous psychopaths. Bryce thought he was more likely to die from a strong gust of wind blowing the house down than from Tyson.

"What am I then?" Bryce asked as the three sat in the car looking at the rundown shack.

"I'll explain inside." Anton said, turning off the car, grabbing a small piece of scrap paper and opening his door. Bryce and Bennett slowly walked to the front door as Anton dragged a large, camouflage tarp over his truck. "Can't be too careful." He chuckled as the two shot him quizzical looks.

CHAPTER 10

Bryce and Bennett followed Anton into the run-down shack. The inside was only slightly better than the exterior. The shack had a bunk bed, a rickety looking shower, a small wood-fire stove, a fridge that hadn't been new since the early 70's, a small standalone sink with cabinets above it, and a large yellow and brown checkered couch stationed just in front of a table surrounded by three wooden chairs. Bryce chuckled to himself thinking of how the Motel would've made a better hiding place than this. At least there he could raid the snack machine. Bryce tossed his bag just in front of the bed and looked over at Bennett who he'd realized had a similar train of thought to him. "Okay Anton, explain." Bennett said, pulling the chair out by the table and gesturing to the man to sit.

"Just a moment." Anton said, walking over to one of the walls and sliding a small picture frame over exposing a keypad. Anton quickly glanced at the scrap of paper before he punched in a seven-digit code and then slid the photo back to its original position. "Just making sure the others know we need to be picked up." He said before he made his way to the chair and sat down with a huff. "Okay where to begin." He thought aloud before he began. "Around 360 B.C.E Plato wrote about his trip to Atlantis." Anton began.

"Yeah, we know, he wrote about the city, and he basically described The Eye of the Sahara." Bryce interrupted trying to speed along the conversation.

"He didn't basically describe The Eye, he described it perfectly, because that's where he went. What history and more importantly Unity left out, was how the inhabitants were not just extremely advanced, they were the next step in evolution. Able to control fire, earth and slow down time. Plato was amazed and reported this back to the world. Well, that's when Unity was formed. Every world power, Kings, Pharaohs, Emperors, Czars, and Jarls, and every other ruler in the world couldn't have their power unseated and so they banded together and launched an attack on the peaceful city. Razing the city and killing all those inside. Or so they thought." Anton said, waving his hands around as he spoke. "Plato helped about five hundred people escape through tunnels the Earth Breakers or Tellus, helped create during the siege, collapsing them behind them as they fled. By the end of the siege, the city looked as it does now. An uninhabitable wasteland in the middle of a desert. The survivors scattered across the globe. And any survivors Unity found they turned into slaves working them until they eventually died. Unity thought they had accomplished something, and it wasn't until 1541 when the first descendant was rediscovered, in the Amazon Rainforest. The sailors reported seeing natives who could control the water, moving quickly through the rivers, with almost superhuman speed." He continued pausing occasionally to ensure he had the correct dates. "That's when Unity began a more aggressive colonization of South America. Clear cutting the rainforest for "resources" when in reality they were killing your people. But much like Charles Darwin would go on to explain in the future the Atlantians had evolved, they'd developed new powers. Besides the Tellus and the Nar-Asam and the Crono- that's what they called those who could slow down time and move extremely fast- they could now control water and they were called the Madzi and some could appear out of nowhere -the Absens or the invisible- with new powers came a new threat. But Unity fought back, enslaving and killing many more, causing the remaining to flee into the depths of the jungle. Unity pushed and pushed but the tribes hid and survived, always pushing deeper and deeper into the jungle. Most of what you know about history was shaped by your people Bryce, the pyramids, made by Tellus slaves forming and shaping the rocks, then moving them into place. The burning of the library of Alexandria, a boy discovering his powers at the worst possible time in the worst possible place." Anton stood up and paced now, his speech speeding up as if a weight was being lifted with each part of the story he told. Bryce and Bennett sat in awe as he continued. "But Unity covered it up, hid them from history. Your people adapted each time growing and learning from each loss just as much as each victory. Unity hunts and your people hide, fighting when they can, fleeing when they can't. But places hidden from the world, erased from history or deemed lost forever, they exist. And that is where your people can hide. El Dorado or The Lost City of Z, those exist. Deep in the amazon where no human can survive, where you can't light a fire without gasoline, how do uncontacted tribes survive? Have you ever asked yourself that? The Nar-Asam. How do they get water or move about the complex river? The Madzi that's how. But as technology advanced so did Unity's ability to hunt your people down. Bryce there's a war waging that you are a part of. I'm sorry we didn't tell you sooner, but you know now." Anton said, placing a hand on Bryce's shoulder and looking the boy in the eyes. "Whether you like it or not, you need to learn how to survive. Rhys did his best to teach you, but now, you are on your own. And you better believe Tyson and Unity will not stop, but you're not alone, like Rhys and I there are others, people who sympathize with your people, generations of them actually. Early explorers altering maps to hide your people, working with natives like Sacagawea, Harriet Tubman helping slaves escape, hell even governments like India placing a protection over North Sentinel Island, though that is no longer a base of operation due to the exposure when Unity crashed a boat on the Island and attacked, framing it as the Natives attacking innocent marooned sailors." Anton sat down as he finished speaking. And looked at the two dumbfounded teenagers.

"Wait so let me get this straight." Bennett began. "Bryce is from an ancient race of more developed humans able to control the elements?" She asked, trying her best to piece together everything that had happened.

"Kind of, but it's more than just elements, Bryce can increase his perception of time, allowing him to move faster, hitting with speeds that allow him to generate force far greater than those unable to move as quickly as him. And his bones are adapted to compensate for that, kind of explains his hard head and history of never breaking a bone." Anton explained. "Some can control or create fire, bend water, go invisible, move great amounts of earth and rock with a single wave of their hand, and hell some can even change their appearance into another person we call those Copia." Anton added, trying his best to explain everything he could.

"So, most world events are just Unity hunting down these descendants?" Bennett asked, reaching over and grabbing Bryce's hand.

"You don't even know the half of it. 1938 Unity found out a large population of Atlantians in Europe scattered across it. And well I'm sure I don't have to explain to you how 1939-1945 went." Anton said, shaking his head as he spoke.

"You can't be serious. Hitler? The Holocaust? World War Two?" Bennett cried out begging for this to be a lie.

"I'm not. Hitler was a figurehead, a puppet. But many of the victims of that act of savagery were Atlantians. But that would be a time when Unity lost control and things quickly spiraled out." Anton said shaking his head in disgust.

"So, then World War One?" Bryce interjected.

"Not quite. It's not confirmed but some believe a rogue Copia turned into Gavrilo Princip and killed Franz Ferdinand who was a high-ranking Unity member, but we can't say for sure." Anton replied, shrugging as he spoke. "But you can see how it's probably true based on everything else that's transpired." He explained simply.

"How has no one ever discovered this?" Bennett asked half knowing the answer but hoping it wasn't true.

"Bennett, Unity is possibly the most powerful secret society, they control the media, the police, the military, and so much more. Anyone who gets close enough to exposing them is either discredited, if they're lucky, otherwise they end up with a quick death." Anton said, dragging his thumb across his throat.

"What the heck am I supposed to do then?" Bryce asked, the mountain of his new reality seeming nearly insurmountable.

"First thing we need to do is get you somewhere safe so you can learn how to control your powers. Then maybe we can think about something more long term. But first and foremost. Survive." Anton said sternly, his eyes burning a hole into Bryce.

"But Unity is everywhere... where can we go?" Bryce asked.

"Leave that to me, for now, you two should rest. You look like you've been dragged through a keyhole." Anton smiled and made his way to the fridge. "I'll fix us something to eat." He said the fridge popping and sputtering as he opened it. "Crap should've known. Empty. Would've been nice for them to leave us something to eat." Anton muttered to himself. "Well, good news for you two, I will make the best canned soup you have ever had." Anton said, rummaging through a small cabinet and pulling out two dusty, dented cans of Campbell's Chunky Soup.

Bryce and Bennett sat and watched as Anton rummaged around for a pot and began singing as he cooked. "So much for rest." Bryce muttered to Bennett as the two watched the performance play out in front of them. Bennett chuckled which earned a glance over from Anton.

"Hey three feet apart you two. Don't need another baby to take care of, I helped do it once, I'm not doing it again." He laughed as he turned around and continued warming up the soup.

"It's not like that, Anton." Bennett called out as she playfully pushed Bryce away.

The rest of the day and evening was spent preparing the cabin, Bennett tidied up the inside as Bryce and Anton gathered firewood for the stove. The two barely spoke, Anton not wanting to push Bryce and Bryce not ready to discuss the events of the last twenty-four hours. When they returned Bennett had brushed much of the dust off of the furniture and swept the interior with a broom she'd found tucked just behind the door.

"Bennett, you really know how to make a house into a home." Anton commented walking in, his arms full of firewood.

"Home economics wasn't a total waste then." She joked back. Sweeping one last pile of dirt out the front door and then returning the broom to its spot behind the door before collapsing into the couch.

"Well, now that we are all comfy, we should go over the plan." Anton said, falling into a nearby chair and fiddling with the stove. "I need to go into town tomorrow and get in touch with the group that will get us out of here and to a facility you can train at." Anton nodded to Bryce.

"You mean we need to go into town, right?" Bennett questioned as she sat up.

"No Bennett, just me. It's too risky for all three of us to go and plus who will take care of him if we're both gone." Anton joked, nodding to Bryce once again.

"What happens if you don't come back?" Bryce said coldly from the other side of the table.

"Well, if I don't come back assume you are absolutely screwed and find the nearest rafter and rope." Anton snapped back. "Probably a better death than if Unity found you considering they'll probably experiment on you."

"But 'WHEN' you come back." Bennett emphasized. "You'll have a plan on where we should go next?"

"Yes, I'll get in touch with the contact and then I will arrange something for us." Anton said more softly than before. "Either way just wait here. Don't leave the house and I should be back tomorrow afternoon. Town is about ten minutes away." Anton reassured Bennett as he spoke.

The group spent the rest of the night in almost complete silence, exhausted from the day's events and aware of the upcoming danger. Bryce struggled to fall asleep that night. *Atlantis? Unity? Am I just going to be on the run for the rest of my life? And what about Bennett, her Dad has to have been contacted. Or will they frame me for some kind of kidnapping? I'm screwed either way.* Bryce's mind was racing when he felt the warmth of a hand touch his; he jumped slightly as he felt the hand hold his. The moonlight lit the outline of a figure, slowly making its way down from the upper bunk. Without a word Bennett climbed into the small twin bed with Bryce and curled up with him. Bryce pulled her in close, feeling her soft skin press against his as the two laid there, Bennett sporting a long-sleeved shirt and her underwear while Bryce had nothing but the American Eagle briefs Bennett had picked out for him. She wiggled further back, pressing further against him as the two remained silent, Anton shifting on the couch as this scene unfolded. Bryce went to speak when he felt Bennett's finger press against his lips. Bryce closed his mouth and savored the moment. His hand sliding up Bennett's hip and stopping just above her stomach. Her skin felt soft and warm. His heart raced. Then as if an alarm made solely to kill the mood, Anton began to snore. Loudly. Bryce accepted his fate and felt Bennett slowly pull away and slide out of the bed, reaching back to squeeze his hand once more before he watched the outline of her toned legs and butt slide out of view and back into the bed above him. Five feet away never felt so far. Bryce slowly began to doze off after that and eventually fell asleep.

The morning sun shot through the window and hit Bryce right in the face, its warmth only overshadowed by its indistinguishable ability to force one awake. Bryce slowly opened his eyes, the blinding light shining right into them. Reluctantly he swung his feet over the bed, got dressed and realizing he was the first awake silently made his way to the front door. "Don't even think about it." Anton croaked, his eyes not even opening. "You don't leave this place without me by your side." He commanded as Bryce slowly closed the door and made his way back to his bed.

Bryce spent what felt like forever waiting for Bennett and Anton to wake up, he counted the logs making up the cabin, went over the pledge of allegiance in his head which seemed redundant now that he thought about it, considering he was now most certainly being hunted by the government. And after his fourth time going over all the defensive moves for a knife fight, and when your attacker has a gun, he heard Bennett shifting in the bed above him. With a big loud moan, Bennett swung her feet down and slowly lowered herself down, before rushing over to her jeans and pulling them on, jumping as she struggled to pull them over her butt. Bryce couldn't help but stare and smile. Which gained him a sharp look from Bennett who turned around and noticed him sitting there watching her. "Is it safe to open my eyes?" Anton questioned, clearly aware of the scene that had just played out.

"Yes, it is. Thanks for not staring." Bennett said, looking directly at Bryce as she spoke. Bryce returned her look with a shrug and a smile. "How did you sleep?" She asked as Anton sat up and cracked his back.

"Well, I have slept on the floor in the deserts of Pakistan, and this has to be one of the least comfortable places I have ever had the pleasure of laying my head." He chuckled as he stretched once more. "What are the chances this shack has coffee?" Anton asked the room as he stood up, stretched his back once more and walked over to the cabinet, opening it and rummaging through it once more.

"If there is some, I'll take a cup." Bennett said, sitting beside Bryce and elbowing him for a response.

"Ouch... umm... me too." Bryce said rubbing his ribs which still had bruises from his fight and fresh ones he was sure were from the stampede yesterday.

"Well, we are in luck." Anton said, pulling a small mason jar labelled instant coffee out of the cabinet. Anton brewed three cups and sat down at the table blowing on his as it cooled. "Really wish there was some honey and milk around here." He groaned as he took a sip of the bitter brown liquid in his cup.

"Good thing you're going into town, you can pick some up." Bennett cheerfully said as she sipped her cup, pulling away and making a face as she did. "This is awful." She called out pushing the cup away from her and sitting back with a huff. "Can you pick up some real coffee and some food for us? I don't think I could take another night of your soup." Bennett asked, batting her eyelashes as she did.

"I can, but what's wrong with my soup?" Anton said feinting pain as he did.

"I think we all know it is not good." Bryce said, taking a long sip before he instantly regretted his choice.

"Harsh crowd." Anton replied before he took his cup, stood up and dashed it out the front door. "I think coffee is the first thing on the list." He chuckled as the two teens followed his lead, throwing their cups out of the door and onto the grass surrounding the shack. Bryce and Bennett spent the next ten minutes making a list as Anton uncovered his truck, punched a code into the keypad behind the picture and then set out, list in hand. Issuing a warning to not procreate while he was gone, Bryce laughed knowing he was only half kidding.

Bryce closed the door and turned to face Bennett who looked up at him from the couch, her blue eyes drawing Bryce in. "About last night." She began. "I don't want to give you the wrong idea." She said softly burying her face in her hands.

"You're not." Bryce reassured her. "It was a strange day yesterday, emotions were high." He continued sitting beside her and pulling her face up out of her hands.

"It's not that. It's just… I'm not that kind of girl. I just needed… I needed to feel you and feel safe in your arms." She said looking at him, her eyes welling up with tears. "Bryce when the man had me and was taking me, I thought… that was it. I was dead and I'd never see my Dad ever again. I thought I'd never see you again." She mumbled, tears beginning to pour down her face as she spoke. "And I was scared."

"I know, but you're safe now. I'm here, and I won't let anything bad happen to you." Bryce said, pulling her into a hug, feeling her sob into his shoulder as he did."

"I know." She sniffled as she broke away from his hug. "But… I'm sorry… for everything… I shouldn't have been so selfish; it was a mistake. I just needed you." She said, trying and failing to wipe her tears away.

"Bennett, it's okay. I'm not complaining. It was nice." Bryce said, pulling her back into his arms. "I'm not mad. I needed it too. You make the world seem less daunting. I wouldn't be here if it weren't for you." He said as she pressed her face into his chest.

"You're sure?" She asked her words muffled by his shirt as she spoke.

"Of course." He replied holding her tight for a few moments, allowing her to cry and feel emotions he was sure she'd suppressed for the last twenty-four hours. "Bennett… Can I ask you something?" Bryce said after he felt her sobbing subside.

"Yes." She replied, pulling away from him and looking at him. Her eyes red from crying.

"Why did you not come back after we kissed in ninth grade?" He asked, holding his breath immediately wishing he could take the words back as they left his mouth.

"Bryce…" She paused looking at him for a moment. "I panicked. You were my best friend, and I kissed you. I freaked out and hid in the bathroom for like thirty minutes, crying and freaking out because I knew how I felt about you but that was the first time it became real." She said hurriedly, watching him sink into his feelings as she spoke. "When I came back you weren't there, and Ashton was. I felt rejected, and he made me feel pretty and wanted. I figured you didn't want to be with me." She said softly as she took Bryce's hands and met his eyes with hers.

The Atlantian Chronicles

"You were all I've ever wanted." He mumbled as a chill went through his body. "I sat there for twenty minutes so excited. And then you didn't come back."

"But I did." She replied, looking at him, her hands in his. "I came back, I promise. I'll always come back to you." A tear rolled down her cheek as she pleaded with Bryce to understand.

Bryce looked at Bennett for a moment, her blue tear-filled eyes pleading with him. With one hand he reached forward and wiped her tears with his thumb. "No more tears." He said leaning forward and pressing his forehead to hers. "I'm sorry I made you feel that way. I wouldn't have left if I'd known how you felt." He whispered, feeling her breath on his lips as he spoke.

"Just promise you won't leave ever again. And I'll promise to always return." She whispered back as she closed her eyes, the tears spilling out.

"I promise." He said softly as he pressed his lips to hers and kissed her. Her lips felt as soft as silk. As they kissed Bryce felt the world slip away for a moment, it was just the two of them. No Unity, no fear, no life-threatening danger, just Bryce Hillcrest and Bennett Douglas.

The two continued to kiss for the next few minutes, Bennett pushing Bryce back onto the couch as she climbed on top of him and kissed him. His hands grabbing her waist, butt and back pulling her closer to him as their tongues danced in each other's mouths. After a few moments Bennett shifted and nearly fell off the couch causing the two to giggle, breaking the passionate kiss. Both took a deep breath and looked at each other before bursting out into more laughter.

"So..." Bryce said, running his hand through Bennett's hair as he spoke. "What now?" He asked before the two giggled again.

"Well... you heard Anton, no procreating." Bennett joked back as she nuzzled her head into Bryce's chest. "Can we stay here forever? Just in this moment?" She asked, listening to his heartbeat. "You're not nervous anymore?" She commented as she listened to his relaxed heartbeat.

"No... just happy." He said as he placed his hand on her back and moved it slowly side to side. Bennett giggled and pushed herself up, giving him a small peck on the lips before she rolled off of him and popped up onto her feet. "Let's play a game." She said dancing over to the table and falling into the seat. "Twenty questions... like when we were kids. Remember?"

Bryce remembered the game all too well, he had twenty questions to guess what she was thinking of, by only asking yes or no questions. He much preferred kissing her, but as he felt the moment pass, he agreed to play. "Fine... but I'll go first." He said sitting up and moving to the table.

CHAPTER 11

"A meerkat?" Bennett shouted as Anton walked through the front door.

"How?! How did you know?" Bryce nodded to Anton as the man set down a brown paper bag and looked at the pair.

"Why did I think I'd come back to find you without a shirt on and you hiding under the covers?" He asked, pointing to Bryce and then Bennett accordingly.

"Maybe because you're a pervy old man with nothing better to do?" Bryce joked as he walked over to the door and watched Anton pull the tarp back over his car.

"Hey, don't forget who has a handgun on them right now?" Anton spat back lifting his shirt up with one hand exposing the grip of the gun he used at the mall.

"Don't forget who can slow down time and dodge bullets." Bryce called back with a cheeky smile.

"Good joke, no Crono has ever moved that fast, believe me they have tried and failed." Anton explained as he entered the house and made his way to the picture, sliding it aside and punching in the numbers once more. "You're not the flash kid. You might perceive time slower and move faster but that doesn't mean it freezes for you." Anton added before he returned to the car for another set of bags filled with groceries.

"What did you get?" Bennett asked, breaking the silence that followed Anton's comment as she began unpacking the bag.

"Everything on the list I could find. Unfortunately, they don't have oat milk in rural Texas, sorry." He shrugged half-heartedly.

"That's fine, I should be able to make something other than old, gross, canned soup with this." She called back as she placed the items away as Bryce handed them to her. "So, what's the plan?" She asked, looking at the stock of supplies and realizing they would not make more than a dinner and light breakfast.

"Well, I got in touch with them. And there's a flight heading out of Dallas Airport to Maine. From there we will travel to Millinocket where my contact will meet us." Anton explained. "We have to remain domestic for now since neither of you have passports that won't immediately flag you as a terrorist. Which fun fact, we are now deemed. Thank you, Unity." Anton said, pulling a folded newspaper from his jacket, flattening it out on the table and sliding it to Bryce.

"They're pinning the mall shooting on us? I didn't even have a gun." He shouted in shock and disbelief, shaking the paper in his hand. The front page showed Bryce and Anton's faces, with a grainy black and white security camera photo of Anton shooting right beside their faces.

"Not only that but congratulations Bennett, you are now a hostage, being kept against her will. So, Bennett now's your chance, doors open, feel free to escape." Anton sarcastically said, flipping the page to reveal a yearbook photo of Bennett smiling, with the word 'missing' in big bold letters across the top and gesturing to the door.

"Funny." She called over her shoulder as she turned back and continued cooking.

"Anyway, the plan is we hang here until nightfall and then go to the airport, it's a four-hour drive from here so, hopefully that puts us there early enough in the morning that the crew will be sleepy, and we can slip by without issue. They're looking for a group of three so Bryce, you will go first, make sure you get a seat on the plane, regardless of what happens you need to get on that flight. Bennett, you and I will pose as a father and daughter, I know I look too young to have a teenage daughter. Well, we can't judge people for their past." He continued joking as he went, trying his best to break the tension with humor. "If all goes to plan, we will all board the flight and make it to Maine in just under six hours. If we've done everything right, there shouldn't be a hit squad waiting for us. If we make it out of the airport, Bryce you start walking and Bennett and I will borrow a car from the long-term parking lot and then pick you up. So, let's hope this goes well, because I do not want to die in Maine." Anton finished, taking a deep breath and sitting back in his chair.

"Well, I hope this meal is better than the soup because I'd hate to eat bad food for my last meal." Bennett said, throwing a pan onto the top of the stove and placing a cover over it.

"Me too." Bryce said nervously biting his nails. "Don't we need a passport to fly?" He added as Bennett joined the group at the table.

"Not for domestic flights. Just a driver's license. Which… I had made for both of you." Anton said sliding over two plastic cards, a picture of Bryce on one and one for Bennett the same photo as the one in the paper but cropped so it was just her face. "How did you…" Bryce began before Anton cut him off.

"Rhys and I have had that made for a while, as for Bennett's I had to work with what I had and after a few minutes on photoshop and a hundred-dollar bill slipped to the printer shop guy, I had one. It won't pass a full scan but I'm hoping they look at mine more than hers." Anton said, taking Bennett's back and slipping it into his wallet. "You hold onto that one, this way if anything happens you have a new name and a valid I.D." He finished as he watched Bryce pick up the card and look at it in the light. It looked almost identical to his actual license. *Did they fake my license?* Bryce thought to himself as he examined the plastic card further.

The group spent the next twenty minutes discussing the plan further and coming up with contingencies for each step ensuring if anything happened Bryce would board the flight. Bennett excused herself occasionally to check on dinner, adding spices that filled the cabin with mouthwatering aromas. Bryce didn't like the thought of leaving Bennett even if it meant him dying in the process of saving her. But he agreed to the plan, hopeful the two groups would pass by unbothered. After more planning Bennett checked on her food and luckily for the group it was ready. Sliding a portion onto each plate Bennett assembled the plates and let each person grab it themself. Bryce looked at the dish and smiled. Bennett had somehow managed to make a skirt steak with asparagus and crispy potatoes. Bryce's mouth watered as he waited for everyone to sit down. The whole group ate in silence devouring the food as quickly as they could.

"Well, as last meals go… I could have eaten worse." Anton chuckled as he wiped his mouth with a paper napkin and smiled.

"It was delicious, Bennett. Thank you." Bryce added, trying his best to make up for Anton's less than ideal comment. Bennett smiled as Bryce cleared the table, grabbing his hand for a moment as he collected her plate. Bryce smiled back and then continued his task. After he'd washed the plates, he returned to the table and looked at the two who were chatting about their plans for Maine, trying to come up with a solid backstory that seemed to calm Anton and Bennett alike. Even when things were unpredictable Bennett loved to plan as much as she could.

"We should get some sleep. It's early but this way we are fresh for the drive." Anton suggested, clearly half asleep after the heavy meal he'd just had.

"Good idea!" Bennett said, leaping up and climbing into her bed. Bryce looked at the two quizzically thinking how he wasn't even remotely tired. It was barely 6 P.M. he thought to himself as he climbed into his bed. With that Anton drew the curtains closed, closed the stove so the fire was barely an ember, before collapsing onto the couch.

After what felt like forever, Bryce heard the snore of Anton. Shifting more and eventually beginning to drift off before he felt the bed above him move. Opening one eye he saw the shape of two legs swing down and with one motion Bennett dropped to the floor, she froze in place for a moment as the two heard Anton adjust on the couch the springs squeaking under his weight. Bryce propped himself up looking at the silhouetted figure in the blackness of the room. Slowly she lowered herself onto the bed and then slid closer to him, her one hand finding his and her other finding his cheek. Together they slowly laid down. He felt her breath on his, and then without hesitation he felt their lips press together. Bryce pulled her close and kissed her again, his tongue touching her lips as the pair kissed. Soon he felt her tongue meet his and then her hand guiding his to her butt. In one motion Bryce swept Bennett on top of him and placed both hands on her butt grabbing and playing with it as the two continued to kiss. Bennett reached for her shirt and with one motion removed it, the small amount of light illuminating her figure, and her simple black bra. Bryce shifted and slowly slid his hand to her bra when a cough and shift from Anton just feet

The Atlantian Chronicles

away stopped him dead in his tracks. Bennett quickly scrambled to find her shirt and slip it on as the pair held their breath, Bennett still straddling Bryce as the two looked through the darkness of the cabin. "Clearly I was the only one actually trying to sleep." Anton mumbled; his eyes still closed. "Could whichever horny teenager is on top confirm it is safe for me to open my eyes?" Anton added unmoving from his spot on the couch.

"Clothes are on." Bryce embarrassingly muttered.

"Good. I guess there's no point in trying to sleep anymore considering I was the only one actually trying to." Anton lectured as he sat up and flicked on the light. "Next time, the heavy breathing and the muffled bed movements are a dead giveaway." Bryce felt Bennett squeeze his arm one last time before she begrudgingly slipped out of his bunk. Bryce shot Anton a look which he returned with a shrug. "Let's pack the truck and go." He said hopping off the couch and slipping his boots back on.

Within an hour, the truck was packed, the shack was cleaned up and the group was backing down the trail leading to the shack. Bryce secretly hoped the next place they stayed had private rooms. Bennett sat up front this time which was fine with Bryce who sprawled out in the back seat as Anton drove the four hours to the airport. Glancing up at the clock the time read 12:15 A.M.

"So… you two are…" Anton started breaking the silence as the road stretched on for miles.

"Figuring it out." Bennett interrupted awkwardly trying to change the subject. "Anton, what will they teach Bryce to do?"

"Well… I don't really know. I kept as much distance from the groups as possible. We didn't want anyone to know where we were. So, I assume they will teach him how to control his power. It's like a muscle. If it is worked out properly it will become stronger and easier to use." He explained.

"Okay, but how did they find Bryce so quickly? Tyson said they were looking in Georgia for Rhys, before he… before he… you know." Bennett questioned trying her best to take the subject as far away from her and Bryce's late-night escapades.

"Before he murdered my Dad." Bryce said sharply. "It's fine you can say it, I'm not going to cry about it." The anger apparent in his voice.

"It's not that Bryce I just don't..." Bennett replied softly.

"It's fine, sorry for snapping." Bryce mumbled in the back as he placed a hand softly onto Bennett's shoulder. It's true Bryce was mad, but he shouldn't take it out on her. She was only helping. Hell, if it wasn't for her getting him onto the roof of the house, he'd probably be lying dead in his burnt down house along with his Dad.

"It's complicated. Essentially, Unity has people constantly monitoring social media for any sign of Atlantians. Thousands of people secretly watching, searching, using keywords to find them. It used to be a lot harder, they'd scour newspapers, track down tall tales, read police reports, and whatever else they could do to find them, but with the invention of social media and people recording everything and anything, it only takes one slip up for a team to be sent out. That's why the Atlantians keep to areas less frequented by people and that's why Unity hasn't been able to find their new headquarters." Anton explained as Bryce looked out the windshield the white glow of the high beams illuminating the otherwise black night. "Why don't we fight back? Unity isn't exactly subtle with their tactics." Bryce asked angrily.

"We do, they do." Anton stated shooting a look back at Bryce as he did. "They can't just run up to a Unity leader and shoot them in broad daylight. I mean think about it. Unity aren't just rich big wigs, they're political leaders, CEOs of billion-dollar companies. The fight might not always make the front-page news, but the fight has never stopped."

"I'm sure we'll find out how we can help when we get to Maine." Bennett called out trying to turn the dark mood around.

The remaining drive was spent in relative silence, save for Bennett's occasional callout of a landmark on the way to Dallas, and the changing of radio stations occasionally as they passed through new areas. About ten minutes before they arrived, Anton turned down the radio and broke the silence. "Okay ladies and gentlemen, crunch time. Bryce, do you remember the plan." He asked with a sense of trepidation in his voice.

"Yeah, you drop me off at a Dunkin' and I get a drink chewing up at least fifteen minutes to put distance between our arrivals. Then I walk the ten minutes or so up the road, enter the airport in the domestic entrance,

I make my way to the gate and buy a ticket, requesting an aisle seat if they have it. 'Nervous flyer'." He explained, placing air quotes on the final part. "Then I make my way to the gate, sitting against a wall that faces the entry to the gate with a clear view of my surroundings, then board the flight with everyone else, trying my best to get into the middle of a group or crowd." He finished, anxiously looking at Anton through the rearview mirror, their eyes locking onto each other for a moment, something feeling eerily off before the moment passed and a calm washed over the vehicle.

"Okay good, and what if Bennett or I get grabbed?" He quizzed, clearly trying to drive a point home.

"I do nothing, I avoid looking and pretend I do not know either of you." He responded, his tone slightly sarcastic considering he had gone over this more than once now.

"Exactly, no hero stuff." He returned, the stern almost father-like tone, the stark opposite of his normal tone. "Now Bennett, what about us?" He asked, turning to the girl in the seat beside him.

"We arrive at the airport first, if people are waiting there, we calmly turn around feigning having forgotten something in our car and make our way back where we promptly leave. If no one is there, we enter and make our way around the airport, killing time and waiting to see Bryce, once Bryce has bought his ticket we will follow a group of people and buy our own, I will stay silent and let you talk to the ticket holder, pretending I could be less than thrilled about our 'father-daughter trip'." She stated matter-of-factly as she mimicked Bryce placing air quotes on father-daughter trip, with a deep breath she then continued. "From there we will go to a store and buy a few snacks and a newspaper and magazine, then we will make our way to the gate, meandering around as much as possible until our flight time. Then we board the flight and next thing we know we're in Maine." She finished with a flourish of her hands.

"And if I get caught?" He asked.

"I keep walking pretending we do not know each other." She replied, her face suddenly turning serious.

"And if Bryce gets caught?" He asked, checking his shoulder and changing lanes, pulling off the interstate as he did.

"I make my way to the nearest emergency exit, or fire alarm, and pull it. Then I move with the crowds out while you get Bryce." She stated, calmly sitting up straight in the seat and playing with her hair nervously. Bryce saw this and placed a hand on her shoulder softly, squeezing it as he did.

"Okay good. If anything happens, Bryce do your best to get on that flight, if all else fails, get to the long-term parking and try your best to get your hands on a car, Toyota Corolla if you can. It's the most common car and it'll be harder to track. Then head South and we will meet up in Fort Worth." Anton said, turning right, signs for the Dallas International Airport passing by as they did. "If we make it to Maine, we'll meet in the long-term parking lot. If they're waiting for us... find the nearest emergency exit and run, don't stop, don't look back, and don't worry about anyone but yourself. That goes for both of you." Anton asserted, his voice calm and cold. "Bryce, we're coming up to the Dunkin', once you exit this car you do not know us, and we have never met. Try to find any group of people other than us to group up with, and try to smile, you might have the personality of a rock sometimes, but you're anything but ugly." He joked, trying his best to break the tension as he spoke.

Bryce nodded as he saw the large, orange, glowing sign approach, the coffee shop almost seemed out of place in the dim glow of the early morning. Anton slowed to a stop and Bryce heard the click of the door. "Good luck." He said, swinging open the door and hopping out. With the sound of tires spinning and gravel kicking up, Bryce glanced back as he watched the car speed off towards the airport. He took a deep breath and pushed forward, shaking the anxiety out of his hands as the cold morning air bit at his exposed flesh. Bryce pulled his hood up and adjusted his hat, looking at his reflection in the large front window. His cream-colored hoodie, black jeans and white shoes looked somewhat fashionable. He couldn't help but smile slightly as he pulled his backpack up. The thought of Bennett and her ability to style him even in the face of grave danger made him feel warm. With one motion he pulled the handle open, and the smell of coffee and baked goods rushed to fill his nose.

Bryce ordered a small, iced coffee and a donut, waited the appropriate amount of time and then set off towards the airport, the morning sun beginning to shine down warming up the once cold air, gradually, as he made his way up the road to the airport. It was 5:30 A.M by the time Bryce entered the airport, throwing his empty cup in the garbage as he passed by, his eyes scanning the faces of the crowd, hoping to catch a look of Bennett or Anton as he did. But he had no such luck. Bryce calmly made his way to the front counter of the airport. A heavier set white man, with a faded ketchup stain on his shirt waved Bryce over, his five o'clock shadow and ruffled black hair clearly not putting the best foot forward for the airline, but a perfect candidate for Bryce to slip through undetected. "H...Hi, could I get a ticket please?" Bryce coughed his voice, seeming to take a moment to catch up to his busy mind.

"A ticket to where?" The man responded, his eyes barely coming off of his screen as he scanned the available flights.

"Maine, Bangor Airport. Aisle seat if you have it." Bryce hurriedly replied, as he nervously looked around him.

"First time flying?" The man questioned as he noticed Bryce's nervous movements.

"Is it that obvious?" Bryce lied quickly, as he watched the man's fingers dance across the keys.

"Definitely, but we do have a flight leaving shortly for Maine with lots of seats left, I just need to see a passport and I can book it for you." The man said, looking up from his screen at Bryce.

"I...I don't have one." Bryce said, trying his best to sound more nervous than he was and play into the part.

"Oh no sweat man, just stay calm, a state issued license will work just fine if you have one of those on you." The man reassured Bryce who took a deep breath and nodded, pulling out his wallet and sliding the fake license across the crisp, white counter. The man grabbed the license and looked at it for a moment. "This isn't fake right?" He asked, looking it over and then at Bryce.

"What?!" Bryce replied, his hands tensing as he heard the words leave the man's mouth.

"Kidding, just a little joke, don't worry, you're good… James… Gilbert, of Highland Park, Texas." He hurriedly said, trying to calm down the ball of nerves in front of him. "Note to self, know your audience." He muttered as he punched in the information and returned the card to Bryce. "And… here you go, one ticket from Dallas Texas to Bangor Maine." The man said, spinning his chair around, grabbing the ticket that printed out, and then spinning back around. "That will be 687.42 after taxes. How do you want to pay?" The man said, holding the ticket in his hand and looking at Bryce.

"Umm… cash." Bryce nodded as he pulled the cash out of his backpack and handed it to the man.

"Wow… big spender." The man joked as he took the cash, counted out the change and tucked it into the ticket, handing the whole lot back to Bryce. "You're going to be at gate seven, just down that way, follow the signs and you should make it there in no time." The man said, gesturing to the left with his hand.

"Thanks." Bryce said as he turned on his heels and set out towards his gate. His eyes scanning the crowds as he walked, looking for…anything. A man reaching towards his jacket, a group of people turning and heading his way, Tyson, but just then he saw it.

Out of the corner of his eye he saw it, it was just for a second, but he knew it. He turned and looked, quickly but that was more than enough time to confirm he was correct.

It was Bennett! A wave of relief washed over him as he saw her bright pink, mud stained backpack perfectly sitting over her tight black shirt, his borrowed red flannel- she'd purposely left open to show off her toned stomach and chest just enough to draw attention away from her face- and her light wash and ripped jeans sitting just below her hips as the fashion of a teenage girl would have them. Turning back around he smiled to himself and hurried his pace to his gate.

Bryce arrived at the gate and looked around, his eyes scanning the rows of seats for the perfect spot. It took him a moment, but he found it. Bryce weaved through the crowd of people half asleep waiting for their flight to begin to board and sat down, his back to the wall, his eyes scanning the area looking for the first sign of trouble.

The Atlantian Chronicles

Bryce sat for a few minutes before he saw Bennett again, her pink backpack bobbing up and down through the aisles of snacks in a small shop just outside of the gate's waiting area. He tried his best not to stare but his eyes kept coming back to her, almost as if they were drawn there. He thought about kissing her, and how her skin felt pressed against him, her laugh and positivity. She was a beacon for him in these last few dark days. He couldn't help but feel guilty for getting her involved in this. *How could he keep her safe when he had no clue what was going on? There seemed to be no end to this. Would he spend the rest of his life on the run, hiding and living under fake names? That wasn't fair to her, she didn't sign up for that. Hell, he didn't sign up for it either. Unity, Rhys, Atlantis, everyone forced him into this.* Just as he began to become frustrated at his situation, a woman's voice came across the intercom. "Hello, All passengers on flight 271 departing from Dallas, Texas to Bangor, Maine, your flight is now boarding. All passengers from first class and seat numbers beginning with row A and ending with row F and all those needing assistance boarding please line up in front of the ticket counter to check in. Again, that is flight 271 Dallas to Bangor First class, Rows A to F and all those needing assistance boarding please come to the gate now. Thank you." The message repeated in Spanish as Bryce checked his ticket. Row G seat E. Bryce leaned forward and watched as the line slowly moved forward. Slowly person by person the flight boarded his heart raced as he watched, his eyes scanning for any sign of trouble, or Bennett.

"Hello, all passengers on flight 271 Dallas, Texas to Bangor, Maine, with seats in Row G to Row J please line up in front of the ticket counter to check in. Again, that is Flight 271 Dallas to Bangor Rows G to J, please proceed to the ticket counter for boarding. Thank you." The intercom woman's voice played over the speakers, the message repeating in Spanish as Bryce stood up and calmly walked over to the counter, handing a well-groomed and dressed man his ticket before he ripped it and handed it back to him, directing him down the walkway to the plane. Bryce took a deep breath and followed the crowd making his way to his seat where he stowed his bag in the overhead and sat down. Bryce drew his hood up, adjusted his hat and pretended to close his eyes, leaning back slightly as he kept his eyes on the people entering the plane. His heart raced as each person boarded the plane, one by one, men, women, children, of all different sizes, races and builds entered the plane, one by one taking their seats.

"Excuse me Dear," A soft, elderly woman's voice broke Bryce's concentration as he stared at the entrance. "Is it possible to change seats so he could sit in the aisle he's a nervous flyer?" The woman continued as Bryce looked at her. Describing this woman as someone's grandma would be an understatement, the elderly woman sported, short grayish white hair, styled into a perm, she had her make-up fully done, her eyes sporting a combination of blues and greens, as her cheeks had a rosy, red blush applied to them. She smelled heavily of a flowery perfume that nearly choked Bryce. He glanced over at her and then the man leaning out from behind her, he was bald on top with bright white hair on the sides of his head forming an almost comical hairstyle he aggressively combed over. Bryce had to stop himself from laughing as he saw the two wore matching Burgundy tracksuits. "What do you say dear? You'd only have to move from the aisle to the window seat?" She repeated smiling as she did, her southern accent becoming more apparent as she spoke.

"Umm… sure." Bryce said quickly standing up and sliding over in the row as the pair took their new seats, Bryce immediately kicking himself for not keeping the aisle seat as Anton had instructed, justifying it by saying the conflict and attention of him saying no would have been worse. Nodding to himself once he'd won the debate in his head.

"Oh, thank you, Sweetie, you know there aren't enough nice people like you in this world." She said as she sat down and quickly buckled her seat belt. "I'm Norma, and this is Howard, but you can just call us Mimi and Beep Bop, everybody does. It's our wedding anniversary this week. We're heading to Maine, to visit our daughter and grand babies, she moved away when she married Devon, oh boy is he so sweet. He's in the milit…"

"Norma, this boy does not care, let him—" Howard chimed in, cutting off the word vomit of his wife.

"Oh, hush up Howie, he doesn't mind, do you sugar?" She continued, cutting off her husband before he could finish scolding her.

"You're fine ma'am." Bryce said over his shoulder as he half listened, his attention remaining on the entrance.

"Perfect, anyways, where was I? Oh right, Devon, well he is just the sweetest, and so good to Florence -our youngest, a real Daddy's girl- but Devon, he's in the military, air force I think, anyways he is just so sweet, even volunteered to help throw Howie and I's 60th wedding anniversary this weekend. Can you imagine it, sixty years? And I ain't sick of him yet." She said her pace was almost too quick for Bryce to keep up with as he waited for Anton and Bennett to enter. "What are you looking at, Sugar?" She asked leaning over onto Bryce, trying to copy his eyeline.

"Norma, what this boy is looking at ain't none of our business, sit back down." Howard scolded as he pulled at the woman's tracksuit. "I swear we can't go anywhere without you bugging people." He huffed as she brushed his hands away.

"Oh, she's pretty." Norma called out as Bennett entered the plane, Anton following close behind pretending his best to be a doting father.

"Umm... yeah I guess so." Bryce said, sitting back as a wave of relief washed over him. They'd made it onto the plane, no issues. Halfway there.

"Oh, hush up Hun." Norma said gingerly, slapping Bryce on the arm as his attention switched to the screen in front of him. "You were waiting for that girl to board. You should go say something to her. Oh, just imagine it, you meet your future wife on the flight. Imagine it, Howie." Norma pestered as she returned to her seat. "Come on Sweetie, just imagine it." She continued elbowing Bryce in the side garnering a wince from him.

"Oh, great now look what you did Norma, you've gone and hurt the boy." Howard scolded her, pulling his wife's arms away from Bryce. "You need to settle down now, I knew we shouldn't have let you have that second cup of coffee." He whispered at her, his tone clearly a tone of frustration.

"No, no it's fine, just a bruise from... football." Bryce quickly lied trying to soothe the building argument between the two.

"Oh, our little grand baby Ryan plays football, just tyke right now but I swear he's going to be the next Tony Romo." Norma stated proudly, gaining her an eye roll from Howard. "What position do you play, with your build I bet you're a kicker. You're a kicker ain't you, I got an eye for this I swear."

"You got it right." Bryce nodded, thinking back to Rhys's teachings. *It's always easier to convince someone of a lie they already believe, let them answer their own questions and then go with that.* Bryce thought, hearing Rhys's deep, raspy voice.

"See I told you; I have a gift!" She cheered triumphantly. "So..." She began as the stewardess closed the plane door, sealing it and pressurizing the cabin. "It's starting." She whispered, elbowing Howard who shot her a look before turning his focus to the woman at the front of the plane.

Bryce listened attentively to the woman at the front of the plane watching carefully as she indicated the different safety points of the flight, where the exits were, and what to do in the case of an emergency. The plane took off without issue and within twenty minutes the seatbelt light flicked off. "Now's your chance Sweetie, make your way back there and talk to that girl." Norma began, trying her best to put as much Southern draw and charm into her words.

"I... I... I can't." Bryce stuttered trying to think of a lie as he did.

"Why not? You ain't got someone you're sweet on at home, do you?" Norma asked, turning in her seat to face Bryce.

"Norma, that is none of your business." Howard said, pulling at the sleeve of the woman's tracksuit once more. "Leave this poor boy alone, if he don't want to talk to her, he ain't got to."

"Ummm... Kind of? We're... figuring it out." Bryce said remembering what Bennett had said earlier that morning.

"Oh Sugar, tell me about this girl then." Norma said shrugging off Howard who huffed and then tapped his screen bringing up a sudoku.

"She's from my high school." Bryce began nervously. "And umm... we used to be friends. But then she dated this guy, who wasn't really nice to her." Bryce said softly a smile coming to his face as he thought about the girl who sat only a few rows away from him, completely oblivious to the conversation about her that was taking place. "And we kind of drifted apart because of it."

"Oh Howie, listen to this, it's like one of those romantic comedies we love so much." Norma said giddily as she tugged at Howard's arm as he typed away on the screen.

"That you love so much." He corrected, muttering to himself as he played the game.

"Oh hush." She snapped back waving her hand at the man. "What does this girl look like?" She asked excitedly.

"She's beautiful, she's got blonde hair, a smile that lights up any room, and eyes that just look through you." Bryce lied picturing Bennett as he spoke and then changing small details as he did, thinking of her kind, forgiving, caring eyes, her brown hair, perfectly layered, small highlights throughout it, and her smile, she might not have powers like him, but when she smiled, it was almost as if she did.

"Oh, she sounds so pretty." Norma cooed, clasping her hands together as she did and smiling wide.

"Yeah, she is." Bryce replied, trying to hide his smile as he thought of her.

"So, she was with this other guy." Norma said, trying to get the story back on track.

"Yeah, right. She was with this guy, and he wasn't good to her, so one day I was at a party, and he hit her." Bryce said, receiving an audible gasp from Norma as he spoke. "So, he hit her, and I stepped between them, and..."

"You better say you beat him up." Norma interrupted the vinegar in her voice very apparent.

"Yeah, I did." Bryce nodded, rubbing his hand on the back of his neck shyly. "And then I don't know we just kind of realized that maybe we should..." Bryce said softly trying to find the right words.

"You realized you were meant to be together. Oh, that's so cute, I love young love. I wish Howard and I's story was nearly as heroic." Norma finished the statement for Bryce who blushed as she spoke. "Oh, look at you, you love this girl." She continued pinching Bryce's cheek as she did.

Bryce spent the rest of the flight listening to Norma discuss everything and anything she could, from her three grandchildren: Juliet, Ryan and Millie, to her entire working career as a hairstylist, she even went so far as to tell Bryce she once cut Dolly Parton's hair when she stopped off in the town on her tour. Howard adamantly denying this is true, only to be shushed by Norma. By the end of the flight Bryce was surprised he hadn't been invited to the anniversary party.

As the flight landed Bryce stood up, and helped the couple with their bag, glancing back as he did to confirm where Bennett and Anton were. Bryce let the couple go in front of him and the group slowly began their departure from the flight. As Bryce entered the bridge connecting the plane to the gate, he saw it. A pair of men, wearing uniforms checking each passenger as they did. Panicking, Bryce slowly moved backwards, before he was bumped into by the person directly behind him. With a grunt the man bumped Bryce forward and back into formation with the rest of the group. His heart raced as he watched the two men stopping each person, taking off any hats or hoods they had on and checking a tablet. "You okay Sugar?" Norma whispered, glancing back at Bryce who nervously looked for an exit.

"Umm… I think they're here for me." He gulped as he ducked down narrowly avoiding the men who waved the next two people forward.

"Sugar, why would they be here for you?" She questioned leaning her head out of the line and looking at the two armed men.

"Well, back home, I got in some trouble, and I think they found me." Bryce lied trying to sound as innocent as possible, glancing around as he spoke. *Should he fight them? How many were there? Should he try to run? Was Tyson here?* All questions he needed to answer and fast.

"What kind of trouble?" Howard asked sternly, pulling Norma close to him.

"The girl, her ex-boyfriend, he didn't like me. When I beat him up, he charged me. So, we're running away together, I'm meeting her here." Bryce lied, the panic in his voice building as he spoke. Howard looked at him sternly before he spoke.

"Don't lie to me boy." He whispered pointing a finger at Bryce as he did. "Norma might like you, but I am not so easy to persuade." He threatened.

"I swear, I'm telling the truth." Bryce pleaded, realizing his time was running out. "She's meeting me in Portland, we took separate flights." Bryce begged Howard to believe him, silently praying he could convince the man to help him... somehow.

"Okay Son." Howard whispered his expression softening as he spoke.

Slowly the trio made their way to the two men, each time the men waved a pair though Bryce grew more and more nervous. Bryce drew his hood up, lowered his hat and tilted his head down. The armed men waved another couple through and then it was just the elderly couple left before Bryce. Keeping his head down Bryce waited, his heart racing, the sweat pooling on his brow. The men motioned for Howard and Norma to approach and as they did, Howard tripped, or fell, or rather he dove to the ground, pretending to stumble the man went down screaming in pain as he did. Norma rushed to his side as the two armed men paused for a moment, then moved to help the elderly man as he shouted, cursed and promised to sue everyone involved. Bryce stumbled as people rushed to the aid of Howard and as they did, Bryce watched as Norma glanced over and mouthed the word "Go." to him. Bryce slowly and calmly stepped sideways glancing around and seeing the chaos unfold before him.

Seeing his chance Bryce began to walk, his pace quickening as he did. Bryce had nearly made it to the door when he heard it. A voice. "Hey Sir!" It shouted from behind him. Ignoring it, Bryce continued to walk, almost breaking out into a run as he did. "Sir. In the hoodie." The voice shouted, the sound of steps quickening behind Bryce. Within seconds he felt a hand grab his shoulder. "Sir. You dropped this." Bryce stopped turning around to see a middle-aged man in a dress shirt and slacks, handing him his wallet. Bryce froze, his brain unable to process what was going on.

"Umm... thanks." He said taking his wallet and nodding to the man, stuffing it into his pocket and continuing his walk towards the nearest exit. Bryce had nearly made it to the exit when he heard it.

"There he is!" The words cut through the air like a knife through warm butter. Bryce's head jerked up as he saw a pair of men pointing directly at him. Bryce took off at a full sprint trying to make it to the exit, but he was too slow. The first of the men, a large black man with a shaved head and a goatee barely distinguishable from his dark skin, blocked the entrance. Struggling to get traction as Bryce skittered to a stop and changed direction, the second man, a stout white man far shorter than his counterpart, dove for Bryce as he stopped.

With a painful thud, Bryce felt the man collide with him and the air leave his body as the two fell to the floor, his backpack absorbing much of the ground's impact. Struggling to catch his breath Bryce gasped and coughed. The man wrestling with him as he did. Bryce quickly wrapped his legs around his attacker and closed his guard, hoping for some kind of protection as he wrapped the man up preventing him from hitting Bryce again. That's when the second man's foot struck Bryce in the side of the head, sending a jolt of pain through his body and causing his whole world to spin. Fighting with all the strength he could muster, Bryce continued to grapple with the first man and dodge the incoming kicks of the second. Tying the first man up as best he could, Bryce was in a bad position that got worse with each second he was on his back and the two men could continue to attack him. He needed to act fast. Crunching his body away from the second man's kick, Bryce saw his chance, the first man posted his leg just high enough for Bryce to grab it. As the first man struggled to break Bryce's grip, Bryce struck, like a snake he coiled his body crunching down once again, but this time he released his grip on the man's back and slid his closest hand under the first man's leg. In one fluid motion, Bryce released his legs from their tight hold around the man's waist and rolled forward, sweeping the man onto his back and reversing the position. Bryce was back to his feet in the blink of an eye and searching for an exit. As the black man swung at Bryce, his large arms generating an alarming amount of force aimed right for Bryce's head, Bryce evaded, dodging backwards and raising his hands, the blow narrowly missing his face. With a sharp inhale Bryce finally felt the air return to his lungs. Looking around Bryce watched as the white man returned to his feet, his hands moving to his waistband as he did.

The man produced a black, Glock 17 handgun and slowly began to raise it. As his barrel came up sighting in on Bryce, a hand struck the man directly in the jaw. In awe, Bryce watched as Anton flew from the opposite side of the man, his hand instinctively going for the barrel of the gun and controlling it. The black man quickly turned, reaching for his waistband as his attention shifted to the more immediate threat. As Bryce watched the man produce a similar gun to his partner, without thinking Bryce threw a kick at the side of the man. Bryce putting as much force as he could into the large man's ribs, feeling them buckle under the force as the man let out a loud scream of pain, before falling to the ground.

"Bryce run!" Anton shouted as he continued to fight for control of the gun with the stout white man. Slowly backing away Bryce watched as two more men -finally free of Norma and Howard's distraction- sprinted over. Turning away Bryce leaped over the black man who struggled to stand as he clutched his side. And took off at a full sprint as soon as his feet hit the ground.

Bryce ran as fast as his legs would allow him too, bursting through the nearest exit, the midday sky and bright sun, hitting his skin as he jumped over railings and down stairs, taking them three to four at a time, not daring to look over his shoulder. As Bryce rounded a corner he heard three short honks of a horn. Looking up he saw Bennett behind the wheel of a blue, Chevy Cruze. "Get in!" She called and flung open the rear door of the vehicle.

"Drive, drive, drive!" He screamed as the tires screeched and Bennett peeled out of the parking lot, hitting the curb with a loud crunch as she exited the pick-up lane and flew down the street. "How did you?" Bryce questioned as he looked back, watching the men slowly disappear from view as the car sped away.

"Don't ask." Bennett replied, the sound of air rushing into the car, throwing her hair around as she sped down the street. It took Bryce a moment to realize she'd broken the opposite window and stolen the car, the fragments of glass littering the seat beside her. "What happened to Anton?" She asked, her voice shaking as she spoke.

"I don't know." Bryce replied in between deep breaths. "He told me to run, and I did." Bryce said, glancing back once more to see if the coast was clear. "I don't think they're following us." He said softly as he turned around, fearing the worst. "We should find somewhere to hide for now."

CHAPTER 12

Bennett drove for well over thirty minutes before she pulled down a side street and parked the car. "What happened there?" She asked looking back at Bryce.

"They knew we were there. As soon as we came off the plane, they were waiting for us." Bryce replied looking out the window of the car. "I slipped past the first two but was spotted by another pair. Then all hell broke loose. I'd be dead if it weren't for Anton, and now he's most likely dead because of me." Bryce said, clenching his fist tightly as the words caught in the back of his throat.

"Don't say that Bryce, you don't know that for certain." Bennett whimpered, fighting back tears herself. "I know you don't want to hear this right now. But I think Anton knew we wouldn't make it to Maine without getting discovered." She continued her voice breaking as she spoke.

"What makes you say that?" He asked looking up from his lap at her.

"After we dropped you off, he… he told me where we needed to go and who we needed to meet. Then he taught me how to do all of this." She said as she gestured to the car and the steering column. "Bryce, I think he knew one of us would get caught, and I think he planned on it being him. He gave me all the information we needed in case he didn't make it out of the airport. I didn't think anything of it at the time…"

"That's ridiculous, why would he knowingly get caught by Unity!" Bryce interrupted, his voice breaking as he spoke.

"Because Bryce, he knew how important it was to get you to Maine. He had to have known you wouldn't agree to this if you knew this is how it would go." Bennett continued. "You know I'm right." She asserted, her voice shaky but forceful.

"You're right I wouldn't have. There had to have been a better way to get us here." He said his eyes beginning to water.

"There wasn't Bryce. Not that quickly." She comforted, her hand finding his cheek. "Bryce, I'm sorry." She whispered as she wiped the tears from his cheek. "I know you don't want to hear this right now, but I think we need to get going. Millinocket is a far drive and it's better we do it now before it gets too late." She said softly. Bryce nodded.

The two stopped by a gas station, filled the tank, and after several minutes of vacuuming glass and a borrowed bag and tape, the window was repaired and the two set out on the five-hour drive to Millinocket. The first hour was tense as the two held their breath every time they passed a police car, or heard a siren ring out. But as the city faded away and the time ticked by the two began to relax.

"I wouldn't be here if it wasn't for you." Bryce said, squeezing Bennett's hand in his as he held the steering wheel with one hand.

"I know." She replied in a faux smugness that drew a smile from Bryce.

"I'm being serious." He said, glancing over at her. "I'm sorry I got you involved in all of this. You'd be studying for a history test right now if it wasn't for me."

"So, I guess it's you who saved me then." She joked back as she took his hand and kissed it softly.

"Bennett, I'm serious." He said sternly.

"I know. It's okay." She whispered looking at him as she held his hand inches from her mouth.

"Okay." He returned softly, pulling their hands towards him and kissing hers. "So, tell me again what Anton told you about Millinocket?" He asked, trying to wrap his head around the next step of their journey.

"He said we were meeting someone named Echo, at an arcade called The Rocketship. He should be waiting there. He's going to ask us: where do you feel most alive? And we have to reply when you are moments away from death. After that he's going to take us to the camp." She repeated pausing as she tried to remember the passphrase.

"I swear this gets more and more cliche with each day." Bryce said, shaking his head.

"Come on, you have to admit, you feel a bit like a spy don't you." Bennett replied, her hands gesturing all around. "I mean look at this, we are on the run, there is a secret society chasing us, if it wasn't so terrifying it might actually make for a good book."

"Maybe, but it seems a bit... made up." He said pessimistically.

"Well, if not a book, I'm sure it will make for a great college essay." She joked back, the thought of what college they might attend in two years' time seemed like an impossibility to Bryce now.

"How are you so positive through all of this?" Bryce asked concernedly. "You're just taking this in stride like it's nothing. Aren't you scared? Worried? Hell, I'll even take startled by everything. Four days ago, your biggest concern was Ashton's party." Bryce questioned.

"Of course I am Bryce." She shot back. "But if I shut down, stop or slow down, we could die. I am terrified! I have spent the better part of two days scared I'll get caught or killed." She said, tears running down her face as we spoke. "I've been almost killed more times than I can count, committed at least two felonies, and abandoned my Dad, who probably thinks I'm dead. It breaks my heart thinking about how he feels, about how you feel, I want to curl up in a ball and cry, but life is hard sometimes and you don't get stronger, you just get better at dealing with it. And that's what I'm trying to do. I see you getting mad, I feel it. I'm mad too. They took my life away from me. And I don't know when I'll get it back." She cried, the emotions from the last few days boiling over.

"I know I'm sorry." He muttered as he listened to her cry, his heart ached. "I'll drop you off in town if you want, you can tell them we forced you, threatened your family if you want. You can have your life back." He suggested knowing the answer before he'd even finished.

"You don't get it." She huffed, letting go of his hand and turning in her seat. "You aren't even listening to what I'm saying. Bryce, don't you get it. Unity knows about me. They know I'm with you. They literally made up a story about me. I can't go back, there's no way I survive without you, no matter what lie I tell, the second they get their hands on me I am as good as dead. So, I try to spin things in a positive way because this is my only hope. If I fail, if you fail, if WE fail! It's all over anyway." She yelled, her voice ringing in Bryce's ears. "So, I'm positive because I have to be. We both can't be doom and gloom." She spat, the anger in her voice almost scaring Bryce.

"I didn't realize." He said softly as she breathed heavily.

"Exactly you didn't. And you're allowed to be considering everything that's gone on. You've lost your Dad and Anton. But don't push me away because of it. I'm not just some bystander you can drop off at the nearest bus stop." She continued her voice returning to a normal speaking volume.

"Okay." He replied, not knowing what else to say.

"Good." She huffed. The two drove in silence for the next few miles, Bennett crying into Bryce's flannel silently.

"It's not that I want to push you away or leave you at a bus stop Bennett. It's just I can't lose someone else, especially not you." He said, finally breaking the silence.

"Well too bad. You promised." She muttered over her shoulder. "You promised to never leave. My mom promised that before she went to the hospital, and she lied." She said keeping her curled position as she spoke.

"I know I'm sorry." He said, reaching a hand out and touching her back lightly. The silence continued as they drove, Bryce rubbing Bennett's back as she curled away from him. "Can you just talk to me?" He asked after he couldn't take the silence anymore.

"About what? I've said all I have to on the matter." She spat back clearly not in the mood to talk about the subject further.

"How does the spy book start?" He said softly trying to lighten the mood.

"You're not funny." She mumbled.

"I'm not trying to be. I'm curious." He replied warmly. "I'm thinking with a handsome guy saving the damsel in distress." He continued trying to bait her into talking.

"I think it's the other way around. I'm pretty sure I have saved you more times than you saved me. Plus, you kind of ruined my life." She said, turning over and looking at him.

"Yeah, I think I might have." He joked. "I didn't have much of a life to ruin myself if it's any consolation."

"It's not." She snorted back. "You know you really suck at apologies, right?"

"Well, I haven't had the chance to stop by any flower shops since you yelled at me." He chuckled back. "What flower would you get to say, 'Sorry I ruined your life, forced you to go on the run and almost got you killed several times?' Tulips?"

"Tulips are ugly. Lillies would probably be a good start." She laughed, wiping her nose with the wrist of the shirt.

"Ha. You laughed; you can't be mad at me anymore." Bryce said triumphantly, remembering back to their first fight as children, Bennett had tripped Bryce at recess causing the whole class to laugh at him. Angrily Bryce told Bennett they weren't friends anymore, Bennett said something funny to Bryce who laughed, and she exclaimed that he couldn't be mad if he was laughing. From then on if one of them was mad at the other, whoever was in the wrong would make the other laugh and all was forgiven.

"You suck." She giggled. "Why couldn't you let me be mad a little longer." She asked, trying to hide her smile.

"Doesn't work that way, those are the rules." He replied, squeezing her thigh with his free hand.

"Quit it." She laughed, wiggling in her seat as he squeezed.

The two drove the rest of the way laughing and playing driving games, trying their best to put the fight, and the fear behind them even if it was just for a moment. The tank was almost empty by the time they pulled into Millinocket. The clock read 5:23 P.M. when the two turned into the parking lot of the rundown arcade and surrounding strip mall. The faded sign and exterior in need of a facelift; as it clearly hadn't been updated since the early 90's. The alien riding a rocket ship, barely distinguishable anymore from years of UV rays hitting the cheap plastic casing, the words

'The Rocketship Arcade' cracked and faded like most of the signs for the neighboring businesses. "Are you sure this is the right place?" Bryce said as he pulled the car into the parking lot and looked at Bennett.

"No, but I doubt there are many arcades in Millinocket, Maine. Until yesterday I hadn't even heard of the place, so I doubt they get many tourists." She replied, stepping out of the car slowly and making her way to the rear door where their backpacks were.

Bryce glanced around the rundown looking strip mall, with a handful of cars dotting the parking lot, the sleepy town seemed almost abandoned to Bryce who grew up in a much busier city. As traffic flowed behind them, Bryce slowly put his backpack on, looked at Bennett and took a deep breath. "I guess we go inside?" He asked half hoping she would say no.

"That's what Anton said. He said to find the man who goes by the name Echo, I'm assuming he's in here." She said, taking Bryce's hand and walking towards the door.

The two entered the building, the smell of fried food wafted through the building, making the pairs mouth water. It had been hours since they'd last eaten. The sound of games ringing, beeping, and buzzing flooded the air. The two made their way through the rows of games, dust flying up as the two walked over the patterned blue and black carpet. "Should we get something to eat?" He asked as the two saw the snack bar at the end of a row of arcade machines.

"I don't think that's the smartest idea." Bennett said as she nodded over to a single man hunched over a game pushing the buttons furiously.

"Umm... Hello are you, Echo?" Bryce asked softly, tapping the man on the shoulder.

"Just a minute." The man said straining as he pressed buttons and threw the joystick in multiple directions. "I've almost beat it."

"We're looking for Echo, is that you?" Bryce repeated to the man's back.

Just as Bryce finished his sentence, the man threw his arms up in frustration. "This game is rigged." He exclaimed, turning around and looking up at Bryce through his thick glasses, his bloodshot eyes looking almost alien in size. The Asian man was five-foot-four at best, with a belly, short, black hair and stubble that clearly showed it had been a few days since his last shave. He wore a vintage video game t-shirt that struggled to cover his large belly, and brown khakis. "And who might you two be?" He asked, glancing up and down the pair.

"Are you Echo? My friend said you might be able to help us?" Bryce repeated again, his arm moving Bennett behind him slightly as he watched the man slowly check her out.

"Possibly, but where do you feel most alive?" The short man asked, raising his bushy eyebrows.

Bennett's eyes lit up as she heard the question. "When you are moments away from death." She replied, trying to contain the nervousness in her voice.

"Ahh... good, thought you might not make it." Echo replied, checking his watch and then glancing at the pair again. "I thought there were supposed to be three of you?" He said, squinting his eyes at them.

"There were, we... something happened." Bryce replied sorely. "Can you help us or not?" He asked, clearly tired of the man's quizzical nature.

"I can..." He said drawing out his reply as he did. "But we need to leave right now." He hurried to the front door and locked it. "Right this way please." He called, rushing over to a door at the back of the arcade and opening it. Bryce and Bennett followed him through the door and towards a handful of broken arcade machines. "Could I get your hand with this?" He asked as he pushed the side of a machine. With Bryce's help the two swung the heavy Pac-Man game aside revealing a hole broken into the wall. Echo ushered the two through the hole and then climbed in himself straining as he pulled the game back into its original position. "Shhh..." The small man said, placing a finger to his lips and rushing down a long hallway, that Bryce guessed ran just underneath the arcade. Echo almost ran down the hallway to a staircase waving his hand in a motion indicating he was not pleased with the speed at which Bryce and Bennett were moving. "Time is of the essence." He whisper-shouted at the pair as they made their way towards and then down the stairs.

Through another door, the tunnels opened into an almost command center like room. "Crap!" Echo said, staring at one of the monitors, as two black SUVs pulled up. "You were followed." He whispered his nasally voice twinging with fear. Bryce and Bennett watched in fear as six armed men emerged from the vehicles and surrounded the car they'd arrived in. "Where did I put it?" Echo muttered to himself as he rushed around the room opening cabinets and drawers quickly. "Ahh here it is." He said pulling a silver CZ shadow handgun from the drawer and waving it around. Bryce and Bennett ducked as he swung the barrel towards them as he spun around to look at the monitors once more. "Walk away." He muttered to himself as he watched two armed men approach the door and peer through the shutters on the glass door. Bryce and Bennett held their breath, Bennett wrapping her arms around Bryce instinctually as the two watched the scene play out.

Two of the men stared through the doors for a few more moments before eventually moving onto the other stores in the plaza. A handsome looking man shrugging his shoulders and barking what look like commands to the rest of the group as they fanned out. The group collectively let out a sigh of relief. "Good. Thought I would have to use this thing." Echo said stuffing the gun back into a drawer and shoving it closed. "Let's go." The man said, swinging open a large green cabinet to reveal yet another secret passage. Bryce and Bennett entered the passage, the smell of dirt and stale air choking them in the long tunnel. "Okay, now we just take this tunnel this way and then we are home free." The man said as he clicked on a headlamp and began to lead the way.

The group walked for over a mile before they reached the end of the tunnel. Echo pulled a key from his pocket and unlocked the rod-iron gate that marked the end of the tunnel and swung it open. Bryce emerged and took a deep breath before he took in his surroundings. The tunnel had surfaced somewhere in a forest. The whole area was filled with pine, maple and birch trees alike, Bryce glanced back as Echo locked the door, the stone entryway tucked into the side of a large hill as if it had been shaped around the entrance. *Was it a Tellus?* Bryce thought looking at the entrance and thinking back to the tunnel and how it seemed to be lacking in any shovel or tool marks of any kind. Plus, the more he thought about it, *the extreme length of the tunnel would have taken months to dig, how did no one notice them, how did they dispose of all the dirt.* The more he thought about it the more probable the theory an Atlantian made the tunnel seemed to be. Echo led the way through the forest to a small trail and after telling the pair to wait there and venturing off for a moment; he returned driving a black, old model Jeep Wrangler, the tires almost half his height. "Well don't just stand there, get in." Echo called over the engine. With a shrug Bennett walked over and climbed into the back. Bryce followed suit and soon the group was back on the move.

"So which one of you is…" Echo began.

"Me." Bryce interrupted knowing exactly what he was about to ask.

"Interesting, what are you? Madzi? Copia?" Echo continued as he weaved down the trail branches snapping against the windshield as he went.

"He's a Crono?" Bennett replied, still unsure if she was pronouncing it right.

"Oh, don't get many of you around here. Lots of Copia, Madzi, Nar-Asam too, a few Tellus -they helped build the tunnels- but not many Crono. You're the first one I've dealt with." Echo stated, his tone very casual as if he'd done this hundreds of times. "Crono don't last too long, takes a lot of energy to shift as they call it. Typically end up getting caught or killed because they pass out. Hypoglycemia sets in and poof, they pass out. Plus, not many of you left you know. Guess that's where you come in." Echo said, gesturing to Bennett.

"It's complicated." She replied looking at Bryce, his hard features accentuated in the low light.

"It always is sister. One time we had a pair of Copia who liked to change faces and genders while they… you know. Now that, that was complicated." He joked, slapping the steering wheel and laughing.

"How much longer until we arrive?" Bryce asked hoping the answer was sooner than later, as his stomach growled.

"Not too much longer, about ten more minutes." Echo said as he slowly maneuvered over a creek.

"Are there a lot of people at the camp?" Bennett asked thoughtfully.

"Maybe ten, most we've had was twenty but that was a while ago, we try to keep a steady flow in and out of the camp, it's safer that way. Most people stay for a month or two until the heat has died down and they've learned to control things a bit better. Then we move you to wherever you can do the most good." Echo explained as branches snapped under the tires.

"How have you guys remained hidden out here for so long?" Bennett asked.

"There's a few reasons. The camp is pretty deep into the mountains of Appalachia, which doesn't hurt considering many people believe they're haunted that reduces the foot traffic, then we've also made friends with the locals who showed us the old rumrunner trails, so we can avoid being seen that way, and on top of that, the old moonshine camp we use is so long abandoned that as long as we avoid making any changes to it externally and keep all our electrical work underground -thank you to the Telluses at camp for that one- we are basically invisible to all but the few who manage to get past all of that. And if that is the case, we have hidden trail cameras that feed directly into a monitoring station, along with a signal jammer. Then if all else fails we have escape tunnels and a lot of guns." Echo explained as he turned his high beams on and off in a pattern.

CHAPTER 13

Echo repeated this seemingly random pattern of flashing the lights of the jeep as he progressed through the forest. Bryce tried his best to memorize the pattern, predict when the next set of flashes would come but he was unsuccessful, it was as if the short, fat man was randomly flicking the lights on and off purely for his own enjoyment. It wasn't until the sixth or seventh time Echo played with the lights that Bennett noticed it. A faint light off in the distance. Within a few moments the Jeep crested a hill and after a far faster than expected trip down the hill, Bryce and Bennett watched in awe as the darkness quickly faded and the thick forest gave way to a small town like camp. "Welcome to the Atlantian Brotherhood's Appalachian camp." Echo called out as he brought the jeep to a sudden and abrupt stop, the tires sliding for a few feet as the short man stomped on the brake.

With a look, a shrug and a bit of maneuvering, Bryce climbed out, turning around to help Bennett -who was already halfway through the process-, offering her a hand which she promptly swatted away, jumping off the edge of the jeep, landing with a thud into the soft ground. For a moment the two took in their surroundings. The camp was in a small clearing, clearly created years ago, the clearing had to be forty feet wide and thirty feet long by Bryce's estimation. A large fire pit in the center of the camp, surrounded by a variety of chairs ranging from old kitchen chairs, to outdoor camping chairs, and stumps of wood that had clearly been placed there and well used, a large, old looking, barn the worn paint barely visible after years of weathering, flanked the fire, it's large doors held open, revealing several dirt bikes, and what looked like a boxing ring of some sort. To the left of the fire was a small shack that made the cabin in Texas look like a castle. With a gulp, Bryce looked around the camp, hoping there was some kind of magic cloaking device that hid the actual camp.

"Cung, what have we told you about your speed entering camp?" A tall slender native woman, in a gray colored hoodie, worn under a pair of blue, faded denim overalls, and black boots, called as she stormed towards the jeep, pushing past the pair and slamming Echo's door closed as he attempted to clamber out of the raised jeep himself. "Do not go anywhere, I will deal with you two in a moment." She said, turning around for a moment as Bryce and Bennett began to collect their bags. "Now Cung, what did we say?" She scolded as the short man hung his head.

"It's Echo, and I know what you said, you don't have to make a big deal about it." He muttered his voice barely audible to the woman let alone Bryce or Bennett.

"Well clearly I do, because for some unknown reason you understand the orders, but you do not follow them." She argued her voice a mix of commanding and scolding now. "You cannot drive into camp with that much speed, you will hurt or even worse kill someone, and the fact that I need to continue to tell you this tells me you are not ready for further responsibility. Now who are these two? Reports said there were to be three of them, where's the third?" She demanded as the small man shrunk even deeper into the jeep.

"I'm Bennett Douglas and this is Bryce Hillcrest." Bennett began reaching a hand out to the woman as she spoke.

"Well, it's good that at least one of you has the balls to talk." She scoffed, turning away from Echo and shaking Bennett's hand.

"Amelia Blackburn, apologies for the less than formal introduction, but we have found the best way to deal with this one, is to treat him like the man-child he is." She said snarkily looking over her shoulder as Echo climbed out slowly.

"It's okay. We are just glad to have made it here." Bennett replied diplomatically, gesturing around to the camp as Bryce stood stoically watching the scene unfold.

"Well, you haven't made it in quite yet." The woman said as Bryce finally took her in, she was a very pretty woman, her sharp features told the story of someone very fit, who spent much of their life training and in a constant state of movement. She had long-braided hair, barely visible in the light of the fire. She stood a little over four inches taller than Bennett, her body, hidden under her choice of warm clothing, seemed to be toned based on how skinny she looked in her bulky outfit. "We had reports of three of you arriving today. What happened?" She questioned, her hand still holding Bennett's but now unmoving.

"We... we..." Bennett began the words not able to leave her now scared body.

"Unity found us at the airport, and we barely escaped ourselves." Bryce said sternly, his voice shaking slightly as he thought of Anton, who was probably dead now, if he was lucky.

"They followed them to the arcade too, the place is probably burned now." Echo chimed in, a tone of certainty in his voice.

"Oh really, it's burned. Did they enter the building, find the tunnels, follow you here?" Amelia snapped, releasing Bennett's hand and turning her attention to Echo as he stumbled over to the group standing behind Bryce as he spoke.

"Well no." Echo replied meekly.

"Then it isn't burned Cung, but we should be more cautious for the next little while. I'm sure they're going to watch the strip mall to see who comes and goes. We will have to move the meeting point for now." She said cautiously, placing her hand over her mouth as she thought to herself. "Well, which one of you is it?"

"It's him, he's a Crono." Echo said, giving Bryce a shove forward. With a stumble Bryce caught himself and stood up straight.

"Cung!" Amelia called out frustratingly. "The boy can speak for himself. But a Crono, are you sure?" She asked giving Bryce a quick up and down with her eyes.

"That's what Anton said." Bryce answered softly.

"Wait, that scene at the airport, was you?" She asked in a worried tone.

"Yes." Bryce said as the memories of Anton flooded the forefront of his mind.

"That is less than ideal. Please leave your bags with the jeep for scanning and we will place them in your rooms when we have cleared them." Amelia said her tone changing back to a cold and concise one, with one motion, she turned on her heels and set off towards the shack. "Come on then, we haven't got all day." She called out as she noticed the two teens did not follow. With a startled jump Bryce and Bennett moved, and quickly fell into stride with the woman as she set out. Amelia swung the door of the shack open and kicked a slab of plywood across the floor, revealing an old wooden staircase that descended into a long dimly lit tunnel, old electric lights wired together filling the passage with a warm light. "Gotta love the ingenuity of moonshiners." She chuckled as she caught the two teens' look of awe. Soon the passage turned from dirt into a smooth almost laser cut stone leading to a large metal door embedded in the wall. The submarine hatch-like door had a large wheel in the center. With a quick spin, and a grunt, Amelia swung the door open. "Welcome to the camp." She gestured to the pair as they entered through the door.

Inside the passageway opened to a well-lit, bright white and gray stone, open area more than triple the size of the clearing above, with high ceilings that almost disappeared in the light, the smell of freshly cooked stew filled the air as groups of people sat at tables in the middle of the hideaway, tucked into bowls of food. To the left was a very nice shower and bathroom area, separated by high walls, to the right were pod-like rooms spanning multiple levels with wooden walkways allowing for access to the higher ones, some were decorated with trinkets, knitted blankets and handmade drawings, while others were left empty and bare or covered up by what looked like a curtain that doubled as a door. By Bryce's count there had to be nearly thirty pods of varying sizes, and more than half remained empty. A large cooking area at the back of the room tied the area together, large ovens mounted into the walls and a vent system leading out of the area told Bryce that whoever helped with the setup had more than a simple construction background, with more doors like the one they entered placed along the walls of each area.

"Wow this place is incredible." Bennett said, looking around at the architectural marvel that laid before her. "How did you guys do all of this?" She asked, her eyes wide with excitement.

"Well, Telluses did most of it, the shack, barn and tunnel, used to be used by moonshiners, but they abandoned it long before we got here after a collapse. We made a deal with some of the hill folks that live in the area to let us live here, and it's just grown over the years." Amelia said as Echo pushed by the group and headed for the food. "We've been here for nearly forty years now, most of us are new, personally I only took over control five years ago, before that a man named Dennis ran this camp, but the history lesson can wait. Charles made his famous stew and he baked fresh bread. Follow me, we will get you two set up with rooms after we eat." Amelia said, leading the way through the bustling camp and falling in line behind Echo who already had a plastic tray and was filling it with slices of bread that he'd buttered.

"I'll take two bowls please, with cheese on both of them." Echo exclaimed as a heavy set, large, grizzly looking white man with a short buzz-cut and long red beard, scooped a thick, chunky, steaming hot, brown stew out of a large metal stockpot. A stained, formally white apron barely wrapped around his bulging waist.

"You'll get one, Cung. If there's more at the end you can come back for seconds. And leave some bread for the rest of the camp." He growled at Echo as he put a bowl topped up with the stew and a small piece of cheese onto the outstretched tray.

"Come on Charles, you know there will be more." Echo begged, his nasally voice somehow seeming to anger the large man far more than it should have.

"No, now get out of here before I…" He threatened, raising a large ladle over his head.

"Charles, that's enough. Cung, take what you have before you get nothing." Amelia commanded, causing both men to jump. "I swear you two are like children." She continued grabbing a tray and a slice of bread, opting not to butter it as she did.

"Sorry boss, it's just… you know how he is." Charles said quietly, his large stature seeming to shrink away as he spoke to the much smaller woman.

"I expect more from you Charles, that's all." She returned softly as he placed a bowl of stew on her plate.

"I know, I'm sorry." He said, hanging his head slightly. "It won't happen again." He mumbled as the woman gestured for Bryce and Bennett to grab a tray.

"It's okay Charles, he annoys me too, God knows I probably act the same way. But I'm just asking you to try." She comforted, her tone soft and caring. "Now this is Bryce and Bennett, they're new here so I expect you to treat them well and make sure they're bowls are filled up good and proper. And you two, enjoy your meal, I need to go attend to some things, but I will find you later and get you each set up in a room." She said nodding to the pair who just finished placing their bread slices on their tray, grabbing a plastic cup and cutlery set from the respective piles and then heading off to a table at the far end of the eating area.

"Of course, Boss." He replied, fixing his apron and turning to the pair greeting them with a big crooked toothed smile. "How's this?" He asked Bennett, tilting a nearly full bowl towards her.

"That's perfect thanks." She smiled back.

"Cheese on top of course." He said taking a large handful of shredded cheddar cheese and sprinkling it on top, the orange cheese almost immediately beginning to melt as it hit the stew. "That enough?" He asked, his hand still hovering over the bowl with more cheese in his hand.

"Yes, it looks amazing. I am so hungry." She replied smiling as Charles placed the bowl on her plate and smiled.

"Well, if you want seconds don't be shy, there's more than enough to go around, and I am more than happy to make more if needed." He smiled back, grabbing another bowl and scooping in two big spoonfuls for Bryce. "That good?" He asked, repeating the process of filling his bowl with stew and adding cheese to the steaming bowl.

"It is. No cheese though please." Bryce said politely garnering a small quizzical look from Charles before he shrugged and handed him the bowl. "Thanks." Bryce replied before he turned and followed Bennett towards the eating area.

"Welcome. Don't be a stranger." Charles said smiling once more, his intimidating voice and size almost washing away with his kind, teddy bear like personality and expressions.

The pair stopped, looking around the area for somewhere to sit and eat. Amelia had joined a table with an older serious looking man, and a younger, concerned and worried looking man. Glancing around the pair looked for the familiar face of Echo but somehow, he was nowhere to be found. The pair stood for a few more moments before noticing a table with two open spots. Bryce glanced at a table towards the middle of the area with a group of two boys who looked to be around their age at it. With a nod the two set out to the table.

As the pair approached, Bryce noticed the two boys were twins. Both boys were strong, bulky looking boys. One of them had a forest green hoodie with the hood pulled all the way up, a pair of black 5.11 tactical pants (Bryce was familiar with the pants as Rhys had worn them often). The other wore a black hoodie with light brown pants similar to his twins, his hood left down revealing a soft face with a slight beard beginning to take shape, his hair was cut close in a military style, a scar running from the upper right side of his head towards the back.

"Hi, do you mind if we sit here?" Bennett asked politely as she gestured with her tray to the table. With a smile the boy without the hood gestured to the table. "Thanks, I'm Bennett and this is Bryce." She said sitting down and pulling her chair towards the formed stone table.

"I'm Michael and this is Taylor." The boy said waving his hand in front of the other boy and moving his hands in a clear form of sign language.

"It's actually Bennett with two Ts and Bryce with a Y." She said, signing her and Bryce's names back at Taylor who had removed his hood and looked at Bennett. With a smile the boy returned back several signs, his hands moving quickly with excitement. "I'm sorry I am out of practice can you repeat…"

"He said, it's nice to meet you, it's nice to see someone else who signs here, typically Michael has to do the talking for me. Most people don't sign and it's hard to find hearing aids in the middle of the forest." Michael said cutting in and flashing several signs at Taylor, that Bryce could only assume was telling him to slow down. With a surprised face and a closed fist Taylor rubbed a circle on his chest and then signed several more signs, causing Bennett to giggle.

"You're so funny, It's nice to meet you too, and no he's not my boyfriend, but I do like him a bit." Bennett said narrating her signs as she spoke, leading both Taylor and Michael to burst out laughing. "What did I say?" Bennett asked, her smile turning down slightly as she spoke.

"No, no don't frown, it's just you signed he's not your 'lover', not 'boyfriend'." Michael said between breaths. "You're close but this is the sign for boyfriend." He explained showing her the correct sign and then looking at Taylor who was still laughing.

"Oh, that is funny." She laughed looking at Bryce and winking.

"Is anyone going to tell me what he said?" Bryce asked looking at the group who all collectively shared a look and then laughed.

"Don't worry about it, he just asked if we were dating or if we were related." Bennett reassured Bryce who nodded in understanding and then tucked into his food.

"It's good right?" Michael asked as Bryce spooned the first bite into his mouth and sat back. "Charles is the best cook, I swear. Hurry up eat, don't let us interrupt your meal." He continued motioning for Bennett to eat as he signed to Taylor. Without any more prompting, Bennett took a big spoonful, blew on it and then put it in her mouth, letting out a loud hum as she did.

"So good." She said as she watched Bryce tear a piece of bread off and dunk it in the stew. "Sorry we haven't eaten all day." Bennett said, spooning more food into her mouth. "Oh, my gosh, I am so sorry Taylor." She said, beginning to sign what she had just said.

"It's okay, he can read lips if you enunciate well." Michael said, waving his hands at Bennett. "Please eat, we will talk afterwards." He said watching Bryce not stop as he devoured his stew. It took the pair only a few minutes before they were mopping the bottom of the bowl with their bread, getting the last few drops of the delicious stew out of the bowl.

"Wow, that has to be one of the best meals I have had, ever." Bryce said, wiping his mouth with a napkin. "Sorry about that." He said, turning slightly to face the two boys.

"Oh, don't worry we get it." Michael said, rubbing his hands over his stomach and smiling. "So, what brings you two to this neck of the woods?" He asked looking at Taylor who nodded in agreement.

"Well, I guess it was the best option?" Bryce said his mind beginning to wonder.

"He says that's fair; we had similar feelings when we got here too." Michael said, watching Taylor sign and then repeating it for Bryce.

"It's just that we only just arrived, so we really have no idea what to think yet, we don't even have beds yet." Bennett chimed in, pushing her tray away from her and taking a long sip of water from her cup.

"Fair enough, well I see Amelia walking over, so I am sure she's sorted something out for you." Michael said, nodding as the slender native woman approached.

"Hello, Taylor." Amelia said, signing the words as she did. "Michael, I see you met our newest additions." She continued nodding at Michael.

"You're getting better." He acknowledged as Taylor smiled. "But yes, only briefly but we have."

"Perfect, hopefully you can show them around in the coming days." She half asked and half commanded. "I expect that won't be too much trouble for you both." She nodded making eye contact with both boys as she did. "But for now, I will need to borrow them. Bryce, Bennett, if you would follow me." She finished turning in her authoritative way and setting off.

"Leave your trays and we will handle them." Michael whispered smiling and nodding as the pair stood up and hurried to catch Amelia.

It took a few strides, but the pair caught up with Amelia who headed towards the barracks area. "I hope the meal was to your liking." She began as she slowed her pace, pulling a piece of paper from her pocket.

"It was delicious." Bennett squeaked as Bryce nodded in agreement.

"Good, Charles might be a bit rough at some times, but as long as you're nice to him he is the same to you and trust me it pays to be on his good side." She said lowering her tone as she finished so as not to be heard by others as she passed. "I've placed you two in pods beside each other, on the second level, now we do have rules here, and we expect them to be followed. Firstly, we expect you to pull your weight, we will teach you skills and train you the best we can here, but it's not for free. You will be expected to work with our group, and follow the instructions given to you no matter what, am I clear?" She asked, looking at the pair who nodded quickly. "Good, secondly, lights out will be called and is to be followed, each room has its own bedside light that may be used but we expect lights out to be followed. You may be alone with each other in your pods, and you may keep your pod decorated however you'd like but we expect them to be kept tidy and clean and your neighbors to be respected." She continued as she climbed the wooden staircase. "Showers may be used throughout the day and night, but never after lights out, and we expect them to be reasonably timed showers, no forty minute showers." She added, looking directly at Bennett as she spoke. "Wake up is at 6 A.M and breakfast is served promptly at 7:30. I will come get you tomorrow and we will introduce you to the instructors. Bennett, I am sure you understand, but you will have more of a support role here and less of a student one. We will help you hone some skills, but our main goal here is helping Bryce learn to hone his abilities and prepare him to help the Brotherhood's cause. I'm sorry if this is not what you expected." Amelia finished as she walked towards a pod dug into the wall and drew the curtain.

"No, I understand." Bennett mumbled softly a clear understanding of what Amelia meant ever present.

"Good." Amelia agreed, ignoring the clear feelings of the young girl. "This is you, and Bryce you are directly to the left of me. I will leave you two to get settled, your bags have been cleared and placed in your room. Goodnight." She said, before setting off back down the stairs and out of sight.

With a smile, Bryce watched as Bennett turned and entered her room, after a deep breath, he did the same. The interior of the room was far more spacious than Bryce had expected, the room sported a fairly large bed with a mattress at the end of the room, a pile of sheets and pillows lay neatly at the foot of the bed. A desk and a chair were tucked to the right of the entryway, with Bryce's backpack placed neatly on top and just as described, a small light was mounted on the wall, the wire running up the wall and out of the room. Bryce paused for a moment to absorb his new environment and then got settled, making his bed and unpacking his bag, placing his clothes neatly in a row of carved alcoves just between his desk and bed that he hadn't previously noticed from the entryway.

"Knock, knock." Bryce heard Bennett say from behind his drawn privacy curtain.

"Come in." He said as he watched her pull the curtain open and enter his room. Bryce stood up and walked over to the girl, pulling her into his arms and hugging her tight. Bryce felt her arms wrap around him, and he just stayed there, unmoving, the warmth of him pressing into her. "How are you feeling?" He asked softly, his chin resting on the top of her head.

"I don't know. I guess I'm a bit disappointed, but I understand. We're not here for me, we're here for you." She murmured through his tight hug.

"We're here for both of us. We're safe here, I can figure out how to protect us here." Bryce said as he willed Bennett to believe him, his hug remaining tight around her.

"I guess so, just promise me this isn't forever." She whispered softly.

"I promise. Not forever just for now." He whispered, pulling back and kissing her softly.

CHAPTER 14

The next few weeks went by as Bennett and Bryce settled into the routines of the camp. Each morning, the pair was woken up by the wake-up call sent throughout the otherwise quiet camp. Bennett typically spent the night with Bryce, having brought her bedding, blanket and pillow over to his room the third night after she'd had a few nightmares; they'd eventually passed. For many nights the first three weeks, Bryce was woken up by a screaming Bennett who he'd calmly wrap in his arms and soothe, slowly comforting her until the panic had subsided and she was able to fall back asleep. With a kiss Bryce would roll out of bed and make his way to the shower as Bennett typically opted to shower in the evening.

Bryce and Bennett would then join Michael and Taylor for breakfast, finding out that Taylor had been deafened the first time he used his ability as a child to burst him from a pool he fell into, the water had filled his ears and when he shot out of the water, the water in his ear had built the same pressure required to launch him to safety, completely bursting his ear drums in the process. Ironically Michael was able to control fire, discovering it when he accidentally burned down the pair's back deck when he attempted to blow out a birthday candle. Shortly after, Unity showed up, claiming to be an insurance company inspecting the damage. The team quickly killed the two's parents, and then kidnapped the pair. While on the way to a holding facility, the Brotherhood attacked the convoy carrying the pair, freeing not only them but several other children and teens of varying ages. During the escape process, Michael was hit with a stray bullet causing his scar and as he put it, winning him the title of most badass twin. Taylor would strongly disagree whenever Michael mentioned it. The boys had been at the camp ever since, nearly ten years since their abduction.

After breakfast, the group would head to their various lessons, some taught by Amelia such as how to spot a tail, how to disappear in a crowd, and what they called being a gray-man, which Bryce basically equated to dressing and acting in a way where you could move undetected through places, looking seemingly indistinguishable from the background. While other lessons such as combat training were taught by Grayson Mills, the younger worried looking man Bryce had seen Amelia sit with their first night there. He had short, brown hair styled into a faux hawk and looked far weaker than he actually was. Bryce had the displeasure of sparring with him his second week there and while he held his own, Bryce was left with several bruises from punches, kicks, elbows, and knees he'd never even seen coming. Amelia allowed Bennett to attend these classes and soon she was picking up the skills, she'd even managed to surprise Bryce and take him down once. Grayson also taught the group how to shoot, and Bryce really took to it, hitting bullseyes consistently from twenty-five yards with a pistol. Once the training portion of the day was finished Bennett would separate from the group to complete some kind of extra chore around camp, typically ending up in the kitchen helping Charles with the prep for the night's dinner, the two forming quite the friendship as they worked together peeling vegetables, mashing potatoes, and preparing meats for cooking later. The boys however would be taught by Samson Gonzales, the other person Bennett and Bryce had seen with Amelia that first night. Samson was an older salt and pepper gray haired man who opted to keep his hair slicked back and beard trimmed nicely. He spoke with a Spanish accent and after a week Bryce discovered he had grown up in Spain, his family fleeing the country when he was ten after Unity discovered his parents were Atlantian resistance fighters in the country. They'd barely escaped with their lives, then spent the next few years bouncing from place to place until they found the camp, opting to stay there, his parents offering to teach other Atlantians how to control their powers. A mantle Samson had picked up since the passing of his parents in a routine Brotherhood mission to secure a group of children and teens nearly ten years prior.

Through the training he received with Samson, Bryce learned his power was unique, Bryce's power required constant energy, meaning when he used it, he would require a surplus of energy for longer durations of use or repeated use. Unlike other abilities that outside of creating water or fire, changing ones features such as facial structure or height, the majority of abilities required quick bursts of energy and could be used without much strain on the Atlantian using them. But much like a muscle, as Bryce used his ability, and honed it he would be able to control it and go longer before needing a break, eventually not even having to worry about passing out from extended use. For now, however, he was never more than an arm's reach from a piece of chocolate or a Gatorade, the hypoglycemia kicking in whenever he pushed himself past his limits. He'd missed dinner more than once, passing out in training only to awake in his room sometime later, Bennett curled up beside him, a small plate of food neatly placed on his desk by her.

The day started much like any other day, Bryce awoke to the sound of the alarm, played across the loud speaker. He laid in bed for a moment, taking in his surroundings. His eyes slowly adjusted to the light that flooded in under the privacy curtain. Rolling over to lay on his back Bryce watched as a still half-asleep Bennett rolled over, his large shirt covering much of her small body as she curled up to him. "Give me your warmth." She whispered, pulling at his arm.

"You know you don't make it easy to get out of bed, right?" Bryce whispered as he reluctantly rolled back onto Bennett, wrapping his arm over her and pressing his forehead to hers.

"Mmmm... shut up, you love it, otherwise you would've kicked me out by now." She mumbled, still half asleep.

"I do." He whispered, wanting today to be the day he finally said the other half of that sentence. *But I love you more*, he thought, before shaking the thought out of his head. It had been a week since he came to the realization, he truly loved Bennett, he'd felt strongly for her long before any of this, before the camp, the airport, before they left Texas, hell before they'd kissed. But now, Bryce knew, he loved this girl and wanted to be with her for the rest of his life. The way she smiled at him when she saw him walking over, her laugh, the way that through all of this; all the danger, all the stress, everything she still could smile. He admired it. It happened all of the sudden, the two sat in his room like any other night, talking and laughing, Michael and Taylor had just left, and Bennett was reaching over Bryce to place a deck of cards -she'd been able to get one day by convincing Echo to bring it on his next supply run- away and he just realized he loved her. It was a collection of everything but in that moment, he just thought to himself; *her, it's her or nothing.* And the rest as they say was history. "I should shower." He said a few moments later when he was unable to fall back asleep as he tried and failed to work up the courage to tell her how he really felt.

"Okay fine." She fake pouted as he kissed her puckered lips and climbed over her, his feet touching the cold stone floor, shocking his body awake.

Bryce grabbed his shower kit and made his way down to the line that had formed for the shower that morning. A smile from Taylor and a less than pleasant look from Michael who was never pleasant in the morning until he had at least three sips of a warm coffee. Their hair somehow messy while barely being long enough to take any shape. 'Morning, how'd you sleep?' Bryce signed slowly, trying his best to ensure he had the correct signs.

'Good thanks, how was yours?' Taylor slowly signed back, mouthing the words as he did.

"Not long enough." Bryce mouthed back not knowing the sign for enough. Taylor smiled and nodded.

"It never is." He signed back as Michael nudged him, getting the boy's attention back and pointing to the shower that had since become ready. With a wave, Taylor grabbed a towel off the pile of them placed out every morning, marched over to the stall, pulled the curtain closed and flung his clothes over the side of the shower. Bryce watched as steam began to rise as he waited his turn, watching Michael enter shortly after Taylor when a stall had opened.

"Bryce, I trust you feel better after yesterday's lesson." Grayson said from behind Bryce as he waited for the next shower.

"I do thanks." Bryce replied thinking back to the previous day where he'd once again been unlucky enough to spar Grayson who left him in a crumpled heap after landing a vicious body shot on him, that hit his liver shutting his whole body down and sending him sprawling to the floor where he laid in a curled up ball of pain rippling out of his abdomen.

"Good, hopefully it taught you a valuable lesson, it won't be so forgiving in the real world." He nodded assertively. Bryce nodded back and saw a stall open up, with a wave, he bid Grayson goodbye and walked to the shower, turning it on and testing it with his hand not wanting to enter it until it reached the right temperature. After a few seconds, Bryce felt the water and deemed it good enough. He stripped off his remaining clothes and hung them over the side with his towel placed on top. For a moment he waited letting the water run over him, allowing his mind to wander as it did.

His thoughts danced from *Bennett to his friends he'd left behind in Texas, Harry and Carter were probably getting ready for Christmas break, Ashton had probably told everyone how Bryce had secretly done something and abducted Bennett. Bennett's Dad was probably worried sick, Bryce hated the thought of Bennett's Dad alone, fearing the worst, not knowing where the one person he truly cared about was.* It tore Bryce up, thinking how he would feel not knowing where Bennett was. Then his thoughts flashed to *Rhys, and to Anton, both dead, because of him. If he'd just listened more, followed instructions, not gone to the party, not existed, two good men would still be alive.* This made Bryce angry, it wasn't fair not to Bennett, not to Anton, not to Rhys, not to anyone he loved. He'd make Unity pay, he didn't know how, but he would.

Bryce finished his shower, toweled off and got dressed, his fresh clean clothes felt cold against his warm skin post shower. Depositing the wet towel in the laundry bin, Bryce made his way back to his room, where Bennett lay her eyes still closed on the bed. "Wake up sleepy head." He whispered kissing her forehead, as he placed his dirty clothes in a canvas laundry bag the camp supplied him to wash his clothes on his given day.

"You know as a boyfriend you should really bring me breakfast in bed." Bennett muttered, emphasizing the title she'd given Bryce two weeks earlier when Amelia commented on her emerging from Bryce's room more often than not in the morning. The two bumped heads often, Bennett wanting to learn more and Amelia not wanting to teach someone she deemed non-essential.

"Oh, should I?" Bryce replied, climbing onto Bennett and rolling her on top of him, his hands finding her soft skin just beneath the hem of the shirt she wore.

"Stop it. Stop it. Stop it." She giggled as he pulled her in, tickling her, and feeling the muscles of her back and stomach she'd developed over the course of the last nearly two months of constant daily training.

"Not until you kiss me." He continued as he tickled her as she wiggled and struggled to escape his hands.

"Okay, okay, come here." She wheezed in between breaths and laughs. Bryce stopped leaning in and sliding his hands a little further up her shirt. It happened in an instant, but with a quick explosive movement, Bennett trapped Bryce's arm to her side, locked his leg and rolled him over, ending up in a full mount position on top of Bryce. "Ha!" She called when her plan had successfully worked. "Do you give up?" She said, pinning his arms down with hers.

"Well done." He said softly looking up at her, her messy hair covering much of her face, strands of it caught in the corner of her mouth. "I give up." He sighed, knowing he could escape but not wanting to ruin Bennett's triumphant moment.

"I think you have to tap out." She whispered in his ear playfully.

"Don't push your luck." He said, kissing her cheek. "Now get off so we can go eat, it's French toast today, I saw Charles dipping the bread when I went for my shower." Bryce said his mouth watering at the thought of Charles' delicious French toast. The fresh brioche bread, perfect cinnamon to egg mixture, with powdered sugar dusted over top. If it wasn't for the constant training Bryce would have weighed five hundred pounds by now, he was sure of it.

"Fine, but I won, remember that next time you try something." Bennett joked, swinging her leg off of Bryce and landing on the floor. Her sleeping shirt now riding up slightly to where Bryce could see her black, boy short cut panties. His eyes glued to her butt as she walked to the pair of jeans she'd brought over the night before, pulling them over each foot and then jumping into them, struggling to get them over her now even more toned butt. "Hey, my eyes are up here." She called, waving her hand at Bryce when she caught him staring.

"Sorry, it's just…" He began losing his track of thought again as he watched her slip her shirt off, covering her chest with her arm and turning around to face away from him.

"Whatever, just hand me my bra." She playfully replied as Bryce continued to stare. "If you're going to watch, you might as well be of some help." She said waving her free hand in the air waiting for Bryce to bring over the bra. Bryce got up and quickly moved over to her, handing her the small black bra that seemed to match the panties, and somehow looked spectacular, while simply being a plain bra.

"You know, I had an idea just now." Bryce said, running his hands up Bennett's soft sides, staring at her black jeans and running his hands up moving them to the front and cupping her bra in his hands as he kissed her neck.

"Fat chance, you got me out of bed, we are not doing that. Not for the first time, not here, and not when you moments earlier wanted me out of bed to go get French toast." Bennett said, turning around and pushing Bryce back onto the bed.

"No, not that." He quickly replied as he stood back up. "I was thinking, maybe we could volunteer to go on a run to town, I still have some of the money we brought, we could each get a Christmas gift for each other." Bryce asked as Bennett was pulling on one of his sweaters.

"I'd like that, but there is no way Amelia lets both of us go into town, she barely lets the twins leave camp and they've been here for years." She said her expression turning sour when she thought of the inevitable no they would receive when they asked.

"Well, I'm going to ask and worst case she says no, but I bet we could pitch it as us posing as a couple visiting the town, we could get loads of stuff, and they wouldn't think anything of it." Bryce said excitedly trying to convince Bennett of the merit of his idea. "Plus, the twins don't like going into town."

"Maybe, I guess it would be fun, but I wouldn't get our hopes up." She said her stern expression softening slightly.

The Atlantian Chronicles

"Perfect." Bryce said, kissing her on the lips and spinning her around so she faced the entrance to the pod. "Now let's go get some food." He whispered, slapping her on the butt playfully.

After a look back from Bennett, the two made their way down to breakfast, greeting Charles who had become quite the fan of Bennett, slipping her an extra slice of bacon, an extra helping of dessert on the days he felt extra culinarily inclined. "Hey Charlie, it smells delicious today." Bennett smiled as Charles placed her plate onto her tray.

"It should, I don't let anything leave my kitchen that's not delicious." He replied, smiling his big grin back at her.

"Oh, me and my waistline have noticed." She joked back smiling just as big back at the large ginger man.

"Oh, hush up, you are tiny. Isn't she Bryce." He asked, waving his tongs dismissively.

"Umm… yeah she looks great." Bryce said half paying attention as he looked at the pile of freshly made French toast.

"See, now here, I cut up some fresh strawberries just for you, they're under your first slice." He whispered, leaning in and lifting the first slice of French toast on her plate.

"Just between us. Thank you, Charlie." She whispered back winking at the large man. As she shuffled down the line gathering cutlery, a cup of water and a cup of coffee and making her way to a table with the twins.

"You take good care of her Bryce… or else." Charles said, handing Bryce his plate and eyeing the boy.

"I will. Quick question Charli…Charles." Bryce began catching himself before he said the nickname exclusively used by Bennett and Bennett alone. "I'm thinking about asking Amelia to go into town to pick up supplies with Bennett, is there anything extra you could use that we could pick up for you?" Bryce asked, laying the foundation for his plan, knowing if he could get Charles extra supplies, his pseudo assistant Bennett would be a logical choice to bring with him on the trip into town.

"Hmmm…" The large man thought for a moment. "Well now that you mention it, I was thinking about making a special wildflower honey glazed, apple stack cake, so if you can get me a jar or two of the honey from the little apothecary shop just beside the general store and the post office that would be great." Charles said with a smile, Bryce couldn't decide if he was smiling because he was going to be able to make a delicious dessert for everyone or if he was just happy to help Bennett, either way Bryce was one step closer to hopefully convincing Amelia.

Bryce joined the rest of the group and watched as Bennett slid some of her strawberries off her plate and onto his plate with a smile. "Thanks." Bryce smiled back, kissing her cheek as he did.

"Taylor says get a room." Michael said as Taylor signed several signs Bryce was not familiar with, and one or two he was.

"He said more than that didn't he?" Bryce asked, cutting a piece of the toast off and stabbing a strawberry with his fork.

"He did, and I will not repeat it in front of a lady." Michael said, clearly more than a few sips of coffee into his day now.

"I can understand what he says, you know that right?" Bennett said smugly, her head down as she ate the delicious breakfast. "But probably better I didn't see anything past the kiss sign." She joked, shooting a look at Taylor who mouthed 'sorry', rubbing a closed fist in a small circle on his chest as he did. Bennett nodded and continued eating her food.

Breakfast carried on fairly typically following that, the group finished their meals and discussed the previous days lessons. After a few moments of talking and laughing Bryce saw Amelia making her way to the command center and saw his moment.

"Amelia, do you have a moment?" Bryce asked, excusing himself from the group's conversation and running over to the woman as she moved through the eating area.

"Yes, Bryce, can I help you?" She replied, halting her hurried pace and turning to face him.

"You can, I was hoping I could go on the next run into town, I'd like to do my part to help out around here, repay the generosity you guys have outstretched to Bennett and I." Bryce said, slipping Bennett into the conversation early in the hopes he could convince Amelia of his plan.

"Is that so?" She questioned her face turning into one of thought as she weighed her options.

"Of course, it would be good to get out of camp, plus if you sent the two of us, we could pose as a couple, stopping off to get supplies before heading to a family cabin or something, no one would suspect a thing." Bryce explained laying out his plan and hoping she would take the bait.

"Oh, it's two of you going now, is it? I was under the impression it would be just you." Amelia said, her mouth turning down as she spoke.

"Well, I just figured..." Bryce began.

"You just figured you would go on a little date with your girlfriend?" She interrupted, her face turning into a frown of disappointment.

"No, not at all, I just figured with Charles asking for a type of honey to make a dessert, it might be a nice treat for everyone, and I know absolutely nothing about cooking so... since she's been helping him, I figured it might be... well helpful if she came along." Bryce pleaded nervously, watching his plan slip away by the second.

"Hmmm..." She thought her hand coming to her mouth in the distinct way she always did when she weighed her options. "Well, it would be a morale boost, and you two have been here long enough for some of the News outlets to have stopped airing your story... and it would be a good chance to test your training, see if you're ready for more important tasks." She paused the silence slowly eating away at Bryce who was waiting on bated breath to hear the verdict. "I suppose that would work, but no deviating from the plan, and try to stay out of trouble." She lamented as Bryce tried not to celebrate too hard.

"Amazing, you won't regret this." Bryce cheered his smile stretching from ear to ear, as a wave of excitement rushed over him.

"Easy there Bryce, at least try and pretend you didn't plan this from the beginning. And get ready, you leave at ten, it should be busy enough then for you to draw the least attention possible. I will let the team know of your plan." She scoffed, turning on her heels and heading to a door that branched off from the main area of the camp.

Bryce watched her disappear through the door as he returned to the table. With a smile and a nod Bryce watched as Bennett lit up, her face breaking into a smile almost as big as his. Without saying anything the twins nodded and ushered Bennett away from the table, knowing full well what the pair had planned.

CHAPTER 15

Bryce and Bennett easily completed the shopping list, getting everything required and even a little extra honey after some expert bargaining from Bennett. After loading the car, Bryce reached into his heavy-duty, black, quilted, Eddie Bauer jacket and pulled out the cash he'd taken from his bag before the pair left the camp.

"Here, nothing too big so we can sneak it back into camp." He cautioned counting out multiple twenty and ten-dollar bills, stripping them from the wad and handing them to Bennett. "We each get twenty minutes then we meet back here." Bryce said his eyes glancing around the sleepy town, the snow-covered streets and roofs creating a scene like one out of a Hallmark Christmas movie. Content with their safety, Bryce nodded and watched as Bennett set out, her bulky, winter jacket pulled tight around her for warmth.

It took Bryce quite some time to find the perfect gift, moving from store to store, holding up various trinkets, snow globes, perfumes, he even stopped at the apothecary thinking maybe he could get her a lotion or serum, but just when he was about to give up hope, he saw it. A small thin gold, chained necklace with a roughly carved pinkish-red stone in the middle. Slowly, Bryce picked the necklace off of the small ornate, metal tree that was filled with several other similar pieces.

"A beautiful necklace, no?" The hunched, older woman said from behind the counter as she watched Bryce examine the necklace.

"It is. What kind of stone is this?" Bryce asked, holding the stone up to the dim light bulb that hung from a unique bone and antler chandelier, watching the lights dance through it.

"That is Mookaite Jasper, and in the way it's carved it has a few meanings. If you'd like to know about them, I can tell you?" She offered her voice frail and soft like a woman who has lived a long hard life but nurtured everyone she met throughout that long journey.

"I'd like that." Bryce said with a warm smile.

"Oh good… I love explaining the meaning of a piece. Mookaite is a stone made to bring peace and wholeness to one in a time of great stress. And when carved in that way, with the techniques I used from the people of the mountains, it is also a love symbol, but be sure the person you give it to is your forever person, because when you do give it to them, your entwined forever, no matter how far apart you stray you will always be drawn back together. Always." The woman said, reaching a wrinkled and arthritic hand out and taking the necklace, pointing out the intricate details with her shaking long finger.

"That is perfect. How much is it?" Bryce whispered, his voice tight with excitement.

"For you, one hundred." The woman replied, smiling. Bryce quickly pulled the bills out and paid, the woman quickly wrapping the necklace up in a piece of brown paper and handing it back to him. He grabbed up the parcel, tucked it into his jacket pocket before he headed back out into the cold mountain air.

With perfect timing Bryce arrived at the car moments before Bennett. Unlocking it and climbing into the cold car, Bryce cupped his hands to his mouth blowing on them and rubbing them together. Content with the warmth he gained, he quickly turned the key. With a struggle, the old car sputtered to life, the air blowing aggressively as Bryce tried to warm up the interior and defrost the now frozen windows.

With a smile Bennett climbed in, shivering as she entered. "It is so cold." She said, pulling her jacket tight and holding her hands over the vents desperately trying to warm up.

"It's definitely not Texas." Bryce agreed, thinking to himself how cold it was in the mountains of Maine compared to that of the Texas winter. With a nod of agreement and a smile Bennett glanced at Bryce who tried his best to hide away the necklace.

"So should we do this exchange now or should you try and fail to hide what you got me?" Bennett asked, smiling and nodding to Bryce's jacket pocket where the corner of the parcel poked out.

"Dang." Bryce said shifting in his seat, trying and failing to block her view. "I guess we could have our Christmas now, here in the car while we wait for it to warm up." He said flicking the windshield wipers that failed to remove any of the frost from the windows.

"Okay, close your eyes and give me your hand and don't open until I say so." She said reaching over and picking up his left hand by the wrist. "There weren't many choices, but I wanted something small and special we could both have, a reminder of our promises to each other. So, I got you this." She said, slipping something over Bryce's wrist. "Okay, open your eyes." She said sitting back and covering her mouth and nose with her hands nervously awaiting his reaction. Slowly Bryce opened his eyes and looked down at his wrist. On it was a bracelet with small, round, black stones encircling his wrist, a metal centerpiece containing a small piece of a light pink stone, shining in the midday sun, two strings crossing and tightening the bracelet around his wrist. "It's lava-stone, it is supposed to mean strength, courage and connection to earth. I figured it couldn't hurt." She said over her hands nervously as she watched him take in the bracelet. "I have a matching one, the stone in the middle is rose quartz. It means unconditional love." She softly continued hiding even deeper behind her hands, the matching bracelet sitting on her wrist just above the cuff of her jacket.

"Bennett... I... I love it." He grinned looking at the bracelet and adjusting its fit on his wrist. "It's perfect." He whispered, choking up as he looked at his gift. After a deep breath, Bryce looked at Bennett and kissed her, her soft lips felt warm and inviting against his. After a moment he broke away. "Okay, my turn, close your eyes." He said reaching into his pocket, and pulling out the parcel, unwrapping it, slowly and carefully taking the necklace out. "Okay, open your eyes." Bryce said, holding the necklace out dangling it off of his middle finger. "It's Mookaite Jasper, it's meant to bring calm and wholeness in times of stress. And the way it is carved is some kind of Appalachian way to carve it, when you give it to someone you are entwined and will always return to them no matter what." Bryce said, nervously dancing around the words he wanted to say but couldn't. *I love you, and this will show you I will always come back to you no matter what, forever.*

"I… I don't know what to say." She said, looking closely at the stone.

"If it's too much I understand we can see if the old lady will give me my money back for something a little less forever-y." Bryce nervously said, panic slightly noticeable in his voice.

"No, it's not that… I love it." She quickly replied, turning and tucking her hair over her shoulder motioning him to place it around her neck. "It's such a sweet gesture." She said playing with the stone, running it over her fingers as Bryce closed the clasp of the necklace.

"You sure? You won't hurt my feelings if you want to exchange it." He whispered looking at the girl whose expression was one of both joy and nervous tension.

"I'm sure, now shut up and kiss me." She said climbing up in her seat and leaning over the center console, planting a big kiss on his lips. The two kissed for a moment, before a car pulled in beside them, the sound of gravel crunching under the heavy tires pulling them back to reality.

"We should go." Bryce muttered not wanting to leave but knowing if they didn't return soon, they'd never be allowed to leave. With a heavy sigh Bennett nodded, and Bryce slipped the vehicle into reverse, backing out onto the road and then speeding off in the direction of the camp.

It took nearly twice as long for Bryce to get back to the camp as it took him to get to town, the evasive techniques Amelia had taught him kicking in as he squared blocks, drove down long stretches of dead end trails only to turn around and head back out, even going so far as to drive past the entrance twice before he finally made the turn, sure he wasn't followed. After a short drive where he flashed his lights in a similar pattern to the one Echo had done when they drove to the camp originally, Bryce pulled into the camp where Amelia stood waiting a stern look on her face. "Took you long enough." She said unmoving as Bryce and Bennett exited the car, making their way to the back and grabbing the heavy boxes of groceries.

"Wanted to make sure we weren't followed. We'll be quicker next time." Bryce quickly called out as he huffed and lifted the heaviest of the boxes.

"If there is one, had us worried you were compromised, I was about twenty minutes away from sending another group." She replied, her arms crossed as she watched the two make their way towards the shack. "Not so fast you two. Drop the boxes." She commanded as Bryce and Bennett froze, the fear beginning to rise in their throats.

"Why?" Bryce said, forcing the word through his tightened lips.

"We need to scan everything, to make sure nothing was slipped in that shouldn't have been." She returned matter-of-factly motioning for the two to drop the boxes. Slowly Bryce lowered his box, with Bennett following suit, his heart racing as he thought of the bracelets on their wrists and the necklace. The thoughts of what might happen if it was found out they deviated from the task they were given leading to them being almost late. Would she even care?

As Bryce stood up, he stretched his arms out in a T position as if awaiting a scan, his breath beginning to quicken. "What are you doing?" Amelia replied as Bryce stood there his arms outstretched.

"Waiting for scanning?" He replied quizzically.

"Not you two, the groceries, now get inside." She shouted waving the two inside as she stood by the large fire in the middle of the opening. A wave of relief washed over Bryce as he opened the door and let Bennett in, following after her. With a deep breath, the two shared a look, smiled and entered the camp.

The rest of the night passed quickly, the pair went about their normal tasks, helping around the camp. Bennett helped Charles prepare dinner and the dessert, Bryce helping with the cleaning and tidying of the main area as Michael and Taylor sat watching a small gun cleaning station set up in front of them. That night Bryce fell asleep quickly, his arm wrapped around Bennett as she curled up into him. The two slept soundly, the alarm of the next day barely waking them, as the pair returned to business as usual.

The following days flew by, the excitement of another possible run driving the two to work harder in the hopes Amelia would tap them for another job. As the days turned into a week and then two the excitement died down. The two settling back into their monotonous tasks of the weeks prior. After nearly two weeks Bryce had nearly given up hope of ever leaving the camp again.

That's when it happened.

CHAPTER 16

The alarm blared louder than ever before, ripping Bryce from his sleep. It was as if someone had poured a bucket of cold water on him. "What's going on?" Bennett asked, the fear and shock clearly having the same effect on her as it did on Bryce.

"I don't know. But it doesn't sound good." Bryce wearily said getting out of bed and pulling on a pair of jeans. Bryce slowly made his way to the entrance of the pod and stuck his head out of it. The whole camp was following suit as people rushed around, red lights flashing throughout the interior.

"What's going on?" Bennett repeated as she walked over to Bryce placing a hand on his exposed back.

"I don't know but get dressed." He said sternly as she rubbed the sleep from her eyes. Bryce quickly turned on his heels and pulled on his combat boots, quickly lacing them up as Bennett wiggled into a pair of 5.11 khaki tactical pants, she'd been given early that week. "Hurry up." Bryce called as he pulled a green colored, slightly baggy, thermal shirt over his head.

"I'm hurrying." Bennett called back between loud bursts of the alarm.

"I know, I know." He returned, handing her a shirt as he stuffed clothes into his black backpack. He watched as she pulled her boots on, zipping them up on the side as she did, her hair messily tucked into a bun.

"Okay, let's go." She said, blowing strands of hair out of her face with her mouth and rushing out of the room. Bryce nodded, zipping up the bag and taking two steps towards the door before he stopped. Looking back at the room he wondered if he'd ever see this place again. *The room where he'd spent so many nights with Bennett wrapped up in his arms, falling more and more in love with her every day.* "You coming?" Bennett said, poking her head back in the room.

"Yeah, sorry, I'm coming now." He replied leaving the room as a controlled chaos erupted in the large central area of the camp. People rushed around, some putting on body armor, others loading magazines and looking down the sights of rifles adjusting them as they did. "What is going on?" Bryce breathed as he watched.

The pair made it to the main floor when the alarm stopped, the lights continuing to flash red as people moved around the area. Bryce and Bennett looked around before a large hand fell onto Bryce's shoulder. "Come with me." Charles said, a large double-barreled shotgun propped up on his shoulder.

"Charlie, what's going on?" Bennett asked the fear in her voice causing it to shake slightly.

"Unity. They were spotted on our trail cameras moving quickly through the forest. Amelia has called for all hands on deck. Told me to grab you two. Now come with me." He said sternly, his calm kind demeanor completely gone. The two followed as Charles led them through the people rushing around preparing for the upcoming danger. Soon the three arrived at a door, with the butt of his gun Charles banged on the door twice, then waited then three more times in quick succession. The door's handle spun and the locks on the door released as it swung open, Grayson standing behind it, his custom colt 1911 pistol with red dot sight and under rail flashlight held close to his chest with one hand. "Quick, get inside." Charles commanded ushering the two inside and closing the door behind them.

"How did Unity find us?" Bryce asked as he moved past Grayson.

"I don't know but it is not good." He whispered as he locked the door and slowly backed away from the metal door.

"Where are Michael and Taylor?" Bryce asked, realizing he did not see them as he moved through the chaos that was the main area of the camp.

"They're safe, they're just up ahead making sure the exit is clear." Grayson replied, pointing his gun down the tunnel before returning it to his chest and continuing to walk. Just as Grayson finished a loud bang echoed from behind them, shaking the walls and causing dust to rain from the ceiling as the lights flickered. "That is not good." Grayson said hurrying Bryce and Bennett up as a second and third bang went off.

"What's going on?" Bryce asked as he quickened his pace, the lights flickering more and more as they rushed down the long tunnel.

"It would seem as though Unity has found us and is attempting to breach the main door." He replied as a fourth charge went off followed by the sounds of gunfire. "Time to run." Grayson said, reacting to the sounds that erupted behind him.

The three took off at a full sprint as they heard the chaos of a gunfight, the screams of people burning, and the sounds of small explosions Bryce guessed were some kind of grenade. Within a minute they group exited the tunnel, Taylor standing guard just outside of it.

The group burst out the tunnel and into the cold night air, the eerie moonlight slicing through the branches of the leafless trees. With a whistle from Grayson, Bryce and Bennett watched as Michael emerged from a nearby tree and joined Taylor.

"Thank God, you're safe." He whispered as he walked over, a black AR15 rifle with a four times scope and suppressor attached to it, resting against his shoulder.

"You know what to do." Grayson nodded as he looked at Michael who returned his nod.

"You can count on us." He said, his voice barely audible over the sound of explosions coming from the tunnel and echoing out into the night-time air. With that Grayson turned and set off towards the tunnel.

"What are you doing Grayson? You're not coming with us?" Bryce hissed as he watched the man place a hand on the rod-iron gate embedded into the wall and swing it closed, locking himself into the tunnel they'd just emerged from.

"No Bryce, I am not, my duty is to protect the camp." He replied before he disappeared from sight completely, the sound of his footsteps crunching on the dirt floor slowly fading into the tunnel.

"What the heck is going on?" Bryce whispered as he glanced around, the snow-covered forest looking eerily dangerous in the night.

"We will explain when we get to safety. Now follow us… and here." Michael answered, pulling a black Sig Sauer P226 pistol and one extra magazine from his leg holster and handing it to Bryce.

Bryce took the pistol, tucking the magazine into his pocket and performing a press check on the gun, ensuring there was a bullet chambered and the gun was ready to fire, a trick Grayson had taught him during one of their more recent training sessions. With a deep breath Bryce reached out and took Bennett's hand, her cold skin pressing into the warmth of his palm as he nodded to Michael who in turn nodded to Taylor who turned, raised his own rifle and set off through the forest. The group moved slowly, stopping and using a combination of hand signals and sign language to communicate as they moved through the dark forest; the light of the moon, their only protection from the black of the night in the forest.

After what felt like an hour of quick paced hiking through the mountain, they heard it before they saw it, and by that time it was too late. "Hands, hands, hands." The man shouted as four red dots appeared on Michael's chest. Immediately they froze, with a frustrated grunt, Bryce watched as Michael raised his hands, his rifle held high above his head.

"You too!" Another man said as Bryce felt the barrel of a gun press into the side of his head. Slowly Bryce raised his arms and released the gun, its trigger guard catching the weight as it slid down his finger. Within moments Bryce, Michael and Taylor were disarmed, and herded into a circle with Bennett as five masked men in white winter camouflage surrounded them and forced them to their knees.

"This is Bravo-Two we have four in sector three." One of the men said into his radio as he looked at the four teenagers. "Remember me?" He whispered to Bryce as he lowered himself down to Bryce's eye level and removed the white mask he wore. It took Bryce a moment to remember the man, but once he did, he was sure of who it was. The man standing in front of Bryce was the same man who tackled him in the mall two months earlier. "Didn't think we'd find you, did you?" He sneered as he stepped back, the barrel of his gun pointed directly at Bryce. "Nothing to say for yourself you little piece of…" The man said as Bryce felt the sound of the world fade away.

His heartbeat pounding in his ears slowly faded, Bryce watched as the man mouthed a curse word and then he struck. Leaping forward he pushed the man's gun into the air with one hand as he punched the man directly in the throat. Then he spun, taking control of the man's gun and firing a burst of shots at the man directly across from him. Moving quickly knowing he didn't have much time, Bryce charged at the next man throwing a flying elbow to the man's eye, feeling the bones and flesh collapse beneath the force. Taking control of his gun Bryce fired another burst as he saw a man moving for Bennett, watching as they struck the man sending him sprawling backwards and blood slowly flew through the air. Looking around Bryce found his final target. The man had a hand on Taylor's collar pulling him upwards as Michael dove towards Bennett in an attempt to shield her from the chaos. Bryce moved forward jumping into the air and planting his foot on a tree in between himself and the attacker. In one fluid movement, Bryce bounced off the tree and performed a spinning roundhouse kick, falling flush on the man's jaw spinning just his head around as the force generated from Bryce's quickened movement landed.

The sounds of the world rushed back as Bryce landed on the ground with a thud, wobbling and trying to catch himself. "Are you okay?" Michael said as he wrapped Bennett up, the bodies of the men spread out around the circle.

"Yeah." Bennett replied as Michael slowly climbed off of her.

"Holy crap Bryce. I thought we were dead." Michael called out as he collected his rifle and backpack from the pile the men had thrown it into when they removed it from him.

"Well, we're not out of the woods yet." Bryce said wearily, the fatigue of shifting hitting him.

"Here let me take that." Bennett said noticing Bryce's pale complexion and motioning for him to hand her the backpack and gun.

"Taylor says thank you, but we have to go." Michael translated interrupting Bryce's silent protest to Bennett's request for the backpack and handgun.

Without another word the group set off, leaving the group of men or whatever was left of them for the other Unity agents to find. The group pushed forward with Bryce struggling to keep up, fear and adrenaline the only things carrying them up each hill and over each small creek they crossed. The sun began to rise as the group broke through the forest making it to a main road about six miles from the tunnel, they'd exited nearly three and a half hours earlier. The asphalt road barely visible under the fresh snowfall, aside from a few tire tracks on either side.

"We should find somewhere to rest." Bryce panted, trying his best to catch his breath as Michael looked around for any sign of where exactly they were.

"I agree, we need to rest." Bennett said, placing her hands over her head and breathing almost as hard as Bryce. Michael glanced back and noticed Taylor had taken a similar position, watching the groups back as the four sucked in deep breath after deep breath.

"We need a car. Town's our best option." Michael said coldly, his brain focused on the task in front of them and nothing else. He could rest when they were safer.

"You mean the town that is probably swarming with Unity looking for us?" Bryce called back between deep breaths as he bent over, his hands on his knees.

"Do you have a better idea?" Michel hurled back, his voice commanding an authority Bryce had never seen before. "If you do speak now, because if not, I suggest you take a deep breath and follow me." He continued, his voice one of a battlefield commander more than a teenager thrust into this role. With a nod, Taylor fell in beside him looking at Bryce and Bennett as they waited. Picking himself up, Bryce slowly fell into line, Bennett joining slightly after him as the group began their march to town.

"Up here, we can get a good vantage point and see what we're dealing with." Michael said, stepping off the road and into the forest once more as the small rustic town came into view.

The group had been walking down the forested road for a little over thirty minutes now, the early morning cold nipping at their exposed skin as they walked. Taylor, Bryce and Bennett followed Michael as he led them through the forest and up a small hill that overlooked much of the town.

"Perfect, they aren't here." Michael whispered as he nodded to the silent town. "Okay, here's the plan. We sneak through the forest, get into the town, find a car, and then hightail it out of here. That good?" He whispered looking around the group to nods of agreement throughout. With all in agreement, the group slowly made their way back down the small hill and through the forest. Slowly watching for any signs of Unity as they moved through the forest keeping distance between each other to avoid another easy capture.

As Bryce emerged from the forest, Michael was already taking cover at the back of the general store, the wooden walled building dusted with fresh snow, outlining the figure in black. His rifle lowered as he peered around the corner to the alley between that and the post office. With a wave of his hand, Bryce moved up and joined him, taking position on the other side of the alley, his back resting against the cold brick of the post office. Soon after Bennett and then Taylor joined, taking positions behind Bryce and Michael as the group paused, waiting for their moment.

"Bryce, you and Bennett go first. Taylor and I will watch you guys and cover you while you get a car." Michael said holding up his rifle as if to say this isn't something I can easily hide and then quickly signing the plan to Taylor who nodded in agreement.

"Okay here goes." Bryce said standing up and leading the way down the alley, Bennett following close behind, the pistol tucked into her jacket pocket with one hand gripping it tightly.

With a hurried pace, Bryce made his way through the alley and onto the main street of the town. Glancing around he quickly looked for a vehicle that fit his desired criteria. Older model, dirty exterior, and high enough off the ground to go off road if necessary. These criteria ensured, the vehicle was most likely not equipped with a tracking device, not uncommon or easily spotted, and could handle going around roadblocks in the case Unity had blocked off roads. Bryce glanced around as he tried his best to blend into the sleepy town. As he walked up the otherwise quiet street, the fresh snow crunching under his boots, he ran through his list. The first car was a newer looking Ford Ranger, with large expensive looking tires, an ornate front grill, and was clean save from the snow that had fallen that night. With a shake of his head, Bryce continued looking, his heart racing as he looked over his shoulder confirming Bennett was right behind him, and no police cars had suddenly pulled down the quiet street. Then Bryce spotted it, an early 2000s black Nissan Pathfinder. As he walked closer, he noticed the basic interior and salt stained exterior. It was perfect. Bryce looked around for a rock to smash the windows when he heard the click of the door. Glancing back, he saw Bennett opening the door and climbing in.

"How did you do that?" He whispered as he held the door to the vehicle open and kept watch.

"I tried the handle; the door was left open." She said nonchalantly as she pulled the steering column off, pulled a set of wires down and began tapping them together. Within a few moments and after several coughs of the engine, the car came to life.

"You are amazing." Bryce said triumphantly as Bennett climbed into the seat, adjusted it and her mirrors as he climbed into the passenger seat.

"I know." She replied as she fixed her seat and buckled up. "Now take this, I always feel weird having one." She said pinching the handle of the pistol and pulling it out of her jacket. Bryce quickly took the gun and placed it at his side, ready to be quickly brought up and fired if the moment called for it. With that done, Bennett pulled the gear shift down and with a slight grinding sound, the car lurched forward, slowly pulling out of the spot and onto the road. Taylor and Michael quickly jumped in, and the group was on their way.

"You know you can drive a bit faster." Bryce muttered as Bennett maintained a speed just under the speed limit as the country roads passed back mile by mile putting distance between them and the attack.

"Don't get caught committing a smaller crime on your way to commit a big crime." Bennett replied, in a mocking tone as she repeated one of the lessons taught to them by Amelia. "I don't want to get pulled over in a stolen car, with guns I'm almost certain are not legal, with wanted fugitives, so forgive me if I drive a bit slower and avoid any issues." She asserted looking around the car.

"You've got a point. But where do we go from here?" Bryce asked as he turned in his seat and looked at Michael.

"Oh, right. Pittsburg." Michael said, snapping out of his own thoughts. "They said to go to Pittsburg and use the communication system to reach out to Atlas and let him know what happened." Michael stated as he looked at Taylor and signed before he returned the signs with a nod. "Yeah, Atlas."

"Who the heck is Atlas? And isn't Pittsburg like ten hours from here?" Bryce asked, more confused than ever.

"Thirteen and a half actually." Michael responded before returning his attention back out the window.

"Who. Is. Atlas?" Bryce repeated this time slower and far louder than before.

"The leader of the Brotherhood. Atlas Mantalou, he runs everything from a secret location only a few trusted people know about." Michael replied as if Bryce should have already known about this.

"Okay." Bryce said, turning in his seat and sharing a look with Bennett, before turning his attention to the road ahead.

CHAPTER 17

The drive to Pittsburg went without incident, as the minutes turned into hours and cities passed by, the worry and fear faded, replaced with bundles of frayed nerves and a tiredness only achieved from a full day spent in constant alert. The journey ended as Bryce pulled into the nearest budget hotel they could find as they entered Pittsburg.

"We'll drop you off here, get us two rooms, anything but the ground floor, adjoining if they have it. Taylor and I will go contact the Brotherhood and figure out what they want us to do next." Michael said as he climbed out into the drop off area of the hotel and then back into the driver's seat.

"Okay stay safe." Bryce said, placing a hand on the boy's shoulder and sliding out of the way as Bennett hugged Taylor as he took her place.

"Meet us in the lobby in two hours." Michael called to the pair as he slowly pulled out of the area and sped away into the night.

Bennett and Bryce wearily entered the lobby, their eyes heavy with the fatigue of the day's events. With a little bit of bartering and the use of a fake ID Amelia had insisted Bryce and Bennett get made properly at the camp, Bryce secured the rooms and left in the hope of getting some rest before the twins returned. Slowly Bennett and Bryce made their way up to their fifth-floor room, noting the fire exits and stairways as they did.

The pair entered the room and fell into the bed, only barely stripping off their muddy clothes, and setting an alarm, as they did. In the blink of an eye the alarm clock beeped, ripping them from their slumber. "I am going to sleep for two days when this is over." Bryce said slipping off of the bed and moving to his clothes that lay in a pile at the foot of the bed, placing a hand on the soft skin of Bennetts lower back as he did.

"Do you think anyone else made it out?" She asked as she rolled over and sat up, sliding off the bed and pulling on her pants.

"I don't know, hopefully." Bryce replied, placing a hand on Bennett's cheek and running his thumb across it gently wiping some dried mud off in the process.

"Hopefully the twins have some news for us." She replied, taking his hand in hers and holding it tightly. "We should get going, the longer they wait the higher the chance we get caught." She whispered softly pressing her forehead to his, placing a hand around the back of his neck holding him there for a moment.

"Bennett... I..." He started his voice quivering as he spoke.

"Don't say it. I know. It's okay." She replied softly, kissing him, assuming he was going to apologize to her for everything once again.

"No... it's not that." Bryce said, pulling away from her kiss.

"It's okay, I don't care." She said kissing him again, harder than last time. "Everything will be okay." She said softly, pulling away and reaching for her shirt, ending the conversation and ending yet another chance for Bryce to say how he really felt.

The pair got dressed and ventured down to the lobby, their less than clean appearance gaining them looks from many of the other patrons as they waited in the typical hotel lobby, the strangely patterned chairs and cheap common furniture positioned to provide a level of homeliness while breaking up the bland colors of the lobby. After only a few minutes Bryce saw the old muddy car pass through the entryway and head towards the parking lot, shortly after Bryce and Bennett watched as both twins entered the building. Like a rehearsed movement, Bryce and Bennett got up and moved to the elevator, calling for it as the twins walked over, pressing the button as if they were separate hotel guests calling for an elevator who just happened to also be covered in mud.

The group entered as the doors slowly opened, riding the elevator in silence back up to the fifth floor where their rooms were. Heading down the hallway two by two, the pairs entered the adjoining rooms and closed the doors, locking and latching the door behind them.

"How did it go?" Bryce asked as he swung open the door connecting the two rooms to see Michael standing there his arms outstretched for a hug.

"Good, we got in touch with them and reported what happened, they told us to wait here, and they would send someone for us." Michael said after a quick embrace.

"Did anyone else make it out?" Bryce quickly asked, hoping for good news.

"No, Unity killed some of them and took the rest prisoner. Amelia is one of the confirmed prisoners, but Samson… he didn't make it." He said, hanging his head as Taylor entered the room and hugged Bennett tightly. "They said they'll have a way out of here, to safety tomorrow night, so we just need to stay put until then." Michael finished, his nervous energy filling the room.

"Do they know how Unity found the camp?" Bryce asked, hoping for an answer to the question that had been eating at him for some time now.

"No, they are looking into it, but they think Unity had inside information somehow." Michael answered angrily, slamming his fist down as he spoke. "If we find out who it was, we'll make sure they pay." He finished, pounding his fist once more into the doorframe before leaning on it.

"I don't know about you two, but I am exhausted. If we are going to wait here, I for one am going to take a warm shower, and then sleep while we have the chance." Bennett interrupted, changing the conversation as she pulled at her mud-covered pants and gestured to the boys who sported similar levels of cleanliness.

"Point taken." Michael chuckled, nodding at Taylor who with another big hug for Bennett exited the room and closed their door behind them. Bryce followed suit and closed their door, leaving it unlocked and unlatched so the twins could enter in the case of an emergency.

"Now that we have a moment." Bennett said, stripping off her shirt quickly, as she walked towards Bryce. "There's something I want to do." She whispered, unbuttoning her pants and slipping them off as she walked.

"Oh yeah you think that's wise?" Bryce said, beginning to remove his shirt as he watched her underdress.

"I think I'm going to shower before you do so I can climb into bed and sleep." She teased as she slipped into the bathroom, dropping her bra out from behind the door and shutting it, the lock clicking into place as he moved towards the door.

"You really suck." Bryce laughed twisting the doorknob in a half-ditched effort he knew wouldn't work. With a sigh Bryce turned and walked to the bed, stripping off his mud-covered clothes before climbing onto the bed and turning on the TV. The local news began to play...

A white toothed, brunette man with a big smile, his hair styled perfectly into a side part, a classy blue suit and shirt combination showing in front of a large gray desk, the station's logo in the center of it appeared. "Good evening, ladies and gentlemen, I am Mason Lancaster, and this is the Pittsburgh News at seven. A string of late-night social media posts has the Pittsburgh Mayoral Race heating up as the front runner Don Ashbury has made claims to have new information regarding his opponent and current Mayor, Russell Nickols and his involvement in last month's construction scandal, more on this in a moment. Our main story of the evening is the daring early morning raid in the mountains of Maine, carried out today by a combined group of local and federal law enforcement agents as they acted in part on a tip obtained from an insider embedded in the cartel-run operation. Police claim the underground operation had been supplying weapons, narcotics and aiding in human trafficking to groups both home and abroad." The man said his smile was somehow unbreaking as he spoke. "Several high-ranking members of the cartel known as the Brotherhood were taken into custody. While this is a large blow to the operations of this group, law enforcement officials still warn that at least four members have escaped, with one of those believed to be linked with the airport shooting in early September that saw at least one man taken into custody." He finished as Bryce watched in a shocked horror as videos of Amelia, Charles and Grayson kneeling before Tyson flashed across the screen.

Bryce shakily stood up moving unsteadily towards the twins' door when he heard a knock. Slowly he opened the door to Michael, the sound of a shower filling both rooms. "Did I just? Crap, bad time?" Michael asked as he eyed Bryce up and down, noticing his state of undress and assuming he'd interrupted.

"No, the News, Tyson, Amelia, Grayson, Charles. And an insider." Bryce choked out; his brain barely able to speak through the shock of what he'd just seen.

"This is not good. So, it's confirmed someone inside the camp told Unity where we were." Michael angrily pounding on the doorframe once again.

"I know, I saw." Bryce replied, still processing everything he had just seen. "This doesn't change anything, we meet the Brotherhood, and we figure out our next move." He continued trying his best to reassure Michael as he watched the anger building in the large, bulky, offensive lineman sized man.

"Yeah, exactly, just got to stay focused." Michael responded, his anger fading away quickly. "I'll let you go, sounds like Taylor's getting out of the shower." He said, stepping back from the door frame as the shower sounds from his bathroom stopped abruptly.

"Sounds good, just remain calm. We'll figure it out and the person responsible will be dealt with accordingly." Bryce nodded, stepping back and closing the door once again.

Bryce continued to watch the News as he waited for Bennett to finish her shower, hoping for any more information he could gather on the attack and try to piece together who might have given them up. After nearly twenty minutes Bennett emerged from the bathroom, a white robe wrapped around her with her hair tucked up into a towel. "I needed that." Bennett cheered her as she walked over and joined Bryce on the bed. "What's wrong?" She asked as she tried to cuddle up to Bryce.

Unity captured Amelia and Grayson; they're saying they got a tip from someone inside the camp." Bryce said, looking at Bennett concernedly. "Someone inside the camp willingly helped Unity capture and kill Atlantians, their own people."

"You don't know that, Bryce. Unity spins the truth all the time, they control the media. Remember?" She comforted, trying to raise Bryce's spirit.

"Why would they lie about how they found out?" Bryce questioned sternly, his frustration building at the thought of the betrayal.

"I don't know Bryce, I'm just trying to tell you, it might not be as simple as someone choosing to help Unity, they might have done it without knowing they were." She pleaded with him to see her point of view, doing her best to calm him down.

"How could someone be so stupid?" He asked as he stood up, pacing the room as he spoke. "Like they would have to ignore the rules Amelia set out."

"Like we did when we bought these?" She said raising her wrist to show off her bracelet. "All I'm saying Bryce, is we do not know how they found out, and while it might be the truth the person might not have known they did it." She explained her voice softening in the hopes it would calm him.

"I guess so." Bryce said, sitting back down beside her. "I'm just frustrated, I'm tired of running, I just want to live without the fear of Unity looming over everything, I just want to be with you." He whispered, wrapping her in his arms and falling back onto the bed.

"You want to be with me?" She giggled crawling up to him, so her mouth aligned with his before planting a big kiss on him. The pair kissed for a moment, Bryce's hands finding their way quickly into Bennett's robe and onto her butt. With some soft moans from Bennett, Bryce pulled her in closely, her soft skin pressing into his as her hands explored him. "Bryce?" Bennett asked as she pulled away from their passionate kissing.

"Yeah?" He replied, his hands still moving up and down her body.

"Can we stop?" She asked nervously. "I don't think I'm ready. It's not you, it's me, I'm just not ready to you know?"

"Of course, there's no pressure, when you're ready I'm here, and never before." He comforted, his hands finding their way out of the robe.

"Are you mad?" She asked softly looking him in the eyes, her blue eyes piercing any defenses he had up.

"Why would I be mad?" He whispered, pulling her into him. "I promised you I wouldn't leave, that means I am here for you no matter what."

"Promise? No matter what?" Her voice clearly pained as she asked.

"I promise no matter what." He responded, kissing the top of her head softly, the smell of the hotel shampoo pleasantly filling his nose.

"Good, now go shower, you smell like sweat and pine sap." She chuckled, kissing him one more time before rolling off of him and pinching her nose. Laughing, Bryce sat up on the bed, glanced back at the nearly naked girl in his bed, and sighed, walking to the bathroom, glancing back one more time before he entered.

The two awoke sometime shortly after noon, Bennett first who after some gentle nudging woke Bryce up. "Morning sleepy head." She whispered, kissing him on the cheek and placing her head on his chest as he rolled over onto his back.

"I always enjoy the few moments of bliss I have right when I wake up before everything hits me." He yawned as he slowly opened his eyes, the light from the hotel room's window causing a warm glow throughout.

"Me too." She said, running her hand up and down his toned stomach as she spoke.

Just as Bryce went to kiss Bennett there was a knock at the adjoining door. With a groan, Bryce called out. "Just a minute." Rolling out of bed and opening the backpack, dried mud crumbling off of it as he moved, pulling out a change of clothes for him and Bennett as he did.

The pair quickly got dressed, Bryce in a pair of dark-washed jeans, a baggy, black t-shirt, and a plain maroon hoodie and Bennett sporting a pair of light blue, acid washed jeans, with a white t-shirt and a borrowed black hoodie of Bryce's.

Once the pair had dressed themselves, Bryce flung open the door and greeted Michael and Taylor who wore beige 5.11 brand tactical pants, black crew neck sweaters, and fitted black baseball hats, the brims curved into a tight U-shape. "We ordered some breakfast sandwiches and figured you might want some while we prepared for the meeting." Michael said, holding up two foil wrapped sandwiches. With a smile and a nod, Bryce took the sandwiches, tossed one to Bennett who quickly unwrapped the food, looking longingly at the delicious croissant bun, cut in half and filled with a scrambled egg, slices of bacon and a piece of cheddar cheese.

"You are the best." She cheered as she smiled and took a big bite of the food. "Come in and sit, we should talk." She said motioning to the pair who followed Bryce into the room from the doorway and sat on various pieces of furniture throughout.

"So, what's the plan?" Bryce asked between large bites of the sandwich.

"Well, the Brotherhood contact said to meet them around 7P.M. at the shipping yard about twenty minutes from here- we mapped out the route earlier today- should be an easy drive, we'll stash the car a bit away from the meet and then walk the rest of the way. Then we just use the passphrase: 'Getting cold out here, isn't it?' And as long as they respond: 'Yeah, it really seeps into your bones.' Then we know they're with the Brotherhood, and we follow them to safety." Michael said an air of confidence in his voice as he sat on the faux wooden dresser placed below the flatscreen TV that hung on the wall.

"What if they don't respond properly?" Bryce asked cautiously, his mind instantly wandering to the worst-case scenario.

"Then we handle them." Michael said coldly, looking at Taylor who nodded a serious expression across his face. The group sat in silence for a moment, what was just said hanging in the air as the group looked around the room at each other.

The conversation changed after that, Taylor signing jokes and lightening the mood as much as he could, the tension and nerves slowly building as the time passed and the ever-present danger became more tangible. After about an hour of visiting with each other Michael and shortly after him, Taylor returned to their room to prepare, packing up their backpacks and trying their best to calm their ever-building stress. Bryce and Bennett took a similar approach, flicking through TV channels and slowly packing their clothes up, wrapping their mud-covered clothes in plastic bags they'd removed from the unused garbage cans in their room. As the time ticked away and the day's sunlight faded, the group checked out of their rooms and left, piling back into the SUV and heading towards the meeting place.

Bryce looked out the window as the cityscape flew by, trying his best to push the feeling that something wasn't right out of his mind. Eventually Michael pulled into a random parking lot the light of the red and yellow sign filling the dark night sky. "Okay we walk from here." He said looking back at Bennett and Bryce who then exited the vehicle and fell in behind him as he led the way and Taylor followed behind, looking over his shoulder occasionally as the group walked through the cold, dark and dirty industrial area.

Pulling their jackets tight and stuffing their hands in their pockets for warmth the group walked for several minutes before they approached a fenced off area between two buildings, a large river just behind it. They climbed through a hole in the fence, just as a hooded man stood at the opposite end of the area, the compacted dirt and mud squishing under their feet as they approached. The sounds of cracking and popping barely audible over the sound of the river and industrial machinery running throughout the area.

"Getting cold out here, isn't it?" Michael called to the man's back once the group was close. Breaking away from the other three.

"What?" The man called out turning around, his scruffy beard and scraggly brown hair hidden under his hood in the dim light of the area. "Talking to me boy?" He asked his voice sharp and raspy most likely from years of smoking and drinking.

"I just said it's getting cold out here, isn't it?" He repeated louder this time, cupping his hands around his mouth to amplify the sound as he closed in.

"Oh, it's you!" The man replied looking at the group and smiling, his yellowed teeth creating a sinister smile in the darkness of his hood. "We were hoping you'd arrive soon." He said approaching Michael and quickly grabbing his wrist. "Come here boy." He said, pulling hard on the large boy's wrist.

"Get off me!" Michael called, pushing the man hard and sending him sprawling to the floor, his hood falling off as he did. Slowly the man picked himself up, the sound of cracking and popping once again filling the air as his face slowly contorted and changed, bulging and shaping into another face as the man grew taller.

"Is this better?" He sneered as the sound of popping and cracking stopped and he looked far more handsome, his once sharp and yellowed teeth now straight, white and perfect, his scruffy face now clean and his once messy hair now perfectly styled into a layered, undercut, hairstyle that suited him well. If it wasn't for the man's clothes having not changed one might think he was a completely different person. "Now follow me, we don't have much time. Unity will be here before you know it." He motioned for the group to head towards a small alley just behind him.

"I'm not going anywhere until you return with the correct phase." Michael said slowly backing away from the man.

"Taylor, there isn't time for this." The man said walking towards Michael again matching his pace as he walked backwards.

"I'm not Taylor, and you're not… You're not part of the Brotherhood, are you?" Michael said, stretching his arms out and slowly backing away, his body shielding Bryce and Bennett who began to back up with him, Taylor following suit as he looked behind them, scanning the shadows, his hand reaching behind his back slowly removing the pistol from his waistband.

"Well, I thought this would be easier, but I guess you want to do this the hard way." The man said, producing a large knife from under his coat as his other wrist came up to his mouth. "We're blown, move in."

Just as the man spoke, the whole area lit up, as floods of heavily armed men rushed out of every alley, and over the fence, quickly surrounding the group. "Get on your knees. And lose the gun." The man's calm voice cutting through the shouts and stomping feet as the group was surrounded.

The four teens did as commanded and kneeled down, the dirt and mud squishing beneath them as they did. Taylor threw away the pistol as he knelt, the metal skittering across the rocky, dirty ground towards the feet of a masked man.

"Now wasn't that easy?" The handsome man asked as he slid his blade back into his coat. "I was hoping you'd resist; it's been a while since I've got to test my skills on an Atlantian." He smiled his white toothy grin turning sinister as he looked down at the four kneeling figures. "What? Cat got your tongue?" He asked as he walked over to Bennett, taking her chin in his hand and tilting her face up to look at him.

"Get off her!" Bryce snapped moving to stand up, only to feel a shove on his shoulders from behind him, forcing him back to his knees.

"Oh, we do have some fight in us? Good. I just have to touch the right nerves." The man chuckled as he released Bennett's face and paced in front of the group, clearly enjoying the anger building in them. "I bet you just want to jump up and snap my neck don't you, just imagining how you'd kill me, maybe with fire, or water, plenty of that here." He continued his charming demeanor only serving to make the group more and more angry. "And to think, if it wasn't for this pretty little girl here, we'd never have found you or the camp." The man said smiling and returning to Bennett once more, crouching to her eye level as Bryce, Michael and Taylor turned to look at Bennett.

"You're lying." Bryce spat, as the man smiled even wider at the realization of what he'd just exposed.

"Oh, you don't know." He said softly, his sinister smile changing to an expression of joy and delight. "Oh, I am so happy I get to tell you this. Little Benny here… can I call you that, considering you signed the letter to your Dad with Benny? Oh, screw it, I make the rules here." He cackled, continuing his monologue. "Little Benny here wrote a heartfelt letter to her Daddy!" He began in a mocking tone as Bryce watched in horror, his mouth wide with shock. "Telling Dear ol' Dad how she was safe, and how it wasn't your fault, she willingly joined you, that she'd write to him again when it was safe, but to not believe everything you see on TV. Oh, it was so sweet. Too bad we got it first." He smiled as he watched her eyes well up with tears. "It was easy from there, once we tracked the letter back to a small town in the mountains of Maine, a little post office in the sleepy backwoods." He sneered as he stood back up and paced the group, the expressions of anger and disappointment filling their faces as he spoke, only serving to fuel him more. "The hard part was following you back to the little hidey-hole you cancerous rats lived in. You might be inhuman trash but you're clever, constantly changing directions and routes each time." He spat as he recalled how Unity found the camp.

"Bennett how could you?" Michael asked as the man stood and watched his hand smugly covering his mouth, trying and failing to conceal a smile.

"I... I didn't... Bryce I swear!" She sobbed as she looked at Bryce, his eyes unable to meet hers. "Bryce, you have to believe me, I didn't do that. Please just look at me, please, Bryce." She pleaded, her voice shaking as she cried, pulling at Bryce's face, trying to get him to look her in her eyes.

"Awww... she's trying to lie yet again." The handsome man mocked. "Oh, Tyson is going to be so glad we found you. We've been looking for you for some time now." The man said, tapping Bryce on the head softly. "It's been years and finally we have you." He bragged, his voice softening as he celebrated his victory. "Well, I for one am glad we had this time together, but now we should get going." He finished, signaling for his men to grab them. The group was forced to stand as shackles were placed on their hands and feet.

The four were loaded into the back of a set of waiting SUVs, Taylor and Michael in one, Bryce, Bennett and the handsome man in another. The SUVs quickly took off, the industrial cityscape passing by quickly as Bryce looked out the blacked-out window unable to look at Bennett who cried quietly. "Where are you taking us?" He asked the handsome man as he fixed an earpiece into his ear and adjusted himself in the front seat.

"Oh, now why would I ruin the surprise?" He asked, his mocking tone only pissing Bryce off more.

"Not important enough to know I guess." Bryce mocked back as he struggled to shrug, trying his best to upset the man.

"Bryce, Bryce, Bryce, try as you might, but I just can't tell you. I can tell you it will be fun breaking your spirit. And even more fun breaking her's." He teased as he reached back and tapped Bennett's leg causing her to wince and pull away.

"I'm going to kill you." Bryce said coldly looking at the man in the eyes, his voice calm and flat.

"I hope you try; I like when they fight back." He returned, looking at Bryce and smiling. Just then Bryce was hit in the side, and everything went black.

Images flashed in Bryce's mind as he went in and out of consciousness, one moment Bryce was in the car, looking around as he watched the handsome man hanging unmoving in his seat, Bennett lay in a pool of blood as Bryce struggled to get to her. Then black, the sound of gunfire barely audible over the loud ringing and screams. Next thing he was being pulled from the car, screaming for Bennett as he was dragged backwards, fighting to get free, only for everything to go black once more. When Bryce came to again, he was on a plane looking up at bright lights as people ran around him, a woman with dark brown eyes looking at him, a surgical masking covering the rest of her face, as a sharp pain filled his abdomen.

"Bryce, can you hear me?" She asked as she shone a light into his eyes. "Pupils are responsive, blood pressure is dropping, he's coding." The images faded away once more, then black.

Bryce awoke again unsure of where he was, the pain in his stomach still there as he struggled to move. His blurry vision slowly sharpened, revealing a green canopy above with small beams of sunlight flowing through. The sound of a boat motor and water rippling filled his ears. "Where am I?" He panicked, unable to move his body as he struggled against straps that held him down.

"He's awake, put him under again." A familiar body-less voice said to his left before a warm stinging feeling filled his arm and he faded to black again.

CHAPTER 18

Bryce 's eyes opened, the bright sunlight and hot, thick air choking him as he struggled to swallow, his mouth dry and pasty, his skin clammy and moist, sweat pooling on him. Slowly but surely, he sat up in bed, looking around at his surroundings as he did. The room wasn't a room at all, it appeared as though Bryce was in a shipping container that had been converted into a living space, the metal walls and floor broken up with a skylight and window that had been installed to let natural light into the space. The bed was a thin mattress placed on a military-like metal bed frame, a small pile of clothes folded neatly and placed on the top of a wooden green footlocker that was pushed against the end of the bed. Bryce examined his body, he was covered in cuts, all scabbed over, some stitched closed, a large bandage was placed along the left side of his abdomen, peeling it back revealed a large cut that was also stitched closed. A panic filled his body as he struggled to remember the series of events that led him here, or why he was covered in cuts, why his head hurt, or why he was only wearing his boxer briefs? With great pain in his abdomen and stiffness in his shoulder and neck Bryce got dressed. He put on the clothes laid out before him, even though he didn't remember ever buying them. The black Columbia brand cargo pants, black Solomon hiking boots, white t-shirt and dark blue linen button up shirt fit him perfectly.

Just as Bryce finished rolling up the sleeves of the linen shirt, a woman carrying a metal clipboard entered the container from a door installed further down. She was petite, tan and blonde with soft features, wearing a pair of pants similar to his with a maroon sweat stained shirt, her hair cut short into a cropped pixie cut. As she approached Bryce slowly readied himself to fight. "Bryce it's okay I won't hurt you." She said softly as she drew near raising her arms above her head.

"St... Stay back! Where am I?" He replied aggressively not trusting anything he was seeing.

"Okay, okay. I won't get any closer." Her soft voice like velvet to Bryce's ears. "You're safe here, no one wants to hurt you."

"Where am I?" Bryce repeated raising his voice as he did.

"I can't tell you that." She answered softly but stern. "But I can tell you that you are safe and that's what's most important."

"Why can't you tell me? How did I get here? You're Unity, aren't you?" The questions flowing out of him as if he were vomiting them up.

"I'm not allowed to, we brought you here, and no I am not." She responded, answering each question as briefly as possible.

"Stop giving me half answers." Bryce yelled as he backed away further.

"Bryce, I am telling you all I can." She said back her tone unchanged. "Please, let me look at you and then we can get you the answers you want. I promise I will not hurt you." She pleaded inching closer to him as she spoke.

"No, don't come near me." He screamed back, his voice booming and echoing in the metal room.

"Bryce, you were injured in the rescue, you were cut badly by a piece of metal, I need to make sure it isn't infected." She pleaded as she moved forward, inching closer and closer.

"What rescue mission? Where are my friends? Where's Bennett?" Bryce called as he backed away, his back foot hitting the wall of the container.

"In Pittsburg, Unity had captured you, we got word of the route they were taking you, and we had to act fast. The extraction didn't go as planned, there were more Unity members than we thought, things didn't go according to plan, we had to get you out of there. Now please sit, let me look at your cut." She gestured to the bed for him to sit down.

"Where are my friends?" Bryce asked again softly knowing the answer before he'd even asked.

"I'm sorry Bryce, you were the target, we weren't able to save them, Unity has them." She said softly, helping Bryce to the bed gently.

"Bennett, the blood, is she?" He asked his mind moving a mile a minute.

"We can't say for sure, but it would appear she is okay, we have confirmation she was removed from the vehicle along with the man who grabbed you. He goes by Dixon." She said lifting Bryce's shirt as he sat unmoving in shock, the will to fight fading from him as she confirmed his worst fear, Unity had the twins, Bennett, Amelia, Grayson, possibly Anton, everyone he had ever known who knew anything about what was going on was now in Unity's hands.

"Why me?" Bryce winced as the woman pulled the bandage off of his skin and examined his cut and stitches.

"That's above my clearance. But you seem to be healing nicely, stitches should be able to be removed soon." She said reapplying the bandage and lowering Bryce's shirt. "If you would care to come with me, I can take you to someone with more answers."

Bryce nodded silently and he stood up. The woman barely reaching his shoulders as she stood, turned on her heels and walked him to the door; the heat of the outside world rushing in and hitting him like a truck. Stepping out of the container and closing it behind them, Bryce took in his surroundings, gigantic tropical looking trees filled the area, the canopy of them shading them as the bright midday sun beamed down, finding little cracks in the dense canopy. The ground a mix of fallen decomposing leaves and dirt, squishing slightly under each step they took. Three more storage containers similar to the one they'd exited lined the perimeter of the area, the logos painted on the side faded and peeling making them completely unreadable as moss and plants coiled around them. Looking around more, Bryce saw an almost ancient looking town stretching out before him, small stone huts, storage containers and several slightly larger looking houses made of stone, encircled a much larger central marketplace looking structure that was almost raised up from the living areas that surrounded. In the middle again on another raised level sat a much larger almost pyramid looking structure, all of it covered in vines and plants, save for a small entrance emitting light from its base. Wires and cables ran overhead on stone carved more modern looking poles. The sounds of bugs, birds, and monkeys filled the air as Bryce looked around in awe.

"Happens to everyone, I still catch myself staring sometimes too." The woman said, noticing Bryce's eyes wide.

The woman led Bryce through the town, pointing out various locations and people moving past them carrying out tasks as they did, nodding or smiling at the woman who greeted them similarly. Finally, she led him to the entrance of the pyramid looking structure, where a muscular, black man stood in a military-like uniform. His sleeves were rolled up slightly to show off the man's large arms, a big faced watch shining brightly on his wrist. "Melanie, how is our patient doing?" The man asked his African accent and voice booming as the two approached, his bright smile sincere and kind.

"Healing up well, should be able to get the stitches out in a few days." Melanie replied, looking up at the man as she spoke. "Bryce, this is Atlas Manatlou, the leader of the Atlantian Brotherhood." She said introducing the man who stretched out a large hand to shake Bryce's.

"Bryce, the pleasure is all mine." Atlas boomed, his hand dwarfing Bryce's as he strongly grasped it and shook. "I hope all this isn't too shocking for you."

"Thanks, I would be lying if I said it wasn't Sir." Bryce answered releasing his hand from the handshake and rubbing it with his other.

"Sir? Call me Atlas, Sir is far too formal. But I understand how it could be a lot let me be the first to welcome you to the headquarters of the Brotherhood. Please, if you would follow me, I'm sure you have many questions. Melanie, thank you for your help." Atlas said with a big showy wave before turning on his heels and leading Bryce into the entrance of the pyramid. Cautiously Bryce followed. Entering the ancient looking stone structure, the wide passage looked small as Atlas walked through it. After fifteen feet, the entrance opened into a large high-tech room, screens and computers lining the wall with a planning table in the center of the room, surrounded by many people typing furiously as various programs, images, and schematics flashed across them. "This is our control center, some of the best Atlantian minds work here, providing critical intelligence and planning for operations." Atlas explained as the two walked through the room and down another hallway to a room full of guns, ammunition, and various tables with cleaning supplies and tools laid out. A serious looking

The Atlantian Chronicles

bald man sitting at one of the tables brushing the barrel of a pistol he held in his hand. "And this is the armory, and of course our expert quartermaster Preston Garry." He gestured to the man who glanced up from his task and nodded before returning to the scrubbing. Bryce returned the nod as he walked past, deeper into the structure, passing a room Atlas explained was a clothing and uniform storage room. They moved into a large room with bookshelves lining the wall, a large ornate dark wooden desk sitting across from the door, a high-back leather chair with a leopard pelt draped over it and two matching wooden chairs sitting in front of the desk, their smaller backs facing the door, with a small bar set tying the room together in the corner.

"Welcome to my office." Atlas boomed as he made a show of offering Bryce a seat and then moved over to his bar, pouring himself three fingers of a brown liquid Bryce could only assume was scotch, before eventually making his way to the chair and sitting down. "Now I assume you have so many questions… where would you like to start?" He asked as he settled in his chair and took a sip of his drink.

"Where exactly are we?" Bryce asked quickly.

"That's a bit hard to answer because we are technically in a place they don't have a name for, however, I guess the easiest explanation would be the Amazon Rainforest more specifically the Brazilian portion, past the point of modern exploration, but previously this place was called: 'The Lost City of Z' you might have heard of it… British explorer Percy Fawcett… " Atlas said quizzically looking at Bryce who clearly hadn't heard of either.

"Okay, how has modern exploration or more importantly Unity not found you?" Bryce asked his mind, trying and failing to come up with a logical explanation.

"A combination of the location, a pact made with the locals centuries ago and some advances we've made in signal and radar jamming tech developed here to prevent Unity from finding us. I'm sure you've heard the story of how the Atlantians settled and mixed with the locals after the fall of Atlantis in 346 B.C.E? They should have discussed this at the camp if they were following our programming for new recruits. Well, when we arrived here, we mated and built lives with the locals creating the early Incan, Aztec, and Kuhikugu. Even now offspring of these civilizations exist, scattered throughout the Amazon. When contact was made, we'd advanced civilizations tenfold, allowing us to live deeper in the jungle than anyone thought possible. Our abilities allowed us to form cities, using knowledge we had to craft pyramids, places of worship, and irrigation systems researchers now still don't understand." Atlas boasted, his chest puffing up as he spoke. "Well, these tribes still exist and since we are so deep into the forest, these tribes act as a deterrent and a warning system, our pacts and alliances still with them, lasting centuries. Their knowledge of the forest and our abilities allow us to coexist with each other. They serve us and we provide them with the help they need." Atlas finished taking another sip of his drink letting out a sigh afterwards.

"Okay, but why did you only save me? Melanie said I was the target?" Bryce asked, hoping for some kind of answer to something that had bothered him since the escape from the camp.

"Hmmm... Melanie wasn't exactly correct in saying that. Saving Atlantians from Unity was the goal, as a Crono you are more important to the Atlantian cause than those of the more shall we say common abilities. When we launched our rescue mission, and things didn't go as expected we had to change the plan and rescue the more important individual of the group. I'm sad to say it came down to this, but we have to do what is best for the people of Atlantis and not what is necessarily right." He said hanging his head and swirling his drink before looking back at Bryce.

"Are my friends alive?" Bryce questioned softly, praying in his mind for good news.

"Our spies inside Unity have reported that indeed they are, both the Maxwell twins are alive." Atlas stated proudly.

"And Bennett?" His spirits lifted after the news of the twins.

"She's hurt but alive, she was injured in the rescue and required some medical attention, but our latest reports say she is alive. However, Bryce it is our understanding that she was the cause of the camp's discovery. And we cannot just let that slide." Atlas said less enthusiastically than his previous statement.

"I don't think that matters, she was trying to help. She is half of the reason I am even here today." Bryce said, wondering to himself how sincere Atlas really was.

"Bryce you must understand, we cannot trust her, she led Unity to our front door and many people died because of it. She is not a priority; she is a maybe right now. And even if we do attempt to rescue her, how can we expect people to want to risk their lives for someone who so fragrantly played with theirs?" Atlas explained taking another sip of his drink once he finished.

"She is a part of this, and we can't just leave her in Unity's hands. It was a mistake; she made a mistake and it's not fair to judge her for that. Not her, not the twins, not Amelia, not anyone. Get them back!" He replied, raising his voice once again.

"I appreciate your passion Bryce, but I don't know if that is how that works." Atlas said looking at Bryce his happy demeanor fading to a more serious one.

"What do you mean? Those are your people, you're the leader here, the leader of the Brotherhood, and you're just going to give up on them? Just like that?" Bryce yelled, slamming his hand on the hard desk again.

"No Bryce, we are not giving up on them, but it is not that easy, it is our number one priority to keep our people safe, rescue missions run the risk of more of our people getting captured or killed. We can't risk this anytime someone we know gets captured, as much as I would like to." Atlas explained his eyes meeting Bryce's in a battle for dominance.

"Not good enough. These are our people, and I will stop at nothing to make sure they are safe." Bryce said sternly staring just as hard back at Atlas who sat back in his chair and took a long sip of his drink and waited.

"That's exactly what I was hoping you'd say." He said smiling wide once more, his eyes sending a completely different message than the rest of his expression. "We are working on something, but I need to know you are committed to our cause before I let you in on it. So, I'll ask you Bryce, what are you willing to do to get your friends back?" He asked, leaning forward in his chair.

"Everything." Bryce responded, his eyes narrowing as he stared at Atlas, his smile growing wider once more.

"Good." He smiled. "We will be in touch, but for now, rest, heal and when we need you, I will come get you. For now, get settled. The town is open to you, but we ask you do not enter the pyramid without authorization." Atlas said, placing his hands on his desk and standing up, walking Bryce to the door and out of the pyramid.

Bryce spent the rest of the day wandering the small, layered city, noticing the ancient town is bordered by walls of large trees like something out of a fantasy novel, the trees so wide they had to have been there for centuries, if not longer. As Bryce wandered the town, he noticed many people whispering as he walked, and pointing when they thought he wasn't paying attention. By his count there had to be nearly five hundred people if not more living in this town; a mix of children, teens, and adults, all living in repurposed containers, modified ancient stone huts, and houses equipped with electrical connections. He came to learn this electrical was fed by solar energy from panels mounted in the top of the trees throughout the perimeter. This place while hidden from the world could rival many places in its access to modern amenities.

As Bryce settled into the community, learning the goings-on of the town, he came to realize how vastly different this place was to the camp. Gone was the daily training and the trips into town, the morning alarms, or the meal times called over loudspeakers. Bryce tried to keep a routine, exercising, shadow boxing and using his ability every morning, trying to maintain his fitness and build his shift duration as he waited for the call from Atlas.

Outside of his visits from Melanie which seemed to come daily for the first week and a half, checking on his injury and then eventually removing his stitches; Bryce never interacted with anyone he deemed higher up in the Brotherhood. While he had grown to be a part of the community, he noticed everyone in the headquarters had some kind of ability. He began helping those he could with tasks like construction, watching children or helping soothe crying babies, teaching martial arts to the young children, and helping run supplies from the stockroom to the kitchen, he never seemed to see Atlas. And he was barred entry by guards stationed in front of the pyramid whenever he tried to enter. He noticed they had shown up shortly after his arrival and by the information he could gain from his hushed conversations with those he helped, Atlas was rarely seen outside of the pyramid, nor did he allow all but a chosen few to enter. Some Atlantians in the town often had never set foot inside the pyramid even after years of living there, and those who were allowed were forbidden from talking about what went on inside.

Nearly a month had passed since Bryce arrived in the town, his anger and resentment growing with each day he didn't hear from Atlas, his stomach fully healed, a pink scar now marking the left side of his stomach where the injury was. A week earlier Bryce had decided if he hadn't heard something within a week, he was going to do something. The morning came, and after Bryce worked up a sweat, showered in his personal bathroom, that was installed in the converted container. He dressed in an outfit similar to that of the first day in town, and then he made his way to the pyramid. Two guards blocked Bryce from entering, both men wearing black combat fatigues, with bullet proof vests and AK-47 rifles slung over their shoulders.

"Tell Atlas I want to speak to him." Bryce called loudly to the men as they stood at the entrance not allowing him to enter. "Call him now!" He shouted, the eyes of those around him watched the scene from afar. One of the men keyed their microphone and mumbled into it as he stared hard at Bryce. Within a few moments Atlas emerged from the entrance, his bright smile and uniform shining in the light from the interior.

"Bryce, I was just coming to get you, please come in, we've made developments." Atlas boomed waving Bryce past the guards and into the pyramid.

"Good." Bryce said brushing past the guard and following Atlas through the various rooms and back to his office.

"Bryce, while I appreciate your enthusiasm, could you please refrain from such displays in the future?" Atlas commanded as he walked around his desk and sat down, a small folder placed in front of him.

"Sure, but tell me you've found Bennett and the twins?" Bryce replied avoiding any pleasantries in the process.

"We have, we believe they are being held with the others in a privatized prison Unity has run for years, under the guise of being an actual prison." Atlas said opening the folder, black and white photos piled up along with papers and copies of documents.

"Well, when are we going to get them?" Bryce asked rifling through the photos, looking at various pictures of Michael and Taylor, Bennett, Amelia, Grayson, their faces bruised with large metal collars wrapped around their necks.

"It's not that simple Bryce. You don't think we want to?" Atlas began, spinning the photos around and pointing to the collar. "These collars we have no idea what they are, how they work and if they are even removable. And we would need to figure this out before we can even think about removing anyone from that prison. On top of this, we need to figure out the best way to get our people out of there. This is not an easy task." Atlas finished before taking a sip of his amber liquid in the crystal cup on his desk.

"It's been weeks, and you're saying we basically know nothing?" Bryce said sternly sitting back in the chair.

"No Bryce, I am telling you we are working on getting all of our people free. Taylor, Michael, Amelia, Grayson, Stephan, Brent, Farrah, Julian, Derek, Kurt, the list goes on and on." Atlas returned, pointing to each person in the photos.

"And Bennett." Bryce called back pointing to the person Atlas conveniently left out.

"Bryce, we will try our best, but our priority here is Atlantians and their safety. Ms. Douglas led Unity to our base, got several good Atlantians killed, and frankly is a security risk at best, she's also human, not Atlantian, and others including myself do not think it is in our best interest to risk bringing her here." Atlas replied, keeping his booming voice flat, his tone unwavering.

"How the heck is that fair, it was an accident, she made a single mistake and you're what? Going to let her rot in a prison because of it? A prison where she does not belong? Like you said she's human, not Atlantian, and she's what? Expected to live the rest of her life there?" Bryce yelled, not caring who he was talking to, his frustration building with each second.

"She made a choice. She chose to send a letter in secret, or did she get Amelia's permission to send that letter? The letter I remind you, by our team's account, led Unity to our secret location. I will caution you as well as to who you yell at, your opinion on her is not a popular one, I am fighting an uphill battle just letting you remain here. People do not trust you, and your aggressive outbursts do nothing to help your cause." Atlas said, pointing his finger at Bryce.

"I didn't ask to be rescued; I was fine going with them to the prison. You brought me here. I didn't ask to be involved in any of this. I didn't fight Unity until I was forced to. Until they killed the person, I called a father and the person I knew as an uncle all my life. So, you'll excuse me if my views don't align with those people who have no idea what Bennett has done to help me and this cause." Bryce said, kicking over the chair.

"Do not." Atlas standing up and walking towards Bryce. "You are here for a reason. One you may not know now but in time you will understand. But do not take our kindness for weakness. Do not take our inaction for a lack of drive, a lack of strength or a lack of bravery. Atlantians are the future, you can either get aboard the train or you can be left behind, but I will not have you act like a spoiled teenager while there are members of our species who died to get you here so you could do what you are meant to do." Atlas said, pressing his finger into Bryce's chest and walking him backwards into the smooth stone wall.

"And what am I supposed to do? Because the way I see it I've spent the last four weeks sitting around doing nothing." Bryce replied pressing off the wall slightly, feeling the pressure of Atlas's finger pressing into his sternum.

"Help lead our people to their rightful place atop the throne of the world." Atlas smiled, his mouth curling into a wicked grin, his big white teeth not matching the stern tone of the conversation.

"What are you talking about?" Bryce asked, standing his ground, the smell of Atlas's breath, a mixture of scotch and chewed cigars, filling his nostrils.

"Cronos are the guards of Atlantians. You see, Cronos were the Royal guard in Atlantis, their ability to move so quickly their opponents were unable to react before they were cut down. They were the perfect soldier. Imagine, facing off against an army of well trained, well-armed soldiers that moved as if time slowed for them, and them alone. We were unstoppable. It was said during the final battle of Atlantis, each Crono took on one thousand men before they fell. Multiply that by hundreds and you'll see why while the others fled, moved to all corners of the globe and hid, your ancestors fought, to buy the others time. Occasionally a Crono will pop up only to be killed by Unity or captured if they're lucky." Atlas said, stepping back slightly as he spoke. "Unity, as well as I, know a Crono is the symbol of the fight; the driving force that will lead our people to victory over Unity, over the humans. And will seat us atop the food chain where we belong, allowing us to make the next step in evolution we should have made so long ago. So, you will understand why we want to keep you safe, why we chose to save you in that convoy. You represent something far bigger than you can grasp. So, I will ask you to try to remember that before you have another outburst." Atlas said, tapping Bryce on the shoulder and turning around, picking up the chair and returning to his position as Bryce stood still trying to wrap his brain around this new revelation.

"Hold on, you're saying I am part of a royal guard? And what's this about evolution?" Bryce asked, more confused than when he had started.

"No Bryce, your ancestors, you are now a symbol showing both our people and Unity, we are not defeated. And that our strongest warriors support our cause. You are a warning, an omen, a prophecy of the impending doom of Unity and the salvation of our people. If it weren't for Cronos like you, all of Atlantis would have fallen, no one would have survived, and Unity would have won. You are what our people need." Atlas said, pounding his fist on his desk triumphantly.

"Okay, but what does that even mean? How do I show our people this?" Bryce asked, confused. His mind trying to take in all this new information.

"Leave that to me. For now, train, show the people of our town, our bastion that you are here. Help out around camp, do the right thing, and when the time is right, we will get your friends, our people, and save the world, one fight at a time." He replied, his voice softening to a low hum as he drew Bryce in with his words. "Now please, understand we are working towards getting our people out of that prison. It just takes time. But do not think we are not just as passionate about it as you are. We just show it differently." Atlas said before bringing his glass to his lips and finishing it in one large gulp.

Confused but reassured about the future, Bryce left the office, walked out of the temple and returned to his room, his mind racing with all that he'd just learned. A new found purpose washing over him...

CHAPTER 19

The next few weeks, Bryce was revitalized; helping out around camp, continuing to join in on the activities at the base, as well as making more public displays of supporting Atlas, their cause and Atlantians as a whole. By the time Atlas finally came to get Bryce, he was on a first name basis with most of the community and had regular visitors from young children to friends he'd made along the way.

"Bryce, it's time." Atlas announced, beaconing him over. Bryce set down the crate of bell peppers he'd carried from the supply boat that he was helping unload, and bolted over to Atlas. Sweat and dirt covering him.

"The prison?" Bryce asked excitedly.

"Yes, but let's discuss this in the situation room." Atlas said, stepping aside and letting Bryce enter the pyramid.

Bryce quickly walked into the large open room full of computers, the screens all lit up with different aerial views of a large central building surrounded by two different fences, guard towers and a large open yard with what looked like a small concrete area and a larger grass area. A group of three soldiers in black, 5.11 tactical pants, black T-shirts that hugged their large biceps, and black tactical plate carriers over top stood waiting. Bryce had never seen them before but with one glance he could tell they were elite soldiers.

"This him?" A gruff looking man with a slight scruff forming on his face, his skin was tanned with the veins throughout his arms bulging out, his hair cut short and tucked under a black baseball hat, the logo of the Cleveland Guardians blacked out on the front of it.

"Yes Colson, this is Bryce, the boy I was telling you about." Atlas smiled his teeth, almost reflecting the color of the screens.

"Doesn't look like much." Colson spat, barely even acknowledging Bryce's presence, before he nodded to the others who agreed with him.

"You know I can hear you right?" Bryce cut in angrily.

"And that means what to me?" Colson shot back standing up and walking over to Bryce.

"It means I expect a little respect from you." Bryce replied unmoving, sizing up the man who approached him.

"Respect is earned, not given." Colson replied as he walked around Bryce, his eyes locked with Bryce's as he circled.

"Gentleman, we are on the same team, with the same goal to save those who Unity has captured. Colson, Bryce is a capable soldier, the reports say he is more than competent in hand-to-hand combat, his pistol scores are in the high 95th percentile so I expect you to have his back just as much as he will have yours. Whether you like it or not, I am in charge here and I say you bring him." Atlas said stepping between the two and bringing order to the situation.

"Yes sir." Colson replied sarcastically, loosely saluting Atlas.

"Thank you, and Bryce, Colson and the rest of his team are the best we have to offer. So please follow their lead and stay alert. This is not a game, there are no do overs." Atlas said, gesturing to the screens. "We have word from a credible source that the collars somehow prevent Atlantians from using their power. However, due to a damaged collar, an Atlantian was able to damage the southern wall of the prison. As such all high level Atlantian prisoners were moved to a central block while the repair is being completed." Atlas said clicking a remote, the screens now showing a wall with damage done to it as if a portion of the earth had been ripped out from under the wall. "We expect more security, but our plan is to infiltrate the compound here, and then blow the wall here." He continued clicking the remote twice showing arrows that pointed to the various points outlined. "We have confirmation that no one will be at this point and once the wall is down, we expect some resistance, I will leave that for you and your team to handle Colson. We will secure a landing zone for a helicopter. Each collar will have to be removed before exfiltration. Our team has been working on a remote that will short circuit the collar and release the lock. From there, we will load all the prisoners onto the helicopter and then make our exit. We expect the mission to be over within fifteen minutes from time of infiltration to the time you touch down in the helicopter at the secondary location where we will torch the helicopter and make our exit in several vehicles." Atlas finished clicking through various slides and images as he outlined the escape plan.

"What kind of resistance can we expect on the ground?" Colson scoffed unmoving from the half sitting half learning position he'd taken up on a desk that faced the screens.

"From what intel we have gathered we assume it will be small arms fire along with most likely gas and less lethal solutions like pepper balls they use on inmates." Atlas answered confidently, his smile beaming almost excitedly.

"Who are the HVTs we plan on getting?" Colson asked again as he readjusted his position pulling a wooden toothpick out of his pocket and flicking it up to his mouth catching it as he did.

"We are hoping to extract as many people as we can, but people to look out for will be given to you directly to prevent any confusion." Atlas said as he gestured over for Preston Garry to come over. The two whispered back and forth with each other before Atlas turned and addressed the group again. "Well, I have some matters to attend to, I will turn the briefing over to Preston here to go over your tools and Colson please meet me in my office when this has… concluded." He bellowed his loud booming voice filling and reverberating around the ancient stone room. Atlas then turned on his heels and marched off towards his office.

"We all know I don't want to be here, I'm a 'get the job done and discuss it after' guy, but beggars can't be choosers… so, your kits will be standard, AR15 modified how you have specified previously, Colson, you will also get a tablet with the information streamed to you. Filly, you will have extra medical supplies, bandages, tourniquets, morphine injectors, the works, for treating any injuries to the team or to the escapees." Preston said, nodding his smooth bald head towards a tall slender, but still muscular looking woman, who's heavily, brightly colored, tattooed arms and neck did not subtract from her stunning features. If she hadn't pursued a career in the paramilitary, Bryce was certain she could've been a model, her purple and black hair was cropped so her bangs swooped over her left eye, while the right side of her head was completely shaved. With a nod back Preston continued. "Mateo, you will like this one, I have added extra C4 and Semtex charges with delay timers for you, they're shaped into breaching charges, but undo one side and you have fully formable charges as well with no other tinkering necessary." Preston explained as he demonstrated. The large stocky man with dark, almost brown skin, clearly a tanning addict nodded. His muscle shirt and thick gold chain, sporting a cross pendant on it, reminded Bryce of the cast of Jersey Shore more than it did of a man ready to kill for a cause. "Bryce, we tried to keep you light, you will only carry a pistol, you shot well according to the reports from Amelia, so we decided rather than try to go further in depth with rifles we'd keep it basic. You'll have a standard chest rig, with level three plates along with everyone else, it should stop most rounds but don't test it out. You'll have a knife and three extra magazines. As always, everyone else's rig has been set up according to their personal preferences I have noted from previous operations." Preston continued, his speed picking up as he glossed over the less important details.

"Yous already said that Presto, can we just call this a meeting? I have places to be." Mateo said with his thick Brooklyn accent very clear.

"Whatever, I don't want to do this anyway. Come to me with any questions. Your boat out of here leaves at 0600 tomorrow, be ready." Preston said, waving his hand at the group, shooting a look at Mateo and walking away.

With that the once bustling room began to empty as various people returned to their computers, Colson, Mateo and Filly, pushed past Bryce, Colson purposely bumping Bryce's shoulder as he walked past, his shorter frame felt like rock as he hit him. For a moment Bryce waited, the weight of what was to come next felt like a boulder had just fallen onto him.

Focus on what you can control… prepare yourself and success will follow. The words of Rhys echoed in his mind as he stood taking everything in as people moved around him. With one final breath, the unique smells of the structure filling his nose, a combination of warm, thick jungle air and slightly stale air pushed through computers, and the smell of sweat, gun oil, cigars and slight mildew somehow comforted him. He was in the heart of the Pyramid, he was going on the mission, he was going to save his friends, be a beacon of hope to the Atlantians, and strike a heavy blow to Unity. For Rhys, Anton, and everyone else Unity hurt.

Bryce spent the rest of the day nervously going over the plan, trying to remember every detail he could, committing everything to memory as best he could. The day passed and outside of a single passing moment Bryce did not see the soldiers again, he didn't really mind not seeing Colson again, but Filly seemed okay.

Sleep came quickly for Bryce, maybe it was a combination of his nervous energy finally crashing after half a day of puttering around waiting for the time to leave or maybe it was his body understanding it will need all the rest it can get, but by the time his head hit his pillow, he was out like a light.

Bryce's alarm went off and he quickly rolled out of bed, got dressed in a pair of tactical pants and a T-shirt and raced out to the Pyramid where Colson, Filly and Mateo already waited. "Took you long enough." Colson called out as Bryce half ran, half walked the path to the entrance.

"Am I late?" Bryce questioned looking at the trio who had all sat waiting for him at various tables in the eating area, just in front of the pyramid entrance.

"If you have to ask, the answer is yes." Colson snapped standing up and walking to Bryce so the two were chest to chest once again.

"What is your problem with me?" Bryce questioned firmly.

"My problem? My problem with you is you're some inexperienced kid, who decided he wanted to play soldier and if I am lucky knows not to shoot me in the back when things hit the fan. This isn't some video game where people can play again this is real life and if you screw up, there's no redo. So, stay out of my way and if you're lucky you won't make a mess in your pants when the bullets start flying." He scoffed his tone sharp and aggressive.

"You know I have been shot at before and fought Unity, right? Or does your small brain not understand that maybe I have some experience and am not just some dumb kid like you think I am. Or do I need to kick your ass and leave you on the floor for you to get it through your thick head?" Bryce snapped back, shoving Colson back as he spoke.

"Oh, a tough guy? You want to settle this, we totally can, but I play for keeps." Colson said, drawing a small knife from his belt line and waving it in front of Bryce. "So, what do you say little boy, ready to die?" He asked with a devilish smile across his face.

"Can't beat me fair and square? Need a knife to win against me? Makes sense, I knew you weren't as good as people think you are." Bryce replied, angling his body slightly, preparing for Colson to lunge at any moment as Mateo and Filly sat unmoving, watching the chaos unfold.

"Colson! Put it away." Atlas shouted, the anger and authority in his voice cutting through the air like a knife. "I will not ask again, and I will not repeat myself, Bryce will be coming on this mission whether you like it or not, he is pivotal to our plan, and if you do not accept this, I will find someone who will. Now fall in or ship out." Atlas commanded. Reluctantly, Colson followed the order slowly sheathing his blade, his eyes only leaving Bryce's at the very end. With a turn he spun and fell in line waiting for Atlas to let them into the Pyramid. "Good choice." Atlas whispered before he turned and the group followed him into the building, Bryce bringing up the rear.

"Is everything ready?" Colson said after two minutes of the group walking through the Pyramid. They walked deeper than Bryce had ever gone before, down sets of stone stairs that felt as if they were perfectly cut from the earth for this purpose. The group passed what looked like shooting ranges, test facilities for new gear Preston would work on, a server room full of large black computer banks with wires running through the ceiling to where Bryce assumed was the computer area at the first open room in the pyramid. The various blinking lights flashed throughout the room; and as the rough stone walls turned smoother and more clinical Atlas responded.

"Yes Colson. Everything is ready and as long as you follow what was discussed and stick to the plan, you and your team will be rewarded as such." Atlas said in a hushed tone almost as if he did not want to be heard.

"And you're sure about this?" Colson added his volume lowering to match Atlas's.

"Yes, now please let's not discuss this anymore." Atlas said, glancing around and then finishing his walk to a large metal door. Like most of the doors and modern additions to Atlantian Brotherhood structures, it looked as though the stone had formed around the door as if it had been there for hundreds of years if not longer. Even now knowing a Tellus just formed the stone this way, Bryce was amazed.

"Gentlemen, and Filly, are you ready?" Atlas said proudly turning around at the door and facing the four figures that flanked him. "I hope you are because you've already passed the point of no return, long ago. Regardless, if you have any opinions, concerns or any other matters now is the time to voice them for once you pass through this door, there is no going back, no leaving, no deviation and no second guessing, through this doorway is the mission and the only goal is completing it. So, Bryce, Filly, Mateo, Colson, speak now or forever hold your peace." Atlas said straightening his posture and looking at the four as if he was some great military leader inspiring his troops to fight a force they surely could not beat. Everyone remained unmoving, stoic and focused. With a nod Atlas continued, turning on his heels and walking over to a keypad on the wall. "Bryce, follow what this group says, you might be strong, and powerful but a bullet to the head can quickly end that. Colson, treat Bryce with respect, he has earned his spot here whether you like it or not and I have the utmost faith he will help this mission succeed." Atlas called over his shoulder as he entered a series of numbers onto the pad before wiping it off with a cloth he pulled from his pocket.

"Understood." Bryce nodded looking at Colson who shot him a look before nodding in agreement.

As Atlas pushed the last of the buttons a loud hiss let out as the door slowly opened, the warm air rushing into the otherwise cool and climate-controlled building. The air almost choked Bryce as the smell of swampy water and jungle filled his nose, as a not so unfamiliar smell of the outside compound rushed in. How could this be they had to be at least five levels down into the Earth? With a smile at Bryce's puzzled look, Atlas smiled and beckoned the group into the grotto. "Amazing, isn't it? Imagine what we would do if we rid the world of the cancer that is Unity and were able to take our rightful spot atop the throne of influence." Atlas said to Bryce as the two walked side by side down a slight ramp-like hill that led from the door to what was a small dock. There a river boat waited with a driver who wore the same uniform Bryce had seen on the guards at the front entrance; several black duffle bags placed on the floor of the boat. The dimly lit path led right up to the boat, the murky water just high enough to allow the boat to pass without issue. Amazed at what he saw Bryce looked around at the cavernous room, the ceilings not visible in the dim light. It took Bryce far longer than he would feel comfortable admitting for the feeling of sheer amazement to pass. "Well team, this is where I bid you good luck, I cannot accompany you for obvious reasons, but I trust you will get the job done. This boat will take you out and up the river where our plane is waiting to take you to the location as discussed in the briefing. Do us proud and do Atlantis proud!" Atlas called as the group got onto the boat, its engine whirling up and filling the area with noise as it continuously bounced off the walls. Pounding his fist to his chest Atlas turned and began the walk up the ramp, the boat slowly maneuvering out of the dock and through a tunnel across the small water filled grotto.

CHAPTER 20

It felt like forever before Bryce finally saw the light at the end of the tunnel, the overhead lights of the boat barely illuminating the water. The boat exited the tunnel and Bryce finally looked around. The jungle seemed to wrap around the river, large trees that had to be thousands of years old hugged the edges of the riverbanks. Bryce took in the beauty of this ever-changing rainforest as the boat flew by.

"Better get comfy, it'll be a few hours before we stop to make camp." Filly said her voice was raspy as her Aussie accent took Bryce slightly by surprise; as he realized he'd never spoken to her before.

"Make camp?" Bryce questioned, the phrase taking him by surprise.

"It's a four-day journey just to get to the airfield." Filly said, throwing her bag against the wooden bench seat on the side of the boat, rolling her tight, black t-shirt sleeves up as she stretched out in the little sun that hit the boat through the heavy forest canopy.

"I figured it wouldn't be that long." Bryce said shyly as he sat down on the bench across the boat and got as comfortable as he could.

"Don't worry pup, there's plenty of food and supplies and it's not half bad, it's like camping with your friends." Mateo said as he joined the pair from the front of the boat, sitting beside Bryce and throwing an arm over his shoulders. "We'll take great care of you, if the anacondas, jaguars, caimans or any of the other hundreds of deadly creatures in the place don't get you first." Mateo said, smiling as Bryce shoved his large muscular arm off his neck.

"Don't scare the kid." Filly said, opening one eye and shooting Mateo a look. "You'll be fine Bryce, we've made this journey dozens of times, technically we made it with you last time, though you were heavily medicated." Filly said, closing her eye once again.

"You never let me have any fun." Mateo sulked as he got up and returned to Colson at the front of the boat.

"Thanks." Bryce said softly to Filly who gave him a slight nod in return. Bryce nodded and returned to glancing out the side of the boat as the river wound its way by.

The rest of the first day went by fairly quickly. Bryce occasionally talked with Filly in between her naps, Mateo would occasionally pop back and tease Bryce who by the end of the day was firing back jabs garnering a few chuckles from the boat driver or Filly. Bryce liked Filly, as the two sat talking he learned she was quite insightful, sharing her opinion on Unity, the Brotherhood and even the fighting she'd been wrapped up in. She'd even gone as far as to tell Bryce how she'd grown up, using her powers to help her become a survival guide and even a military special forces member until she'd been discovered by Unity and fled, leading her to join the Brotherhood and Colson. Bryce hung on every word as she shared some stories and showed off some scars she'd received over the years. It didn't hurt Filly was beautiful, her tight, muscular body, accented by her tattoos, her soft but narrow face, and her raspy voice created a vision of beauty. Bryce even caught himself shooting a glance over at her as she laid out, before he snapped out of it feeling guilty for even thinking about another girl while Bennett was out there in Unity's hands, even if she had caused it. His chest tightened at the thought.

When the boat finally dropped an anchor close to the edge of the river, Bryce's back was ready for solid ground and a break from the bumpy ride of the river and the hard wooden bench he'd sat on the last eight hours.

The group unpacked and set up a small camp, stringing up several hammocks with bug nets over them, breaking out a small amount of food, as Filly easily lit a fire. Bryce helped where he could, avoiding Colson as much as possible, while the group set up the camp. The boat driver, LJ, was a short, stout, Peruvian man who Bryce came to find out was a Tellus who'd lived on the river his whole life. His English was very good though his accent made certain words tougher to understand and occasionally he would slip a Spanish word into his speech when he couldn't think of the translation. His dark, tanned skin showed a life of working outside and surviving in the unforgiving environment Bryce found himself in. After camp had been set up the sun faded quickly, the group encircling the fire as a fish was roasting atop it.

"So, Bryce, you really think your girl hasn't cut a deal to get out of Unity control?" Mateo chirped as he sat rotating his third piece of fish over the fire.

"You don't have to answer that, Bryce." Filly snapped just as Mateo finished his sentence.

"It's a valid question Filly, need to know if she's worth saving, because based on what I've heard, she isn't worth the gas it takes to get out there." Colson chimed in as he leaned back biting a piece of fish off the stick he'd used to cook it. "Go on kid, you want to be a part of this team, you answer the question."

"Bryce, you don't…" Filly began.

"Filly shut up and let him answer. That's an order." Colson called his voice sharp and pointed.

"She wouldn't do that." Bryce said, sitting up.

"You're sure about that? From what I've heard she's a snake who went around our back and basically told Unity where to find our base in the Appalachians." Colson said prodding.

"She made a mistake, I'm sure you have NEVER made one yourself, right? You're always perfect?" Bryce called back his temper, getting the best of him.

"I know better than to send a letter to my Daddy telling him I'm okay and that my little boyfriend and I are safe with people who are hiding us in a freaking mountain." Colson snapped back in a mocking tone, as Mateo 'oou'd' and 'ahh'd' at his comments.

"What is your problem with me?" Bryce called back frustrated.

"My problem with you is that you have gotten dozens of good people killed while you played make believe as someone being chased and hunted, while all those who have helped you have gotten killed. And personally, I don't trust you enough to carry my laundry let alone be a member of my team who I need to rely on to have my back and not freeze when bullets are flying because frankly, I'm not impressed with what I've seen so far." Colson said standing up and walking around to Bryce.

Without a second thought Bryce stood up and faced the man. "I didn't choose to be wrapped up in all of this. I was living a normal life before Unity killed my whole family and left me to try to figure out what was going on. Until they showed up to my house and set it on fire while I was inside. I didn't even know who Unity was. Who I was. So, if you have a problem with how I have handled everything, please feel free to screw right off and leave me alone." Bryce said, his chest pressing into Colson's.

"Shhhhhh!" LJ whispered as he glanced around the trees. "They are here."

"Who's here?" Bryce asked as he glanced around.

"Shhhhh! Los Guardianes." LJ said, slipping the Spanish word into his sentence. Bryce strained his ears to listen. But all he heard was the sound of howler monkeys similar to the ones around the headquarters. He listened closely as he stood still, trying to filter out the sound of the fire. Then he heard it, something about the sound of the monkeys wasn't quite right. It wasn't like the sound he'd heard the last few weeks as he fell asleep in his room. Something about the monkey calls wasn't right. Just as he'd made this realization, he heard the sound getting closer and slowly surrounding him.

"Filly, they're close enough, do your thing." Colson whispered as he slowly crouched, yanking Bryce downwards as he did. Bryce stumbled but caught himself as he crouched down beside Colson. On cue, Filly began to wave her hands around, making the fire dance and move before she pulled a large ball of flames out of the fire and danced it around the camp. Bryce watched as the fireball slipped between trees, dodged rocks and moved around the camp. Then he saw them, the things LJ had called Los Guardianes. A man with black paint around the upper half of his face stood in the forest behind a tree, he was naked save for a loincloth made of vines and leaves, in his hand was a large wooden bow with an arrow that had to be seven feet long at least. Bryce's blood ran cold as he stared at the man who was maybe twenty-five feet from him. Frozen in fear Bryce tried his best to keep his breath steady as the fireball circled the camp illuminating several other men who looked similar to the first man with various bows, clubs and spears. As Filly finished the display of her power and returned the fireball to the original spot, Bryce listened as the darkness and the sound of the monkeys echoed around him, slowly getting farther and farther from him. Bryce then watched as Colson stood up and returned to his spot at the opposite side of the fire.

"They're not going to hurt you kid; you can return to your seat." Mateo chirped as he returned to his spot and continued to cook another piece of fish.

"Who was that?" Bryce whispered as he slowly turned around and sat back in his original spot.

"Los Guardianes, they're the protectors of the village." LJ said his voice was quieter and softer than previously.

"What do you mean?" Bryce asked in a whisper, still listening intently to the sound of the forest.

"A long time ago our people found themselves here, looking for somewhere to live, far away from Unity. That's when they came across the first tribes. At first, they fought, but when the elders of the tribes realized what your people could do, they welcomed them into their society. And soon we began mating with them, that's how the first Madzi were made. They were able to use the river to their advantage, carving out cities deep in the jungle, building water systems and farms. As the years went by the tribes made a deal with the Atlantians, we helped them build cities deep in the jungle and helped them fight off the colonizers, and in turn they protected us. At all times, that city back there is surrounded by Los Guardianes who use the forest as she was intended to be. And in turn when they need us, we help them, with water, fire, and earth moving, building, and protecting. That city was actually the last Atlantian city, you may have heard it called El Dorado or the Lost city of Z." LJ explained his soft voice as he spoke quietly and quickly.

"So, you're telling me, that city was the last city of Atlantis?" Bryce asked, confused.

"No kid, it's not, Atlantis is what we left. What my man over there is trying to say is that the city you were just in, the one in the middle of the

The Atlantian Chronicles

jungle, so far in that we have to take an underground tunnel for over an hour is El Dorado. The city of gold, the place that all those explorers from Spain, England, France and everyone in 'The Pirates of the Caribbean' wanted to find. Congratulations, you have now been somewhere no one but Atlantians can go." Mateo said inspecting his fish before he took it off his stick and flung it into the river. "Dang burnt it. Filly, can you?" He continued gesturing for Filly to cook him a piece of fish. She nodded back and began preparing a piece for him.

"Wait. So those guys?" Bryce said his mind still processing.

"Yeah, they kill anyone who can't do what I did, well they will also accept a display from a Madzi, but the fire typically works best. Learned that the hard way a few times." Filly said waving a hand in front of her and cooking the fish quicker.

"What do you mean the hard way?" Bryce asked, already aware of what the answer would be.

"Well, if you can change your appearance that's all well and good but those guys don't get close enough to see that, and water doesn't make a good display in the darkness of the forest, going invisible can work but again it's tough to prove at night. Best thing is to have someone who can do what I did. And well you're the first Crono who I've heard of, so I am assuming they would've killed you before you even realized they were here." Filly explained as she finished cooking the fish and passed it around the fire to Mateo.

"Okay." Bryce said softly sinking into his seat more. A wave of fear washing over him once more.

"We should get some rest. Boat leaves early tomorrow." Colson said ending all conversation as he walked to his hammock, climbed in and pulled his bug net over himself. Everyone followed suit quickly. And once everyone had entered their hammocks Bryce watched as the fire quickly snuffed itself out, the sound of rushing water filling the air as Bryce stared off into the darkness, his mind fighting off the fear he was being watched by the man he'd seen just moments earlier.

Bryce barely slept that night and by the time he did doze off it felt as though he blinked before he was shaken awake by LJ. The heat of the early morning hitting him as he slipped out of his hammock. "Come on Mister Bryce, we are leaving." LJ said his voice was far more cheerful than it had been after the run in with The Guardians. Bryce glanced around as he packed up his hammock and helped tear down camp. "It is okay Mister Bryce; they are not here anymore." LJ whispered as he caught Bryce glancing around the forest.

"I know. Thanks LJ." Bryce replied softly patting the shorter man on the shoulder.

"Good, I don't like them either. They creep me out." He whispered back as he helped Bryce load the last bag onto the boat and climbed into the driver seat.

The next three days were like the first, eight hours of driving the river, a nightly display of the fire when the monkey sounds returned and then a night of fear, sleep only coming when Bryce's hammock finally rocked him there. When the group finally left the jungle and made it to the airstrip Bryce wanted nothing more than a long flight he could sleep on, no matter how uncomfortable the seats were, he was going to sleep, as far away from The Guardians as possible.

Chapter 21

Bryce was surprised when they approached the airstrip. The large dirt runway was surely easily spotted from the sky, large portions of the jungle had been carved away to make this structure and it seemed to Bryce like it was an ongoing fight as he saw a pile of branches and shrubbery just behind a white two story building that looked as though it was half house half air traffic control tower. As the group approached the building, LJ said his goodbyes and ran into the building that Bryce presumed would be for preparing for the flight and calling back to Atlas to report their successful arrival to the airfield. Bryce helped carry the bags onto the back of an older looking military plane he assumed was used in the early 1970s.

"Pretty cool right?" Mateo asked as they approached the plane. "Old smuggler's plane, actually this whole place is an old cartel's, like Escobar's stuff. So, freaking cool, it never gets old." He exclaimed as he threw his bags into the main part of the plane and claimed a small section of the seats that ran the length of it.

Bryce agreed, placing his bags beside Mateo's and claiming his own section of seating across the plane, and using his pack as a pillow.

"Hope you don't think you're sleeping this entire flight kid. We've got prep once we reach cruising altitude." Colson said, walking past Bryce to a seat closer to the cockpit.

"Of course we do, how long is the flight?" Bryce sighed, shifting to a more upright position.

"Eight hours and change." Colson said roughly his voice was quickly becoming something Bryce hated to hear.

"And we're spending all that time prepping?" Bryce asked sarcastically.

"If I say we are then we are." Colson chimed back a stern look on his face.

"Understood. Let me know when prep begins." Bryce said back, buckling himself into his seat and watching as Filly took up a similar position to Mateo on Bryce's side of the plane.

With a loud knock on the wall he shared with the cockpit, Colson shifted in his seat and buckled himself in. Bryce watched as the plane's loading doors slowly closed. And a few moments later he felt the plane gaining speed, the force pushing him sideways slightly in his seat as the plane took off from the ground. The sound of the engines muffled much of the noise inside the plane. Bryce watched as Filly and Mateo slept and Colson glanced around the plane. Eventually Bryce felt the plane level out and watched as Colson unbuckled himself and walked to a large duffle bag. Unzipping it he pulled out a small folder and returned to his seat opening it and leafing through several pages. "What are you looking at kid?" Colson asked as he read a page.

"Just waiting to do the prep you mentioned." Bryce replied smugly.

"How about you sleep and I will wake you when it's time." Colson said his tone unchanging as he continued to read.

With a smug smile, Bryce stretched out and tried to get as comfortable as possible. Before he quickly fell asleep. It felt as though no time had passed, but when Filly shook Bryce awake, he could tell he'd slept for hours, judging by the lack of sunlight he figured it was at least seven o'clock.

"Care to join us sleeping beauty?" Colson called over as Bryce groggily glanced around the plane, locating the source of the sound. Sitting up he rubbed his eyes and face and smoothed his hair out before walking over to the trio who sat by the cockpit looking over the folder Colson had before. Bryce sat beside Filly who handed him a water bottle, which he quickly took and began drinking. "Now that the kid has joined us, we can start." Colson began shooting Bryce a look and tilting the folder more so Bryce could somewhat see the pages. "Should be a quick one in and out, we enter here." He said pointing to a spot on a small map of the prison. "Then we make our way down to the fence here, cut our way in, and then enter the prison here. We should arrive at a time when they are out of their cells and in the main area. Mateo you're on crowd control, there are going to be a lot of people trying to get on this chopper, but we can only take those on our list, Filly you're watching the towers, take out anyone who you see. Kid, your job's the easiest and should require the least brain power. You're going to use this..." Colson began holding up a small device about the size of a small walkie-talkie with several wires wrapping around connecting to various parts of the device. "It's made to remove the collars around the prisoner's necks. If we don't get all the collars off before we leave, they can track us, and we don't want that. So, you take this go to the back of the neck of the prisoner and find the small locking device, it should look like this." Colson continued flipping the map over and pointing to a photo of a thick, metal collar that was clearly wrapped around someone's neck, on the collar there were two lights beside a small black square. "Point it here, press the button and wait, the light will go from red to green and then you can pull the collar off, it should separate just below this part and fall off. Get every collar off no matter what." He said his voice was steely calm and slightly intimidating. "Provided the kid doesn't mess it up, we will load each of the eight prisoners without a collar onto the chopper, and then take off. Put anyone who you see in a guard uniform down. They're not a prison guard just doing their job, this is a Unity run prison, they front it as a regular prison, but the guards and staff are Unity. They lie and say the collars give the prisoners the freedom to go around the prison freely when in reality it's a black site for Unity prisoners. We estimate ten percent of prisoners are actual non Atlantian inmates." Colson's voice seemed more gruff and even more raspy as he spoke. Bryce felt his heart rate increase with each sentence. His hands began sweating.

Then he felt a hand clench his, he looked up and saw Filly who slyly shot him a look. Without saying a word Bryce knew Filly was saying, "Calm down you'll be fine, I have your back." With a deep breath Bryce continued to listen as Colson laid out the rest of the plan, where they would evacuate and what happened once they'd left the prison grounds. Bryce felt as if he were going to throw up as he sat there. From time to time he would glance over to Filly -for reassurance- who would nod to him, and it was as if each time they repeated this ritual a weight was lifted from him. He couldn't understand why but he felt comfort in her presence.

When Colson finished his brief, he nodded to everyone, closed his folder and headed over to the back of the plane sitting down on the last seat away from the others. Bryce returned to his makeshift bed and after receiving one more glance from Filly nodded and laid down, going over the plan again and again in his head. "Repetition creates a habit, a habit creates a skill, a skill produces results." Bryce whispered to himself as he laid out pretending to be calm as he prepared for what would be the most dangerous thing he'd ever done. *He wasn't a soldier, he wasn't a trained killer, he wasn't even a senior in high school, and he was expected to carry a gun and if necessary, use it? His hands began to feel clammy again. He'd shot guns plenty of times, he'd fought Unity and most likely killed or at least severely injured several men but that was in the heat of the moment, this was different, what if he froze, it wasn't just his life, what if he missed a shot and a guard killed Filly, or Mateo, hell, even Colson, he'd blame himself forever. These people were here because of him, because of his trip with Bennett into town, because he chose to try and be a good boyfriend, Rhys, Anton, Michael, Taylor, Amelia, Grayson, and Bennett, all these people were either dead or trapped in a prison because of him and his choices.* Bryce began to spiral his mind running away with the thought of all the people he failed, hurt, caused pain, and loved who would have been better off without him. Just as Bryce felt his heart rate rising, his breath becoming heavy and his chest tight, he was interrupted.

"Hey kid?" Filly said, sitting at Bryce's feet and giving him a nudge.

"Yeah?" Bryce said shakily.

"This is normal. First time in the thick of it, everyone gets anxious. Freak out now, but when we land, you need to take all of those emotions, all the fear, anxiety and stress, ball it up and shove it so far down that you can't find it no matter how hard to look. We need you to focus and do what we are here to do." Filly said, looking straight into Bryce's eyes her gaze unwavering.

"Easier said than done." He replied, fighting back tears, a lump the size of a golf ball filling his throat.

"If it was easy everyone would do this job, but it's not and like it or not you wanted this so cowboy up and get ready." Filly said, squeezing him one more time and then standing up before Bryce could reply. She then walked over to the pile of gear in the middle and pulled a backpack out of it. Bryce stared at her for a moment, his mind turning over what she said on repeat. Without realizing it, his anxiety slowly faded and soon he found himself just staring at Filly. He couldn't place it but somehow, she understood exactly what to do or say to calm him down.

"Twenty minutes until touch down." A voice came across the intercom and snapped Bryce out of his mindless observation.

CHAPTER 22

The flight touched down and within minutes Bryce and the rest of the group had deplaned, unpacked their gear, dividing it up amongst themselves into their individual kits. Bryce dressed quickly, sliding into his plate carrier and tightening it to a point where it felt snug but like he could move without restriction. He then checked his gun, and placed it in the thigh holster he had, counted his magazines- he had four including the one in his gun- and a knife he tucked into a sheath on his left hip. Filly quickly checked him over and after tightening his leg holster slightly she seemed content with his kit and gave him a nod.

Once everyone had checked over each other, the four made their way to a helicopter Bryce couldn't identify, but figured was one repurposed from the military made for carrying troops into and out of battlefields. The black metal sides and sleek but large design looked similar to that of ones he'd seen through playing various military themed video games growing up. With a deep breath he boarded the helicopter first and sat in the seat closest to the door and within minutes the short flight began.

Bryce looked around as they flew, his eyes scanning each of the well-armed soldiers who sat near him. All were wearing black fatigues similar to his with a black plate carrier, their various weapons made him feel as if he was bringing a sling shot to a gunfight with his Sig Sauer P226 pistol. Filly had a marksman rifle version of an AR15, Mateo had a drum magazine version of an AR15, and Colson had an AR15 modified to suit both close and medium range filling in the gaps left by Filly and Mateo's weapons. Bryce felt like the odd one out but trusted his pistol shooting far more than his ability to use a rifle. Rhys and then Grayson had taught him pistol techniques far more than they had rifle ones.

Bryce didn't have long to inspect his comrades before the helicopter touched down and they quickly exited the helicopter in a small, wooded clearing. "We will signal you when we are ready, stay in the air just outside of the prison." Colson shouted to the pilot as Filly and Mateo scanned the area, their guns sweeping across the landscape searching for any threats. With a nod Colson left the helicopter, and it slowly floated up out of the clearing and back into the sky.

"Prison is one click out, let's get moving. Kid, stay close and don't slow us down." Colson said, looking at Bryce and then gesturing towards the tree line. The group set out at a pace that felt as if Bryce was back running with Rhys. He managed to keep pace as they weaved through the forest dodging trees and rocks moving quickly through the rough terrain. It wasn't long before their pace slowed and Bryce could see off in the distance a large fenced in building, with an open yard, area surrounding it. A large double layered fence with guard towers and razor wire encircled the compound. The treeline was at least two hundred yards from the first fence. Any attempt to get close would leave them as sitting ducks. "Filly, find a covering position and ensure the towers are clear." Colson barked as he scanned the fence looking for the best course of action. Then just as Bryce began to fear there was no way to achieve their goal, Colson vanished.

It took Bryce a moment or two before he realized Colson was an Absens! Momentarily stunned by this new revelation Bryce stared unaware of how visible he might be. Then with a violent jerk Mateo pulled Bryce down to the floor. "What are you doing kid? Stay down." Mateo whispered his voice both harsh and stern. Bryce replied with an embarrassed nod and remained as low as he could, allowing the foliage to absorb him. It was then that he heard the first shot. Bryce's attention snapped to the fence first scanning it to see any sign of Colson, then it dawned on him, his eyes immediately moved to the closest guard towers. That was when the second shot rang out. Then a third. When the fourth shot sounded, Bryce saw the guard stumble backwards before falling out of the tower onto the ground below. Filly had fired four shots and killed at least one guard, but judging on the lack of movement or reaction from Mateo Bryce, figured the more likely body count was four.

A lump swelled in Bryce's throat for a moment before he swallowed hard and choked back his ever-growing nervous energy. He was stuck waiting, hoping that Colson could get the fence cut, then that he could make the run to the fence and into the prison yard. His pulse raced as he waited, then he caught the glimpse of the fence moving, he rubbed his eyes and strained hard trying to make sure what he was seeing was right, then he saw it again, and again. Slowly but surely the fence was being clipped away and a small hole began to form. Bryce watched amazed as Colson clipped more and more of a hole into the chain link fence.

"Get ready kid, we're going to make a break for it when Colson moves to the second fence. Run as hard as you can and don't stop no matter what, we're sitting ducks until we get to the fence and into the area between the first and second fence." Mateo said tightening the sling his weapon was in and adjusting his plate carrier slightly. Bryce's pulse raced as he watched Mateo stand up and back up several steps. Then like he was fired out of a gun he took off at a full sprint. Bryce was surprised by the speed of Mateo as he made his way across the clearing quickly. Bryce scrambled to his feet and took off at a full sprint with his pistol in one hand. Bryce felt the world slow and the all too familiar feeling of his power kicked in, the sound drained from the world as Bryce watched the once fast Mateo slow to a near stop. To all those but Bryce it was as if he scrambled to his feet, took two strides and then disappeared into a blur only to appear at the fence line a moment later.

Bryce slowed just before the fence and within a moment was through the hole taking cover against the small concrete wall the second fence was built upon. As the sound returned to Bryce's ears and the world sped up Bryce watched as Mateo crashed through the hole and slammed into the concrete harder than he had.

"Wow kid, that was impressive." Mateo huffed as the stocky man caught his breath.

"Thanks." Bryce huffed back taking a deep breath and trying to return his breathing to a normal rate. Bryce watched as a small way down the fence line another hole appeared. Link by link Bryce watched an invisible Colson opening another hole this time into the prison yard. As he watched the last part of the fence open, he heard a thud off in the opposite direction.

His eyes immediately snapped to the slumping body of another guard he could only assume Filly killed. She was an incredible shot and an even better lookout.

Bryce watched as Colson reappeared on the other side of the fence, his gun up as he gestured to Mateo and Bryce to move up. "Okay kid, count to forty then throw this smoke, it'll signal both Filly and the chopper to come to us, keep an eye out for any other guards and do not let them get through that door." Colson said, pointing to a white scuffed metal door that appeared to be an entrance into the facility. He threw Bryce a silver canister smoke grenade. "Mateo and I will round up the prisoners and then when the chopper is here, we will bring them out, help each one of the people get the collar off and onto the chopper, then we get the heck out of here, copy?" Colson commanded as he scanned the area.

"Copy." Bryce replied readjusting his gun in his hand after he took the smoke grenade from Colson and placed it in a pouch on his vest.

With that, Colson and Mateo made their way to the door Bryce in tow. Without a second look, Mateo gripped the door and flung it open, raising his gun as he entered the building with Colson right behind him. Bryce began his count, each second his eyes moved around the open areas looking for any sign of another guard. By the time Bryce reached twenty he hadn't seen a soul, then thirty came and went, at forty Bryce gripped the grenade in his hand, looping it's ring around his finger he paused then as if something out of a movie, he pulled the pin and threw the smoke grenade into the large open area Colson had pointed to.

He waited his gun up, his eyes moving from side-to-side scanning, looking for anything. But nothing came, except the sound of the approaching helicopter, then the wind picked up, smoke and dust filling the air. A few moments after that the helicopter began its descent, Bryce watching as Filly jogged over to him with a nod, raising her rifle high watching closely.

It felt too easy. Maybe inside was more of a fight? Bryce thought as he waited. Then an explosion rang out from inside the building. After that, the first person exited the building. Bryce quickly turned his gun raised. But when he saw the light blue jumpsuit and collar, he quickly lowered it. Reaching for the device at his waist Bryce gestured for the prisoner to come to him. It took a few moments for Bryce to figure out how to get the collar off but when he did the man hugged him tightly. Bryce tried to remove the man's grip, but it was no use, the bald man was not letting go. "Get to the helicopter!" Bryce yelled into the man's ear as the sound of the whirling blades filled the air with a cacophony of sound. Peeling free Bryce pointed to the helicopter with his finger the rest of his hand holding the device. With a nod of understanding the man ran to the helicopter and climbed in. Slowly, person by person, Bryce removed the collar and pointed them to the vehicle.

By the time Bryce laid eyes on the first person he knew from the camp a wave of relief washed over him. Michael emerged from the door, shielding his eyes from the sun. He looked thinner as if he'd barely eaten since he'd gotten there, but there was no mistaking it, this thinner, battered, bruised, and rough looking person was once the cheerful, boisterous and funny Michael. The pair hugged tightly for a moment overtaken with the emotion, but soon Bryce's focus returned, and he quickly unlocked the collar. With another quick embrace Bryce pointed to the chopper and Michael nodded, turning around once he clambered into the helicopter, waiting for what Bryce could only assume was the same thing as him, Taylor and Bennett.

As Bryce waited, he watched another familiar face exit, but it wasn't Taylor or Bennett, it was Grayson. Shocked slightly Bryce blinked, unable to believe his eyes, he was sure they would have killed Grayson and Amelia. But as Grayson grabbed Bryce he snapped back once again. Quickly he popped off the collar and Grayson nodded in thanks before moving quickly to the helicopter. Bryce turned and did a quick head count, five people were now in the chopper, just Taylor, Amelia and Bennett were left. His heart couldn't help but race. He missed Bennett, he was hurt that her letter led to all of this, and he knew a conversation would have to be had, but he had been sick to death thinking of how, because of him, she was involved in all of this.

Taylor emerged next and the two exchanged a hug as he was unlocked from the collar Bryce waiting on bated breath for her to come out soon, he'd get her out of here, get her safe and then they'd figure out everything else. The anger, heartache, and everything dealing with all that awaited them would come. But not until she was safe. As Bryce waited, the seconds felt like hours. Then he saw it, the door swung open, then his heart sank. Colson and Mateo emerged, their guns pointed at the door, dirt and debris covered them from what Bryce assumed was a full-on firefight inside.

"That's everyone, let's go." Colson shouted through his radio to the group.

"What about Bennett? And Amelia?" Bryce screamed back. As Colson pushed him towards the helicopter.

"Amelia got hit, shot in the head with a stray. She's gone. As for the girl, I'll explain on the chopper." Colson shouted as he forced Bryce onto the slowly rising helicopter.

"Tell me now!" Bryce shouted back, shrugging off Colson's grip as he spoke.

"Now is not the time to argue! Get on the freaking chopper." Filly yelled as she shoved Bryce with her rifle. Bryce stumbled forward landing hard into the edge of the vehicle and reluctantly climbed on.

"Fine. I'm on. Now where is Bennett?" Bryce called back looking at the group of people before him. But no one spoke. "Someone tell me!" Bryce said standing up in the chopper holding the door frame to steady himself.

"Bryce, she's one of them. She was only here a few days before she was released. They walked her right out of here. Taylor and I heard it from one of the guards." Michael said, stepping forward and embracing Bryce who stood dumbfounded in utter shock.

"That's... im... impossible... she wouldn't... she couldn't..." Bryce choked as he spoke, the uneasy movement of the raising helicopter only making his shaky legs feel even worse.

"Well kid, now you know the truth. She was a traitor, and you fell for it." Colson said, removing Michael from Bryce as he stood by the open chopper door alone. "Makes this next part much easier. Sorry about this but Atlas made a deal." He said as he lifted his right foot up and in one quick motion kicked Bryce hard in the center of his chest.

Before Bryce could even react, he was falling, his body launched out of the floating chopper as it rose. Helpless, he fell backwards as he watched his escape plan fly away, the last thing he saw was Mateo restraining Michael and Taylor, as Colson slid the black side door of the chopper closed. Then he landed flat on his back, the impact sending a shock through his core. The nearly twelve-foot drop onto hard, compacted grass radiated pain through his entire body. Then as if the pain wasn't bad enough everything faded to black.

CHAPTER 23

The cold splash of water woke Bryce from his pain induced slumber. The cold-water chilled Bryce as his clothes stuck to his skin and the water dripped down his face. Groggily he tried to wipe the hair and water from his face but quickly noticed his hands would not move. With his eyes drifting in and out of focus Bryce tried to look around and survey his surroundings, but alas it was no use. After a few moments a familiar voice cut through the silence.

"Bryce Hillcrest, as I live and breathe. How have you been?" The voice said from behind him.

"Who are you? Where am I?" Bryce muttered his brain still struggling to piece together all that had happened.

"Oh Bryce, you don't remember me? I'm hurt." The voice said as it drew closer to Bryce. "I know it's been a few months since we last spoke, but I'd like to think I had a slight impact on you and your life." The voice said softly as it reached Bryce's ear, and a gloved hand touched his shoulder. "Let me remind you." The voice said as the chair spun around the metal legs screeching on the wet concrete floor. And there he stood, Dixon, the handsome man from when Bennett, Bryce and the twins were captured by Unity in Chicago. When Dixon saw the realization on Bryce's face his wicked smile spread. "So, you do remember me?" Dixon said his smile not faltering for a moment.

"Screw you." Bryce spat as his body began to shiver from the cold water still sliding down him.

"Oh, now that isn't nice Bryce." Dixon began. "I'm trying to do this nicely but if you want to, I can start with the stick rather than the carrot." He stepped sideways and motioned to a table full of various tools, blades, and syringes set up to look even more menacing than they would just sitting on the table. "So, carrot then?" He chuckled as he watched Bryce's eyes scan the table.

"What do you want?" Bryce asked, his eyes locked on the pair of pliers that looked far rustier than anything else on the table. *Or was it dried blood?*

"Well, it's not as much me as Unity, but it's simple. We want to know how to get to the headquarters of the Atlantian Brotherhood. Tell me that and I will let you live out your days here in this prison free of pain and suffering." Dixon smiled stepping back into Bryce's eyeline, blocking the view of all the torture instruments.

"Why are you working for Unity? They literally kill your kind every day, without remorse, and you're just helping them do it." Bryce replied his curiosity getting the better of him.

"Bryce, you have been 'drinking the Kool-Aid' far too much. Unity isn't the big bad guy you think they are. We're just leveling the playing field. The Atlantian Brotherhood are the real villains here." Dixon said, walking over to the table and picking up a knife and spinning the point in his forefinger.

"Ha. That's rich coming from the guy literally about to torture me." Bryce sneered back.

"The Brotherhood has tortured just as many people; you just aren't privy to it." Dixon replied, placing the knife back onto the table and picking up the pliers. "You know, I've found it's best to explain what I'm going to do if you don't comply before I actually do it, give you one last chance to comply before the actual pain begins. So here goes. I'll ask you one last time, and if you don't answer with exactly what I want to know... I'll clamp this to the side of your left nostril and rip it down. It'll feel like fire tearing through your face- but in the end- no real damage. Just pain. If after that, you're still holding out like all you brainwashed morons do, I'll switch to the right side and do it all over again. But soon we get into the gruesome stuff, I'll pull teeth, beat you, inject pure capsaicin into your blood. That will really suck, that stuff is what makes peppers hot, do you have any idea how painful that will be in your blood? It'll literally feel as if your entire circulatory system is burning as well as a pain increasing agent just to really make it all tickle. Finally, if nothing else works, I'm going to pull off each of your finger nails. If you still won't talk after all of that, well let's just say I start hurting other people. People you love, people who should have never been involved in this brutal business." Dixon smiled as he saw Bryce's eyes widen with the idea of all that laid in front of him. "So... I will ask again. Bryce, how do we get to the Brotherhood's headquarters?"

"You say I'm 'drinking the Kool-Aid' but then sit there and lie about the Brotherhood like you know them? You're a joke." Bryce replied, readying himself for the pain promised.

"Oh Bryce, I was hoping you'd pick the stick. It's so much more fun breaking the spirits of dimwitted kids like yourself." Dixon said, pushing off of the table the pliers in his hand and grabbing Bryce's head as he struggled trying to dodge the incoming pliers before they locked onto the side of his nostril and clamped on tight, the pain shooting through Bryce's head. "Bryce, you realize you're protecting a man who literally traded you to us right? Atlas made a deal, think about who just left, all for you, and you're going to sit here and defend them? Call me a joke? When you sit here going through pain for what? Your pride in being an Atlantian? You've been one for all of six months and you have this pride for a group of people who a year ago meant nothing to you. Remember that while you suffer through every bit of pain I am about to unleash onto you." Dixon whispered as he began slowly pulling the pliers out of Bryce's nose. The pain was like nothing Bryce had ever felt before, it radiated out as he screamed, his eyes watering as the smell of blood filled his nose. Eventually the pliers broke free, and the pain subsided.

"Atlas wouldn't trade me, what would he even get out of it, I'm a symbol for him. It was all Colson." Bryce spat back as blood dripped from his nostril onto his sopping wet pants. Vanishing into the black fabric.

"No Bryce, Colson did as he was told, by Atlas. He makes deals with Unity constantly how do you think he got information about this place, it wasn't some amazing spy craft he managed, the man is a terrorist leader living in some hidden hole playing with house money and the lives of people he convinced to follow him for no other reason than some that two thousand plus years ago they shared a relative. Hell, even the gun you had was useless, we checked, it had no firing pin, so even if you were able to recover from your fall, you wouldn't have been able to do anything with the paperweight you called a gun. You see how idiotic that sounds now don't you?" Dixon said his smile fading as a twinge of anger spread across his face. "Now cut the crap and tell me how to get to the headquarters." Dixon said, switching the pliers to his other hand and moving towards Bryce's face.

"One person's terrorist is another person's freedom fighter." Bryce said, tilting his head back and presenting his nose to Dixon defiantly.

"You really are Rhys's kid." Dixon muttered as he repeated the process, clamping down on Bryce's nostril and slowly pulling until the pliers gave way. Again, the pain was excruciating but Bryce bared down and took it.

"Don't ever talk about my Dad, you piece of garbage." Bryce spat back his voice hoarse from screaming, his teeth hurting from biting down on them as he took the pain.

"You don't even know your Dad. Rhys kidnapped you after your stupid mother got herself killed. You idiot." Dixon chirped back as he set down the pliers and looked at the table of tools.

"He taught me enough to know that the only idiot here is people like you following a group out to kill their own kind." Bryce said with a smile coming across his face now. Just before the all too familiar feeling of a fist connecting with his jaw wiped it from his face. Dixon followed his first strike up with a second, then a third and a fourth. Bryce's nose and mouth began to bleed heavily, his lips split from the punches.

"You stupid child. You know nothing." Dixon said frustrated. "Atlas leads a group of cult followers he's brainwashed to follow his teachings. All so he can feel important while he removes anyone who would actually challenge him for his position. God, you are so dumb, and you don't even know it. There's no escape for you, this is your new home, your new life and eventually your tomb, you don't get to leave here, no one is coming for you." Dixon said wiping his hair from his face before he began another onslaught of punches, hitting Bryce not only in the face, but the chest, and abdomen, making Bryce quickly realize the fall from the helicopter definitely left some lasting damage to his ribs.

Each punch felt harder and harder as Bryce's face swelled up, soon his eyes began to puff up and shut, it was only then that Dixon stopped. Out of breath and his gloves covered in Bryce's blood. "Oh boy, I got carried away there, sorry about that. I'm sure you don't mind too much." He said taking a deep breath and placing a hand on Bryce's shoulder. "Well, we both made mistakes today, but I promise if you tell me what I want to know I will get you the best pain killers we have, because believe me that will hurt a lot more in a few minutes." Dixon said as Bryce watched him barely visible through his swollen cheeks and eyes.

"You should stop lifting your foot on your cross, it'll help you generate more power." Bryce said softly through his bloody lips as he let the blood slowly drip out of his mouth onto his chest and legs.

"Thanks, I'll keep that in mind. But that isn't the answer I asked for, so I'm going to give you one last chance, then if you don't tell me what I want to know, I'm going to make you feel pain like you have never felt before." Dixon threatened as he walked out of Bryce's eyesight and picked up two syringes. "These are chemicals that will intensify your pain. I could go into the long nerdy explanation as to what exactly they are, how they're enzymes we synthesize in the lab specifically for people who are about to experience large amounts of pain. How they make it ten times worse and can actually lead to people begging for death just to end the suffering, but instead, I will just tell you this first one will make all the pain you're in far worse, and the second one is that capsaicin I told you about. Now Bryce one last time, how do we get to the headquarters?" Dixon asked, his voice softening as he slowly set up Bryce for the first injection, finding a vein, inserting an IV, and then sliding the needle into the port, his finger on the plunger.

"Ask Atlas since you guys are best friends." Bryce said his face began to throb from the beating.

"Well…" Dixon sighed heavily. "Enjoy these next few hours, when you're ready I'll come back, and we can try again. Try not to die for me." Dixon said as he pressed down the first plunger. The liquid entered Bryce's blood and after a few seconds the pain in Bryce's body amplified, his ribs felt as if they were stabbing through his skin, his back felt as if he'd fallen from ninety feet, his face as if he had broken every bone, then he felt the second liquid enter his blood, it felt as if his whole body was on fire. He writhed in pain as he tried to escape his bindings. Bryce heard the door slam shut as he screamed, his eyes filling with tears which felt like acid as they rolled down his bruised and swollen face.

For the next hour Bryce felt as if he was being burned alive, his body feeling as if his heart was pumping acid throughout it, the capsaicin burning his body, then the pain of the beatings kicked in, that lasted for another three hours until it slowly faded, Bryce's heart, voice and teeth were the last points of pain to leave as he screamed and bit down on his teeth as the pain wretched his body with no escape. By the time it finally ended Bryce was exhausted and as the darkness slowly creeped in, he welcomed it, his body spent from the torturous few hours it spent awake.

Bryce awoke sometime later, in a bed, both his hands cuffed to the bed frame, his legs strapped down and a needle in his arm. Bryce tried to move but couldn't. His body felt numb, whatever they were giving him felt good, but his thoughts felt disjointed, fuzzy and as if he couldn't string together a full thought. "Bryce, oh my God you're okay!" A familiar voice filled the air. "I thought it would be hours before you woke up." Bennett said as she came into view.

"Bennett?" Bryce whispered, his throat dry and raspy.

"Yeah, it's me, here, here drink." She said, grabbing a Styrofoam cup with a straw, and placing the straw in his mouth. Bryce sucked and the cold refreshing feeling of water filled his mouth and throat as he sipped mouthfuls of the liquid. "I'm so glad you're alive. I was worried when you got grabbed from the cars." Bennett said as Bryce strained to focus on her, as confusion and anger filled him.

"Why are you here?" Bryce asked, slurring his words as he spoke, the medication making his speech delayed.

"Bryce, they helped me, I was hurt, and they saved me, then they explained how things really are, the Brotherhood lied to us, Unity isn't bad they want to help the Atlantians they want to make humans just like Atlantians and you can help." Bennett replied, taking Bryce's cuffed hand in hers. "They want to understand why Atlantians can do the things they can and want to use that information to usher in a new level of prosperity. They're helping everyone can't you see?" Bennett continued her voice sounding different than Bryce remembered, it had been almost three months since Bryce had seen her, but he could swear something was off.

"Bennett, are you okay?" Bryce asked as he fought off the drugs trying to focus.

"Am I okay? Silly, are you okay? You've been through a lot, but you're safe now, and they said if you work with them, they'll let us go soon." She said taking Bryce's water and letting him get another sip of the cold liquid.

"Bennett, what did I get you for Christmas?" Bryce asked softly.

"Christmas? What does that have to do with anything?" Bennett replied, her voice shifting to a higher tone as she spoke.

"Just answer, please it's important, then I'll tell you anything you want to know." Bryce said softly, unable to think straight as he spoke.

"You got me a teddy bear, but I lost it in the attack on the camp. It was so nice though I loved it. I love you." She said leaning in for a kiss.

"That's right. What do they want to know?" Bryce replied, turning away from the kiss as he spoke, causing Bennett's lips to land on his cheek, the sting of it hitting his bruises lasting only a moment.

"I think they want to know about where the Brotherhood is. They said something about The Lost City of Z, right? That's in Brazil, right?" Bennett asked softly, her voice excitedly picking up pace.

"No Peru, Fawcett wasn't in Brazil he got the location wrong." Bryce replied softly, his eyes struggling to focus. "I'm getting tired Bennett." He whispered as he spoke.

"That's okay Peru, where in Peru, near the Amazon River?" Bennett asked, her voice breaking as she spoke. "You're doing great love." Bennett continued. "Just a little longer then you can sleep, and we'll get these cuffs and straps off of you."

"Okay." Bryce whispered. "What else do they want to know?" Bryce whispered, closing his eyes softly.

"Come on, love open your eyes." Bennett said, shaking Bryce slightly. Bryce opened his eyes partially and looked at her once more. "Are there any traps or defenses around the city?" She questioned as she took Bryce's face in her hand cupping his cheek.

Bryce thought hard, the image of The Guardians flashing through his drug addled mind before he spoke. "No… No, they think the forest is enough." Bryce lied. "Also, Bennett?" He asked, his voice straining.

"Yes Bryce?" She replied tenderly.

"I didn't get you a teddy bear for Christmas and you never called me love." Bryce smiled. "Screw you and screw Unity." He continued as Bennett sat back in her chair.

"You're smarter than they give you credit for." Bennett said her voice was much harsher now, then her face slowly morphed, her features changed, her hair darkened to a black that looked as if it absorbed light. Within moments a completely different person sat before him. A woman who looked at least thirty years older than Bennett, her brown eyes sported crow's feet at the side, her teeth were yellowed from years of drinking coffee, her cheekbones sharp and pointed, making her upturned nose look even more pointed and as Bryce watched her face change, her thin lips curled into an evil smile. "You know I thought we had you when you agreed to answer the questions. I assume your answers were lies then?" She asked half-heartedly.

"Maybe." Bryce shrugged.

"That's fine we'll make you talk one way or another. Oh, and obviously these pain meds stop now." She said ripping the IV out of Bryce's arm, blood spurting out of the wound as she wound up the line and stood up. "These next three hours will feel good but after that, enjoy the pain." She said leaning in for another kiss on Bryce's cheek.

"Kill yourself." Bryce snapped back softly the drugs, still making it difficult to put any real effort into speaking.

Bryce was soon taken from the hospital wing and wheeled out of the room still trapped in the bed as the lights overhead drifted by blurring together as Bryce struggled to keep his eyes open. The last thing he remembered was being dumped out of the bed onto the cold concrete floor of a cell, the heavy black metal door slamming shut after him.

Chapter 24

The woman who impersonated Bennett was right, after what felt like moments of bliss, the drugs wore off and all of the pain they blocked hit Bryce as if he had jumped head first into it. His face felt as if it would fall off at any moment, his legs, back and neck were no better, and his ribs were emitting a hot, sharp pain anytime he put pressure on his right side. Needless to say, Bryce was almost completely immobile, the pain filling his every moment with agony. He screamed again until his voice gave out begging for help, relief or something. Cursing every person, he could think of as he laid propped up against the back corner of the small cell he was in.

Over the next few weeks Bryce endured torture after torture. They starved him, beat him, deprived him of sleep and threatened him, but he didn't break. Something in his heart told him that Rhys wouldn't want him to break, so he didn't. He suffered, over and over, the end nowhere in sight, but he persevered, not for himself or for The Atlantian Brotherhood, or as a screw you to Unity but for Rhys, if Rhys protected Bryce from this life and these people for seventeen years then there had to be something Bryce was missing. So, he suffered over and over again. Unbroken and unwavering.

Bryce spent the nights in pain, his body barely holding on, sleep would come when he physically was unable to stay awake any longer or when he was knocked unconscious. That was until one day it stopped. After multiple days of him being strapped to a chair barely able to move, his blood was taken, and his head and body were scanned. Then he was treated for his wounds, fed and given a change of clothes. While this new version of hospitality was refreshing, he didn't trust it. Each meal was met with skepticism, the new prison blue jumpsuit was inspected thoroughly before he took off the rags of his former clothes and dawned what he felt would be his outfit for the rest of his life only he wasn't sure how long that would be.

After another three weeks of regular food, medical care, and relief from the other tortures Bryce began to feel as though the worst parts were over. Then the faithful day arrived, and two men entered the room, Bryce wanted to fight but feared if he did the torture would begin again. So, he didn't and much to his disappointment he was fitted with one of the same collars he had helped remove from the necks of several people just a few weeks earlier. He had come full circle, and it didn't look like it would get any better than this.

After he was fitted with his collar he was handcuffed, shackled, and handed a plastic bag with two changes of clothes and a gray blanket, fitted sheet and pillow. Then he was led down a hallway and into a new part of the prison he hadn't seen before. He was brought down long corridors and through a series of doors before he arrived in a large open area. Round metal tables filled what he assumed was a common area, and glancing around the room he realized he was in a prison pod.

"You're in 210, top floor end of the row." One of the guards said as they ushered Bryce along, leading him up two sets of concrete stairs and down a row of ten cells, people watched banging on the doors as he passed, the eyes of the other inmates watching him.

"Piece of advice kid, don't let them into your cell." The other guard chirped as the pair arrived with Bryce to the door and signaled another guard to open it. With a loud buzz the door popped open and slid to the left revealing a room with a small desk with a single plastic chair tucked into it, a small metal toilet with a sink attached and two beds, one on top of the other, a man laid on the top bunk, a book blocking his face from view.

"Meet your new cellmate." The first guard said to Bryce as he gave him a shove and signaled for the door to be sealed once more.

With another buzz and a loud mechanical locking noise Bryce watched as the guard tested the door with a pull, then walked away leaving him locked in his new forty-eight square foot home.

Bryce quickly got settled, placing his new clothes into a small cubby under his bed and made his bed up. Once he was settled, he stood up and looked at his new cellmate. "Hey, I'm Bryce." He said looking at the man who still had his nose in a book.

"Yeah, I know." The man replied from behind his book, his voice sounding very familiar.

"Do I know you?" Bryce questioned as he tried to move around to see the man behind the book.

"Probably not as good as you used to." The man said, closing his book. Then Bryce realized who it was. His new cellmate was Josiah Douglas. Bennett's father.

"Mr... Mr... Douglas... How did you..." Bryce began before he was met with a hand telling him to stop.

"I think we both know how I ended up here. I was picked up at the Japanese airport about a year ago now and I've been here ever since." He said as he fixed his glasses and adjusted his shaggy blonde hair out of his face. He swung his legs off the edge of the bed and slowly lowered himself down. He looked frail and the bruise around his eye told Bryce he didn't have it easy here.

"I'm so sorry... I never... This is my fault." Bryce mumbled hanging his head as he spoke, unable to hide his shaky voice or his feeling of guilt.

"Not here Bryce, not now." Josiah said hopping down and grabbing Bryce by the shoulders shaking him. "Don't show weakness. That's what they want. What Unity and The Atlantian Brotherhood want. They want to break us. And we can't let them."

"What do you mean The Atlantian Brotherhood?" Bryce said looking up at Josiah, anger in his eyes.

"Bryce Unity and The Brotherhood, they work together." He said looking at Bryce, their eyes meeting for the first time.

"I'm not falling for this." Bryce said, grabbing Josiah by the collar and pushing him backwards into a wall. The smaller man struggled as Bryce pressed his weight, strength and size into the man applying a simple collar choke by grabbing both sides of Josiah's collar with the opposing side's hand and twisting his hands together creating a blood choke on the man using the leverage to squeeze the carotid artery.

"Bryce… Bryce… Stop… It's me…" Josiah said kicking and struggling against the choke as he watched Bryce's cold demeanor unchanged, the choke getting tighter and tighter.

"Give me one reason why I shouldn't kill you right here and now." Bryce said through clenched teeth as he tightened his grip even further prepared to kill whoever was in front of him right now.

"In…. In…. fourth grade… you fell and… hit the door in the house…. It… it… left a scar under your chin!" Josiah choked out as Bryce stared at him.

"It's really you." Bryce said, releasing the choke and falling backwards onto the bed, covering his face in his hands. "I'm sorry it's just…" Bryce began.

"I know, they did it to me too, right when I first got here, they had one of those shapeshifters pretend to be Bennett." Josiah interrupted. "It's okay, I get it, if I'd been through what you went through, I would have reacted the same, hell, I would have done the same having been through what I went through so I couldn't imagine what you've been through." He began sitting on the plastic desk stool across from Bryce.

"What do you mean?" Bryce said, looking up at Josiah who was still a shade of red, fixing his collar as best he could.

"Well, just what I have heard through other prisoners. They don't particularly like me so very little, but I heard about the mall, and the attack on the camp, many prisoners were in here during that time, not so many now." Josiah said, hanging his head as he spoke.

"What do you mean you aren't particularly liked?" Bryce questioned.

"Bryce The Atlantian Brotherhood they aren't as good as you think they are." Josiah began. "Your father didn't tell me much about it, but he told me enough when we thought you and Bennett might be something. I must admit it made me colder to you, I wasn't trying to, but I had to think about my daughter's safety… a lot of good that did." He continued looking at his feet when mentioning how he had treated Bryce, and when Bryce thought about it, it wasn't until he started noticing Bennett that Josiah started sending her away for summers, keeping a watchful eye on them when they would spend time together and was generally far colder to Bryce.

"What did my father say to you?" Bryce blurted out. The mention of Rhys causing a small catch in his throat.

"Well, basically he told me you were going to be in danger at some point in your life, and it was better I knew about it rather than getting surprised by it when something like this happened." Josiah said, gesturing around the cell. "He said to trust Anton, if he wasn't around, and to help you if I ever had the chance to." Josiah spoke and Bryce felt a twinge of guilt thinking about how much he disliked Josiah when he was younger because he was always so harsh to Bryce. "He later spoke to me about Unity, briefly, and The Atlantian Brotherhood. It wasn't much but he spoke to me about how Unity was far more reaching than anyone knew, they've infiltrated governments, fortune five hundred companies, infrastructure we could not live without, and more importantly they did not work alone. As for The Atlantian Brotherhood, he didn't tell me much but just that they shouldn't be trusted. He didn't say why but from what I've been able to eavesdrop here, Atlas makes deals with Unity. He's also a blood purist." Josiah explained, leaning forward as he spoke trying to keep his voice as low as possible.

"A blood purist?" Bryce asked not understanding what Josiah meant.

"Yes, he believes you guys are the next step in human evolution and should be running the world under his control. He believes humans should be slaves and nothing more." He explained as Bryce sat there dumbfounded.

"But there were regular humans at the camp." Bryce blurted out.

"Yes, but what happened at the camp?" Josiah questioned.

"It was taken by Unity, because of a letter Bennett sent to you." Bryce explained matter of factly.

"No, it wasn't. Atlas made a deal; Amelia was a thorn in his side. He wanted her gone, but he couldn't take her out himself. She liked humans, and believed we could work in harmony. Atlas believes we shouldn't. But the problem is she was well liked, and everyone respected her, so when she'd challenge Atlas people backed her." Josiah explained. "Bennett never sent a letter, think about it, she's not dumb." Josiah continued sitting back, his posture becoming more upright when he spoke of Bennett.

"Yes but, Amelia was captured and brought here, she was killed in the escape." Bryce retorted back, still not believing what he was hearing.

"No Bryce, she wasn't. Yes, she was here, I even spoke to her, she was quite nice, when we had yard time, after she saw Bennett and I speak she approached me. And after Bennett was taken, she and I would walk the fence line discussing many things. She was quite smart, but she knew Bennett didn't send the letter. The general store and post office worker was a secret member who reported any suspicious people, or letters going in and coming out of that town. Then she'd check it out, follow the person, or have Samson do it. She knew Bennett didn't send the letter. Atlas sold her out. She couldn't prove it, but she knew he was working with Unity." Josiah said to Bryce whose mouth was wide open.

"Impossible, he hates Unity. Hell, they want to know how to get to the headquarters, they tortured me for the information." Bryce said, shaking his head in disbelief.

"Yes, he does, and that is true, I haven't quite figured out how he communicates with them, but I am assuming he uses a proxy of some sort, a go between, because from what I can tell no one here has ever heard of him leaving the compound once he got power." Josiah answered his hands shaking from the adrenaline dump that he was experiencing after Bryce choked him.

"But, why? Why kill your own people? Imprison them? Why make a deal for me?" Bryce said, trying to wrap his head around everything he had heard.

"Have you ever heard; the enemy of my enemy is my friend? That's why Amelia was an enemy of Atlas. When you try to run an organization with members around the world, it's hard to do, even harder when a well-respected, well liked, and strong-willed individual challenges you. Plus, Amelia had lots of secrets, and as you know Unity is more than willing to resort to enhanced interrogation techniques to get what they want. Why wouldn't you make a deal to remove a thorn in your side, give yourself a martyr and use her as an example as to the savagery of your enemy? It's a smart play on his part, Unity gives him what he wants while removing a threat to his leadership, and Unity is happy because the camp was a refugee site, a training ground and occasionally a headquarters to operations in and around the area. Plus, they removed what they thought was a big player on the Brotherhood's team. As for your other questions, I haven't really been able to glean much more from that. I don't know if you've seen my eye, but I'm sure you can tell I am not well liked. Atlas has certainly spread the rumor of Bennett betraying the camp and shortly after that, my talks with Amelia stopped when the yard time did. We spend twenty-three hours a day in our cells and the hour we get of free time typically involves several threats, attacks or both on myself. I spend my time in the library avoiding any and all issues as they nearly always refuse to talk to me." Josiah said, gesturing to his face. "People don't want to share what they know with someone they believe to be a traitor."

"I'm so sorry." Bryce said, unsure what else to say.

"It's okay." Josiah said softly back to the clearly guilt-ridden boy.

"I'll do my best to protect you." Bryce said looking up at Josiah once more, seeing the eyes he shared with Bennett. "I promise I will do what I can."

"I'm sure you will." Josiah said softly back.

CHAPTER 25

Bryce spent the rest of the night explaining what he had been through, the fight with Ashton, the escape at the mall, the airport, Anton sacrificing himself to save Bryce, the camp, and even explained the headquarters, being sure to leave out the location, but Josiah never questioned him, or pushed for the location. While Bryce didn't fully trust he wasn't another fake placed by Unity, he felt better with the lack of questioning. By the time the lights went out, both Bryce and Josiah were well acquainted with each other.

The next morning came with a loud buzzer signaling the start of the day. Bryce decided if he was going to protect Josiah he'd have to get back into a better shape. He wasn't out of shape by any means, but he'd lost muscle mass in the weeks following his capture, between the starvation, constant fear of more torture, the torture itself, and the fatigue he'd certainly lost a step, and while he spent a few weeks recovering he never trusted that he could exercise without the fear of upsetting his captors further. As such he did as many push-ups as he could- forty before his form declined- the same number of squats and then double the amount in crunches before repeating the cycle. He then did some static exercises; back exercises and any other form of bodyweight exercises the small cell allowed him to do. It wasn't much but it would ensure he kept the muscle he had and also hopefully added to it. Josiah watched Bryce before returning to the book he'd had his nose in when Bryce arrived.

Shortly after his exercises finished, Bryce watched as a hatch was opened on the cell door and two food trays were slid in. Josiah hopped down and grabbed a tray placing the second on Bryce's bed who was quickly washing his face in the sink. The pair ate and then spent the remainder of their day speaking further on their past year. Bryce again avoided the subject of the headquarters' location.

"Josiah?" Bryce said getting the man's attention as he pushed his lunch around his meal tray playing with the gray, mushy meal he could only assume carried the bare minimum nutritional value needed to maintain someone's health and not a spec more.

"Yes Bryce?" Josiah said lifting his head and setting down his plastic fork.

"I didn't believe Bennett. I'm sorry, I didn't." He apologized, this large weight sitting on his chest as he spoke, clutching at his heart as he spoke. "I knew she wanted to tell you she was okay, and I believed Dixon when he said she'd written to you. It was just so believable, he mentioned how you called her Benny, and I just believed him." Bryce said continuing to play with his food.

"It's okay Bryce, it's hard not to when you're faced with half of the story. When they first took me into custody, they walked out someone who pretended to be Bennett, spending hours with me. I stupidly didn't know someone could change their appearance, voice and body that way, and I told them everything, I'm certain they used that information to sell this lie. It's not your fault." He comforted as Bryce hung his head in shame.

"It isn't that. I should have trusted her." Bryce replied remembering how he couldn't even look in her eyes.

"It's okay Bryce. When I spoke to her on the yard…" Josiah began before Bryce cut him off.

"She's here?!" Bryce said, nearly leaping out of his seated position on his bunk.

"No, she isn't. She was here, not long, long enough for her to see me, just once. She spent the whole time talking about you. Telling me how I shouldn't blame you, how she chose to help you, and how you told her how she could leave if she wanted." Josiah said looking at Bryce who sunk back down into his seat once more.

"Do you think…" Bryce said.

"She's alive? Yes. Unity has paraded a video feed of her in front of me threatening her if I didn't tell them about what Amelia and I spoke of. So, I did." Josiah explained frankly.

"And she's okay then?" Bryce asked eagerly.

"From what I could tell, the feeds they showed me were her in a psychologist office, and another from her at school, it seemed like she was back in Broadway Hills." Josiah said, returning his view to his sad lunch.

"I promise, if I can get out of here, I will make sure she is okay." Bryce said, looking at Josiah trying to meet his gaze.

"I'm glad you said that." Josiah said quietly. "Now let's finish this awful food so I can go back to reading my book. I'm hoping to get to the library today."

With that the pair choked down their meals in silence, before Josiah returned to his bunk and Bryce listened as the man flipped pages. Bryce wanted to talk more, *ask about Bennett, or about Anton, had Josiah seen him? Was he ever here? What about Michael and Taylor? Or Grayson? Bryce spent the better part of his time thinking about how he'd gotten there, and what Josiah had said. Atlas had betrayed him, set him up? But why? Why was Unity so willing to trade so many people for him? Was it because he knew Bryce wouldn't leave without Bennett? Was it just a crime of convenience? Or was there something more to it? Tyson hunted Bryce for years, for revenge on Rhys?* It didn't add up and Bryce was only becoming more and more confused as he tried to connect the dots. He needed more information.

The days went by without incident and Bryce joined Josiah in the library where he strolled through the stacks of books. Josiah scanned the library for particular books, often looking in the non-fiction section and spending a long time there. While Bryce just glanced through the stacks settling on a thriller novel by Jack Carr the first time and the sequel when he had finished the first book. If he was going to spend hours in silence with Josiah, he might as well have something to occupy his time he thought.

The days went by like that, more and more time passed, Bryce sometimes skipping the library as he hadn't finished the book when Josiah decided to go. Bryce was astonished that he read nearly a book a day.

Bryce tried to keep to himself, the occasional Atlantian coming into the doorway of his cell often looking to torment Josiah only to find the much bigger Bryce sitting on his bunk. After a couple of weeks Bryce was getting restless.

"What book did you get today, Josie?" A deep voice called from outside of the cell. Bryce slowly lowered his book to see a large, broad shouldered, black man making his way towards their cell just after Josiah had returned from the library. Bryce stood up in a flash. Placing his book down on the table.

"Washington, could we avoid any unpleasantness today?" Josiah sighed as he lowered himself down from his bunk landing just in front of Bryce.

"I don't know Josie, can we?" The large man known as Washington replied. Bryce had heard of him, but he was in solitary confinement until that day, so the pair had never met. While Josiah stood five foot seven, one hundred and thirty-five pounds, on a good day, Washington had to be nearly six foot six and probably closer to three hundred pounds of muscle, he clearly avoided the library instead opting for working out with whatever equipment he could get his gigantic hands on.

"Washington, for the last time, I do not know what Unity is planning as I do not work for them." Josiah said, straightening himself and moving into the door frame of their cell.

"Well, what about your slut of a daughter? Is she letting every Unity worker have their way with her so her Daddy can get another book checked out?" Washington chuckled clearly trying to get a rise out of Josiah.

"Do what you must to me but leave my daughter out of this, she has done nothing wrong." Josiah said softly his voice sounding like he knew what would come next and had already come to terms with his fate.

"Why should I? It's her fault half of us are in here, had she not tried to contact you, Unity would have never found the camp." Washington replied angrily.

"Amelia told you she didn't do that." Josiah said, looking the large man in the eyes.

"Like I actually believe that. Unity probably tortured her so she'd go along with their plan and keep their mole safe so her dumb boyfriend would serve his purpose." Washington said matter of factly back to the smaller man.

"And what purpose would that be?" Bryce asked from behind Josiah.

"Leave it alone." Josiah said, glancing over his shoulder. And that was all it took, a moment of distraction and Washington pounced. Punching Josiah hard in the side of the face, his whole fist taking up more of Josiah's face than not, the force sent Josiah spilling back into Bryce who caught him and quickly switched places with him, heaving the disoriented man onto the bunk.

Bryce stared at the large man who was now entering his cell, without thinking he struck, throwing all his weight at Washington in a well-placed Muay Thai push kick, using his lead foot to drive a forward kick into the man's knee. The sound of the crunch was sickening. Seizing the opportunity Bryce let his weight fall forward loading his back leg up for a vicious knee he drove directly into Washington's solar plex, with a loud huff a look of shock went across Washington's face as he realized the athletic teenager was no normal kid. Without thinking Bryce was in a full-on attack, grabbing the kneeling man's head and driving multiple hard elbow strikes into the side of it. As he watched Washington's head bounce with each strike Bryce kept going. Soon blood was flowing out of Washington's face as Bryce followed each strike up with another. *Keep going until the enemy is unable to fight back* Rhys's advance rang through Bryce's ears as he continued his onslaught. Driving more elbows into the nearly unconscious man's head as the pair fell back into the hallway and Bryce assumed a full mount position raining down even more hard elbows making sure to not use his hands to avoid hurting them on the hard bones in the man's now rapidly swelling face.

It wasn't until Josiah regained some sense and pulled Bryce off did he stop, his jumpsuit arms stained red with blood. "Oh no what did you do?" Josiah asked worriedly.

"I did what I had to." Bryce replied.

"This is not going to end well. This has accelerated things." Josiah said as he peeled Bryce off of the limp body of Washington, a faint snoring emitting from the man's collapsed nose.

"Accelerated what?" Bryce asked, looking at Josiah who pulled him into the cell.

"We have days now, not weeks like I'd hoped." Josiah said, pushing Bryce onto the bed and waited, as a voice came onto the loud speaker and instructed all people to return to their cells immediately.

"What are you talking about?" Bryce asked, completely lost.

"This changes things." Josiah muttered to himself as he wrote symbols into the air.

"What are you talking about?" Bryce asked as he watched several guards enter and carry Washington's body out of the pod, locking down the rest of the unit following the incident.

"I'm talking about us escaping." Josiah whispered, staring at Bryce with a crazed look in his eyes.

CHAPTER 26

The pod was in lockdown for three days following Bryce's fight with Washington. Shortly after the fight Bryce sat waiting for his inevitable removal from his cell and relocation to solitary confinement as was the policy during a violent altercation. But for some reason, it never came. During the lockdown the pair heard Washington had to be medevacked to a nearby hospital. After they had concluded Bryce was going to remain in the cell, Josiah quietly laid out his plan with Bryce ensuring he knew how each part worked. Some time ago, Josiah had found that the library's history section shared a wall with the infirmary and along with that, the infirmary had a device that removed the collars in order to transport inmates who required immediate surgery. They would heavily sedate the prisoner, transport them to a hospital where they would keep the person unconscious until after their surgery at which point they would be returned to the prison and their collar would be returned to their neck.

The plan was simple, as soon as they could they would make their way to the library, where the pair would break through the hole Josiah had been making, once through they would locate the tool used to remove the collars, and after they'd gotten their collars off they would use the door and make their way quickly across the parking lot to a car where Bryce would hot-wire it and the pair would escape. Sounded easy enough to Bryce. But all plans have a way of quickly going wrong in the heat of the moment.

As soon as the doors popped open Bryce and Josiah sprinted to the guard and requested a trip to the library -it had been three days of nothing but sitting in their cells a new book was a reasonable request- with a sigh of complaint the guard radioed the request in and with a relief guard arriving, the guard escorted the pair to the library.

Once in the library Bryce and Josiah deposited their books and then as discussed slowly feigned looking through the stacks trying to ensure the guards attention was anywhere but on them when they finally made their move. When Josiah gave Bryce the signal, he quickly bolted across the library using the stacks as his cover and made it to Josiah. "Okay now we have to be quick about this." Josiah said, pulling out a piece of bent metal from the hole he'd uncovered during the time Bryce was watching the guard. The piece of metal looked as if he'd pried pieces off the racking of the bookshelves and fashioned it into a makeshift pick. Bryce finally got a good look at the hole; Josiah had been busy. The hole was practically all the way through the painted cinder block wall and several other layers of material Bryce couldn't quite identify. It would be a tight squeeze, but Bryce figured he could make it through the hole without much struggle.

In turns one of the pair would walk by the stacks pretending to look for a new book as the other dug. Not caring about the mess, the pair made good progress and by the third time Bryce had made his rounds, Josiah had broken through the other side. With a nod and a gesture of pressing his finger to his lips Josiah peered through the tiny hole he'd made in the wall as Bryce looked on, his heart racing. "Coast is clear." Josiah said, handing the piece of metal off to Bryce and dusting himself off before making his third round.

Bryce quickly dug the wall slowly breaking faster and faster as he did, pulling larger and larger pieces off of the wall, until it was big enough to squeeze through. Bryce climbed back out and glanced around looking for Josiah when he saw the guard walking towards his area. Thinking quickly Bryce dusted himself off and moved to intercept the guard. "Hey, speed it up, this isn't an all-day event." The guard said sternly.

"Right, sorry, I'm just looking for the next book in the series I just read, I think it's called 'Savage Son'? Maybe you've heard of it. Maybe you could help me look?" Bryce asked, trying to sound like he was genuinely struggling to find a fiction book in the non-fiction section.

"What do I look like? A librarian? Hurry up, you have five minutes and then I'm bringing you back with or without a book." The portly guard said getting red in the face as he did.

"Right five minutes understood." Bryce nodded in agreement looking around for Josiah. With a huff the guard turned and marched back to his post just outside the rows of books.

Frantic Bryce looked around for Josiah but without any luck. Fearing something had happened he returned to the hole. "What are you doing? Hurry up." Bryce heard from the hole, just as Josiah poked his head out. "We're running out of time." He continued gesturing for Bryce to hurry. With a nod Bryce began the short crawl through the hole which he realized was far tighter as he tried to squeeze his lower half through. But with Josiah's help and a little bit of anxious squirming he was through.

"Where is it?" Bryce whispered as he looked around the white clean room, the typical medical cabinets he'd seen in every hospital he'd ever been to as a kid lined the wall with a pair of beds and some trays. Various medical instruments on them finishing off the oddly bare room.

"I don't know, just look quickly." Josiah responded looking in one of the cabinets. "We are wasting time." Josiah said panic beginning to set in as the pair rifled through the cabinets. As time ticked away each cabinet yielded no results. Bryce began to fear the worst, the thought of the punishment he would face, the torture he may be forced to go through again, he couldn't take it a second time. His heart was nearly beating out of his chest as he yanked doors open and looked. Just as he'd given up hope and thought of maybe climbing back through the hole, pretending nothing had happened, Josiah spoke. "Yes, oh God, yes! Bryce get over here." Josiah said triumphantly holding a small black box that looked like a sleeker and cleaner version of the one he'd use to free the prisoners.

"You first." Bryce said, reaching a hand out for the device.

"No, you, just in case, better to have someone with some kind of powers." Josiah gestured for Bryce to turn around so he could remove the collar. With a beep and a click the collar was off. Bryce felt oddly naked without it. He shuddered at the thought of becoming used to the collar.

"Okay now you." Bryce said taking the device and quickly removing the collar from Josiah who rubbed his neck as if he was not used to the lack of weight around his neck. "How do we open the door?" Bryce asked as an all too familiar sound brought his new found freedom crashing down. The buzz and pop of a cell door. Or in this case the sound of the door from the hallway into the infirmary buzzing open.

"Do not move." A guard shouted from behind Bryce. Slowly turning around Bryce sized up the guard. The man was about five-foot-eight and quite stocky; his hair was nestled under a black hat that Bryce had seen many of the guards wear. He was clean shaven and pointed an extending baton at Bryce.

"We don't want any trouble." Josiah said, putting his hands up slowly. Bryce followed his lead, just as the man moved forward. "Get him." Josiah whispered as the man took another step towards the pair. With those words Bryce bolted at the man, as the world lost its sound. As it had done plenty of times now, Bryce felt the world slow down, and as if he was the only person unaffected, he moved quickly delivering a hard punch to the man's jaw. Then as if on cue the world began to slowly return to its normal speed and sound returned to him. "Well, that was quicker than I expected." Josiah said almost in awe of Bryce.

"Thanks, but I don't think we're done here." Bryce said as he picked up the man's baton and listened as the sound of running got louder. Bryce readied himself for another fight. "Figure out how to get through the door." Bryce called over his shoulder as he waited anxiously.

The second guard crashed through the door seconds later and was met with a swift strike from the baton as Bryce brought it sideways in a sweeping motion connecting flush with the man's jaw sending a second guard tumbling to the ground. The third guard entered swinging, Bryce easily parried the two incoming strikes and countered with a kick to the stomach sending him backwards into the hallway as he captured another oncoming strike from another guard, extending his arm and hitting it hard at the elbow upwards breaking the joint instantly. The man yelped in pain and Bryce struck him down with a follow up strike with his free baton wielding hand. It felt almost too easy, these guards were barely trained, and Bryce had been fighting and training unbeknownst to him for this his whole life. He didn't regret those early morning runs or training sessions anymore. Bryce quickly closed the door and attempted to buy some time by forcing the baton into the handle preventing the door from swinging open.

As the third guard clambered to his feet he smiled as he looked down the hall. A group of what had to be ten guards rushed towards the room. Bryce knew how to fight but ten people trying to fight him all at once was not something he wanted to wait around for. "Josiah, any luck?" Bryce said his attention focused on the door as he backed away creating as much space as he could.

"Yes. Here. Go." Josiah said as the sound of a door swooshing opening filled Bryce's ears.

"You first." Bryce said, turning to look at Josiah who held a small gas cylinder in his hands as his back pressed against the wall.

"Not how it works Bryce." Josiah said shifting slightly to show Bryce a switch he'd pressed his back up to.

"What do you mean, the plan was for us both to get out of here." Bryce said, trying to pull Josiah who resisted, keeping the tension on the switch.

"No Bryce it wasn't. The plan was never that. It was for my cellmate to press the button and me to escape leaving them here. But you, you weren't part of the plan. You are more important than you know." Josiah said looking at the door as a team of people tried to force their way in, the metal baton straining to hold the door closed.

"Then tell me, on the outside. I'm fast enough I can get us both out of here." Bryce pleaded, a ball forming in his throat.

"We need a distraction to escape. I can't make the run to the forest. They'll shoot me before I even clear the yard. But you can. Go, save Bennett. Tell her I love her. Don't make me tell you again. Go! I'll make sure you get enough time to make it." Josiah said tears were running down his face as he faced the truth of his situation. "Now Go!" Josiah screamed.

"Josiah." Bryce said softly.

"Go!" He returned, his voice breaking as he screamed. Bryce turned and looked over his shoulder at the door, the baton bending to a near breaking point. Bryce looked at Josiah who nodded an unspoken agreement with Bryce to save Bennett and pass the message along to her. Then the world got quiet, and Bryce began to run at a full sprint to the treeline.

When Bryce hit the treeline, he paused and looked back, the sound of the world returning to him as he looked in shock as flames burst from behind a large metal sliding door. Bryce didn't know how he did it, but he knew Josiah had waited until the guards entered the room, then opened the gas cylinder and ignited it, causing a large explosion in the room. It had bought Bryce the time he needed to escape, but *at what cost? Why was he so valuable?* He didn't understand. But now wasn't the time to try and solve it. Bryce needed to get as much distance between him and the hellhole he'd just escaped from, as quickly as possible.

With one last glance back, Bryce took a deep breath and started running.

CHAPTER 27

The alarm buzzed on her watch as it had since she'd bought it after her father barged into her room early one morning to catch her changing. She'd started setting it five minutes before her alarm clock so she could be up and have her pink fuzzy robe wrapped tightly around her covering her entire body in protection. Bennett knew something wasn't right with her Dad ever since she'd arrived home. So, every morning she would beat him to waking her up.

"Bennett honey, good morning!" Josiah said, bursting through the door into the room as if trying to catch her off guard.

"Hey Dad, I'm up. Going to go shower now." Bennett replied, collecting her clothes she picked out the night before, then brushing past Josiah, rushing down the hall to the bathroom where she promptly locked the door behind herself, as Josiah followed her.

"Okay Benny, I'll start making you breakfast. I love you, Honey." Josiah said as he jiggled the doorknob before his footsteps stomped disappointedly down the hallway.

With a sigh of relief, Bennett took her clothes and set them on the vanity before covering the mirror with a towel. It was too tough to look in the mirror. Bennett quickly showered and then got dressed before she removed the towel from the mirror and looked at herself, rubbing her neck where the collar had been. It had been months since she was there, but her dreams took her back often. She looked at her bruised knuckles and sighed. The bruises were finally fading weeks after she'd received a week-long suspension for fighting, well it was more of a one-sided beating. Becky Collins had mentioned Bryce and how he was better off dead after he kidnapped Bennett and how he'd died in a shootout with the police. Bennett didn't know what caused her to snap and rip her out of her chair by her hair, slamming her head into the desk and then proceeding to punch Becky in the face over and over again. But it felt good. It took two football players to finally pull her off. That had earned her more sessions with her therapist Dr. Cynthia Wren, a skinny red headed lady in her early forties who dressed quite provocatively for a therapist. Or at least Bennett found the low-cut tops, often far too unbuttoned, and the short, tight skirts, inappropriate for someone who specialized in helping children, teens and young adults with issues. But Bennett was forced to go to her by Josiah when she returned to Broadway Hills. She hated her. She hated this house. She hated this life.

Bennett brushed her hair, applied some light makeup around her eyes and styled her hair back in a ponytail. Her light blue American eagle jeans, black Chuck Taylors, white, notched neck t-shirt and oversized red flannel button up continued to be her go to look. It allowed her to hide away slightly while at school. She knew people talked about her and it only added to her anger. They didn't know what had happened, they believed the lies, and no one believed her. She was the crazy girl who got kidnapped by the kid who murdered his father and burned his house down to cover it up. It was all lies and whenever she said so Cynthia would say it was her Stockholm Syndrome acting up again, or her PTSD, or her anxiety. Or some other thing that witch would make up so she could put her on another medication. Just as her anger built Josiah interrupted her.

"Bennett honey, breakfast is getting cold." He called up to her. Bennett hung her towel on the hook over the door and stepped out of the bathroom fully dressed. "You know you have a room you can get dressed in silly." Josiah commented as he watched her from the stairs.

"It's easier this way." Bennett replied knowing full well it wasn't, but her room didn't have a lock on the door.

"Whatever you say. Foods getting cold sweetie." Josiah said, almost skipping down the stairs.

Bennett followed and soon was in the breakfast nook table where he'd laid out bowls of oatmeal with berries in it. Bennett tucked in and began eating. No point in starving, she thought. She hated oatmeal, always had, Josiah wasn't a fan of it either, so she didn't understand why he suddenly changed his mind after leaving the prison. Had he been gone from home so long that time he developed a love for the stuff? Bennett shrugged off the thought and forced herself to eat.

"Don't forget your pills, Dr. Wren says you need to take them consistently if you want to improve and put all that horrific stuff behind you. I couldn't imagine what you've been through honey. And Benny, why do you insist on wearing all these baggy flannels? I keep telling you, you should dress to show off the body you have. Might get yourself a new boyfriend, maybe one who plays football. Or some friends. That would be nice. That could get you out of your shell, instead of just holing up in your room all night playing video games." Josiah said as he shoveled oatmeal into his mouth eagerly.

"I like my clothes. I feel comfortable in this. And I have friends, they're playing the games with me." Bennett replied, stirring her oatmeal before she poured a large amount of syrup on the oatmeal trying to make it more palatable.

"Whatever you say, I just wish you'd find more friends to bring around. This big house is always so empty, might help you to not fly off the handle and fight as much if you socialize more. Bring some girlfriends around here, it could be fun." Josiah said between mouthfuls of oatmeal. Clearly enjoying the gray food more than Bennett.

"Maybe." Bennett muttered and she forced herself to eat the now overly sweet slop in front of her.

"Don't forget the pills." Josiah said gesturing to a small napkin with five pills on it, two green, one yellow and two blue. Bennett sighed and picked up the pills, placing them in her hand and looking at Josiah who gestured for her to take them. Bennett tilted her head back and placed the pills in her mouth. Placing them on the side of her mouth with her tongue. She then took a glass of water and took a sip, pressing her tongue onto the pills in her cheek slightly, trying her best to not show she was holding them there as she swallowed the water. "Good, now finish up and I will drive you to school." Josiah said getting up from the table and clearing his bowl.

Bennett nodded and turned her attention to the slop in front of her. Pushing around the berries she watched Josiah leave the nook. Once he was out of sight, Bennett spat her pills back into the napkin and quickly wrapped it up, stuffing it into her pocket, before choking down the rest of her breakfast.

Bennett then pretended to be in the stupor her pills should have put her in. Slowly moving to the door and getting into the car with Josiah. Looking out the window on the short drive as she did. The drive didn't last long and soon enough her and Josiah were pulling into the school. Bennett looked over at Josiah who scanned the crowd that was gathering around the entrance, teens hanging around the various entrances of the school waiting for their friends, and the first bell of the day. She watched as he looked at girls who walked by, checking them out. It made her sick. She quickly got out of the car and walked away. Ignoring him as he called out after her saying how much he loved her. With a huff, Bennett entered the school, walking immediately to the computer lab.

As she entered the room, the lights were out and only one computer's bright white screen illuminated the room. "Carter? Harry? Are you here?" She whispered as she slowly entered the dark room.

"Lady Skyfall?" A voice chimed back in reply.

"Right, sorry, Sir Galahad, Knight Juno?" Bennett replied awkwardly.

"Yeah, we're over here." Another voice chimed back as Bennett walked over to the computer to find Harry and Carter scrolling through news articles.

"Remind me again why we can't use our real names in person?" Bennett asked jokingly.

"Safety, if you're telling the truth then these people could be anywhere, even impersonating you. Every good spy has code phrases they use, tell me something only the real Bennett would know." Carter replied, looking at Bennett.

"Well, you once tried to hit on me over Snapchat sending me photos of you shirtless flexing." Bennett replied with a chuckle from Harry.

"Yeah, that's something you would do." Harry laughed as Bennett took up a position behind them looking over their shoulders.

"Shut up, it was freshman year, I had hit the gym with Bryce and figured I would put the option out there. It could have worked." Carter said, elbowing the laughing boy in the side.

"It didn't." Bennett replied as she read the screen. "You don't think it should be more... I don't know, more direct?" She asked reading the script the pair had been working on.

"I mean it's pretty cut down already, you think it should be shorter?" Carter asked, looking at Bennett whose eyes were scanning the script again.

"I don't know we need to make sure it's good, we'll only get one chance at uploading it." She replied, reading it over once more mouthing the words as she did. Just as she finished reading the warning bell rang. "Oh shoot, save this and we'll talk about it tonight online." She said making her way to the door and heading off to class.

The next few hours dragged on as Bennett suffered through her classes. Her eyes always focused on the window as she gazed out into the world, replaying everything from the fire to the prison and everything in between. The entire time Bryce was there protecting her. She missed him. Then she remembered how he couldn't look at her when that man said she was the reason Unity attacked the camp. The hurt in his eyes, the look of disappointment. It broke her. How could he not have trusted her? A tear began to roll down her cheek. "Miss Douglas... excuse me? Are you okay?" Mr. Jones stopped his lesson to ask her.

"Huh?" Bennett asked, not realizing what was going on. And quickly wiping her tears away with her sleeve.

"Never mind, please focus on the lesson. As I was saying, The French Revolution started when a group of hungry citizens attacked the Bastille which was a large prison in Paris. This kicked off a bloody revolution that saw many royals and high-status individuals beheaded by guillotines." Mr. Jones continued as Bennett slowly lost focus again, her mind returning to Bryce. He needed to know she didn't do that. Her mind played through how she'd tell him if she saw him again. Running up to hug him, his strong arms wrapping around her holding her tight enough to press her into him but not so tight it hurt. She missed his warmth. Curling up next to him in bed at the camp, his arm over her as he slept. She'd give anything to see him again, but she might not ever see him again, he could be dead, he was bleeding a lot when he was pulled from the car, then again so was she. Her hand went to the scar on her arm where the piece of metal had cut her.

The bell pulled Bennett from her train of thought and as she finished out the day of school, dreading the appointment she had with Dr. Cynthia Wren afterwards.

Josiah picked Bennett up promptly from school, and much to her displeasure, parked right at the front the way he always did as of late. Watching every girl leaving the school attentively. "Hey Benny, how was school today?" He asked as the door opened, his attention not leaving the short jean cut-offs Stephanie Armstrong was wearing.

"School was fine, can we get this over with?" Bennett sharply asked her anger, getting the best of her.

"I'm not sure what this attitude is but I'll be sure to mention it to Dr. Wren when I speak with her." Josiah replied in his condescending tone.

"I don't need a therapist, I'm fine, and if anyone would just believe me then I wouldn't be getting so angry. You should believe me; they abducted you too." Bennett said her eyes welling up with tears from the anger seething inside her. "Can we just go?" She yelled in the car banging her fist against the door.

"I do believe you honey, but there is no reason for you to be attacking your classmates when they say what the news has led them to believe. I know you are struggling to adapt but the best thing for you to do is to accept this new reality and let go of all of these delusions that Unity wants anything to do with us at all. We are pointless to them, unless you are in touch with Bryce again which you are certainly not right?" Josiah asked as he started the car and drove off, once again taking a look at any girl he could.

"I can't just let it go, not after what I have seen, maybe it's easier for you because you were barely involved, but I can't." Bennett said angrily, staring at him.

"Dr. Wren said diminishing anyone else's experiences only leads to conflict, so please do not diminish what I have gone through, and furthermore I have asked you to not mention it. I also asked you a question and expect an answer. So, I will ask you again, you haven't been in touch with Bryce, right?"

"Right." She replied, ending the conversation before it could go any further.

CHAPTER 28

Bennett hated this office, hated the smell of calming oils that Cynthia always had filling the air, the place smelled like a store run by someone who believed a cult leader would bring them to salvation. She hated the uncomfortable chairs that were meant to promote relaxation and open communication. She hated the dim lighting that only had a spotlight on her when she sat in the chair across from Cynthia. But most of all she hated Cynthia. She wasn't a real psychologist; she wasn't a real therapist, and she wasn't even a real person. Bennett was sure of it.

"Bennett, how have you been? Your father tells me you are still having a lot of outbursts. Is there anything you want to talk about?" Cynthia asked, her red hair medium length and layered, covering her face slightly as she wrote in her notebook. Bennett looked at her with hatred in her eyes. She didn't want to talk, she wanted to get an excuse to give her more medication so she would be compliant with whatever Unity wanted. She couldn't prove it, but she knew.

"No, I'm just tired." Bennett said, looking down and rubbing her bruised knuckles as she spoke.

"So, you're having trouble sleeping then? Maybe we should up your dose? Your father also tells me you're always awake when he comes to make sure you're up for school?" Cynthia questioned, crossing her legs, her tight black pencil skirt tightening around them.

"No, I don't need more." Bennett answered her rage rising.

"Come on Bennett, I can't help you unless you open up to me." Cynthia continued adjusting her hair out of her face with the pen she was holding.

"Why, so you can prescribe more medications that don't address the issues?" Bennett said sharply.

"Bennett, there's no need to act this way. I prescribed medications that will help calm you so we can have productive conversations and get to the root cause of these outbursts you're having. Your father tells me you spend all night playing video games and are withdrawn from your old life. You used to be so full of life and were involved in so many extracurriculars and now you're not. Why do you think that is?" Cynthia asked, trying to look thought provokingly at Bennett.

"Well probably because I know there's bigger issues than padding my College application. The Atlantians are being hunted down and killed and no one gives a crap about it." Bennett muttered clenching her fist and digging her nails into her hand to prevent her from hauling off and attacking Cynthia like she wanted to.

"Bennett… we've discussed this. There is no such thing as Atlantis, Atlantians or…" Cynthia began before checking her notes to ensure she had the correct wording. "Unity, they are fictional things Bryce made up in order to make you complicit in the crimes he was committing. It may be hard to believe, but it is true. If you remain in these delusions, then you will not be able to move forward in your life." Her tone was that of someone talking to a child trying to explain that Santa isn't real.

"I'm not delusional, I wasn't tricked by Bryce, I'm telling the truth." Bennett said as tears streamed down her face.

"Bennett, I know it may seem that way, but it just isn't true." She said shifting in her chair and adjusting her blouse that was one button short from being appropriate.

"You don't know what you're talking about!" Bennett screamed as she threw her chair backwards and stood up. Her chest heaving with the deep angry breaths she took.

"Bennett, I think we are done here, I will be writing a prescription for your father and upping the dosage on your medications, hopefully this new dosage will correct these delusions and fits of anger, and we can work towards some kind of progress." Cynthia said, standing up and fixing her skirt. "I think you know the way out." She gestured towards the door with her hand as she clutched her notebook beneath her chest pushing her breasts up as it did.

"You dress like a whore." Bennett said angrily over her shoulder as she flung the door open and marched out. "Unlock the car." She demanded looking back at Josiah who had stood as she exited.

"Bennett Madeline Douglas, you come back here and apologize right now to Dr. Wren." Josiah demanded as he stood firmly.

"Josiah, it's fine, these outbursts are to be expected, therapy is an emotional experience." Cynthia explained as she scribbled on a note pad and handed it to Josiah. "Fill this prescription and give it to her each morning and before bed accordingly and I will see you in a few days for our next session. Goodbye Bennett." Cynthia finished leaning against the doorframe and watching Bennett with a smile.

"Screw you." Bennett said behind her back as she flung open the glass door of the office and left.

The drive home was spent with Josiah berating Bennett for her behavior. When they arrived home, Bennett ran upstairs to her bedroom. Tears of anger and sadness at her father filled Bennett's eyes. It took her a few moments to collect herself before she turned on her gaming computer and logged into Heroes of the Realms, placing a pair of gaming headphones on and then shifting them to one side to allow for one of her ears to be out so she could hear if Josiah was approaching.

"This is Lady Skyfall logging on." She said into the microphone as she joined the game and quickly accepted an invite from someone with the screen name Knight Juno.

"How was therapy?" Harry asked his voice coming in crystal clear as the name Knight Juno glowed overtop of an armor-clad figure with pointy ears.

"Because I'm sure she wants to discuss how she was gaslit by a Unity plant so much." Carter chimed in as his character a large green skinned orc with black armor that smoked arrived, the name Sir Galahad glowing over his head.

"I called her a whore so that was nice." Bennett replied as her character, a much smaller human woman wearing purple and blue robes carrying a wand that glowed yellow stood in between the two metal clad figures.

"Oh yes! Lady Skyfall!" Harry cheered as his character did a random dance on the screen prompting a laugh from Bennett.

"Okay enough of this time wasting, are we going to discuss this script? We need to get it sorted sooner than later, I don't want anything interrupting this upload, or for one of us to get caught." Carter said, trying to steer the conversation towards the matter at hand.

"Right, and we're sure they can't find us here." Harry asked cautiously.

"Not that I'm aware of, both indicators in my room weren't tripped. And We checked the place for cameras when you came over to build this computer just as they instructed, so unless there is something we missed, I doubt they have the ability to monitor anything we do here." Bennett whispered while listening with her exposed ear for Josiah's footprints.

"Plus, the VPN we are all running." Carter added quickly.

"Okay good. Are you sure you can't tell us who they are?" Harry breathed in a sigh of relief before asking the same question he asked over and over again.

"It's safer that way. Are you two sure you want to keep doing this, I don't need you guys to risk everything for me?" Bennett asked softly.

"Not just you, Bryce and all the other Atlantians, Unity is putting in danger. People need to know." Carter said authoritatively.

"Agreed." Harry chimed in. "Plus, it's a little late now, no?"

"I guess so I just need you both to know it could get very dangerous once we make sure the program is running and upload the video. As soon as it's out there they'll be trying to discredit or alter it and they'll be after me and possibly you two as well." Bennett coached as she glanced around her room cautiously.

"Agreed, and you're sure you want to be on camera, not one of us because that's the most dangerous part of this." Harry asked ever the chivalrous one.

"Of course, that way if it does go sideways, I am the only one to blame. So where did we leave off?" Bennett asked as the trio slowly played the game, more focused on the video and their plans on when and where to film it.

The group played until late into the night, finishing their plans and sorting out everything. The recording and uploading would happen the next night, after that no matter what happened, no matter who said what, and no matter what people said, the three would have done all they could to help. Exhausted, Bennett climbed into bed, a feeling of accomplishment washing over her as she fell asleep.

The day began like any other, Bennett woke up early, gathered her clothes and prepared to quickly move to the bathroom when Josiah opened her door. Like clockwork her alarm sounded, and Josiah flung open the door. In a dexterous move, Bennett slipped passed Josiah and into the bathroom locking the door behind her and showering, the warm water on her skin transporting her away from this horrible reality and back to the showers she'd take at the camp, where she would finish and smile as she approached Bryce's room. He would wait to wrap her in his strong arms and hold her, the smell of him, the warmth of his hug rivalling that of the shower on her cold skin. But just as she felt as if he was right beside her, Josiah fiddling with the doorknob brought her back to her nightmare of a reality.

She choked back the oatmeal with fruit, faked taking her pills and it was off to school. She glanced out the window as she could have sworn, she saw someone... not just anyone... someone in particular... it couldn't be... or could it? Then just as quickly as she saw them, they disappeared. Bennett rubbed her eyes as Josiah came to a stop at a red light, looking hard at the spot where she'd seen the figure, but he wasn't there. Chalking it up to her new medication and how long she'd had to keep it in her mouth playing tricks on her, Bennett shrugged it off, as playing tricks on her.

CHAPTER 29

Bryce kicked himself for being so careless, how did he know who he saw was really her? How did he know anyone he saw was really who they appeared to be. He'd spent the last two and a half weeks on the run, trying to get to Broadway Hills, avoiding Unity every step of the way, he'd barely slept, his face caked with dirt and his facial hair producing a stubble he'd barely noticed until mud started sticking to it more and more as the days passed. He was in desperate need of a good night's sleep and a hot shower. The trucker he'd gotten a ride with forced him to shower before he allowed him in the truck, but that was over a week ago. Luckily Texas was fairly warm in September otherwise his level of cleanliness would have been the least of his worries.

Pulling his green and black plaid shirt up and adjusting his loose-fitting blue jeans Bryce went to the only place he could think of. He went home. When he arrived, he noticed a completely new house. The lot had been sold, torn down and rebuilt into a new more modern style. Bryce paused for a moment a lump forming in his throat as he remembered the last time he was here, Rhys lay dead in the kitchen, the house burned around him and all he could do was run, run and never look back. Just as Bryce stood there with a thousand-yard stare a voice broke him free of his nightmarish memories. "Yeah, yeah, yeah I know, I'm working on it." Josiah said as he exited his black Chevy Malibu and talked on the phone almost as oblivious as Bryce had been. Without thinking Bryce sprinted down the drive of his former house, hopping the fence and sprinting through the backyard to the woods he knew all too well.

After he reached the trees, Bryce slowed to an almost animalistic stalking pace. Each step carefully thought out to bring him one step closer to his prey. As he made his way deeper into the woods shielding himself from sight from the houses Bryce closed in on Josiah.

Once he could see Bennett's house Bryce sat and waited, taking position in a small bush that provided him perfect sight lines of the back side of the house, the back deck of the house clearly visible as Bryce sat unmoving, his heart racing. It was a few hours before anything happened, Bryce was beginning to think maybe nothing would happen, then he saw movement. Then a figure emerged from the house with a cellphone pressed to their ear, it looked like it was wearing the same clothes as Josiah had but he seemed younger, taller, and once he spoke British? Bryce could swear the figure on the back deck was speaking in a British accent. "I know bruv, I am trying but these teens are making it tough, ya know?" The voice echoed as he spoke on the phone, pacing the deck before he took up a position on the edge, leaning over the railing and fiddling with something in his hands. Bryce strained his eyes and realized it was a cigarette, the red embers glowing as he took his first drag. "It's not even like that, they got me in this house with this bird who is an absolute piece innit? But she dresses like a nun, let me tell you, I've tried to sneak peaks but she's bear clever, never letting a man open the bedroom door while she's asleep, or the bathroom while she's showering, I knew she's an absolute piece because Unity showed me the pictures before I got on this assignment." The voice continued taking drags from the cigarette as he listened to the other side of the call. Bryce's blood boiled as he heard the man talk about Bennett, pretending to be Josiah, the man who had just sacrificed his life to save Bryce, and this man was tarnishing his memory in his daughter's eyes. Bryce could kill him right where he stood. "Let me tell you, this bird was hot. But now all she does is get in fights and complain about everything, then spend all night playing video games. It's a waste man, such potential wasted. Unity better come through soon or I'm going to make things happen myself. The therapist bird they got me paired with is a fun lay, but this girl blood let me tell you she's worth it if I can get a crack at her." The man said, taking the last few drags of his cigarette before walking to the side of the deck and flicking the cigarette into the backyard of another family. "I've got to go but I'll call you tomorrow bruv, these chats are saving me big time, this place is boring otherwise, but the girls at the school, mad potential too.

The Atlantian Chronicles

Anyway, I'll check ya tomorrow." The British man said before he hung up the phone, pocketed it and headed back inside.

Bryce watched the house for another hour before he realized the man would not be coming back out. Slowly Bryce backed out of his hiding spot and made his way back out onto the small path that ran through the woods. Once there Bryce made his way through only leaving the protection and concealment of the woods when he had to. It only took him a few minutes before he saw his next destination. Harry's house.

Bryce watched as Harry arrived, looked over both shoulders and then removed a key from a potted plant, unlocking his door, rechecking each shoulder before he placed the key back and then entered the house. A smile crossed his face as he recalled how Harry would do that exact motion every time he had gone to Harry's house after school. Bryce was confident this was Harry but to confirm he watched for another few moments.

Harry was a madman inside his house. Making multiple pieces of food, packing a backpack, rushing in one room and then out the next and on and on like a man on a mission. Curious Bryce slowly moved forward, watching the house as Harry flitted around. Bryce creeped up the steps, removed the key from its hiding spot, unlocked the door, placed the key back and slowly entered the house. Harry was moving around the house as Bryce made his way into the kitchen where he waited for Harry to return.

As Bryce heard Harry coming, he prepared himself and as soon as Harry was visible Bryce grabbed him. Placing a hand over his mouth immediately, the sound and pressure of a scream muffled by his hand. "Harry, it's me. I'm going to remove my hand from your mouth, do not scream. Okay?" Bryce asked, pressing his hand against the pudgy boy's mouth. Harry nodded and slowly Bryce removed his hand.

"Bryce? Is that you?" Harry asked as he struggled to catch his breath.

"Yeah, it's me. It's good to see you." He said hugging Harry tightly.

"I thought you were dead for sure." Harry said cautiously, returning the hug.

"I guess I'm just hard to kill." Bryce chuckled before realizing Harry was staring at him confused. "It's me. You set up a date with Serena Polland at Ashton's party." Bryce said with a sigh of understanding that Harry didn't trust him.

Upon hearing that, Harry hugged Bryce once more, his mind at ease after confirming his friend's identity. "It really is you." He continued through the hug.

"Yeah, it is. But I don't have much time. Bennett is in danger. Her Dad, well he isn't who he says he is." Bryce explained.

"He's Unity, I knew it!" Harry cheered, before he realized and retracted some of his excitement. "Well, he won't be an issue much longer." Harry said softer.

"What do you mean?"

"Well Bennett, a little over a month ago, she approached Carter and I, and well she had a plan. She was in touch with another group." Harry began.

"Not the Atlantian Brotherhood right?" Bryce interrupted.

"Oh God no, that Atlas guy seems like a jerk if what that Amelia girl says is true." Harry replied.

"Said. She's dead. I'm pretty sure he had her killed." Bryce replied, looking at his shoes as he spoke.

"I'm sorry. Bennett spoke highly of her. Said she really took care of her in that prison when Bennett was there." Harry said, placing a hand softly on Bryce's shoulder. "But Bennett was contacted by a group after she beat up Becky Collins for talking bad about you. Broke her nose in two places and knocked out four teeth before she was stopped! But that's beside the point. She was screaming about Unity and apparently, she was approached by a different group. She won't go into any details, but they told her they were trying to make a world where Atlantians didn't have to hide, and Unity was no longer a threat. A world where everyone lived in harmony, the way it was intended to be. After that she realized she needed our help, and we kind of came up with the idea of uploading a video. This group has a program that reposts it to as many groups as it can until it is too viral for Unity to stop. The video will expose everyone and everything that has happened. They even have footage of people using their powers!" Harry stated proudly puffing his chest up as he spoke.

"How does she know they aren't a fake group created by Unity?" Bryce asked.

"She said something about Amelia being in touch with them and then how the contact was able to prove to her they weren't a fake group. So, I just took her word for it." Harry shrugged. "Anyway, that's what I'm getting ready for now. We're going to sneak into the school tonight and upload it." Harry continued proudly.

"I guess once we deal with Bennett's Dad, I will be joining you guys." Bryce said cautiously.

"Not looking or smelling like that you're not." Harry said, pointing to Bryce's current state.

"Well, we don't really have time, do we?" Bryce shrugged.

"Of course we do, because I do not want to be in a car with you smelling like that. Bennett and Carter are heading to the school two hours early to get set up and get everything running and then I am arriving after with the car for a getaway. So, the way I see it you have at least an hour to get clean and go grab some clothes from my Dad's closet before we leave, he's about your size. So go do that while I finish packing." Harry said, ushering Bryce out of the kitchen and up the stairs to the bathroom. "Oh, and Bryce, I'm glad you're not dead."

"Me too Harry." Bryce said before rounding the stairs and heading into the bathroom.

Bryce spent the better part of thirty minutes scrubbing his whole body, and it felt euphoric. Once done he quickly toweled off, threw his clothes in a plastic bag he'd pulled out of the garbage can in the bathroom, picked a pair of blue jeans and a black sweater that fit far better from Harry's father's closet, the all black hoodie had a yellow faded Ohio Buckeyes logo on it. Once dressed Bryce made his way down to Harry who had placed two backpacks against the front door.

"Well, that is better I would say. How do you feel?" Harry chimed as he saw Bryce.

"Much better." Bryce replied with a smile, the feeling of clean giving him a new refreshed feeling.

"Good, we should probably get going. I assume you'll want some time with Bennett's Dad?" Harry asked unsure what the answer would be.

"You would be correct." Bryce said playing over in his mind what exactly he would do to this imposter Josiah. "But Harry there are some things we should talk about." Bryce said as Harry handed him a sandwich wrapped in foil paper.

"You should eat something; Bennett said a lot about your power? Skill? Mutant abilities?" Harry said as gestured for Bryce to eat the sandwich he'd handed him. It was delicious, a steak and pesto sandwich on a French bread with a bit of what Bryce could only guess was Swiss cheese.

"I think it's a power, but they call it shifting? A shift? I haven't given it much thought but let's go with that." Bryce said, rubbing the back of his head with his free hand before taking a big bite of the sandwich, standing in silence as he chewed and swallowed the delicious food. "But listen, a lot has happened since Bennett and I split up, and I need you to know about it, in case something happens I need you to do something for me and tell Bennett everything." Bryce said as he stood explaining everything, The Atlantian Brotherhood Headquarters, Colson, Mateo, and Filly, the rescue plan, the betrayal, the torture, and meeting Josiah. Then how Josiah had helped Bryce escape, and the last few weeks Bryce had spent on the road trying to get to Bennett to help her, finally ending with how he'd watched the imposter, and Harry.

"Wow that is a lot." Harry said, unable to think of anything else to say. "Are you okay? Like mentally?" He asked, placing an arm on Bryce's shoulder.

"I haven't stopped to think about it. And now isn't the time to start. We need to go, but when I know I will tell you." Bryce returned softly, placing an arm on Harry.

"Okay, we should go then." Begrudgingly knowing Bryce was right. It took only minutes for Harry to drive to Bennett's house but to Bryce it felt like hours. His mind raced as he played over everything he wanted to do to this imposter.

When the car finally pulled up to the all too familiar house Bryce sat for a moment, his heart racing knowing what he was about to do. Once he entered the house, he was sure there was no going back. "Harry, you can still back out if you want, it's not too late but once we go inside the house, we can't turn back and we have to see this through." Bryce said looking at Harry who had pulled the car up to the curb and threw it in park.

"I'm not scared Bryce, if that's what you're thinking." Harry replied, puffing his chest out.

"It's not a matter of being scared, if you go through with this, Unity will be after you. You can't go back." Bryce said looking sternly at Harry trying his best to convey the seriousness of the situation.

"What would I go back to Bryce, one of my best friends is with your girlfriend right now, and the other is sitting across from me about to risk his life to save people a year ago he knew nothing about. Without you two I'm a fat loser who would be all alone. Maybe I make it to college, get a job and live out a life of sadness and regret, or I stand up for people who need help and make a difference. I think the choice is already made." Harry said, adjusting his glasses and unbuckling his seatbelt. "The real question is are you coming or not?"

"Harry, I mean it." Bryce said one last time as Harry opened his door and clambered out.

"So do I, Bryce." He said, closing his door and marching around the car towards the front door of the Douglas house.

Bryce quickly pulled the hood of the sweater up and climbed out, hanging his head as he approached the door. The pair made their way up the front steps and onto the porch. The faded blue paint with white accents reminded Bryce of the days he'd spent playing with Bennett on the front lawn growing up. His expression softened for a second but with a shake of his head he snapped back to the task at hand. Harry knocked loudly on the door as Bryce waited off to the side, trying his best to remain out of sight until the door was fully opened.

The seconds felt like minutes as the pair waited for the response from the knock, Bryce held his breath as he watched the door anxiously. His heart felt as if it would pound out of his chest. Then he saw the door handle begin to move. A moment later the door opened, and Josiah stood in the doorframe staring at Harry.

"Uhhh… Hi Mr. Douglas is…" Harry began to stutter but was cut off before he could finish as Bryce bulldozed into the house grabbing the shorter man, catching him off guard as Bryce quickly took hold of the imposter, placing him in a standing head and arm choke until he felt the man go completely limp in his arms, carrying the man into the house as he did.

"Get the door Harry." Bryce called through gritted teeth as he applied the choke and noticed that Harry stood in the door bewildered by what just happened.

"Oh right." He said springing into action and closing the door behind him, locking it. "You didn't kill him, did you?" Harry asked softly after he entered the dimly lit house.

"No, he's alive, should wake up pretty quickly after I release the choke fully, but let's try to restrain him a bit. Grab some towels and tie them together." Bryce said as he began to give Harry instructions, to create a makeshift rope, and then how to bind the imposters hands together, all while Bryce held the choke, loosening it just enough to ensure the man didn't die in his arms, reapplying the choke when he felt the man begin to awaken.

Once Bryce was satisfied with the restraints, he let the man slump into a chair Harry had pulled up and waited for him to regain consciousness. After a few moments the pair watched as the man began to wake up. Groggy and unsure of what was going on the man struggled against the bindings Harry had tied his hands with.

"There's no use struggling, the moment you get free, I'll put you out again." Bryce warned.

"What the heck do you want?" The imposter said his voice was rough and nothing like Josiah's.

"Well, your name for starters." Bryce responded, his eyes not moving off of the man as he hung his head trying to regain some semblance of his surroundings.

"Why's it matter you're going to kill me afterwards." He replied looking up at Bryce, his face some half-molded combination between the British man Bryce had seen earlier and Josiah.

"I never said that. I just want to know your name and why Unity has you here?" Bryce replied softly, slightly repulsed by the disfigured visage in front of him.

"You really are dumb, aren't you?" The imposter chuckled as he hung his head, and the sound of cracking bones filled the air. "I'm here watching the girl, we figured you or someone would come for her, plus we can't have the little girl making too much noise shouting about Unity and Atlantians. And then there's the leverage. Once we got you, we figured we could use her to make you, or her Dad tell us everything we wanted. Just had to wait for the right moment. But look where that got us." The imposter continued looking up at Bryce, his hair slowly fading to a brown as he completed his transformation to the man Bryce had seen earlier in the day.

"What the?" Harry blurted out watching the man completely change his image in a matter of moments.

"You think that's cool, wait until you see the other things Unity has cooked up, right cracked innit?" The man said dropping his American accent and adopting a British one.

"What is Unity cooking up?" Bryce asked.

"What do you think they just kill us?" He replied smugly. "Bruv, they are making us better. Using our genetics to make new Atlantian's, new soldiers. Imagine a whole army of you, they'd control every battle before the enemy even knew they were under attack. Or me, I've been here for months and none of you twits ever even noticed." The man bragged.

"We noticed; we just didn't know for sure. Plus, you didn't know what we had planned either." Harry chimed in trying to assert his knowledge of the situation.

"Whatever you say big boy." The man chirped back. "You think we didn't know something was up? The girl might have covered her tracks, but no one goes to a school at night on a random Tuesday. Took me about an hour before I figured out she wasn't coming back. Closet was missing clothes and random other items. So, I quickly phoned the big boy and his squad about ten minutes before you arrived. Should be rolling up to the school any moment now. Probably going to just cut our losses and kill her. I only wish I got a chance to ride her before we did. Oh well." The man said as Bryce and Harry shared a look of horror at this startling revelation.

"Crap, Bryce we have got to go." Harry said, starting for the door.

"Not yet." Bryce returned coldly. "What does Unity want with me?" Grabbing the man by the shoulders. The man smiled and just laughed, his cackle filling the room.

"Bryce, we don't have time. Bennett and Carter could be in danger." Harry pleaded as he moved back and began pulling on Bryce.

"TELL ME!" Bryce screamed as he shook the man harder, his laugh piercing through Bryce's mind.

"BRYCE LET'S GO!" Harry shouted back, shaking Bryce who released the man.

"Fine let's go." Bryce said before turned back and roundhouse kicked the man in the jaw as hard as he could, sending the bound man clattering to the floor unconscious.

"What was that for?" Harry asked in shock.

"I bought us more time." Bryce explained as he hurried out the door. "He would have struggled to get free the moment we left, maybe even escaped with enough time to warn Unity we were coming to the school. At least now there's a chance he doesn't." Bryce explained nervously as he climbed into the car.

The tires squealed as Harry sped off, pushing the car to its limit as he drove racing to the school. Within minutes Harry was pulling up to the rear entrance of the school. "They're on the second floor World History Room." Harry said as he came to an abrupt halt. "Oh no!" He cried as he and Bryce watched the beams of flashlights illuminate the dark school's first floor, moving quickly.

"Stay here Harry." Bryce said, climbing out of the door.

"But Bryce, I want to help." Harry protested as he watched Bryce prepare to take off.

"Stay in the car Harry, I mean it." Bryce commanded before he was gone in an instant.

CHAPTER 30

Bryce reappeared just outside of the school's rear entrance, slowly opening the door fractions of an inch at a time before slipping into the empty main hallway. The hard floor echoed the sounds of the moving soldiers as they cleared each room, the sound of their boots filling the otherwise dead silence of the school. Bryce took a deep breath and tried to steady his nerves. Then he began to move with purpose, just how Rhys had told him to during a crisis. Move with purpose, make each movement count and when necessary, strike hard and fast and do not stop until the threat is gone. At the time Bryce thought it was training for a threat that would never come, an overprotective father who served in the military and transitioned to civilian life knowing the dangers this world had and having the knowledge to equip his child with the skills to protect themselves against it. Little did he know Rhys had spent the last seventeen years preparing for a moment like this.

Trying his best to balance, speed and stealth, Bryce moved quickly staying slightly off the wall as he did -another lesson he'd learned from Rhys when school shootings rose across America, walls bounce bullets, if you are around a foot away from the wall you are less likely to be hit-unsure of what he would do when he reached the source of the sound, Bryce moved as if on instinct. He knew this school better than these men. The men knew Bennett and Carter were in the school but not sure where, because of this they had to search the whole school room by room.

As Bryce approached a corner he slowed to an almost snail's pace, straining his ears to listen using an angle to see as much of the hallway as possible while exposing as little of himself to an open space where his foes would have more time to react.

As Bryce strained his eyes trying to adjust to the dark, he saw beams of light scanning the hallway just before the corner he was at. Moving back a half step Bryce readied himself to attack. "Hallway One is clear, Charlie team is moving to the second sector." A rough voice said from around the corner as Bryce listened closely.

Bryce watched as the beam of light swept side to side the movement becoming quicker as the beams got more and more narrow. Soon the beams became three separate points of light! Bryce felt his heart pounding in his ears. Just as the first muzzle broke the plane of the wall, Bryce moved. Grabbing the muzzle and forcing it upwards as bullets sprayed from the gun. Bryce acted quickly and using the strap of the gun attached to the soldier, he performed a one-armed shoulder throw rolling with the falling man and bouncing off of him into a three-point stance. Pushing off the floor Bryce felt the all too familiar feeling as the world became silent and everything slowed. Quickly Bryce zig-zagged trying to dodge flying bullets as he closed the distance to the second man who was in the process of sighting in the spot Bryce had previously been. If you watched from afar, it would have looked as though Bryce was there one moment and gone the next, a blur just reappearing beside the second of the three men, throwing a flying knee into the man sending him flying backwards into the wall, slumping down his body devoid of any signs of life.

Bryce watched as the man he'd just kneed in the head slowly slid down the wall, a small streak of blood following his body down. But there was no time to waste, Bryce, still in his enhanced state, turned his attention to the third man who was panicking, wildly swinging his gun around scanning. Bryce quickly moved towards him, pulling him forward by the strap of his gun, before delivering a crushing elbow to the man's nose, the feeling of the impact being a definitive end to the man as a threat. Bryce felt the world begin to return to its normal speed, and then he quickly moved to the first man hitting him with a soccer kick in the head as he clambered to his feet. The man collapsing before him. Moving quickly down the hallway Bryce recalled the best way to get to his destination.

Bolting down the hallway knowing the sound of the scuffle and gunshots would have alerted the other teams he turned the corner at the end of the hall. Unfortunately for Bryce he ran right into another team of three armed men, this time they had him dead to rights. "Don't move!" One of the men said, training his gun on him before the second of the trio moved up to stand almost level with the first, both of their guns pointed at Bryce, their flashlights blinding him. Bryce was quick, and even quicker when he was able to channel his ability, but Bryce knew he couldn't move that quick. "Bravo team to Alpha, we have one." The first man said into his radio. Before pausing for what Bryce could only assume was instructions as to what to do with him.

Bryce waited as he felt what would be his last seconds tick by. Rhys, Anton, Josiah, Amelia, Harry, Carter and Bennett, he'd failed them all. He came so close. So close to saving Bennett, so close to escaping, only to fall short. Bryce felt a tear roll down his cheek as he stared into the lights that would ultimately deliver the bullet that would kill him.

Time seemed to tick slower as he awaited his fate. But just as Bryce prepared for his death the first man fell forwards, and a moment later the second man did too. Bryce looked on in astonishment as the barrel of the third man's gun smoked. Frozen in place he watched as the third man stepped forward and removed his black mask revealing... "Anton!" Bryce shouted as he moved towards the man hugging him tightly.

"Hey Kiddo, did you miss me?" He said back, smirking.

"How did you? Why are you? What are you doing here?" Bryce asked, his mind, trying and failing to understand how Anton was here.

"Don't really have that much time Kid, I'll answer what I can, but we need to move, Tyson is here and he's closing in on Bennett, second floor World History Room, we're supposed to converge on the room once we deal with you. We've got to move." Anton said, pushing Bryce forward and directing him towards a stairwell.

"Long story short, after I was arrested at the airport, I was taken to a prison but cut a deal to get out promising to help the Unity raid teams carry out their missions. Took a lot of convincing for them to believe I wasn't going to turn on them again, not proud of what I've had to do, but it was either help them or be killed. I took the deal hoping I'd get a chance like this." He said as he moved up the stairwell Bryce following a few steps behind.

"Anton, I'm sorry, this is all my fault." Bryce said the weight of what he knew Anton would have gone through stinging his heart.

"It's not Bryce, I made just as many decisions to get here as you did, we can only play the hand we're dealt. Now focus up, we've got two guards and one big goon to deal with. I'm sure Tyson will want to kill Bennett and whoever she's with by himself, so he's probably put the other two outside. Let me get their attention and then I will take the guard on the left. Are you any better at shifting?" Anton explained before he and Bryce exited the stairwell.

"Much better." Bryce said confidently.

"Good, we're going to need it." Anton said as he pulled his mask back down and nodded to Bryce.

Bryce watched as Anton walked towards the two men, his black clothing, vest and guns nearly disappearing in the darkened hallway. "Where's the rest of your squad?" One of the guards asked as he watched Anton approach.

"Mutt got two of us before I finally put him down like the dog he was. Big man inside with the girl?" Anton said, moving towards the two men who stood watch just outside of the door.

"Hoorah. And yeah, Boss is in there with some girl and some skinny kid, they were recording some kind of video." The guard replied as Bryce watched Anton slowly take an angle allowing him a clean shot on the left guard.

Seizing his moment, Bryce slipped out of the elevator and quickly focused his mind, the sound of the world drifting away again, until it was completely silent. Bryce then took off at a full sprint, before pushing off the opposite wall from the guards and delivering a powerful cross to the right-side guard's jaw, his head pounding off of the wall he stood in front of. Time resumed as he watched Anton quickly raise his gun and squeeze off two rounds into the man who'd been caught off guard by the near sudden appearance of Bryce. The splatter of red blood spraying across the wall and onto the door. "Now or never you ready?" Anton asked as he reached for the door. Bryce nodded and in one movement Anton swung open the door as Bryce entered the room.

"Hey ugly!" Bryce called as he watched Carter shielding Bennett as Tyson slowly and menacingly approached them, his giant frame almost blocking the pair completely from view as they were cornered Bennett holding a phone and tapping away on the screen as she sheltered from the large rage filled man. Bryce knew he was big but never realized how big Tyson really was until he was standing so close. The giant man made the six-foot-one frame of Bryce seem tiny. Slowly Tyson turned around, a sinister smile appearing across his scarred face. "It's me you want, let them go." Bryce called getting into a fighting stance, the door closing behind him as Anton slipped in behind him.

"Bryce Hillcrest, I have been waiting for this moment for eighteen years." Tyson chuckled his deep raspy voice echoing around the room. "You're taller than I expected."

"Well, I guess it's your lucky day then." Bryce said as he watched Tyson face him and slowly move across the classroom slipping in between rows of desks.

"You are going to die like the filthy dog you are, then just for fun I'm going to kill your pretty little girlfriend and your stupid friend too." Tyson said closing in on Bryce.

"I see two of us and one of you, I like my chances." Bryce laughed, glancing over his shoulder to see Anton behind him slowly removing a knife from his vest.

"Is that so?" Tyson asked, his wicked smile becoming even larger.

Just then Bryce felt a sharp pain in his left side, then a warm liquid trickling down him. Bryce turned and looked at Anton then down to his side, the handle of a knife sticking out of him. "Anton, what?" Bryce asked as he stumbled back into a desk, Anton's face grinning wide, his features changing, the aged features of a man Bryce had known his whole life turning into a face he knew and had grown to hate. A moment later Dixon stood in front of Bryce, his perfect teeth, hair and face curling into a sinister smile. The sounds of bones cracking and popping stopped as the transformation was complete.

"My lord, you are easy to trick, it's been me since the mall we picked up dear old Anton on the way there. Dang shame too, he really did have your best interest in mind when he raced over to the mall not checking for tails. I stuck him with that same knife you have in you right now. He went down a little harder, granted I got him right in the stomach and didn't stop pulling up until I hit bone. But you'll go soon enou…" Dixon bragged as Bryce watched Bennett and Carter move towards the door, the two men's attention on Bryce. "Tyson! You idiot, why weren't you watching them." Dixon called as he dove towards the door just missing Bennett and Carter as they slipped through. Tyson started towards the door before Dixon put up a hand stopping him. "I'll deal with them, you handle him."

"Just you and me now Bryce." Tyson sneered as he closed in. Pushing off the desk he'd fallen into, Bryce stood up and raised his hands in a fighting position, the pain of lifting his left side shooting through him.

Bryce watched as Tyson lumbered over to him and with surprising speed threw a punch that caused Bryce to fly over a row of desks. Scrambling to his feet Bryce watched, Tyson threw the desks aside with ease. Clenching his jaw, he struck, throwing a haymaker overhand to Tyson's face, connecting perfectly, sending the man stumbling back, but the large man was quick and caught himself before Bryce could follow up with anything.

"You're not as weak as you look." Tyson chuckled, wiping his lip and readying himself, before lunging at Bryce. Bryce felt the world go silent and Tyson slowed, quickly avoiding the attack and countering with a two-punch combo that caught Tyson off guard and sent him sprawling into another set of desks. Then the sound returned, and Bryce danced backwards like a boxer in the ring.

Tyson moved quickly again this time catching Bryce -who typically ended fights with a punch from his shift, the force he generated typically lethal as he could throw it so quickly the force nearly always broke bones on impact- and swept Bryce's feet sending him stumbling. Bryce caught himself but not before Tyson connected with another powerful punch, the force dazing Bryce, who fell to his knees, Tyson following it up with another punch before he grabbed Bryce by the collar pulling him to his feet and placing him against the blackboard. Bryce watched as Tyson lined up another punch. But just before he could deliver it, Bryce kicked hard into the side of Tyson, sending the man off balance, his large hand colliding with the blackboard, bending it around the impact. Bryce slipped out of the hold and pushed Tyson into the board grabbing his bald head and slamming it against the wall for good measure. Stepping backwards Bryce watched as Tyson picked himself up and looked at Bryce, a cut across his forehead trickled blood down his face.

Setting his jaw Bryce readied himself for the next attack, as Tyson gritted his teeth and rushed forward once more, a battle cry falling on deaf ears as Bryce watched Tyson slow once more, this time even slower than normal. Bryce quickly delivered three punches and a roundhouse kick, causing the large man to go crashing into the opposite wall. The sound of clattering desks and books filling the air once more as Bryce returned to normal speed, exhausted, his eyes blurry, his face throbbing almost as bad as his side, the knife still in him. Bryce tried to raise his hands, but the pain and fatigue was almost too much. He couldn't survive much more of this, and as Tyson picked himself up, his face beginning to swell where Bryce had just hit him. An even more angry Tyson screamed this time Bryce heard every bone chilling note of it as the large man threw himself at Bryce and landed two strikes that sent him to the floor.

The room spun as Bryce felt Tyson pick him up and slam him into the wall once, then twice, and then he felt hands wrapped around his neck, barely able to see he watched as Tyson's gritted teeth and blood shot eyes faded in and out of sight. Bryce's hands weakly pawed at the large man's hands that were squeezing the life out of him.

Just as the tunnel of vision had begun to close in, he felt the pressure on his neck release, Tyson's grip lamenting. Air filling his lungs Bryce felt his world come back to him. Just in time to see Harry wielding a thick textbook backing away from Tyson who was walking him down his back to Bryce who lay on the floor coughing.

"You stupid kids never learn." Tyson screamed as he slapped the book out of Harry's hands and grabbed him by the collar.

Harry watched as the large man picked him up and raised a giant fist. Harry closed his eyes and prepared for the impact and subsequent death, when the feeling of a spray bottle hit him, and the man's grip loosened completely. Harry opened his eyes and saw Bryce standing just behind the large man, a knife in his hand, as the man clutched his throat slowly

The Atlantian Chronicles

choking to death on his own blood, the low gurgle the final sounds of the large barbarian.

"That's for my Mom and Rhys Hillcrest, you piece of trash." Bryce said, spitting on the man and collapsing into a nearby chair.

"Holy crap Bryce what did you do?" Harry stammered as he rushed over to the boy who held his side and breathed raggedly.

"What I had to." He replied harshly as he tried and failed to pull himself to his feet.

"Where's Bennett?" He asked as he helped Bryce to his feet.

"Job's not done Harry." Bryce said weakly as he leaned heavily on him and tried to regain his composure. "What happened to staying in the car?" Bryce chuckled softly.

"I saw flashlights on the roof and figured something was wrong, so I ran in here, and heard the commotion from the stairwell." Harry explained as he walked Bryce to the door.

"We need to get to the roof." Bryce said, pushing himself up, picking up a pistol off one of the guard's bodies and hobbling to the stairwell.

Adrenaline pumped through Bryce as the pain faded and he pushed himself up the stairs as fast as he could, bursting through the roof access door and onto the gravel covered roof. Bryce scanned the roof quickly looking for Dixon, for Bennett or for Carter. And that's when he saw it.

Carter sat leaning against the electrical box on the roof, blood coming from his arm. The pair rushed over, before Carter waved them off. "Go get Bennett." He whimpered as he clutched his arm, the bullet wound pumping blood out and down it.

"Harry get him out of here, I'll get Bennett." Bryce ordered as he scanned the area for the others.

Then he heard it. "Give me the phone or I will shoot you!" Dixon shouted in the cool night air. Bryce ran as fast as he could to the source of the noise, passing another access room and a caged electrical and gas connection area before he finally saw Dixon. The disheveled man approaching the last air conditioning unit on the roof. With his gun pointed at Dixon, Bryce assumed Bennett was hiding behind the unit.

"Put the gun down Dixon." Bryce called out to him as he placed the man in his crosshairs.

Just as Bryce spoke Dixon dove to the ground. Moving forward cautiously until he heard a scream and saw Dixon emerge from his hiding place holding Bennett, the gun pressed into her back, the larger man hiding behind her much smaller frame. "Don't move Bryce or she dies." Dixon said as he walked Bennett around the roof using her as a shield as he made his way to the closest access door.

"Okay Dixon, no one else has to die, just let her go, I'll let you live, and you can go back to Unity." Bryce bartered as he kept his gun trained on the pair trying to find an angle to hit Dixon without risking Bennett.

"You don't get it do you. She messed it up for us all." Dixon yelled back the desperation in his voice. "This stupid girl ruined everything." Dixon continued sticking the barrel of his gun angrily into Bennett's cheek.

"That doesn't matter, let her go and you'll live." Bryce repeatedly trying and failing to shift.

"I'm dead anyway. We all are. She exposed everything." Dixon screamed as he yanked Bennett towards a door.

"I'm sure Unity can fix it; you're telling me this has never happened before?" Bryce asked, stepping towards the pair.

"Ah... Ah... Ahhhh... don't get any closer I will ventilate her I swear to God." Dixon screamed, gesturing to Bryce to back up.

"Dixon don't do anything stupid." He called back as he stopped his onward movement. Bennett remained silent as she tried and failed to will sound out of her mouth.

"Stupid? Stupid? Like uploading videos of us changing our face, or exposing everything? Atlantians, Unity, everything? In a ten-minute video? Like this STUPID GIRL DID!" Dixon cried out as he moved closer to the door.

"Who cares Dixon?" Bryce called back, taking another step towards them.

"Stop moving Bryce!" Dixon screamed. "We can't all be like you, precious and unique. We can't all be the bloodline of the Kings." Dixon mockingly continued.

"What are you talking about?" Bryce asked as he cautiously stepped forward.

"Your powers, they are from your Father. The last Crono we have on record. We can trace him all the way back to the King, the one who started this all by not giving up when he had the chance!" Dixon called out as he continued to move back glancing over his shoulder every so often as he did.

"You're wrong Crono were warriors, the King's Guard. Atlas told me so." Bryce corrected matching Dixon step for step.

"You really will believe whatever we tell you, won't you?" Dixon laughed, his voice shaky with panic. "Crono were King's they were a warrior culture. The strongest led us, like the Spartans, the royal family were all Crono and passed it down to their children who led after them. Unity wants you; they can't figure out how you move so quickly, hit so hard and don't break bones." Dixon explained stopping entirely as he spoke. "Why do you think we didn't kill you the moment you fell out of that helicopter? Or why we scanned you and took your blood? We want to create thousands of you, win every conflict before they can even start."

"Enough of this Dixon, let her go." Bryce said as he saw Dixon getting closer and closer to the door, he was maybe ten feet from the door when it swung open and a figure in a gray trench coat and a fedora emerged from the opening. Bryce couldn't make out the figure as his eyes were trained on the front sights as he scanned for an angle.

"I think that's quite enough, Dixon." The figure said in a familiar voice.

"Are you kidding me?" Dixon called out as the sound of a suppressed pistol cut through the air. And Dixon slumped to the ground, releasing Bennett who ran forward towards Bryce whose gun moved from one figure to another.

"Who are you?" Bryce called out in the quiet night as the figure held their hands up the gun hanging off their pointer finger by the trigger guard.

"Bryce it's okay he's with us?" Bennett said, trying to push Bryce's arms down.

"I want answers." Bryce replied softly, not taking his eyes off the figure.

"I believe you know who I am, Mr. Hillcrest." The figure said removing their fedora, revealing a close-cropped white hair.

"Mr. Jones?" Bryce said, lowering his gun and looking puzzled.

"He's the person who's been helping me. Bryce, he's been working with a group the whole time, watching over you." Bennett said pushing Bryce's arms down finally, the gun clattering to the gravel, before Bryce hugged Bennett tight.

"Not quite the whole time, Miss Douglas, but we've been watching students who fit a certain criteria for a long time. You're not the first young Atlantian of whom I brought to safety but if the delay in my timing is any indication you will most likely be my last." He stretched his old back and took a deep breath before he fixed his grip on the gun.

"Oh my gosh Bryce you're bleeding." Bennett said, removing her hand from Bryce and looking worriedly at him. "We need to get you to a hospital." She whispered the concern in her voice, making Bryce even more nervous.

"What about Carter and Harry, are they okay?" Bryce asked more worried about them than himself.

"They're okay Mr. Hillcrest. Mr. Wilson was given instructions to drive Mr. Pearson to the safehouse, where they are already prepped for an event such as this. Now if you would be so kind." Mr. Jones said, gesturing to the door he entered from.

Bennett walked with Bryce towards the door when they were interrupted. "Piece of advice, always make sure the bad guy is dead." Dixon coughed as he raised his gun and pointed it at Bennett. Just then the whole world went quiet. Bryce screamed but no sound came out as he watched the smoke burst from the gun. But something wasn't quite right normally when bullets were fired Bryce saw a sound wave and heat trail, but never the bullet. Making it impossible to avoid since it moved faster than he could.

This time Bryce saw the bullet and it was moving almost slow enough to catch. Bryce grabbed Bennett and dove to the ground avoiding the bullet entirely as he covered her with himself awaiting another shot. The sound of the world came crashing back hitting Bryce like a brick wall. Then the sound of two shots from Mr. Jones's pistol filled the air.

"Bryce?" Bennett said softly.

"Are you okay?" Bryce asked hurriedly, rolling off of Bennett who looked scared but fine as he patted her down looking for the bullet wound.

"Yeah, did the bullet hit you?" Bennett asked doing the same to him.

"No, I'm okay." Bryce replied wincing as Bennett grazed his stab wound. "Okay maybe not fine, but it didn't hit me." Bryce finished standing up slowly.

"Mr. Hillcrest, I believe we have much to discuss." Mr. Jones said, helping Bryce and Bennett to their feet and ushering them out of the door. "But first we must get to safety." He finished hurrying them down the stairs.

By the time the group reached the ground floor, Bryce was fading fast. The fatigue, adrenaline dump, and blood loss had caused Bryce to nearly lose consciousness. Bennett carried him as the pair followed Mr. Jones to his Toyota Camry. Bennett loading Bryce into the back seat and pressing the sleeve of her gray blood covered sweater into his stab wound. "Mr. Jones, we need a hospital!" She shouted as the older man started up his car and drove out of the school's parking lot, bottoming it out as he popped over the curb and onto the street.

"Miss Douglas, we have more than capable people at the safe house, and they will not ask questions, now you got the program uploaded and running along with the video, yes?" Mr. Jones asked, looking at the pair in the rearview mirror.

"He's bleeding to death! Why does the video even matter now?" She yelled as she watched the color drain away from Bryce's face, his eyes struggling to stay open. "Keep your eyes open Bryce, we're almost there." Bennett begged as the blood spilled over her soaked sweater, covering her hands and the seats.

"We only had one shot at this, if everything was not done right, we have wasted our only shot at exposing the truth and bringing this war into the public eye. If we don't succeed here, we will never end this war." Mr. Jones said back calmly as he zoomed through the neighborhoods, the passing houses a blur.

"Bryce, come on please, don't leave me, not again, please." Bennett cried as she watched Bryce's chest rising slower and slower. Bryce placed a weak hand on her cheek before it fell off the strength needed to keep it up too much for his failing body, the color from the world fading to a black and white as the dark walls of his vision closed in. "No, please don't go." Bennett begged as Bryce closed his eyes.

CHAPTER 31

It had been hours since the three had arrived at the safehouse, shortly after Bryce closed his eyes, his chest barely moving as he struggled to breathe in and out. The group had been met by several people in gloves and surgical dress who carried Bryce into the house quickly only asking "What is the biggest issue?" Noticing the blood on Bennett, Bryce and the seat.

"His side." Bennett cried as she watched the limp body dangle as people carried him into the large, faded gray, farm house with white, aged and chipping painted accents. Bennett tried to follow the group of people but was stopped by Mr. Jones.

"Miss Douglas, please, let them work. He is in the best hands possible." He comforted her, as he held her in his arms, his old frame deceivingly strong.

"If he dies, I quit." Bennett whimpered as she was held tight by the old man.

"Well, let's pray he and you remain with us then, there is a lot of good you and he can do." Mr. Jones whispered as he held the crying girl in his arms. "We need to debrief and discuss everything that has happened with the others. I think it's best if we look to move as soon as it is safe to do so. Unity will be scrambling and struggling to cover everything up. But they will also be out for blood. This is far from over. And there are now targets on many of us." He continued as he pulled away from Bennett and looked at her, his old eyes meeting hers as she sniffled.

"Not until he is okay." Bennett said sternly. "I did my part, until I know he is okay I won't be doing anything else for you or for your people." Her rage building as she spoke. "We have sacrificed everything for you, if my Dad is alive, he will certainly not be after this, and if I lose Bryce then there's no point in continuing." She said marching towards the house.

"Miss Douglas, I know you are upset but they will need time and the less we interfere the better." Mr. Jones said, shuffling over to Bennett and taking her by the hand. "I hope Mr. Hillcrest makes a full recovery, but we cannot sit and wait for the news, he would not want us to sit and wait around." He pleaded as he held Bennett's gaze.

"You don't know him or what he would want." Bennett replied, pulling her hand back.

"Bennett?" Harry said as he stood in the doorframe of the house looking out at the pair's argument.

"Harry! Is Carter, okay?" Bennett asked, turning to look at the pudgy boy who sported bruises on his arms, his collar crumpled from where Tyson had grabbed him, the spots of blood still staining his face and shirt.

"He's okay, they say it'll be a bit before he's out of surgery." Harry said, accepting a hug from Bennett who squeezed him tight in her arms. "He told me what happened. I'm sorry I wasn't there sooner, but Bennett there's some things I need to tell you, some things Bryce told me." He began looking at Bennett and guiding her inside the house.

The interior was far homier and cleaner than the old exterior appeared to be. Bennett pulled off her gray Broadway Hills High School Cheer Squad sweater and placed it in a bag offered to her by a nurse who moved throughout the space bringing various items back and forth down a hallway where Bennett could faintly make out the sound of two different heart monitors beeping back and forth. Bennett sat in her blue jeans and a plain black T-shirt, her once bright white Converse sneakers, now dirty, with scuffs from running, sliding and hiding on the roof, drops of blood staining the tongue and laces from her carrying Bryce down the stairs and into the car.

"Why don't you wash your hands at least, I can make tea?" Harry suggested as he looked at Bennett who slumped into a small, cushioned seat at the front of the spacious front entrance, in a room with a TV and couches off to the left, a fairly modern kitchen just off to the right.

"Harry, I don't want tea." Bennett said rubbing her fingers together, the sticky blood feeling almost necessary.

"Bennett, please." He asked, looking at her shell-shocked appearance.

"How do we have so much blood?" She replied quietly.

"Come on, I'll go with you, we can talk while you wash your hands." He compromised as he helped Bennett to her feet and walked her over to the nearby bathroom, feeling her shaking body as he walked. "I don't know how to tell you, other than to tell you." He began opening the door to the bathroom, a small vanity with a single deep white sink, a matching white toilet and a towel rack with black hand towels inside, a picture of a starfish hanging just behind the toilet. Harry sat on the closed lid of the toilet and began. While Bennett washed her hands, the blood taking a long time to wash off, as Harry had experienced only moments earlier.

Harry explained everything, Josiah's imposter, and how Bryce described their escape and Josiah's death and how he'd spent two weeks running from Unity, trying to get here to rescue Bennett. Harry held and hugged her a lot, the pair moving to the couch in the room with the TV, once Bennett had removed as much of Bryce's blood from her hands as possible. They spent a long time in silence after that, Bennett, in shock and Harry unsure how to help her. He brought her tea, explained what he knew to Mr. Jones, and recounted how he'd come across Bryce as Tyson was strangling him, and how Bryce subsequently killed him.

"Harrison, the boy who was shot has made it through surgery, he should make a full recovery, but it will take some time, his shoulder blade was cracked by the impact of the bullet, luckily it did not fragment or bounce around his chest cavity. It was a relatively easy procedure. We will check on him over the next couple of hours, but he should come to in the next twenty minutes." A doctor said not removing the mask as he spoke, his lanky body towering over the much shorter Mr. Jones.

"Ahh, yes thank you so much Gabriel. Do you happen to have any updates on the other young man we brought in? The one with the stab wound?" Mr. Jones asked softly as he pulled Gabriel away from Bennett and Harry who were celebrating after the update as relief washed over them.

"Not yet Harrison, he lost a lot of blood and while we are working to repair the wound it looks like it punctured the large intestine, causing bleeding into the digestive tract. It is touch and go right now, but he's in the best hands we have. I will update you when I have more information." Gabriel said as he lowered his tone. "Now if you'll excuse me, I should scrub back in and see if I can't be of any help." And with that Gabriel turned and walked back down the hallway to where Bryce and Carter had been taken.

Mr. Jones turned around and walked over to the pair who sat attentively watching the older man as he discussed Bryce with the doctor. "What did he say Mr. Jones?" Harry asked as the elderly man settled into a seat just to the left of the pair.

"Bryce is doing well; they say he should make a full recovery. They're finishing up and then he should be out of surgery and resting, but he will need time to recover, and he will need time to himself." He lied, the old man not having the heart to tell the pair the truth. Not wanting to believe Bryce might not survive himself.

"Really? That's amazing! Did you hear that Bennett, Bryce is going to be okay!" Harry cheered "We should go see Carter, I'm sure he'd love to wake up to us there." Harry said as he rose to his feet, pulling Bennett up to hers as he did.

"Well actually Mr. Wilson, now that we are sure Mr. Hillcrest is safe, I was hoping to steal Miss Douglas and discuss some things." Mr. Jones said, extending a hand out and stopping Harry before he pulled Bennett down the hallway. "Miss Douglas if you would be so kind." He continued stretching out his arm and gesturing to a room on the opposite side of the house.

"It's okay Bennett, go talk to him and I'll wait for Carter, come join us when you can." Harry said hurriedly as he saw a moment of hesitation on her face.

"Are you sure?" She asked quietly to Harry.

"Of course, it's not like we're going anywhere in the meantime." Harry laughed as he reassured her.

Bennett followed Mr. Jones as he led her to a small room with a desk and a pair of high-backed fabric chairs set opposite the large chair at the center of the desk, facing the door. The room had walls covered with old books and various nicknacks. "Miss Douglas, I know today has been trying for you, and the news Mr. Wilson delivered was undoubtedly hard to hear. So, before we begin anything else, I will ask you, how are you doing?" Mr. Jones asked softly as he guided the puffy eyed girl to a chair before walking around the desk to the large chair, removing a small black leather notebook and pen from his jacket pocket.

"I don't know. I don't know what I am feeling right now. My whole world has changed, and Bryce is the last person I have in my life. Harry and Carter are great but they don't know what we've been through, they don't know how I think, or what I mean when I say things the way Bryce does. He understands me like no one I have ever met before." She said her eyes were welling up with tears that she quickly wiped away.

"It is okay to cry Miss Douglas, it is a part of dealing with the trauma of life." Mr. Jones said opening a drawer on the desk and producing a small wooden box where he removed a fresh white linen handkerchief and placed it on the desk in front of Bennett.

"Thank you." She said, picking up the piece of cloth and wiping her eyes before she continued, her eyeliner staining the white fabric as she began playing with it in her hands as she spoke. "On the other hand, my whole world is gone, my father is dead, because of me, because of Bryce and because of this whole situation that neither of us asked to be in, and nothing I can do will ever fix that. So, it's tough to want to do anything right now besides either breaking things, or curling up next to Bryce and waiting for him to wake up, because I know the second he looks at me, he will know exactly what to do, and he will know exactly what I need. I didn't think he would come back to me after everything that happened so it's just kind of confusing, I know what I did was right, but Harry and Carter helped me because of Bryce, and because they're good people. I don't know how I can repay them, because their lives are gone now too, they can't go back to living a normal life, not until this is over." She said, exhaling deeply after sitting back and pulling her knees up to her chest in the large seat of the chair.

"Well, I may not know exactly what you need, but I do know how you can repay those two boys who risked their lives to save the lives of a group of people they have never met." Mr. Jones said, looking deeply at Bennett who met his eyes over her knees as she pulled them in close. "You can make their sacrifice mean something. Help me, help us, and help end this conflict once and for all." He said, leaning forward and quieting his voice. "Miss Douglas, what you have done tonight is more than what most humans will do in their entire lifetime, and no one would fault you for wanting what we promised, a safe place to remain, away from Unity and away from Atlas's Atlantian reach. Based on the report I received earlier, you were successful, so the Coalition will gladly hold up their side of the bargain, but we need people like you, like Bryce, and like those two boys who quite frankly looked as if they saw a ghost tonight when they saw me. So Bennett, I will ask you one time, will you continue to help the Human Atlantian Coalition in order to put an end to the secret war that has gone on for millennia and bring peace to the innocent people on both sides of this conflict, by whatever means necessary?" Mr. Jones said looking at Bennett who seemed taken aback by the use of her first name.

CHAPTER 32

It was hours before Gabriel emerged from the room Bryce was taken into, and after a brief conversation with Mr. Jones in hushed tones, Gabriel entered Carter's room. Inside was a large hospital bed. Harry, Bennett and Carter sat in the room, Carter in the bed, Bennett leaning against a window ledge, and Harry sitting in the only chair in the room, a gray, cloth fabric chair with a deep comfy seat.

"Excuse me, sorry to interrupt, but Harrison, told me to let you all know Mr. Hillcrest completed his surgery, it was successful and though it took far longer than we expected we wanted to be sure of our findings and no further damage was done, he should make a full recovery. Gabriel said to the cheers and smiles of the group. "He will be asleep and groggy for some time, but we will get you when he is awake and able to take visitors." Gabriel finished placing his hands behind his back giving a quick nod and turning on his heels, his scrubs stained with blood, his eyes showing the clear signs of fatigue.

Once in the hallway Gabriel closed the door and walked over to the office Bennett and Mr. Jones spent over an hour in while Harry waited with Carter. Once inside he closed the door and looked at the old man sharply. "Harrison, I will not be a pawn in your game. These are teenagers, and you want me to lie to them about their friend? This is unfair to both them and me." Gabriel said, walking over to the desk and removing a rocks glass from a small bar set up just inside one of the recessed bookshelves that lined the room, pouring himself two fingers of whiskey and taking it all down in one gulp, exhaling hard before pouring himself another two fingers.

"That is two hundred dollars per glass Singleton Dufftown fifty-four-year single malt. Please treat it with some respect." Mr. Jones said, sitting forward in his chair and looking at the tired looking man.

"Screw you." Gabriel responded, gulping down the second glass. "These kids deserve to know, their friend died on the table four times, had two and a half inches of his intestines stitched back together, and then had his spleen removed after we found it beyond repair. Not to mention muscularly, it looks as though he was in a forty-five mile per hour car crash, but his bones are perfectly fine. His recovery will be months and that's not speaking on his mental battle from what I can tell all of these kids have been through a traumatizing experience." Gabriel said furiously as he made little attempt to keep his voice down.

"First of all, keep your voice down. As for what these children should and should not know, that is for me to decide. I am their handler, and I am in charge of them. I will do what I think is best for them and that will be that. Yes, he had trauma, yes, he had injuries, but he is fine and will recover. We need him to; he did something incredible last night and we need him. He is the last Crono on record. As such will be the person we have been searching for, the person the founder wanted. This war has killed millions, with casualties on both sides. Hell, this boy killed at least five people last night alone. Gabriel, he moved faster than a bullet. Do you understand what that means?" Mr. Jones said sternly. "It means he is the most powerful Crono ever, he is our best shot at rallying the people and she has said she will help him do it. So, if a little lie here and there must be told to ensure this war ends in a way where we can live and be harmonious as our goal has been from the start of this organization, an organization I will remind you, you work for. Then I will gladly be the one to tell that lie. Now if I cannot count on you to do your job and ensure this secret is kept, then I will find someone who can." Mr. Jones said an air of excitement and passion in his voice.

"Harrison, this boy should know what is ahead of him. Not just in terms of recovery, but in terms of what he most likely has not signed up for." Gabriel said, sliding his glass across the table to Mr. Jones and walking out of the room.

Bryce awoke about an hour after the news was given, and after a private meeting with Gabriel and another Doctor, Bryce was allowed one visitor. He chose Bennett without a moment of thought.

Bennett who had anxiously waited for the news he was awake and could be seen. She burst into tears as soon as the door opened, and ran towards Bryce, prompting a warning from a nurse who reminded her, he was recovering and to be careful not to rip any stitches internally or externally.

He looked as though he had been hit by a truck, his face was bruised and swollen, his neck had large almost giant hand prints around it, and blood vessels in one eye were burst, but that was just what Bennett could see she could not imagine what the inside looked or felt like. "I'm sorry I lost your bracelet." He said weakly, breaking the silence.

"You still came back to me though." Bennett said through tears.

"I'll always come back to you. I promised." Bryce said, reaching out a hand, the bruises on his knuckles already a sickly purple.

"Then we can get a new bracelet. As long as I have the original you." Bennett said, pressing his hand to her lips softly.

"I made a promise to your Dad to save you, and to tell you he loved you, right until the end." He said his eyes watering the tears painfully stinging as they rolled down his face.

"Thank you." Bennett whispered, the ball in her throat preventing any more words than that.

"Bennett?" He asked softly.

"Yeah." She replied to the word barely audible in her shaky voice.

"I'm sorry I got you involved in this." He mumbled, squeezing her hand softly with his.

"It's okay, I am right where I want to be." Bennett replied, tears rolling down her face in a steady stream now.

"I'd rather be on a beach." He joked, his smile hurting almost as much as his tears.

"A beach would be nice." Bennett chuckled back leaning into Bryce.

"Bennett, I will never question you again. I should have believed you from the start." Bryce said softly as he felt her skin on his body as he lay there in the cold room. Her placing her head on him.

"I forgive you." She replied not lifting her head.

"I love you." Bryce said the words just leaving his mouth before he could think about it.

"What was that?" Bennett asked, sitting up straight and looking at Bryce.

"I said I love you." Bryce said louder this time.

"I know I just liked hearing it, because I love you too." Bennett replied looking at Bryce, his swollen and bruised face, his hands looking as if they'd been painted purple, and a whole mess of injuries she couldn't see meaning nothing to a girl who loved a boy, who loved her back. They'd won the fight, but Bennett knew the war was just beginning.

Epilogue

It was a few days before Bryce was taken off the pain medicine that caused him to be groggy and barely able to string together a thought. Bennett spent every moment she could with him during those days, talking about the weather, or the story of The Terminal List, a series of books she found out Bryce read while in the cell with her father. It hurt her to think of all she'd lost and the loss she knew she would encounter in her future. She had decided she cared more about the people who were being manipulated, tortured, punished, and killed for something they couldn't control, than she did about herself and she decided if she was going to be involved, she was all in. She'd lost almost everything, and after the events at the school, she could never go back.

It surprised her how easily the decision came to her, after she'd beat up Becky Collins for telling lies about Bryce, an event she didn't even really remember, when she found herself in Mr. Jones's classroom. Apparently having blacked out during the violent outburst, and more importantly screaming how Unity was hunting people, and killing them. Ready for a quick trip to the office, Bennett was surprised that Mr. Jones didn't take her there immediately, instead he offered to listen as she spoke about her time on the run, in the camp, and in the Unity run prison. They spent hours talking over the next few weeks and eventually Mr. Jones offered Bennett an opportunity to get her revenge, but not just on Unity, but on The Atlantian Brotherhood as well, explaining to her that it wasn't such a black and white conflict. And they were by no means the good side.

Mr. Jones explained there was another group in play. The Human Atlantian Coalition -or The Coalition for short- wanted to create a world where both groups lived in harmony. Unlike Unity who wished to level the playing field, or Atlas who Bennett came to find out wanted nothing more than to enslave the human race and take what he considered Atlantian's rightful place atop the throne of the world. Mr. Jones explained how The Coalition was founded on the idea of cooperation and prosperity gained through the groups working together, how they had with various indigenous groups around the world, created monuments that baffled and amazed even the smartest of people. He explained how he'd been placed in Boardway Hills as a preventative measure citing that Broadway Hills as a town fit many characteristics as a place that someone aware of the conflict might hide out. Unfortunately for him he realized too late who Bryce was and Tyson had beat them to the punch. He would go on further to explain how he'd been in touch with many Atlantians who were embedded in The Brotherhood and how he even spoke with the leader of a camp in the Appalachian Mountains, not realizing it was someone Bennett was familiar with.

Eventually Mr. Jones outlined a plan to Bennett that involved her bringing this conflict to light once and for all, and not only bringing it to light but putting it on the center of the global stage. Mr. Jones had been cleared to give Bennett footage, and with editing and access to a bank of computers, Bennett would write and record a video, splicing in the footage, to expose the existence of Atlantians to the world, to expose what both Unity and Atlas were doing. Once recorded, the video would be uploaded to social media, and then a program would share it, creating exact copies, reposting it, and sharing it hundreds of times flooding the airwaves with it, making it impossible for Unity to create copies that would prove the original was fake and ensuring every single person regardless of algorithms would see the footage. The whole internet would be flooded with the truth. Then it was up to the people to do the rest, to demand answers, pursue the truth and for those who could, to come forward unleashing a firestorm. And that is exactly what Bennett had done. She lit the fuse that blew up the entire secret world.

When Bryce was able to, Mr. Jones arranged for him, Bennett, Carter, and Harry to be taken to a remote Coalition base, from there Bryce slowly started to return to normal, the bruises faded, his energy increased and soon enough he was exercising, training, and being the person Bennett fell in love with, what felt like so long ago. Time would tell what they would face, but Bennett knew, just from how Bryce looked at her, that regardless of what it was together they would get through it.